Dealers in Death

The authors assert the moral right to be identified as the owners of the work. This novel is entirely a work of fiction. The names, characters and incidents portrayed in it are the work of the authors' imaginations. Any resemblance to actual persons, living or dead, events or localities is entirely coincidental. All rights reserved.

No part of this publication may be reproduced, stored in a retrieval system or transmitted, in any form or by any means, electronic, or otherwise, without prior permission from the publishers.

This book is sold subject to the condition that it shall not, by the way of trade or otherwise, be lent, re-sold, hired out or otherwise circulated without the publisher's prior consent in any form of binding or cover, other than that, in which it is published and without a similar condition including this condition being imposed on the subsequent purchaser.

Copyright Written Work: © Arthur Cole and Nigel Williams. 2023.
Copyright Front Page Image: Karen Cole. 2023.
Publisher: AC Imprints.
ISBN: 9798860222779
First Edition 2023.

Acknowledgments.

The authors wish to thank Mike Paddick for his early feedback and all the readers of the books in the series. They also thank Karen Cole for the cover design and the two Caroline's for the unending support.

1
Michigan USA. June 1992

Secrets. A soft voice, barely audible. The sounds muffled by the closed door. He knew they were deliberately hushed to avoid his young ears, but he could still hear everything if he pushed his blackened cheek against the wood panel. It was man's voice, deep, resonant, but this wasn't pa talking; "...nothing anyone could do. You were lucky. You and your boy."

Now he heard pa's voice, even deeper, and a notch lower on the volume control; "Lucky? You wanna tell my boy we were lucky?"

Then silence, for what seemed like an age, then clacking steps on the tiled floor, getting louder – that meant closer.

The young boy recoiled and hurried back to the plastic bench where pa had left him and had told him to wait. He made the bench just as the door opened and pa stepped out into the corridor. Pa smiled, a weak, sad expression. He hadn't noticed the soot mark where Abe's cheek had pressed against the door.

"Alright, boy?" The humourless smile was briefly replaced by an expression of abject fear as their eyes met. They had indeed been lucky.

Abe nodded, but he felt anything but alright. How could anything be alright ever again? Ma was dead and his burns hurt like hell. The nurse had said lots of nice things as she cleaned his hands and dressed the damage. She had reminded him of his good fortune too many times for it to be true. The more she said the words, the less lucky he felt - but luckier than ma, for sure.

Pa's hands were wrapped in thick white bandages, just like his own. Pa's hands had been burned worse than Abe's. They would both be okay. The damage wasn't too bad, but it would hurt for some time to come. The nurse had promised he'd be playing softball again soon.

"Let's get out of here." Pa extended a mummified hand and quickly withdrew it as Abe's eyes fixed on it, the lad's bottom lip trembling, threatening to unleash another wail of anguish. "No more of that, boy. Plenty of time for crying in private. This is not the place," pa said through gritted teeth.

Even at the age of ten, Abe knew *anyplace* was the right place for wailing when you'd just seen your mother die.

The walk along the corridor was a blur. It seemed to last forever, like mile after mile of sterilised, white passageways. Hundreds of doors leading to rooms with job titles he could never hope to pronounce, let alone understand. Pa seemed to know where he was headed. Abe would never have found his way to the exit. He would have been lost in the sterile maze forever.

The corridor ended in a wide expanse of grey plastic chairs – lines and lines of them. Most were occupied by sorry looking characters waiting their turn to be called to triage.

"Jeff!" The voice was loud and even deeper than pa's, like the voice of Darth Vader, but a million times more friendly. "Jeff! Over here!"

Pa stopped and turned. He nodded to the enormous bulk of a man rocking his way towards them on stiff legs, bulging legs that had played too many games of college football.

Abe smiled at Trucker. The man was a human juggernaut. Skin as black as a star-less night, Trucker was blessed with a face that had done more smiling than frowning over his forty years of life and showed it in the lines that etched the skin around his eyes. Not that he had never had reason not to frown. Abe knew Trucker's story. He knew he had been treated badly for most of his life, but the big man had never let that affect his relationship with friends. Warm, generous, and blessed with the tightest of enveloping hugs, Trucker could never meet anyone without throwing his big, hefty arms around them and squeezing the breath out of them. Pa was a big man too, but Trucker was something else. They had been friends for years and Trucker had always been a constant presence for Abe. Trucker had been coming over to the house for barbeques and parties and he could make any gathering into a celebration - even a wake. If there was a party, Trucker had to be invited. That seemed to be the unwritten rule that the whole neighbourhood seemed happy to comply with.

Trucker stopped short of pa and scanned the damage to his friend. "Sweet Jesus. What happened, man?"

Jeff Quince – pa - shook his head, eyes avoiding contact with his friend. "Couldn't save her, Trucker. God knows I tried."

Damage assessment scanned and processed; Trucker smothered Jeff with the gentlest hug Abe had ever seen. He held Jeff for several seconds, burying his own head into his friend's shoulder before breaking off, wiping away tears and then turning his attention to Abe. Trucker moaned as he bent low to pull Abe into another of his hugs. "Trucker's here now, Abe. Everything will be OK."

2

Francine slumped in a hard chair, listening to Bob Marley through her earbuds. The white walls, ceiling, and white-washed wooden floor of the waiting room was matched with the desk that the white-clad receptionist sat behind. Even her face mask was white. Francine had been happy to see the end to face coverings and understood why some people still insisted on wearing them even though the British Government had ruled them no longer necessary a week ago. Covid-19 had messed up more than just the regular lives of ordinary people. It had also screwed up some pretty serious on-going investigations. Perhaps the receptionist was vulnerable to infection? Perhaps she was a jab refuser? Francine thought that was unlikely in a place like this. Perhaps she had vulnerable family? Whatever, the reception room screamed it was free from infection. God help any germ that tried to infiltrate. Only a large seascape that hung on one sterile wall added any reference to a world outside that was far from clean and sterile. Francine watched the receptionist shuffle papers and tap the occasional clatter of words into a white laptop in the centre of the desk. The receptionist avoided eye contact. When their eyes did meet on rare occasions, the smile was practiced and lacked any connection with a soul. Francine knew her appearance, no doubt, contributed to the woman's discomfort, but that was strange because she certainly wouldn't have been the only seasoned undercover operative from the Metropolitan Police that would have visited for the compulsory psychological assessment.

This would be the second of her bi-annual meetings with the Force forensic psychologist. It was a procedure that all undercover operatives had to go through, but that didn't make it any the less of an awkward inconvenience. She had been through the process many times during the last couple of years. She'd been working undercover for the last six months, busting a south coast gang of heroin smugglers. It had been a stressful job, and on occasions life-threatening.

She checked her sports watch. Arriving early in her new powder-blue joggers and a tight-fitting, blue Lycra top, she knew she looked like a stereo-typical twenty-something woman from the underclass of low-income housing estates that were littered around the town. That was the impression she needed to convey and knew it was a look that didn't sit easily with the immaculately presented receptionist who had probably never set foot in a council estate in her thirty-something life.

A white door to an adjoining office opened and a round shaped woman no taller than a Space Hopper appeared. The woman scanned the waiting room and smiled at the receptionist. The returned smile was warm and comfortable and nothing like the versions reserved for Francine. The small woman was a Pantone period, a full-stop of bottle green that was at odds with the all-white facility. "Ah, Francine, good morning," she smiled warmly. "I'm Dr Ralston," she held out her right hand as she wobbled towards her.

Francine removed her ear buds and paused the song playing on her phone.

"I don't believe in formality, so call me Pru," the doctor said.

Francine stood and extended her hand. "I'm pleased to meet you, but I was expecting Dr Ahmed. He normally does my assessments."

Pru nodded sagely. "Sadly, Dr Ahmed has some family business to take care of, so I'm filling the breach. Come on in and take a seat, just relax, help yourself to a coffee," she said as she stepped back into her office and pointed to the percolator on a white-wood drawer unit against the right-hand wall.

"I don't mind if I do," Francine mumbled as she spat a ball of gum into her hand and found a waste bin.

The doctor shuffled into a white high-back leather chair and sank almost out of sight. "We've never met, but I've read your personal file. I see you've been an undercover operative for the last five years?"

"Yes, closer to six, actually," Francine said over her shoulder as she poured herself a strong coffee and pierced a small carton of milk with her powder-blue thumbnail.

"How have you coped with lockdown?"

Francine shrugged. "Bit of a pain. I was undercover when it first happened, and I ended up getting stuck in with the crew I'd infiltrated. No way of getting away from them and that was awkward."

"Wow! I hadn't even thought of someone being locked down like that."

Francine shrugged. "Thankfully it's Spring. New season, new start without the masks."

The doctor smiled and nodded. "Yes. It would be good to get back to normality."

"I'm afraid normal has gone forever. Now we have to suffer twats like Putin dropping bombs on their neighbours."

Again, the doctor nodded. "I must admit that you're the first undercover officer I have had to assess, so this could be a bit of a sharp learning curve for me. I hope you don't mind if I go over old ground with you?"

"I've got all the time in the world, fire away." Francine stirred the milk into the coffee and walked to a matching white chair that had been set off to the side of the desk. She knew the idea was to make the space between them open and not divided by obstructions such as furniture. It was some sort of psychological nonsense she had read somewhere; about making connections to get her to relax and open up.

"Now, let's see, you joined the Met in 2008?" she looked to Francine who nodded. "After training, you were posted to Brixton, where you worked until you joined SO10 five years ago… sorry, nearly six."

"Yes, I loved my time working Brixton, but just fancied a change. So, I volunteered for undercover work, the opportunity arose, so I just went for it. I was trained and here I am today," she smiled a well-practiced smile, honed to perfection. Few, if any, were able to read her expressions.

"I notice from reading your file, you were born in South Wales, so why join the Met?"

"Spur of the moment thing," she shrugged. "I'd finished my A-levels, didn't fancy going to university, or into the family business. I think I made the right decision."

"I see you're multi-lingual, French, Spanish, German and of course Welsh," Pru said, clearly impressed.

"My parents made me pursue languages. I think they would have liked me to be a teacher, or a linguist, but I never really fancied that."

"You're also a black belt in a number of martial arts, I bet these skills are handy for someone undercover?"

"If I ever have to use it then the job has gone tits up. Thankfully, I'm good at what I do. Talking is my best skill."

"OK, after years undercover, perhaps you should think about calling it a day? You know you can't do it forever, and you have plenty of time to progress within the Force."

"I thrive on it. I've no commitments. No children. I'm not ready to finish."

Pru smiled again, her eyes boring into Francine's soul, searching for something Francine knew she would never find. She picked up a pen and notebook from the desk. "How do you sleep?"

"Never had a problem."

"No waking up in cold sweats, flashbacks, things like that?"

"When I'm on a job, I must stay in character. I know that can seem hard to understand, but I cope. It's probably a lot like being a method actor."

Pru smiled again. "What about drink or drugs?"

"No, thank you, this coffee will do fine," she laughed. "I always use moderation on a job," she added with a wink, "and I get tested often. No issues there, I assure you."

Pru sat forward, elbows on knees, chin resting on knuckles. "Tell me what it's like being undercover, Francine?"

"Well, not a lot I can say, not specifics anyway," she looked towards Pru who raised her eyebrows and tilted her head. "It's sometimes dangerous, stressful, sometimes there are sights that I would rather not see, and of course, I mix with the scum of the world."

"So why do it?"

"I suppose I thrive on it," she answered honestly. "I've got a good support team behind me. I just get on with it and try not to think too much about the possible consequences of getting things wrong."

"Do you feel lonely and isolated..." she paused for a breath. "...when you're on an operation?"

"Not really, I know what I'm doing. I treat it like acting. I studied drama at college, and I was bloody good at it. I thought about applying for a course in Dramatic Arts at uni. I've always had a talent for hearing an accent and instantly being able to mimic it. It was a skill my friends loved. So, I suppose I'm acting all the time. The only difference is, when you're on stage there's no likelihood of being killed or injured."

Nodding, Pru's eyebrows scrunched together. "Are you acting now?"

Francine grinned. It was a fair question. "Don't we all act all the time? Aren't we all acting when we meet different people in different situations?"

Pru said nothing, her expression impassive. "Would I be right in describing you as a thrill seeker?"

"No, most certainly not. I do my job," she said, careful not to be defensive in her tone. Francine knew the questions were loaded to test responses, to judge the manner in which they were answered more than the answers themselves. The interviews were always a minefield. "I have a job to do, that's all it is and ever was. If things are getting too much, I know when to pull the plug and get out."

"What about your parents, do they know what you do?"

"No. They might have guessed I'm not walking the beat anymore. I see them when I can. If they ask, I tell them I'm on the crime squad in Brixton. I even invite them up now and again."

"How do you think they'd react if they knew you were working undercover?"

"I doubt they'd be pleased. I'm still their little girl. They weren't keen on me joining the job, but they knew it was what I wanted to do. So, in that respect, I guess they'd be OK about it. They'd have no choice. But they won't ever find out from me."

"Does it bother you that you lie to them?"

Francine sat back and crossed her arms defensively, and then realised she needed to look relaxed and engaged. She had allowed a crack to appear and hoped Pru had missed it. "It's my job. I suppose you could say I'm paid to lie. Whether I like it or not is irrelevant. I have to lie to survive."

"How does that sit with you, though?"

"It is what it is. I have a job to do."

"That's not really answering my question."

"OK, I found it difficult to begin with, but when my life depends on it, and the lives of my family if they were ever drawn into it, that is more important than the lie."

"A means to an end?"

"That's a leading question," she smiled.

"Well?"

"Yes. That's all it is. A means to an end. I feel less of a liar than our politicians who lie to get elected and then continue to lie throughout their careers."

"That's cynical. Aren't they doing the same as you?"

"No. There's a difference. They lie to gain power, to fill their pockets and the pockets of their friends and families. I lie to undermine and derail the power of those who exercise it over people who are unable to fight back. There's a difference. I sleep well at night."

"Do you?"

"Yes, I do." Francine said emphatically. "I know I'm doing the right thing for the right reasons."

"But you are acting on the information of people like politicians. What if what you are doing is just helping unscrupulous people with their own agendas?"

"That could well be true, but I must trust my supervisors, my handler. I can't make a judgement call on things that are above my pay grade. I just have to do my job to the best of my ability. I'm a tiny cog in a big operation. Small cogs in a machine have no idea of what they are a part of. Cogs turn and do what they must. If they break down, then the whole machine stops too. I'm just a cog."

"What if you discovered that your work is for the people who don't deserve your trust? What if everything you've done, the risks, the lies, are all... well... for a lie also?"

Francine knew the questions would come. It was an obvious extension of the line of those gone before. "Then I will still sleep well at night because I've always acted in good faith."

"Faith? Are you religious?"

"Not since I was old enough to think for myself."

"You think people with religious faith don't think for themselves?"

"I know they don't. Following religious doctrine, for whatever reason, is inherently unthinking. How can you think about life and science and the universe and believe we are the product of a divine power, a power so confused and fucked up that it gives rise to terrorism and other acts of insanity in the name of God?"

"Can I infer from what you said that you used to be religious?"

"Yes. I was born into a devout Protestant family. Church three times on a Sunday."

"Not for you?"

"It was until I began to question the nonsense being spouted from the pulpit. I realised it was just about social control, a manmade load of old bollocks."

Pru smiled. "I must say Francine, you are very forthright. Is there anything you'd like to ask me?"

Francine checked her watch. "Not really, only whether I've passed? It's funny, really, if I get the all-clear from you, I'm off to South Wales tomorrow, re-charge the batteries. I think my next op is going to be a long one."

"Any idea what it entails?"

"Now, that would be telling, my lips are sealed," she grinned.

Pru laughed. "I understand." She picked up a sheet of paper and waved it before Francine's face. "After reading Dr Ahmed's previous reports, I must concur with him."

"So, how would you describe me, Pru?"

"That's not for me to comment."

It was what Francine expected. People like Pru liked to make career decisions for people like her. They expected straight answers, but they would never give a straight answer in return. "Am I OK to get back out there?"

"If you ever show any signs of what I call battle fatigue, I'm here any time you feel like talking."

"I'll bear it in mind."

"You look after yourself, Francine. See you in six months."

That was as good as a verbal confirmation that she'd passed the assessment. That was good enough for Francine. The bi-annual assessments were a pain, but she understood the politics behind them. They were a necessary evil in a world where she believed box-ticking had become more important than doing the job on the streets.

3

Judgement day for all Swansea soccer fans. The city buzzed in anticipation, the atmosphere electric. The rivalry between Cardiff City and Swansea was deeper than just a game of sport, it was tribal. Two warring factions segregated by policing systems born in the fires of the headline grabbing battles of the seventies and eighties, and scenes of violence had become few and far between as a result.

A mid-day kick off Sky Sports had deemed the game worthy of televising. A sell out; the Liberty stadium would be packed to the rafters, and the majority of Swansea's pubs were well frequented by fans who had failed to get tickets.

Quince was glad he had no direct involvement with football since his promotion. The only football he loved was the one played with the egg-shaped ball in the land of his birth. He enjoyed rugby though and had excelled in school when he had moved to Wales with his pa many years earlier. Trawling through paperwork he had scanned twice already; he was glad of the distraction of his best mate Andy Stokes calling him on his mobile. "I'm popping up to the Adam for a couple of pints. Going to watch the match on their telly. Do you fancy it?"

There was nothing urgent in the pile of files. They could wait until he got his head back in the game. "Why not? I'll top and tail what I'm doing and meet you there in twenty minutes. No doubt the Adam'll be packed?"

"No problem." Stokes said with confidence. "I've had a chat with Speed. He'll keep us a couple of seats."

***

"A good crowd in for the game," Stokes observed. The pub was indeed packed but a small corner table for two with a good view of the wall-mounted television was marked with 'reserved' scribbled on a piece of folded card.

"Always do, Andy. Got the usual suspects, but they're no trouble. They know the score. Any nonsense and they're out," he said with conviction. Then he grinned. "So, what are you having?"

"A couple of pints of IPA, please. Quince will be joining me later."

"Haven't seen him for a while," Speed said as he took two glasses from a rack above the bar and began pouring the beer. "He normally pops in for a pint."

"You know what he's like, hundred bloody miles an hour."

Speed nodded. "And caught the curse of the detectives... marriage went to shit. Never understood why they put the job before their families."

"Not so much of that these days, to be fair. But Quince isn't fucking normal, is he," Stokes laughed.

Handing the pints to Stokes and taking the cash, Speed nodded to the reserved table. "There's a couple of chairs and a table near the window for you both. Should be a tidy match."

"I hope so. The last one was a load of shite. Like watching paint dry it was."

No sooner had Andy sat down, Quince made an appearance. He waved at Speed and sat down with Andy. The first pint didn't touch the sides. "I needed that, Andy. I'll get a couple more in. Do you fancy a chaser with them?"

"Why not? Are we going to push the boat out this afternoon?"

"Like you said…Why not? I think I'm due a blow-out, truth be told."

Quince took the glasses and pushed his way through the huddle littering the bar and beckoned Speed. "Give me a tab, and just keep them coming. I'll settle up when Andy and I fall over."

"Your wish is my command, Abe, enjoy!"

"All local?" Quince gestured to the noisy group around him.

"Mostly regulars, Abe. Not a Bluebird in sight," Cardiff City football Club was nicknamed the Bluebirds. "…they dare not show their face in here."

Abe grabbed the drinks and wrestled back to the table. He sat with his back to the window, where he had full view of the big screen, and anyone who came into the bar. It was a habit he couldn't break.

"Who do you fancy, Andy?"

"The Swans of course. Cardiff is struggling at the minute. Three points in the bag I reckon."

It made no difference to Quince. He just didn't get the rivalry.

As it got closer to kick off, the volume of the locals rose several decibels. With the beer flowing, Quince knew their brains would go down the toilet with the alcohol. "I hope they win, Andy. The boys in blue will have their hands full later if they don't."

"I bet you did a few big matches in your time?"

"Always been some kind of aggro between opposing fans, and I've put a few away."

It was midway through the first half when the pub erupted. The Swans had gone one up after dominating the game. They were in control, and if they kept playing the way they were, Cardiff was in for a drubbing.

Quince knew his day was about to go down the toilet with the supporters' brains when he saw three leery characters enter the bar. He gave Andy the nod.

"Look at these three beauties who've just come in. Don't look like soccer fans to me, more like Nazi FC fans."

"I know the one with the shaven head and piercings," Stokes agreed. "He's bad news. Kirk Smithers, got cons for affray, possession, and offensive weapons. He's one of our regular clients." Stokes knew more of the villains than Quince. He worked as a clerk for a local solicitors', tasked with taking statements for the defence.

"What about the other two, Andy?"

"Never seen them before."

All three sidled up to the bar and ordered three pints, although it looked like Speed was at first reluctant to serve them. Quince couldn't hear what he was saying but Smithers retort was loud enough for everyone to hear.

"You'll have no bother off us. Just serve us a beer."

Smithers scanned the bar as he waited for his drink and saw Andy. Beer now in hand, he made a bee line for him.

"Mr Stokes, how are you doing? Long time no see."

"Not long enough Kirk. What are you up to? You don't normally drink in here."

"You know the score, Mr Stokes. Been banned from most of the pubs. Not my fault though," he said with false pain. "We were going to go up the Liberty, but the filth have got it tight as a drum up there."

"Well, you behave yourself, Kirk. You don't want to end up

inside again, do you?"

"It's a piece of piss, Mr Stokes. No bother."

A sudden roar from the crowd; the Swans had now gone two up as Smithers' mates joined him, crowding Stokes and Quince.

Smithers grinned then shouted, "Come on Bluebirds, shove it up them!"

The pub fell silent, and all heads turned to the three newcomers.

Smithers feigned shock. "What have I said, Mr Stokes? It's only a fucking football match. You'd swear it was life and death."

"Tone it down, Kirk. Maybe it would be best if you and your mates drunk up and left?"

Quince looked towards the bar and gave Speed the nod. Sped knew that meant he should give the boys in blue a call. Trouble was brewing.

"Who's your mate, Mr Stokes, never seen him before. Where's he from, Africa? Look good in a loin cloth, I reckon."

Smithers' mates laughed.

Quince stood, towering above the three of them. "You couldn't be further from the truth. Now I suggest you, and your mates, do yourselves a favour and leave."

"Who the fuck do you think you are, big man? You come over here and order us about as if you own the fucking country. Get back in your dingy and fuck off."

Quince put his hand into his inside coat pocket and produced his warrant card. "Look numb nuts, the boys are on their way, so you either go peaceful or you go out headfirst."

Speed had come from behind the bar and now hovered behind the three troublemakers.

"Everything is sound, Speed," Stokes said. "The boys are going to drink up and leave, isn't that right, Kirk?"

"Fuck you, Mr Stokes, and your mate."

As if rehearsed, which Quince later guessed it was, all three threw their pint glasses in the direction of the big screen. One of them smacked Speed on the top of his head. Then all hell broke loose. The locals made their presence felt.

Smithers' pals began kicking and punching anyone and everyone around them. But Smithers stood his ground and faced off against Quince. He pulled a lock-knife from his leather jacket and took another step towards Quince. "I've always fancied carving one of your lot."

"Kirk, don't be so fucking stupid," Quince warned. "If you use that you'll get a ten stretch. Use your head."

Smithers made a lunge toward Quince, but he was too slow. Quince had already taken his own advice and drove his head into Smithers' nose. He felt the man's face crack in several places. Smithers was tougher than Quince had anticipated. That blow would put ninety percent on the deck. The thug regained his balance, but Quince drove a right hook into Smither's solar plexus, dropping him like a stone. The knife fell from his hand and hit the floor a microsecond before Smithers did the same and it was about to get worse for the man. Quince could see his blow had had the desired effect. Smithers struggled to catch his breath. Then Smithers stepped over the line. "You're dead. You hear me?" he screamed. For Quince, the red mist had descended. The little voice that usually warned against taking things too far was lost in the din of the fight. He pushed the crowd away and grabbed Smithers by the throat.

"Abe, be careful. You're fucking throttling him," Stokes shouted. This voice was heard. "He's done. Just get him out."

Quince's own little voice now shouted too. STOP! He grimaced, and let Smithers go. Andy stepped in and dragged the injured man through to the door and launched him out onto the pavement.

Smithers' mates had been kicked senseless and were lying unconscious on the floor as two uniformed constables burst in to quell the riot. With the job done by the fans, the appetite for destruction quickly subsided. Apart from a few choice insults thrown at the coppers, they were allowed to drag the unconscious men to join their pal outside.

"Speed, two pints and a couple of chasers please," Quince shouted as the fans resumed their viewing of the match. "In your own time of course. How's the head?"

"Had worse!"

4

The air conditioning was set to a temperature that would keep milk fresh for a month, not that it was needed. Kelvin shivered, a combination of the blown-air chill and the soul-chilling prospect of the pending interview. A great deal depended on the impression he presented to the man sitting opposite at the table bolted to the floor. The man looked more like a drug dealer than a probation officer. Tall, emaciated, and dressed in jeans and a T-shirt proclaiming the virtues of a punk band Kelvin had never heard of. The man's hair had thinned to a handful of strands that reminded him of Homer Simpson, but he had let the back and sides grow into a ponytail. A pierced nose and earlobes completed the confusing picture.

"How are you, Kelvin?" the man flashed a gold tooth. "I'm Russell Gibbs. I work for the probation service, and I'll be your supervisory officer when you're released next week."

"Yes, I was told that you'd be coming, Mr Gibbs, and that you'd be supervising me when I got out."

"Good. So... let's have a look now," he opened a brown card folder and shuffled a sheet. "You were sentenced to five years and you've served four. So, you'll be out on licence for twelve months from the date of your release, do you understand that?"

"Yes, I do, Mr Gibbs."

"And you know that there will be stringent conditions regarding your licence," his eyes rose to meet Kelvin's, "due to the nature of the offences that you've committed?"

"Yes, Mr Gibbs."

"I've got the reports relating to the offences. But I usually like to get it straight from the horse's mouth. Would you like to tell me in your own words?"

"I'd rather not, Mr Gibbs. What I did was wrong. I admitted it all, it'll never happen again, I swear."

"Fair enough. I can understand that you've never met me before, however, I'll be looking after your best interests when you're on the outside, do you understand?"

"Yes, Mr Gibbs."

"I suppose you've had a hard time inside during the last four years?"

"That's for sure. There have been times when I wished I was dead, to be honest. I've had all sorts done to me in here. The screws just let it happen, they turn a blind eye. I'm supposed to be segregated, but they still get to me. It's no-good complaining because some of the prisoners are raving loonies, they'd slit your throat without blinking. I know what I did was wrong, but I've paid the price."

"That's as may be, but you may find it even harder on the outside. It's not going to be easy for you, but that's my job, to settle you and make sure you adhere to the terms of your licence."

"Yes, Mr Gibbs, thank you."

Gibbs sat back in his chair and folded his arms. He watched Kelvin for a moment before speaking again. "You play ball with me, Kelvin, and everything will be alright."

"I will, Mr Gibbs. You can count on me. You'll never see me inside again, I promise."

"That's what I want to hear," he smiled and leaned back to the table and the folder of notes. "Right then, the first thing is accommodation. I've sorted a one-bedroom flat for you in York Street. It's nothing fancy, but it's a start."

Kelvin nodded his thanks.

"I've also sorted out a job for you, on a local building site, general labouring. Are you okay with that?"

"Well, it's not what I'm used to, but this is a fresh start for me, Mr Gibbs. Beggars can't be choosers."

"That's the hammer, Kelvin. Think positive. Bit different from your old job. I.T. wasn't it?"

"Yes, I worked for a local electrical company, in Bridgend. I was doing well until I fucked it all up."

"Do you want to tell me all about it, Kelvin? I can understand if you don't."

"Not just yet, Mr Gibbs. You've got the reports, you know what happened. I didn't mean any harm; I knew it was wrong. As I say, I've been punished for it. I just want to forget about it all, start afresh, a new life."

"What about family, Kelvin, have they stood by you?"

"Not really. I've only got my mother. I don't blame her, I let her down. I haven't seen her since I was sentenced."

"Well, I'm sure you and I will get on, Kelvin. You just listen to me and things will work out fine, I'm sure of that."

"To be honest, Mr Gibbs, I can't wait to get out of here."

"Okay. I know I'm repeating myself, but you know there will be stringent conditions to your release on licence because of the offences you've committed?"

"Of course."

"Well, I'll just go over a few for you to be sure."

"Okay."

"The first thing you must do is attend Swansea Central Police Station and give all your details so that you can be entered on the Sex offenders register. They'll want to know the ins and outs of a cat's arse, and, as you know, you'll be on the register indefinitely because of the length of your sentence."

"I've no problem with that. Mr Gibbs."

"Once you've registered, you'll be assigned an officer by the Public Protection Unit, usually a detective constable. They'll be part of the Management of Sexual Offenders and Violent Offenders. You'll hear it referred to as MOSOVO. He or she will probably visit you in a couple of days. They usually go through all the old bollocks, like going abroad, declaring electronic devices like computers, and mobile phones. They'll be watching you like a hawk. The next few are a bit more complex and will tie you down a little. You must never go near any schools, do you understand?"

"Yes, I understand."

"You must never be alone with anyone under eighteen years of age or attend any premises where children frequent. In other words, Kelvin, the system has you by the bollocks, do you understand?"

"Yes."

"I'll be calling on you as and when I feel like it, as will the public protection team. So, whatever you do, stay on the straight and narrow or you'll be back inside in the blink of an eye."

"So, can I have a computer, or mobile phone?"

"They're not a problem, but like I say, you'll have to declare them to the MOSOVO officer." The acronym stood for Manager of Sexual Offences and Violent Offenders. "If you do get them, they've all got to be in your name, the same with social media, no using a false name or they'll have your legs. My advice is, keep your head down for a while, forget about all that crap."

"I understand. I'm so glad I've only a few more nights here. Four years seems like thirty."

"You were lucky. By pleading guilty four years ago, you saved yourself another five stretch."

"I couldn't do any longer, Mr Gibbs. I would definitely top myself you can be sure of that."

"OK, Kelvin. I don't think there's anything else. I'll see you on the day of your release and take you to the flat. I'll settle you in and then we'll register you."

"Thank you, Mr Gibbs, and you'll look after me, I have your word on that?"

"No problem. You take priority at the moment. Once you're settled, you'll only see me now and again. However, I must warn you now, it will be unannounced, you understand?"

"I know the score, Mr Gibbs, I won't let you down."

"I'm sure you won't."

***

The choice of a VW campervan had nothing to do with taste. Russ Gibbs had laid the foundations of a monumental deception that had played out exactly as he had planned. No one could beat the system. You had to join them and play them at their own game. Like the American's liked to say, 'stick it to the man.' Gibbs had stuck it well and truly to the man. His job as probation officer had brought him into contact with the scum of society that others went out of the way to avoid. But Gibbs had exploited those connections and made a pretty penny for himself in the process. The camper van just added the icing on his chosen persona.

He dropped the glovebox door and removed a tin of ready rolled reefers. Lighting one, he pulled down the blinds he had fitted to his windows and turned on the extractor that he designed to suck the tell-tale stench from the interior. After several long drags, he tapped a number into his phone.

"Alright mate, Russ here, I've sorted Kelvin out. He's opened his heart out to me this morning, I feel a little bit sorry for him to be honest, he's had a torrid time in nick."

"Then we're on course, yes?"

"Yes."

"Any time frame?"

"I reckon three or four weeks. Then I'll start doing the business with him. He's naïve, so it should be plain sailing from here on in."

"What's your plan?"

"I think I'll do it with a mobile, you know take a few snaps and store them, then leave it lying around the flat. I'll check in with you in a week or two, when we're good to go.

5

Russell Gibbs drove Kelvin Spearman to the one-bedroom flat that was to be his future home, a future that would be at best challenging. The flat was a typical nineteen-seventies box of concrete crammed into a mean plot where a dozen homes were stacked without thought for outside space. They took a lift that stank of urine to the second floor and walked a short graffiti painted corridor to a battered red door that had been patched with metal plates where it had been kicked in at sometime in the past. Gibbs fished for the key and shoved the door open with his shoulder as it caught on a curl of ripped linoleum.

"Well, Kelvin, here it is. What do you think?"

"It's very nice, Mr Gibbs, thank you." Kelvin hated it but had to be careful. He wasn't in a position to complain.

"I bet it's very strange, being locked up for four years? Must have seemed like a lifetime?" Gibbs shut the door and squeezed past Kelvin to enter the lounge.

"I had it rough," Kelvin agreed, following his probation officer. "Initially, things weren't too bad, but once the others found out about me, that was it. I was terrified. All sorts of things happened." He had never tried to block out those things, as terrible as they were. He knew they were the things that would keep him from ever going back inside. "No one cared, you know I tried to kill myself when I was inside, don't you?"

Gibbs sat in a well-worn armchair. "I *did* read somewhere in the report that you attempted suicide. Do you want to talk about it?"

"I suppose now I'm out perhaps it would help if I spoke to someone." Kelvin sat at one end of a two-seater settee that didn't match the chair.

"Well, I'm a good listener, and I can set the wheels in motion for you to have some counselling if need be."

"Where do I start, Mr Gibbs?"

"Well, wherever you want, Kelvin."

"I don't want to talk about what I was locked up for, I can understand why I was arrested. I've not blocked out what happened. I don't deserve to forget it. I know I was wrong but what was done to me was something I struggled to get my head around."

"What do you mean?"

"I did wrong, Mr Gibbs, and I will never repeat what I did. But when I was jailed, I should have been protected. I wasn't. I was treated like crap. Warders turned a blind eye to things that went on. It was their job to protect me, and they didn't."

"Did you ever complain about your treatment?"

"Complain? If I had, do you think I would be here today? That's why I tried to kill myself."

"And when was this, Kelvin?"

"I was about eighteen months into my sentence. I tried to hang myself." Kelvin had rehearsed this in his head many times. He knew he would have to talk about it if he was ever going to get his life back on track. He had read all the books on this kind of thing. But even he was surprised at how easy it was now for him to tell Gibbs. Afterall, if Gibbs was going to believe in him, he had to trust Gibbs and show him he had nothing more to hide. Of course, that wasn't strictly true. He did have something to hide back no one would benefit form knowing that secret.

"Why?"

"I'd been raped by my cell mate."

"By another sex offender?"

Kelvin nodded. "Up until then, I was in a cell on my own. That was great. I used to cry myself to sleep most nights without anyone knowing. Then, that all changed."

"Have you told anyone else about this?"

"No. You are the first. I didn't even tell the doctors. I was in the prison hospital for months being treated and evaluated."

"That's terrible, Kelvin. I've heard these things happen, but what happened then?"

"He threatened me, telling me not to say anything or he would kill me. I thought, if he was capable of doing that to me, he would be capable of anything. I just wanted to die but I didn't want someone to have that control over me too. Does that sound crazy?"

"Not at all. He controlled a part of your life and you didn't want him to control your death too. So, you decided to take that control off him and kill yourself?"

Kelvin nodded.

"So, when did you attempt that?"

"Early that morning. I ripped up a blanket and made it into a rope, tied it around my neck, then fixed it to the top bunk rail. I climbed up and just jumped off."

"What about your cell mate, didn't he try to stop you?"

"He laughed. I can see him now, before I jumped, just laughing. The next thing I know is I wake up in the prison hospital. I'd been unconscious for a day and that's about it, Mr Gibbs."

"How long were you hospitalised?"

"About three months, and to be fair, I wasn't bothered at all in those three months. Everything was calm. The doctors and nurses were brilliant with me. When I was released from the hospital wing I just kept myself to myself. They gave me a trustee job in the library, and I kept my head down."

"You've been through the mill, for sure."

"Yes. I just want to be left alone to get on with my life." He sighed and forced a smile. "I feel a bit better about it, now that I've told you." As the words came out, he realised it was true. He did feel ever so slightly better. He'd never be the same again, that was for sure, but even a tiny improvement was better at this point in his life. Perhaps he could begin to live again? Things could never be the same again, but who knew what the future held.

"That's good, Kelvin," Gibbs also smiled. "I'll give you a couple of hours to settle in and then you can meet me down at the police station. We can get you registered and then you can look forward to work on Monday. There'll be no problem there, just keep your head down. If there are problems, you can ring me anytime."

"Thank you, Mr Gibbs. I'm very grateful."

"Kelvin, you fully understand all the restrictions that go with your licence, do you want me to go through them again to be sure?"

"No Mr Gibbs, I understand them all, I will do nothing to contravene my licence, I don't want to go back to prison, and I'll make sure that I never will."

"I have no doubt you'll find it strange on Monday, Kelvin, swapping the computer for bricks and mortar."

"I'm sure I will, Mr Gibbs."

"OK, I'll leave you to it. I've stocked the cupboards and fridge for you, so you should be fine until you get your first wage."

Russel Gibbs left Kelvin's flat and headed back to the car. He checked no one was near before making the call.

"Alright mate? Russ here. I've sorted Kelvin out. He's in the flat and I'm meeting him later to register."

"And he hasn't a clue what sort of shit storm may be heading his way?"

"No. Not long to go now."

6

He'd been on the building site for a day short of four weeks, and he hadn't encountered any problems. In fact, it seemed like nobody cared. Kelvin got on with his job and nobody got into a conversation with him. As far as they were concerned, time was money, and that's all they were concerned with.

He often wondered if any of his work mates knew about his past, and if they ever found out, how they'd react.

As far as Kelvin was concerned Russell Gibbs was a saint. He'd sorted everything for him, and things couldn't be better - considering.

There were times when he thought about his mother. Since his arrest and incarceration, she had shunned him. If she only knew the truth.

Kelvin had sacrificed his future, and even to this day had never divulged the truth to anyone, least of all to his family.

The work was mundane, heavy going, but stress-free. At the end of his shift, he headed for home on a service bus, just another face amongst thousands walking the streets and going about their business.

He microwaved a tv dinner when Russell Gibbs banged on the door and announced his arrival.

Opening the door to the probation officer. Kelvin smiled warmly. "Nice to see you, Mr Gibbs. I was just having dinner. Fancy a cuppa?"

"No, I'm fine. You look tired," he said.

"Yes. The work isn't what I'm used to, but hey, it's cool."

"I'm glad, Kelvin. And you're keeping your nose clean?"

"Of course. There's no way I'm going back to prison."

"That's the attitude. I must say you're one of the easiest offenders I've had to supervise, and it seems the public protection team are happy with the way you're conducting yourself. DC Penny's been keeping me in the loop."

"Yes, he's popped in a couple of times unannounced. It's all down to you, Mr Gibbs, and I'm more than grateful."

"That's good," his eyes wandered the room. "Can I sit down?"

"Of course. You sure you don't fancy a coffee or something to eat?"

"No, I'm sound. I won't keep you long. Just a few questions."

"Shoot!"

"Are you encountering any problems?"

"No, it's all going well."

"Have you had any contact with your mother since your release?"

"No. I'm on my own, Mr Gibbs. The past is the past as far as I'm concerned."

"Well, it's still my job to ensure that you adhere to the conditions of your licence."

"I understand. I suppose you want to check the flat out again?"

"Well, if the truth be told, I don't think I really need to. But it's in my brief."

"You carry on, Mr Gibbs, feel free."

Gibbs stood and walked through the flat, poking his nose into cupboards and drawers. In less than five minutes, Gibbs seemed satisfied. "Well, everything seems in order. I think I'll have that coffee now."

"Of course," Kelvin grinned.

Gibbs sank between two cushions on the sofa.

"Two sugars, Mr Gibbs?"

"You got it."

Coffees brewed, Kelvin handed a mug to Gibbs and sat on a worn armchair opposite.

"You've got it nice and comfortable here, are you happy?"

"As happy as anyone who has just done a four stretch, Mr Gibbs."

Gibbs balanced his mug on the arm of the settee and made a show of stuffing his hand down the side of the sofa cushion. What he produced made Kelvin freeze. He felt his blood run cold.

"What's this, Kelvin?" Gibbs held a Nokia mobile phone out towards Kelvin.

"That's not mine, Mr Gibbs, I swear. It must have been there when I moved in."

Gibbs shook his head. "Oh, Kelvin. What did I tell you, no computers, no mobiles without express permission, for fuck sake. And I know you haven't had permission."

"I-I s-swear that's n-not my phone," Kelvin stammered.

"Please tell me that there's nothing incriminating on this phone, because if there is, you're going straight back inside, you know that?"

"It's not mine, I swear, Mr Gibbs. For fuck sake, please believe me."

"This is disappointing."

"It's not mine, it must be from the people who lived here before me. I swear it's not mine."

Gibbs switched the phone on, "Bloody good battery if this has been here for over a month." He flicked through to photographs. Gibbs started scrolling the menu and frowned. He held the phone towards Kelvin to show ten images of children playing in a school yard. "What have you done, Kelvin?"

"Mr Gibbs, I've nothing to do with this, honestly. This is all wrong, please believe me."

"You've let me down badly. I thought you were different. You know what this means?"

"Please, Mr Gibbs, this is all wrong. That phone is nothing to do with me. You don't understand. I'm no paedophile, for fuck sake. You don't understand, you don't know the truth."

"I'm sorry, Kelvin. I've no choice. I must inform the police. You'll be arrested then returned to prison, in breach of your licence."

"Please, Mr Gibbs, I beg you. This is all wrong, it's not my phone, I swear."

"Kelvin, I've been doing this job for many years. Why should I believe you? I've been let down so many times in the past. I thought you were different."

"I am, Mr Gibbs, you don't understand how different. If I go back to prison, I swear I'll kill myself. Do you want that on your hands?"

"To be honest, I don't give a fuck really," Gibbs snapped.

"What are you going to do?"

Gibbs scratched his head. "I thought rehabilitation was the answer for you. Obviously, I was wrong again."

"No, Mr Gibbs, you weren't wrong. This is all wrong, I'm no paedophile."

"No paedophile? You've just done four years, you've been

raped, and yet you go and do this," he said, waving the phone in Kelvin's face. "How the fuck am I supposed to believe you?"

"Please don't report me, Mr Gibbs. How can I make this right?"

"My hands are tied, Kelvin. I have to report it. You've breached your conditions. I told you what would happen, didn't I?" Gibbs took a deep breath, considering his options, of which there were none.

"Right, and what if I believe you? Where does that leave me? I'm damned if I do, and I'm damned if I don't."

"What can I say? You must believe me. I can't go back to prison, I just can't."

Gibbs stood and dropped the phone into his pocket. "I'll have to sleep on this, Kelvin. I 'm going to go out on a limb here. I've never done this before, but you seem different. You should heading to a cell now."

Kelvin sighed, the tension plug pulled, he was deflating as fast as a balloon. Was there hope? "Thank you, Mr Gibbs, please don't have me recalled."

"I'll speak to you tomorrow. Just carry on as normal. But I'll keep the mobile."

Kelvin watched Gibbs leave. Stunned by the find, he ran his own hand down behind the cushions even though he didn't expect to find anything. Surely, the place would have been cleaned and searched properly before he moved in?

***

Gibbs walked down the stairs to the car park at the rea of the flats and made another call.

"I've done the business, got him by the bollocks. He's shitting himself. I'll give him a few days to sweat, then I'll make him an offer he can't refuse. If things work out, we can go ahead. Just let the others know, the future looks bright."

***

The discovery of the mobile by Gibbs was devastating, and although he carried on working, Kelvin nerves were shattered into tiny, fragile pieces. He hadn't heard from Gibbs for two days and was expecting to be nicked at any time. He was on the edge, constantly scanning the site for faces he hadn't seen before. Would the cops stake him out before arresting him or would they just barge onto the site and drag him away in front of everyone?

He couldn't get his head around it. He knew the mobile wasn't his but had no idea what was going on. The dark thoughts and flashbacks to his time in the nick consumed him. Clocking out at the end of the day, he felt a glimmer of hope. He hadn't seen any new faces and hadn't been arrested. No one waited for him outside his flat either. Perhaps Gibbs had decided to give him a break.

Kelvin dumped his work clothes in the old, battered washing machine, dressed in a pair of shorts and T-shirt and sank into the settee. He didn't feel like eating but he'd have to force something down. The work at the site was hard and he needed energy. Just at that moment there was a knock on the door. He sprang from the settee. Was this the cops? Had Gibbs sold him down the river? More knocking. He couldn't hide. Where could he go? Kelvin eventually cracked open the door and there was Gibbs.

"Aren't you going to invite me in, Kelvin?"

"M-Mr Gibbs," Kelvin stammered. Gibbs was not someone he wanted to see but he was better than having the police barging through the door. "I wasn't sure if you'd come... yes, come in. What's happening? Have you reported me?"

Gibbs frowned, seemingly troubled by the question. "To be honest, Kelvin, no, I haven't."

Kelvin felt the tension drain from him instantly. "Oh, thank you, thank you.2 he sobbed. The relief was palpable. The release of tension freeing his emotions. He didn't want to cry in front of Gibbs back couldn't hold it back. "I can't go back inside, Mr Gibbs, I'll do anything, anything."

Gibbs sat where Kelvin had been seconds before. "Now, listen, Kelvin, listen to me. Your future is in the palm of my hand. I've got the mobile and you're fucked. From now on you do what I say, do you understand?"

"Anything, Mr Gibbs."

"I've got a job for you."

"Of course." Kelvin smiled and sat in the armchair opposite.

Gibbs frowned again. "For God's sake, are you thick, or

what?"

Confused, Kelvin leaned closer. "Sorry?"

Gibbs shook his head. "You do the job I have for you, or you will go back inside."

Kelvin was still none the wiser. He knew his freedom depended upon doing what his probation officer told him to do. Why was Gibbs saying this now? "What have I got to do, Mr Gibbs?"

"I want you to go to Jersey?"

"Jersey? What for? I can't, my licence doesn't allow me to. I'll have to inform DC Penny."

"Don't worry about the licence and fuck DC Penny. I've sorted that out. Y,ou can go no problem."

Now things were getting very weird. "Why Jersey?"

"I want a package picked up and brought back."

The penny had dropped. This was not right. "Package? What the hell's going on, Mr Gibbs?"

"I want you to pick up a package."

"You've set me up, haven't you, Mr Gibbs," Kelvin seethed. He knew he had to be careful, but Gibbs had stitched him up. "You're just like the others I've spent four years with."

"Calm down, Kelvin," Gibbs grinned. "I don't want you bursting a blood vessel. Good to see you're not as thick as I thought you were. So, you either agree or you're back inside tout suite. What's it to be, the collection, or the nick?"

He had no choice. There was nothing he could do. He had to find some way out of this and had to be careful. "I'll do it, but only this once."

"Kelvin, you'll do what I ask, no you'll do what I tell you to do, as and when I tell you to do it. You got that? Now listen and listen good. You're booked on the early morning flight to Jersey. You'll go to the Apollo Hotel. Your room has already been reserved. All you have to do is spend the night there."

"But what about the Police? I suppose they're in on it as well?"

"That's all sorted," Gibbs said dismissively. Just do as I tell you and everything will be alright." Gibbs stood and patted Kelvin on the shoulder.

Kelvin pulled away from Gibbs and strode to the window.

"This nightmare is never going to end, is it?"

"OK, Kelvin, you've had your blow out. Nothing will change until I say so. When you book out of the hotel, there'll be a package at reception for you. All you have to do is bring it back and give it to me, do you understand?"

"What's in this package?"

"The least you know the better." Gibbs pulled an envelope from his pocket. "Here are your tickets. Just get to the airport, get over to Jersey and get the package. Simple as that."

"And if I get caught?"

"Well, you go back to jail. Just don't get caught, not that there's any chance of that," Gibbs smiled. "Remember, what future have you got? No family, a registered sex offender, brilliant mind working on a fucking building site and holed up in a shitty flat. Do I give a monkeys about you? I'm sick of dealing with scum like you."

"Just give me the tickets, Mr Gibbs," Kelvin snatched the envelope, "and get out of my sight."

Gibbs laughed. "So, you do have a pair of balls somewhere in those shorts. See you same time day after tomorrow. And don't open the package," he warned him. "I'll let myself out."

He slammed the door and threw the locks. He had to do something. If he was caught, no one would believe him. It would be another nail in his mother's coffin. His mother hated him but she didn't know the truth. He found a pen in a kitchen drawer and tore a sheet of lined paper from a notebook.

Dear Mum.

I know that you think I've let you down, and I'm so sorry for the pain I've put you through. But now is the time to let you know the truth. I've just spent four years in prison for something I never did. In the eyes of the world, I am some sort of monster who preyed on young children. It's so far from the truth, you wouldn't believe.

I don't blame you at all for not standing by me, it was probably better for everybody all round. If you'd known the truth at the time you'd have been mortified.

At the time of writing this letter, I am between the devil and the deep blue sea. I've lost everything. I would end it all now, but I can't whilst you think I'm a monster. You must know the truth. I went to prison for something I didn't do. I was protecting someone

I loved, and still do.

When the Police raided the house and took possession of the computer, the images they saw were nothing to do with me.

I would love to explain to you one day face to face, I know it will be hard for you to take in, but I'm innocent.

I'm writing this letter, because I have nowhere to turn. I'm in deep trouble and I may end up back in prison.

If anything happens to me, I have deposited this letter, along with other evidence showing my innocence, with my solicitor, Mr David Spencer.

I've already instructed him. He knows the whole story.

I hope you can forgive me for putting you through this ordeal, but I think, if at the time of my arrest you had known the truth, it would have been even more devastating for you.

I love you Mum, and always will.
Kelvin, XXXXXX

7

Is it possible to drown in files of evidence? Abraham Quince wondered. He certainly felt like he was drowning and there was no one on the riverbank able or willing to toss him a lifeline. His paperwork was regarded by management as amongst the best, but Quince hated it. He sometimes wished he had stayed a beat bobby. At least the files *they* put together rarely had lives riding on them.

Topping and tailing a recent murder file for the CPS, before heading off to the pub for a celebratory drink, Quince's team had worked hard during the investigation of a domestic murder where the wife had stabbed her husband to death after suffering years of abuse. Quince felt for the woman but the fact she had planned the killing, and severed his head, too, had made it impossible for the team to seek a reduction in whatever sentence was eventually decided upon by the Crown Court. The woman had clearly lost the plot during the lockdown. It must have been terrible for the poor woman, having to stay within the house with an abusive husband. Still, the team deserved the plaudits for tying it up so swiftly. Now it was up to him to ensure the evidence was all neatly presented for the Crown Prosecution Service.

Quince had no time to get his head around the appointment of a new Detective Chief Inspector. There had been strong rumour that the rank was going to be mothballed, but the powers-that-be had decided otherwise.

Checking his watch, Quince closed the file and tucked it in his desk drawer. Grabbing his coat, he closed his office door and strolled through the dimly lit CID office. The team had gone on ahead and would be halfway to being pissed by the time he rolled into the pub.

"Boss?"

Quince spun to find Bill Daniels, the Crime Scene sergeant, standing in the shadows. "What the hell are you doing here? Thought you'd be down the pub."

"I hung back. I wanted to speak with you."

"Why didn't you knock my door?"

"I could see you were busy. I'm not in a hurry. I wanted you to know who they've appointed to DCI before you hear it from some drunken detective."

"OK… and?"

"They've appointed Norma Cross."

"What? Norma Cross?"

"Yes, boss," Daniels said, the apology clear in his voice.

"Cross couldn't detect a fart in a crisp bag."

Daniels laughed but Quince could see he was just as unimpressed as he was.

"Jesus!"

"It should have been you," Daniels offered.

"I'm not that bothered, but Norma Cross is not going to be good for us."

"It came as a shock to us all."

"You all knew?"

Daniels fidgeted. "An email came out earlier. No one wanted to tell you."

"I haven't had time to check my mail."

"Sorry, boss. Things won't be the same again. Cross will be a thorn in all our sides."

Pulling on his coat, Quince nodded. "I guess it's up to me to make sure she knows where she stands."

***

Sitting in her office at Swansea Central Police Station, Norma Cross smiled at her reflection in the compact she carried in her handbag. Pat would be pleased by the news.

Cross snapped the compact shut and got up from her chair, she opened a window and took out a packet of Gitano's cigarettes. Lighting the end, she smoked it with her head out of the window, blowing smoke circles, watching the rings dissipate on the evening breeze.

Finishing her smoke, Cross flicked her cigarette butt down to the road below to join a huddle of others in various states of decay.

The desk drawer contained a bottle of gin. She poured herself two fingers and thought about the evening ahead.

A celebratory drink with Quince had been arranged for the team. It was a tradition within the department – something Cross wanted to end, but it was also an ideal opportunity to meet Quince's team and rub a little salt into the wily bastard's wounds.

She knew the dislike was mutual. Quince had made it clear what he thought of her on several occasions, but now the worm had turned. She would be his boss and he'd have to answer to her. There was no doubt that Quince was a good detective, but he was also a pain in the arse as far as she was concerned. She finished her drink and tucked the glass away in a drawer, shuffling a file over the top to hide it. Standing, she pulled her coat from the back of a chair and headed for the door.

Quince stood by the bar, surrounded by rowdy colleagues, as Cross entered the pub. He'd be buying the drinks. That too was tradition. There was no way he would steal all the limelight. Cross smiled warmly as she pushed through the crowd and stood alongside Quince as she made a show of putting three-hundred quid over the bar as a tab. It was going to be a long night, and Cross was going to enjoy herself.

"That's very generous of you," Quince grumbled, clearly overshadowed by the new Chief Inspector's gesture.

"The least I can do for *my* team," she said, clearly leaving no doubt as to who was in charge. She turned to the others huddled around. "The drinks are on me."

A cheer from the detectives annoyed Quince. Loyalty of detectives could sometimes be hired for a night, but it was the day-to-day operations, the shoulder-to-shoulder fight against crime that really dictated respect. "Don't forget there's still money left in my pot too," he shouted and necked the dregs of his whiskey. He turned to the smiling barman. "Since she's paying, I'll have a double and a pint of bitter."

Cross grinned and shook her head. She leaned close and whispered in his ear, "You'd better get used to it. There's a new top dog in town."

"I wasn't going to call you a dog," he whispered back. "But if that's how you see yourself, who am I to argue?"

The smile slipped from Cross' face. "Remember who you're talking to."

"That's the problem," Quince said, the smile now on *his* face, "I remember only too well."

Cross moved away, pushing back through the crowd with the

smile back on her face. Finding a young DC sitting at a table of older detectives, she ushered him from the seat and climbed up. "Attention please," she shouted and waited for silence. "I'd just like to say that, as your new Chief, I'm delighted to be in charge of such a distinguished group of detectives," her eyes singled out Quince. "I know things haven't been the same since DCI Reynolds retired..." smiles suddenly slipped to be replaced by embarrassed expressions as some eyes turned to Quince. "But I'm here now to get this team back to where it belongs... at the top." A subdued cheer failed to mollify most. Cross knew the detectives loved working for Quince. But Quince was a thorn that needed removal and she would do her best to pluck it before it festered and ruined her new posting. Quince knew her too well. He was outspoken and would make things difficult for her. "Thank you all," she said as she jumped down from the chair.

Finishing her drink, her mobile rang, she checked the caller ID, it was Pat. She headed to a narrow passageway leading to the toilets before speaking.

8

A light but warm breeze rustled the logo festooned umbrellas of the eateries and fashionable bars of Wind Street – the nightlife epicentre of Swansea City centre. Dressed in half-blues (a stripped down, off-duty version of his uniform), Gareth Dix focussed on the day ahead as he trudged towards the Central police Station. He had spent the last three months with his 'puppy walker' – an experienced constable entrusted with showing a probationer constable the realities and practicalities of real policing. Today would be his first day out on his own. He had passed the assessments of his progress to date and was deemed to be competent enough to venture out on his own.

He barely glanced at the ruins of the Swansea Castle, founded by Henry de Beaumont in 1107. To be fair to Dix, not much of the old fortress remained, not after three nights of heavy bombing during the Blitz of World War II. But he did notice the shrapnel holes in the old red brick work of the former Central Police station as he cut through a lane to the new monstrous city police HQ opposite the Magistrates Court. The old station was now another fancy café and formed part of the art school. A large stainless steel fingerprint sculpture stood proudly outside the new black and blue tile station, linking the past with the present and hinting at the possible investigative developments of the future.

Entering the vehicle yard to the right of the main building, Dix tapped in his key code and pushed the steel gate open.

Geoff Lyons locked the doors of his Toyota as Dix headed to the charge room door.

"Well, Dix, this is the day you've been waiting for," Lyons grinned. "Today you lose your umbilical cord and go out into the big bad world on your own. How are you feeling?"

Dix stopped and waited for his sergeant to catch up. "A bit nervous, Sarge."

"That's good. If you said you weren't I'd be a little bit concerned. You'll be OK. If you have any problems just give me a shout."

"Cheers, Sarge."

"After you've made the tea, one of the boys will drop you down on the marina beat. Should be a nice quiet shift for you."

"I'd rather have a walk down, if that's alright, Sarge."

"Whatever, Dix, but like I said, if anything out of the ordinary crops up, you get on the blower, you understand?"

"You bet, Sarge."

Making the tea was a rite of passage. It had always been normal practice in the police for the youngest in service to make tea for the rest of the shift. Times had changed and some new recruits saw it as demeaning, but not Dix. The grandson of a retired copper, a man who had become something of a legend within the division, his grandfather, Frank, had drummed it into him that it was important to fit in. If that meant making gallons of tea all day and doing nothing else, then so be it.

After the morning brew, Dix donned his helmet and the rest of his uniform and took a deep breath as he stood on the threshold. The safety of the station was just a step behind him. The unknown lay ahead.

There had never been a time when Dix had wanted to do anything other than be a copper. He had grown up listening to stories of his grandad. His mother had raised him on the tales of daring, outstanding police work, and occasional serious bending of rules. Frank Dix had been an old-style copper. There had been no phone cameras to record events and a clip around the ear was mainly acceptable – in preference to a spell in the cell.

Walking the regulation pace – a speed slow enough to see everything and be seen, but not too slow to make beat coverage impossible - through the city centre towards the marina, Gareth Dix suppressed a grin. This was what he had wanted for as long as he could remember, since he first heard the stories of his grandfather's exploits. Of course, modern policing is nothing like it was back in Grandad Frank's day. The body cam, the mobile phone cameras in everyone's hands these days mean a copper has to be sure to do things right.

Conscious of his uniform, determined to fix a confident expression, even though he felt anything but confident. The training had been good, thorough, but now he doubted he'd remember any of it if something happened. What if there was a personal injury RTC, and he was first on the scene, how would he cope? Sergeant Geoff Lyons had talked him through potential incidents time and time again. He kept rehearsing them in his head, Road Traffic Collisions, suicides, sudden deaths, shoplifter, domestic disputes, assaults. He had not dealt with a great deal since his posting to Swansea Central, but he knew enough, probably as much as anyone in his position.

Castle Gardens ahead, in the shadow of the castle ruins. An expanse of concrete slabs and steps of waterfalls surrounded by benches and an enormous video screen broadcasting whatever the local authority deemed was suitable for the locals. Frequented by daily visits from a handful of homeless and youths flaunting local byelaws on skateboards, if there was somewhere he'd encounter a problem then this would be it. Apart from a group of teens snarling at him as he walked past, he was beginning to feel comfortable out on his own. As sergeant Lyons said, no-one would know if it's his first solo run or his hundredth marathon.

Abertawe, the Welsh name for Swansea, which loosely translated means 'the mouth of the river Tawe,' had undergone another one of its transitions. Not quite a butterfly emerging from a cocoon but the new theatre build; on the seafront and the gold-coloured bridge spanning the width of Mumbles Road had certainly brightened up the area. Dix was unsure about the bridge. He had heard it described as a marmite structure – you either loved it or hated it. Dix didn't like Marmite but was therefore in a minority. He liked the bridge. Being the second largest city in Wales, Swansea had a lot of potential. At the gateway to the Gower Coast in the south, it was just fifty or so miles west from the capitol Cardiff and about the same distance east of Tenby in the west of the country. It should have enjoyed growing prosperity, but over the last decade, big retail chains had either gone through or bailed out of Swansea. The shopping centre had more empty retail rentals than open stores and the increase in charity shops was a sure sign to Dix that the city was dying. Not even a new three-thousand seat theatre could breathe life into the place.

By the time he arrived at the marina, the boat owners were busying themselves on the dockside. He nodded and smiled at a wizened fellow, bent by years of labour that Dix knew had made his fortune. Dressed in a wet suit, he looked like a bloated penguin. He had been introduced to many of them over the past weeks when he was accompanied by experienced colleagues – part of his training period.

"Let you out on your own have they, Gareth?" the old man grinned. "They're taking a bloody chance, aren't they?"

Peter Gilchrist owned a forty-foot powered yacht, one of those gin palaces that had never seen a sail since it had been built twenty years ago.

"Aye, my first solo patrol."

Gilchrist slipped a key into a wire gate that secured the jetty for exclusive access to owners and stepped aside. "Come a-board. I'll make us a coffee."

"I don't know whether I should. If the sergeant catches me, I'll be for the high jump."

Gilchrist shrugged those hunched shoulders. "I reckon, in a few weeks, if I ask you again, you'll bite my hand off for a quiet coffee. Enjoy your patrol and stay safe."

Dix flashed an even-toothed smile, nodded and strolled on, breathing in the fresh salty air and admiring the yachts and speed boats moored alongside the old man's vessel. It was like a poor man's version of Monaco. The only thing that spoiled the impression was the litter floating amongst the boats and gathered in flotillas of detritus around the steep walls of the marina. Plastic shopping bags, aluminium beer and soft drink cans, crisp packets and even a coat. Dix stopped and sighed, disappointed. Why would anyone throw a coat into the dock? The arms were splayed wide and something at each extremity looked remarkably like hands. He stepped closer to the edge and bent down lower. They looked like hands because they were hands. Shocked, Dix sprang to his feet and ran back to the gangway. "Peter, I think there's someone in the water, can you let me through?"

Gilchrist was still in his wet suit and shuffled surprisingly quickly back to the gate and followed behind Dix. "You sure it's a body?"

"I'm sure."

Gilchrist pushed Dix aside and dropped off the edge of the wooden walkway extending between two large yachts into the cold dark water. His bald head disappeared for a moment then appeared alongside the body. Other boat owners had been altered and were hurrying to the scene.

Dix remembered his radio and put a call into the control room.

Gilchrist flipped the coat over and a face appeared, white as the ghost he had become. "Gareth, it's a youngster," Gilchrist shouted, then let the body go and swam towards something else bobbing nearby. "There's another one floating here as well, we need help a bit sharpish."

"They're on their way, Pete."

The whip-whip sound of the cavalry arriving, several minutes later, eased the sense of panic. Led by Sgt Lyons, two black-clad constables ran with him towards the gathered crowd. Dix realised he should have dispersed them as some began taking photos and video shots on their cameras.

"Move away, now!" he shouted. "Anyone posting photos or videos will be prosecuted, understand?" There was a reluctant grumble from the lookie-looks as they shuffled back but remained close.

"Bloody hell, Dix, I can't leave you alone for a minute. Your first day out on your own, and you give me two stiffs. Let's have a look at what we've got."

You want me to tow them to the gangway?" Gilchrist shouted.

"If you can. We'll get a better look at them there," Lyons called back.

Gilchrist was surprisingly strong and at ease in the water. He grabbed the nearest body and kicked towards the gangway. Lyons and the two constables dragged the body onto the aluminium jetty.

"Keep those nosey buggers away, Dix," Lyons snapped and nodded at the crowd.

Like the tea making, there was no point in arguing. There was a pecking order of responsibility and Dix knew his place.

"They look foreign to me Sarge," Gilchrist said. "I'll get the other."

Both the bodies were laid side-by-side on the jetty.

Lyons took a cursory look and checked the bodies. Both were young and male, and their features did look East Asian. No obvious signs of violence on the bodies, and it was obvious they had not been in the water that long. They were bloated - bodies full of the gasses of death and early decay - but not nibbled by fish yet.

"Get some tape from the car and help Dix cordon off the area," Lyons said to the younger of the two uniforms with him. "I'll get

CID, CSI and the FMO down here a bit rapid." Any suspicious death would warrant the attendance of the Criminal Investigation Department, Crime Scene Investigators and the Force medical officer.

Gilchrist flopped onto the decking of the gangway and wiped the water from his eyes. "I'll get some tarp from my boat, Sarge, just to cover them over. Give them a bit of dignity, if that's OK with you?"

"That would be great, and thanks for what you've done. Saved us from getting the frogmen out or me getting my bloody feet wet."

After Dix had cordoned off the area, Lyons gently pulled him to one side.

"How are you doing, Dix? It's a hell of an initiation. Do you want to go back to the nick for a break?"

"No, Sarge. It's a first. I'm OK. A bit shocked, that's all."

"As your supervisor, I've got to offer you counselling. It's a load of bollocks really, but are you up for it?"

"Leave it there, Sarge. I don't need counselling. But I'd like to deal with the case, if I'm allowed."

"We'll see what the CID make of it first, but obviously, your statement will be important. If it was just one, it could well be an accident, but two? I've got a funny feeling about this one, Dix. I think you've found and opened a can of worms."

"I've got it all recorded on my bodycam, Sarge. In fact, I videoed the recovery of the bodies too."

"Cracking. Thinking on your feet. Preserve the scene as best you can. Difficult when they're floaters but well done. There'll be post-mortems, of course. Do you want to attend them?"

The question needed no thought. "If I could, Sarge? I've seen a couple already. I'd like to be involved in some way."

Within twenty minutes, the Crime Scene Investigators; DS Bill Daniels, and new side kick, DC Ted Farmer arrived, closely followed by Dr Wayne John the Force Medical Officer. They were given free rein to do the necessary business - examine the bodies, photograph the scene, and take any samples they felt were needed, and some that might not be. It was better to have too much than not enough. Ten minutes later, a dishevelled suit appeared on the dock. Quince looked the worse for wear. Six-foot-three tall and built like a modern-day rugby centre, his physique was entirely the result of genes. Although Quince had played a lot of sport, and was naturally good at most, he had never really applied himself to any. Not an ounce of muscle had been forged in a gym for vanity. A career copper with twenty-two years in the job, he had joined as soon as he was old enough – keen to leave the children's home behind. Born in the USA, he had emigrated with his dad to Wales shortly after the death of his mother. With dad part of the management team at Ford's in the States and then in Bridgend, the move had been hard on Quince. With a black dad and a white mother, growing up in Wales had been no more difficult than that he had experienced in America, but when his dad died, two years after the move, he was left with no one who was prepared to take him in. Even though his mother's family were from Port Talbot, and his dad thought it would be wise to bring young Abe closer to his maternal line, it soon became apparent that his Welsh family wanted nothing to do with him. It was years later that Abe Quince discovered why.

"Morning, Geoff," Quince groaned in his typically gruff way – just the hint of an American accent could be detected by those who met him for the first time. "The Ops room gave me the heads up. I hope it's something that makes my braving this headache worth it?"

"You look like shit, boss," Geoff Lyons frowned.

"I've had a heavy night. Feeling a bit fragile this morning. Should be having a nice kip."

Lyons laughed.

"They tell me a probationer found the bodies?"

"That he did, boss. And it was his first morning out on his own. He's bagged a couple of floaters on his first day. Looks like his grandad's luck is rubbing off on him."

Quince looked confused. "His grandad?"

"Aye. Frank Dix. Retired when I was in my probation. Legend of a man."

Nodding, Quince had heard the tales of Frank. He was a man whose tales of daring do were still talked about over a few beers by those who had worked with him. Every time Quince heard one of the stories, the events and actions were just a little bit bigger and more incredible. He glanced at the young copper standing nearby, just out of earshot. He was tall, slim and looked nothing like he'd expect from the genes of the legendary Frank Dix.

"So, what's the score?"

"I think they're of foreign origin, boss. Possibly brought in from some place in Asia. Probably illegal immigrants. No injuries on them, from what I can see. I can understand one body, God knows we've had more than our fair share, but two? Together? Doesn't take a genius to work out there's something not right and that's why I think they're illegals."

Quince donned a white paper suit and blue shoe covers supplied by the Crime Scene Officer and strolled carefully over to the bodies. He walked along a narrow line of raised plastic steps laid out by the CSI team to prevent any more scene contamination. It was a pointless precaution. There had already been too many tramping around for anything of use to be found and the bodies could have entered the water anywhere.

"Morning everyone, nice to see you all bright eyed and bushy tailed."

"Unlike you, you mean?" the doctor grinned.

Quince shrugged. "What have we got, Doc?"

"From what I can see; two teenagers, Abe. I'd say around seventeen years old possibly twenty at most. No injuries that I can see so far. I'd say they've been in the water no more than twenty-four hours. As usual, I'm going to tell you my stock response… the PMs will give us a better idea."

"OK, I'll get in touch with the DCI, let her make some decisions for once." The doctor laughed. "That's what she gets the big bucks for, after all," Quince added. "The day staff can crack on with some enquiries. I'll sort the PMs for after dinner. I don't fancy one on an empty stomach."

***

Cross answered the call after Quince's third attempt to connect. "We've got a big one down at the marina. Two male bodies of foreign origins, no sign of any injuries. I'm going to fix the PM's up for later. Are you going to attend?"

"No, Abe. I don't see any need. As long as everything's covered down there, I'll get in touch with Clive and get the Incident Room opened. We'll take it from the top. By the way, you had a few drinks last night. I thought you were taking a day off."

"Got a head like a bucket, but the call woke me. I told them not to bother anyone else until I'd assessed it. I've already got the Incident Room opened and everything's up and running."

"Great! So, your initial thoughts?"

"Unless it's some kind of suicide pack or they were both unlucky to fall in like some drunken diving team, I'd say it's foul play, boss."

9

The on-call Home Office pathologist; Professor Geraint Smallwood, was clearly on the ball and, unlike Cross, answered Quince's call on the first ring. The post-mortems were arranged for the two victims at two that afternoon.

Quince had heard of PC Dix's request to attend and as promised, picked him up and headed to the mortuary at Singleton Hospital overlooking the expansive sandy horseshoe of Swansea Bay. It was a shame the mortuary customers couldn't appreciate the view, but even if they weren't dead, the mortuary was at the rear of the towering, sixties, concrete block and devoid of even a glimpse of the stunning view.

Even though it appeared that both the young men had drowned, it didn't answer the question of what they were doing together in the water prior to becoming flotsam and jetsam.

"What do you reckon has happened to these lads?" Quince asked Dix.

Surprised that the DI was remotely interested in what he thought, Dix was keen not to waste the opportunity to impress. "Well, boss, it was a shock when they were fished out of the marina. I suppose drowning will be the cause, but I've no idea how they got there. I assume they were on some boat?"

"Why? Couldn't they have fallen in off the side of the dock?"

Dix shook his head. "Don't think so, boss. Have you seen how busy the marina is at night? Someone would have seen something or heard a splash. All those apartments around the dock, someone would have seen something."

"Bit of advice, always think outside of the box. Never be blinkered, and don't assume. Take things one step at a time. Personally, I think there's more to these deaths. You are probably right about the boat, but they could have been fighting and fallen off the marina into the water in the early hours, after the locals had gone to bed. Who knows? We'll have a better idea once the Prof has done his magic."

"They didn't seem to have been injured in any way, boss. Fighting is unlikely unless it was a push and shove thing, you know, handbags at dawn sort of thing. They hadn't been in the water long, the marina's a busy place. Like I said, they'd have been spotted quickly. But I would have thought there'd have been some evidence of injuries even if it was an accident."

"I'm glad you're thinking of options, I like that. It's nice to see you're keen. Many young bobbies would have been happy just to fill out the sudden death forms and leave it at that. Here you are, seeing it through. That's a good sign. If there's something suspicious about the deaths, it's a different ball game, and we need to start ramping up our play."

They arrived at the morgue, a few minutes before two, and met Professor Smallwood, Bill, and Ted.

The bodies of the two victims were already on the tables and had been prepped by the mortuary assistant for Smallwood to commence his grizzly duty.

Quince had been involved in countless murder enquiries and serious incidents over the years where Smallwood had carried out the post-mortems. Smallwood was a seasoned campaigner in the world of forensic medicine. A diminutive man standing no more than five feet in his Cuban heeled boots, he looked like he would be more at home line dancing than performing a post-mortem. Bald on top, his unruly white hair stuck out from his ears like Ronald McDonald. But he was an expert in his field, and on many occasions had given evidence both for the prosecution, and defence. In his mid-fifties, he was a straight talker. He liked to get right to the point, speaking in layman's terms to avoid any possible confusion.

"Ah, Abe. I got here a bit early, and as you can see we've done a little prep work on the two victims. Definitely teenagers. As I said earlier, they are no older than sixteen or seventeen. I would say they are possibly Vietnamese. I've carried out a cursory examination of the bodies. The only obvious injuries I can see at his time are on the wrists. There appears to be very slight bruising on all four. I would say at some point they've been bound together. I also found what appears to be puncture marks on their arms, where they've been injected. We'll have to wait for the tox results, probably have them within twenty-four hours for you."

"The plot thickens, Prof."

"The next thing is to determine the cause of death. To find that

I'll have to open them up."

To watch him work was hypnotic. He was a master of his craft. His commentary throughout was inspirational, talking his audience through every stage and always showing respect for the victim – a difficult balance to maintain.

He examined the lungs of the first young man, handling them with care before taking to dissection.

"OK," he said after carefully inspecting his handiwork, "I can tell you with certainty that this man didn't drown. There is no sea water in his lungs. That means he was dead before going into the water and I'm afraid that I don't need to tell you that this changes things somewhat."

"It certainly does, Prof. What about stomach contents?"

"Eaten hardly anything in the last twenty-four hours. Some rice and noodles, and that's about it. I would say they are both well under weight for their age."

"So, what we've got, Prof, is possibly two Vietnamese youngsters who haven't drowned, possibly been drugged, and have hardly eaten anything." He sighed. "God knows what they've been through."

"You've got it in one, Abe. If the tox comes back with something sinister, I think you'll have got yourself a handful."

"OK, you've given me enough to get on with. I'll start the ball rolling." He turned to Bill standing behind the professor. "Have you got all you need, Bill?"

Bill was the antithesis of Smallwood. As tall as Quince but showing the weight gain of later life and lack of exercise. "Yes, boss. Got all their clothing bagged and tagged. I'll get it off to the lab straight away."

"I'll ring you early tomorrow with the tox results," the professor said.

Quince had seen enough. He gestured for Dix to follow him outside. "So, what's your theory now, Dix?"

"I think it's people trafficking, and I wonder if they are the only ones, or are there others on the loose?"

"You're on my wavelength there. We'll have more idea when we have the tox results, and if it reveals what I think it will, we're looking at a double murder. The quicker we find out who's responsible, the better. The answer may lie within the Vietnamese community here in Swansea. We need to get them to open up and talk to us."

10

The Incident Room had been set up at Swansea police station. Desks for the team, equipped with computers linked to the national network had been allocated, and a new digital board to replace the old whiteboard and telephones affixed to one wall. The team had already been briefed on the causes of death, and Quince knew in his heart, that the enquiry into the deaths of these young men was going to be a convoluted investigation. He also knew that his right-hand-man; DS Ken Lewis would keep the team on their toes. Ken was a career DS. He had no interest in climbing further up the promotion ladder. Ken saw the role of the DS as the most important in the team and Quince believed he was probably right. Although the DI controlled the day-to-day investigation policy, the DS was the officer with closer ties to the troops and micro-managed the enquiries. This wasn't a case that was going to be sorted in a few weeks, and only God knew how far around the globe the enquiry would take Quince, Ken and the team.

The first bullet-point on the agenda was to identify the victims. Quince had already organised a press release, in the hope of gleaning some information - anything.

It was late morning when Quince received the call he'd been waiting for - an update from Professor Smallwood.

"Morning, Abe. I've got the tox results for you and they're very interesting."

"Don't keep me dangling, Prof."

Smallwood looked ten years older than his birth certificate claimed. Lined cheeks, drawn and littered with red thread veins, anyone who didn't know him would assume he was a heavy drinker, but Smallwood never let alcohol pass his lips. He sat at his laptop in his office as he began to run through his findings on Zoom. "Both the young men had exceedingly large amounts of methamphetamine in their systems, enough to kill them. In fact, they both had enough to kill an elephant."

"Jesus!" Quince gasped. "Any other drugs, Prof, or just the meth?"

"Just the meth. They wouldn't have known what hit them. I'm

reliably informed that they'd have had an initial feeling of pleasure and then their hearts would have given up."

"So, the puncture marks are significant?"

"Most definitely, Abe. In my opinion, the drugs were administered by needle."

"Probably against their will, then." Quince thought out loud. "That would explain the injuries to their wrists. I'm reluctant to speculate, but I'm going to anyway," Quince said. "I believe they were being trafficked and the drug was administered to keep them quiet, or for some other reason," he sighed. "That's no way for two young men to die, Prof."

"No, indeed, Abe. I'm seeing too much of it these days."

"I'm having a briefing later, Prof. So, in a nutshell, what am I going to tell my team?"

"Quite simple really, Abe. Cause of death would have been heart failure due to massive overdoses of methamphetamine. There were no other significant injuries to their bodies, except the wrist bruising. No defensive wounds. In my opinion, these deaths are therefore suspicious."

"Thank you, Prof. I'll upgrade the enquiry to a double murder status. I had a bad feeling about this one from the outset."

***

"OK team, this is what we've got. For those who weren't here earlier..." Quince took a sip from his oversized mug of black coffee, "...just after six yesterday morning, the bodies of two young men were recovered from the marina. There didn't appear to be any injuries on the bodies and, initially, it was thought they'd drowned. At this moment in time, we haven't identified them. We believe them to be Vietnamese. Since their discovery, things have certainly changed, and this has now become a double murder enquiry.

"Professor Smallwood carried out the PM's yesterday afternoon. His examination at that time revealed that the victims hadn't drowned. There was no sea water in their lungs. The Prof also noticed bruising to their wrists, probably caused by cable ties. There were no other significant injuries, and certainly no defensive wounds. The kicker to all this is that I've just got off the blower with the Prof, and the actual cause of death is heart failure due to extreme doses of methamphetamine. They wouldn't have known what hit them. My theory is that they were deliberately overdosed while their hands were bound. The Prof found puncture marks on their arms consistent with being injected.

"That's about it, really," he shrugged. "We've got a shit-load of enquiries to make, and I have no doubt this will take some sorting. My theory is that these two men were being trafficked into the UK, ending up here in Swansea for whatever reason. You've each got a briefing sheet showing what enquiries need to be carried out as a matter of priority. Pictures of the two deceased men are attached. These have not been released to the press at this moment in time and I want it to remain that way until I decide otherwise. Are there any questions?"

DS Bill Daniels looked ill at ease in anything other than jeans and T-shirt and tugged at the tie he felt duty bound to wear. The remains of a pasty clung to his jacket lapels. "Boss, all their clothing has been bagged and tagged, and it's been forwarded to the lab, in view of these developments I've told them it's a priority."

"Cheers, Bill."

DC Connor Harrington, a short, red-haired Irishman thrust his hand into the air. "We haven't got a large Vietnamese community here in Swansea. I'll crack on and start some enquiries with them. Shouldn't take long."

"Connor, you never fail to amaze me. Look at your briefing notes and you'll see I ear-marked you for that task. You're the man for it. Top priority, OK? Get amongst them and tell them I don't give a fuck if there are illegals working in their community. I just want to find the bastards responsible for the deaths of these men."

"Sorry, boss. I didn't have the old bins on. I'm on it."

"I'll liaise with Immigration and Customs. I'm sure they'll have intelligence that may be useful to us on this one. Now, let's get out there. Be back by ten for the next conference and make sure you have something useful for me."

Clive Purcell, a Detective Constable with six months short of thirty years' service had worked as Quince's office manager for nearly a year but had done the job for the previous DI after Purcell had fallen from the roof of a building and shattered his hips.

Although he could hobble along with the aid of two sticks, his days of working the streets were well and truly over. He knew he had been lucky. His injury should have seen his career come to an end but with just a few years left before his retirement, a campaign to keep him in post worked only because he was well respected and admired by all who had worked with him. Quince could rely on him, even though Clive Purcell had set him straight on more than one occasion. Clive Purcell said whatever he thought and seemed to not have any brakes on his tongue. But no one ever seemed to mind because he always spoke sense.

"Right, Clive, all systems go?" Quince asked.

"Yes, boss. All up and running. Phones are manned. It will all come through me, and I'll keep you and the DCI updated."

"That's the hammer," Quince placed his bucket-mug on Clive's desk and pulled up a hard-backed chair. "You've worked the division for many years, have you ever come across anything like this?"

"No, boss. We've always had a few illegals, but I can't recall any of them being found dead in the marina."

"Any scrotes you can put in the frame for trafficking?"

"Not really, boss. If it is trafficking, I reckon it would be international. The net could spread far and wide and head for any place they think might let them slip under the radar. They might have seen Swansea as an easy touch."

"You're probably right. Did they come in by boat or am I being blinkered? If they did, which boat? Have you seen the hordes of gin palaces in the marina?"

"They could very well have just been dumped from a fishing boat, boss. Perhaps they landed somewhere else and were transported here. These traffickers are cunning. Life means nothing to them."

"Perhaps the CCTV down at the marina may throw some light on it."

"Bit of a bummer, I afraid, boss. Geoff Lyons got straight onto that yesterday. Seems their system has been down for a few days. No help there, I'm afraid."

Quince cursed. "Well, that's a good start, Clive, but I swear we'll get justice for these two lads and the dealers in death will get their just deserts."

11

The two young men had been born into poverty and spent much of their formative years living on their wits to survive. Dreams of getting to the UK for a better life had been their focus for months; knowing that even if they defied the odds and managed to get there, they would be forever looking over their shoulders, hiding from authorities. But even life like that was better than what they had. They were both prepared to take that chance.

Their families had begged, stolen, and borrowed the twenty thousand pound each to the unscrupulous people smugglers to make the perilous journey halfway across the world by sea.

Treated no better than cattle, they had no idea where they were at any one time, always concealed below decks, living off meagre scraps of food and occasional plastic bottles of water.

If, and when they were transferred to different ships, they were blindfolded, and their hands bound with plastic tie grips. Even though they had paid for passage, they had no idea where in the UK they would end up.

The smugglers didn't care, they already had the money. If someone died, they were dumped into the sea.

Both men were now targets for unscrupulous gangs who knew their status and would use them to their own end, be it supplying drugs or working illegally, off the books for a pittance.

As night fell, it was imperative that the men found some place to shelter, somewhere they wouldn't be discovered by the police, or any other authority. Swansea had not even figured in their thinking before setting off on their quest. They had hoped for a coastal town in England, somewhere closer to London, but at least they were in the UK.

A Salvation Army soup wagon parked in a side street offered food that smelt of boiled potatoes, peas and cheap coffee.

A handful of homeless men and women queued for cups of the vegetable soup, a bread roll, and coffee in paper cups wrapped in corrugated cardboard rings.

The two men quietly waited their turn, and without any questions were served. They wolfed the soup and bread down as though they hadn't seen food for a fortnight, which was close to the reality of their situation.

Avoiding eye contact, they found a wall to lean against and a dumpster to rest their coffees.

"Hello, I'm Dawid."

The voice startled them. The man was perhaps ten years older than them and smelt of a sickly mixture of fresh soap and cannabis.

"I'm Chi, and this is Danh," Chi said, cautiously.

"You look new here. Haven't seen you before."

Chi shrugged.

"Have you anywhere to stay tonight?"

"No, nowhere," Danh said and received a sharp and surreptitious kick in the ankle from Chi.

"Don't like to see anyone on the street," the man named Dawid said. "I come here often to see if I can help people like you," he smiled. "Sometimes, we can't help, they're either addicted to drugs or are hopeless drunks."

"We?"

Now Dawid shrugged. "A small group of us, like a charity, you know?"

Chi shook his head, but Dawid continued, clearly not wanting to elaborate on his group. "You two look like you could just do with a little help. Perhaps some work?"

"What work?"

"Lots of work around, if you know where to find it, and I know where to find it," Dawid smiled like a shark, gnashing his white teeth with prominent gold fillings. "I've got a friend who needs people like you to do some delivering…" he paused briefly – that grin again. "You know… that kind of stuff. Another friend is looking for men to do a bit of building work. All cash in hand," he held up his hand when Chi began to shake his head. "Don't worry. I'm a friend. It's quite obvious to me that you're illegals."

Neither answered.

"We've got a place in Neath, a little bed-sit. It's nothing fancy but it would be ideal for you boys. You'll get cash in hand. You'll be picked up every morning, no questions asked. I've got the van around the corner. We could go now. What you think?"

Danh and Chi looked at each other, nodded yes, and followed Dawid.

"Well done boys, you won't regret this."

The van looked new. White Transit. No signs, plain and clean. No windows in rear cargo area. Danh and Chi clambered in the back and sat on the wheel arches as the van headed to the Neath bed-sit.

After just fifteen or twenty minutes, the van slowly pulled up outside an isolated property just on the outskirts of Neath. The back door opened and Dawid nodded to the property. It was a three-storey building in need of some paint and new windows. The front door was new though; a heavy, solid looking thing that stood out against the peeling and chipped paintwork of the rest of the house.

"Don't worry boys, don't be deceived by first appearances, it's not too bad inside, but there again, beggars can't be choosers in your position, can they?"

Chi and Danh said nothing, but both picked up a new, more sinister tone in Dawid's voice.

Dawid unlocked the front door, the three of them walked into the hallway.

"This is your room boys," he said as he unlocked a room off the hallway into what had probably once been a sitting room. Two pairs of bunks were pushed up against a corner of the room. There was an old, battered and stained table in the middle of the floor and some hard wooden chairs abandoned around it. The floorboards were covered in mismatched pieces of greasy linoleum and a single, torn bean bag seat was looking sorry for itself under the old bay window. The panes of glass were coated in a white paint and dark, heavy drapes hung precariously off a broken rail. "I think you'll like it. There's a little cooker in the kitchen and you have a pick of the beds. Just the two of you in here at the moment. The bathroom and communal shower are just down the corridor, gets a bit crowded now and again, but I'm sure you'll manage. By the way, I've been meaning to ask, where are you from? I guess Asia, but where exactly?"

Chi said, "Vietnam."

"You're the first Vietnam boys we've had. It's getting like the fucking United Nations in here. Got all sorts upstairs; Chinese, Indians, Iranian, you'll be at home here. Make yourselves at home. I'll pick you up at seven sharp in the morning, and will put you to work, just a bit of door-to-door stuff at first, delivering charity bags. Nobody will take a bit of notice of you, so don't worry."

"Do we have key?"

"No boys, the door won't be locked. One of the other boys will make sure you're safe and sound. My advice is, stay put, that way everyone will be happy, get my meaning?"

Both Chi and Danh nodded.

Once Dawid left the room, both Chi and Dahn began getting second thoughts, they were in between the devil, and the deep blue sea, however they knew they were, at least for the time being, trapped.

Chi waited for the sound of the front door closing behind Dawid and then stepped out into the hallway to be confronted by the biggest man he had ever seen. .

"Where are you going?" The man-mountain growled in a Polish accent.

"Bathroom, please?"

The monster pointed down the passage.

"First on the right, and don't be getting any fucking ideas about going anywhere else, got it?"

12

Quince donned his charcoal grey suit and rummaged through a rail of ties and smiled sadly at the bright, multi-coloured silk one Jess had bought him for his fortieth birthday, along with several equally bright shirts and a tan pair of trousers and brogues. The tie was something he would never feel comfortable wearing to work. He had worn it once, to make Jess happy, but she had needed more than just his willing compliance in his wardrobe habits to keep her smiling. It took a special kind of woman to put up with the life of a detective and it took nearly ten years for Jess to come to the realisation that she was not one of those women. It had taken Quince a lot longer. He had been blind to her increasingly dour moods. Why hadn't he seen it? The job was all consuming. There were many times when he had had to let her down; date nights cancelled, dinner with friends where only she would attend. He had just taken it for granted that she would understand - that she would accept that a detective was always liable to be called away at the most unsociable of times. Her affair with her work colleague had devastated Quince but, after several days of plotting how he would rip the man's arms off without detection, he grudgingly accepted that he was to blame; or to be more accurate, his job was to blame. The work was his mistress and he had been more committed to it than he had been to his marriage. That wasn't true. He silently berated himself. Jess had known what he did for a living. He had talked about cases – whenever he could – and she had enjoyed the group socials – whenever they were possible too. He had never cheated on her and all he expected from her in return was her love, patience and the same level of commitment to the marriage.

He removed a plain blue tie from the jungle of silk vines and slammed the wardrobe door. He had to stop thinking like this. How on earth could he expect Jess to stay committed to a marriage where the third party was an all-consuming career? No, she was right to walk away. It had cut him to the core, but he knew it was right for her. There had been a few dates with women since, but none had ever come close to capturing his heart quite like Jess had. The truth was, he would never get over her. He sprayed some aftershave on his chin and winced, not because of the sting but because it was a bottle Jess had bought for him. Her favourite scent on a man. He looked around the bathroom. The place was full of reminders of their time together. He would have to clear it sometime soon. He couldn't keep living like this, under the memory of their marriage.

The office was quiet when Quince arrived. The team were out, working through priority actions. These actions had to be thoroughly investigated, every detail, no matter how minor had to be covered.

Quince was determined to find out who was responsible for the deaths of the two dead men. In any enquiry of this sort, the first forty-eight hours are the most crucial, and the investigating team were always hoping for that initial break, the break that would crack the case wide open.

***

The sun had set below piles of actioned files and the team regathered in the office when Ken Lewis opened the second case conference.

"OK, team, let's see what we've got, eh? I've no doubt, you've all been busy little beavers. Perhaps Clive can start the ball rolling with the CCTV and ANPR actions?"

"No problem, Sarge," Clive remained seated. "The marina CCTV has been out of commission for a few days, so as far as the timeline is concerned, we're knackered. But I can tell you that we had access to the coastguard logs and there were no boat movements in or out of the marina during the relevant timeline. I've trawled the ANPR records and there were hundreds of vehicle movements in and around the marina. However, we did have one hit on a white Ford Transit van. Now for the good and bad news. The good news is; we're sure it's the vehicle we need to trace, but the bad news is; the reason we think this is; the van had false registration plates."

"OK, Clive, any idea of general direction of travel from the scene?"

"Last sighted heading out of Swansea towards the Mumbles. Then it just disappeared off the radar. I've circulated it nationwide, but I don't hold out much hope, boss."

"Well, it's a lead. I'm not saying the van is involved, it could be up to some other nefarious activity," he grinned, "but you never know. Make it a priority action, Clive."

"Already have, boss," Clive grinned back. "Nothing more to add."

"Connor, what have you got from the Vietnamese community?"

"I've spoken to Force Intelligence; they've got loads of intel. The Vietnamese are very tight lipped and don't trust us. The photographs have been circulated, so we'll just have to wait. There's a strong rumour on the street that there's a Polish gang on the loose, threatening and using the homeless as cheap labour."

"Any Vietnamese involved in this, Connor?"

"Not to our knowledge, boss. If they hear anything about the two dead lads, they'll let me know."

"Excellent. Clive, get an operation set up. Have it run from midnight right through the week. If these Poles are at it, I want them identified and nicked, whether their involved in this shit or not. Whatever it takes. I want a surveillance team on stand-by."

"Not a problem, boss, I'm on it as we speak."

"OK. So, Bill, how are we fixed with forensics?"

"All their clothing is at the lab and they're making it a priority. They've promised me something tomorrow."

"OK. Any theories? Don't be afraid, let's chuck it all in the mix," Quince said.

DC Kevin Small stood and said what most were thinking. "I think it's safe to say that these victims had been trafficked, boss. Looks like they didn't come in by boat and didn't die where they were recovered. They must have been dumped and that would suggest a vehicle, possibly the Transit. We need a bit of luck to I.D. those responsible, boss."

"I think you've summed it up, Kev. We have other problems to work round too. Customs, Immigration, and our Special Branch are all snowed under. They all have loads of operations either under way or in the pipeline but are under resourced. The only thing they can say is that there's been a big increase in trafficking along the south coast, all sorts of nationalities; Chinese, Vietnamese, Eastern European… need I go on? They've smashed a few gangs, but in their eyes they're small fry. They believe there are bigger fish running them. I'm afraid this one is going to be down to us, so let's crack on. Go home, get some rest, be back at eight in the morning and we'll have a conference later tomorrow evening."

Quince and Lewis spent a little time mingling with the troops as they tidied their desks and left the office for the night. It was a good time to catch up on gossip and things that were perhaps never wise to say in front of others in a case conference. Rumours were never good for evidential purposes but certainly helped to focus attention to substantiate or rule them out. Many cases had been cracked by a simple piece of hearsay that triggered a follow up and ended in evidence to prove the case.

Walking slowly back to the office with Ken in tow, both were pondering what the next move could be. The team needed a break, and they needed it quickly. Time was always of the essence.

Ken gratefully accepted a whiskey and closed the office door behind him before they began discussing options. Ken looked tired. He had not been home since the bodies had been found. Quince had walked in early on many occasions and found Ken dozing on a pair of chairs pushed together to make an impromptu bed.

"You need to get some kip, Ken."

Ken took a gulp of his whiskey and dismissed Quince's comment. "Don't worry about me, Abe. I'll get a curry and kip here tonight."

"Again?"

Ken shrugged. "It's OK. Got used to it."

"What about the missus?"

Now Ken snorted. "So, you haven't heard?"

Quince shook his head.

"She's thrown me out. Got all my clothes in the boot of my car."

"Jesus, Ken. No wonder you look knackered. Drink that up and you're coming home with me. I've got a spare bedroom. You can kip there for a while, at least until you find yourself some place."

Blushing, Ken shook his head. "I can't impose on you like that."

Quince necked his whiskey and dropped the half full bottle into his coat pocket. "Come on. I won't take no for an answer, and we'll finish this off over that curry."

13

Ken had emptied his car boot and thrown his holdall into the wardrobe of the spare room. Now he slept soundly, the whiskey and a soft bed quickly carrying him off to dreamland. Quince had stayed up to watch an American cop show on a streaming channel. It had passed midnight when his mobile rang. He looked at the caller ID. 'Stokes.'

Quince answered and spoke quietly, "Hey, Andy, what can I do for you? It must be months since we spoke last. You got something for me?"

"You got another woman there with you, Abe?"

"Sorry?"

"You're hardly audible. Why are you whispering?"

Quince laughed. "Nah. Nothing like that. Got Ken crashing with me for a while. Been kicked out of his home."

"Another copper's marriage down the tubes, eh? Anyway, I know you're busy with theses bodies in the marina, but I may be able to get some info on an armed robbery committed a few years ago. I've done an old villain a favour and he's willing to spill his heart out. Early days at the minute though. I should have the full SP in a couple of weeks. He's even on about giving us the sawn off that was used and the toe-rags behind it. Are you interested?"

"Too royal, just give me a bell when it's a goer. I'll get the boys to sort it."

"I'm down the Morgan's Hotel at the minute. Can I pop around to yours and I'll bring a four-pack. We'll have a swift half, what you think?"

"Sounds like a plan, it's not as if I've got a nice warm backside to cwtch into…"

"What about Ken's?" Stokes laughed.

"Have you seen the state on him lately? Even if I were a sailor, like you were, I'd not go near that arse if it was the last on the planet."

Quince and Andy Stokes had spent two years in a local college and had developed a sense of humour common to both, but few others. Quince had gained his qualifications and joined the police while Andy joined the navy. He returned to Swansea after seven years, rekindling their friendship.

Andy had been out of work for months after de-mob and had been finding it difficult to adjust. Quince pulled a few strings and managed to get him some work with a local solicitor. Initially, it had been on a temporary basis, however, he took to it like a duck to water, and had not looked back.

It took a little over twenty minutes before Quince heard the muffled tapping on his door. Andy stood smiling in the light from the hallway, two packs of four beers in hand. "Thought I'd bring a few extra in case Stokes sticks his head in."

"You've done well," Quince said, taking in the expensive shoes and designer labels. "Bearing in mind the job was just a start for you, it's clearly worked out well?"

Andy handed the beers to Quince and closed the door. "I took to it from the outset. I think I'd have made a cracking detective. I should have joined up with you when I had the chance."

"You shot your bolt there, Andy boy," Quince whispered as he walked past Stokes's temporary bedroom. "I can tell you now, I never saw you as a sailor. Came as a shock when you joined up. I saw you more as a delivery driver with Tesco, something like that, know what I mean? Click and collect."

"You cheeky sod," Andy laughed. "I had seven cracking years," he followed Quince into the lounge and slumped down on an oversized sofa. "Yes, it was tough, but it opened my eyes, Abe. There's so much conflict around the world, people don't know they're born. I had enough, I was worn out. Had to get out."

"I often wondered why you jacked it in and didn't make a full career of it. You were certainly capable of going a long way."

"I did go a long way," he grinned.

"I'm not talking about Airmiles." Quince cracked open a can and handed one to Andy.

"Well, shit happens!"

"Seems your new career suits you. You've certainly gained a reputation in the legal profession; practically every villain in South Wales asks the custody sergeant for Stokes as legal representative."

"That's only because the briefs don't want to get out of bed. I reckon I could represent them in court as well," he snorted. "The briefs are even asking me for advice, can you believe that?"

Quince shook his head. "That says a lot, eh?"

"They know they're on a winner with me, that's why they pay me so well. I'll travel anywhere if there's a few extra quid in it. That's why you haven't seen me for ages."

A photo of Quince and his ex-wife stood on top of the coffee table.

"Thought you'd have dumped that by now?" Andy said, nodding towards the picture.

Shrugging his shoulders, Quince smiled sadly. "We had some good times, you know? She's my... *was* my soulmate."

Andy nodded.

"Ever thought of getting married, and settling down?"

"Not really, Abe. My life's a bit like yours, not enough hours in a day."

"So, what's this information you have for me?"

Andy took another swig from his can and wiped his mouth on the back of his hand. "You remember a villain by the name of Toby Walters? He's got to be in his late sixties now."

"Toby, is he still alive? I thought he was long gone. A prolific burglar. High-end houses. Always nicked cash, and credit cards."

"Aye. Well, he's been very ill. Lung cancer. Hardly ever leaves the house now. His boy, Toby junior, got into a bit of bother in Neath a few months ago. An alleged GBH. I got called out and did the business for him. Made a few enquiries and the CPS eventually offered no evidence."

"So, where where's this going?"

"The old man asked to see me. So, I popped along. Seems he was grateful for what I did and then he offered up the robbery info. Like I say, when I get the full SP, you'll be the first to know."

"Sounds interesting. You sure he's not feeding you bullshit?"

Andy shrugged. "Why would he? No reason to."

"I'm up to my eyes at the minute. Got a conference with the CPS tomorrow," Quince said. "But I'll certainly act on it if it smells OK."

"Thought you'd take it," another sip of beer, "anyway, I'm guessing you're dealing with these floaters?"

"Yup."

"Nasty business."

"Gangs, drugs, and knives, Andy. That's all it is now. Where have all the honest villains gone?" Quince grinned.

"Abe, why burgle when you can make a fortune running drugs or people? It's a no brainer. Half the inmates in the nick are high as kites when I interview them. You tell me how they're getting it past the screws?"

"Anything for a quiet life, Andy, otherwise there'd be riots."

"Aye, suppose you're right. Look, I've got to shoot," he finished his can and placed the empty on the low, glass coffee table next to the photo. "I'll give you a ring when I get something off Toby."

14

The bedroom door burst open and standing there was Dawid, accompanied by one of his many henchmen. This one was also built like a brick shithouse and wore a scowl that would sour eggs in their shells.

"OK you two, up you get. It's time for you to earn your keep," Dawid said. "Get washed. There's some toast on the kitchen table, you can eat it on the run."

Dahn and Chi, were equally terrified but didn't argue. They'd been held against their will for a couple of nights, so they did as Dawid commanded without question. They'd come halfway across the world to seek a better life only to be exploited and treated like cattle from the time they left Vietnam.

As soon as they were ready, Dawid blindfolded them and pushed them roughly into the back of a different Transit van. This one was dirt-ingrained and parked under a sickly-looking tree at the rear of the house.

Dahn and Chi had no idea where they were being taken, or what fate awaited them.

The journey seemed like an eternity. Then, the van came to a stop. Both Dahn and Chi were dragged out of the van and ushered down a flight of steps.

Their blindfolds were removed, revealing a large underground basement room filled to the rafters with cannabis plants. It was incredibly hot, totally insulated, blindingly light, with the sound of running water somewhere.

There were two other young men laying on makeshift camp beds in a far corner. They were sleeping. Both had lengths of chain attached to their ankles.

"Here we are, your home for the foreseeable future," Dawid said. "Just do as you're told, and no harm will come to you. There's enough food and water here for a few days, all I want you to do is make sure the plants are watered regularly and don't dry out. We wouldn't want that, would we?"

Chi was visibly shaking. "Can we just go, please?"

"Go? Go where? You're mine. Just get used to it. You listen, do as you're told, and you'll be OK. If not? Well, who knows what will happen. Don't think about escaping, you'll never get to the trap door, and nobody will hear your shouts, so don't bother. Now, we'll leave you to get acquainted with these two."

The henchman rolled out two lengths of chain and shackled both Dahn and Chi by the ankles before climbing up the steep concrete steps and slamming the trap door behind them.

15

Quince arrived at the office earlier than usual. He had wanted to get an early night but, events had slipped beyond his control. That wasn't true. He could have excused himself but a few drinks with an old pal had been too tempting. He had been thinking about how he had messed up his marriage, how the temptation of drinks with mates had messed things up at home. He had also always put the job before the love of his life and just watched, like some soap opera, as his relationship had fallen apart. The job had become all-consuming – a lover who took all and gave little back in return. No, that wasn't true either. He had been promoted and promotion meant a better life for them. Of course, he knew it also meant more time away from home. He had made loyal friends, friends who would die for him and he for them. But life was more than just a career and a bunch of friends who had their own lives when they got home. Quince knew what Andy was doing. Andy knew how hard the break-up had hit him, even if Quince would never show it.

He'd resisted the temptation of finishing the rest of the beers Andy had brought and was glad he had as he ran through the priority actions until his mobile rang. It was Andy.

"Morning, Abe. I had a bell from Toby Walters this morning…"

"That was quick."

"I told you it was for real. He'd like to meet. He'll give us everything and knows you'll be dealing with it."

"Pick me up in a couple of hours, Andy, after my briefing. I hope it'll be worth it."

"We'll soon see. He's got no reason to string us along, he's on his last legs."

A few hours later Quince and Andy rolled up to Toby's flat, a converted former council owned semi-detached house that had, like many, been bought by the tenant and split into two flats for rental. Quince had never understood how the council had built social housing in such a stunning location. The street sat atop a valley rise with unobstructed views of Swansea Bay. If the land was ever put up for sale for private development, Quince reckoned it would be worth tens of millions. He had read somewhere that the estate of houses was built during the rebuilding of the city after World War Two. The city had taken a hammering over a few nights of Luftwaffe bombing. Many died during those attacks and the city centre paid the price of being adjoined to the docks.

Andy rang the bell and after what seemed like a few minutes, but was probably nowhere as near as long, Toby let them in.

His skin was jaundiced, Quince was reminded f Homer Simpson, and he was a skinny bag of bones. It didn't take a doctor to see that he wasn't long for this world.

"Long time no see, Abe. Take a pew. I take it the boy here has given you the full SP on what I got for you?" He said, nodding at Andy. "I think you'll be pleasantly surprised by what I have for you."

"You sure you're up for this?" Quince said, feeling a stab of sympathy for the man who had been on the other side of the law for most of his life. As much as Quince had dedicated his career to putting people like Toby behind bars, Toby had dedicated his life to making Quince's job difficult. Perhaps the spectre of imminent death made a man like Toby think about his life in a new light? Perhaps it was fear that made someone like him repent – a fear of everlasting torment in purgatory? Whatever the reason, Quince still had his doubts.

"Aye. I've only weeks left to me. Not even months, they say. Everyone wants me to go into a hospice but fuck it. I'll die here watching the old box and swigging a few cans. I've done some bad things, but it was all I knew. Never had much of a chance, you know?"

Quince snorted. "Look Toby, everyone has a chance. You might have been dealt some bum hands, but you chose to play them your way."

Toby laughed and coughed. "Aye, I suppose I did. Never any bullshit from you, is there, Quince? Even when I tell you I've got a few weeks left to live and that I want to give you the heads up on some shit, you still tell it as it is."

Shrugging his shoulders, Quince smiled too. "It's just the way I am."

"Aye. Well, I've still got a few contacts."

"No doubt. You were an old school villain. Been in the game a lifetime. I bet there's no one you don't know. But you were never a nasty piece of shit."

"Nah, never laid a hand on anyone, and never did a poor house. Like Robin Hood, I was, except I stole from the rich and gave to myself," he grinned.

"So, what have you got for us, Toby?"

"Do you remember that spate of bookie robberies about five years ago?"

"We had about seven or eight around the area, if memory serves me correctly?"

"Aye those were the ones."

"They were cleared up, Toby."

"Cleared up, my arse! Aye, the team doing bird cleared them all up, but there's the rub. They didn't do them all. The two in Maesteg were done by a local pair. They were only kids at the time, eighteen and nineteen, but a brutal pair of fuckers."

"Both had sawn-offs, and they gave a few of the staff some hidings. Got away with about twenty-grand from both shops," Quince nodded.

"Did you work on any of them, Quince?"

"No, but I was in the loop."

"Did you fancy anybody for them at the time?"

"Not really. The Crime Squad nicked a couple on the job, after a tip off, and they cleared them all."

"Exactly! Case closed, and the books cleared. Well, let me tell you who actually did them. You'll know them once I mention their names."

"Don't keep me in suspense."

Toby coughed blood into a paper hanky before he could continue. "Dai 'Squeaky' Nash and Conrad Villis."

"Never! I can't believe that they wouldn't have the bottle," Quince scoffed.

"I don't give a shit if you believe me. That's my info, and it's from a good source. They're still at it, but are travelling far and wide, doing the odd job here and there. They've still got the shooters and think they're untouchable."

"I'll need something more concrete to get them lifted."

This made sense to Toby. He knew the score. "They've got a storage unit on the Viking Way Industrial Estate. Queensway

Storage, and it's jam-packed with goodies from all over, plus the sawn-offs."

"And the number of the unit, Toby?"

"NC401. Here, I've written it down for you." He pulled a scrap of paper from the pocket of a threadbare cardigan that was drowning him in food-stained wool.

"They've got a little garage and forecourt nearby as well, where they buy and sell second-hand cars. It's a cracking cover for them to travel."

"Well, I hope your informant is not messing us about."

"Quince, it's on the up, take my word for it. On my boy's life," he said as he tapped his chest above where he should have had a heart. Quince wasn't sure there was one in there but was prepared to give him the benefit of the doubt.

So, the info had come from Toby's boy as a thank you to Stokes for sorting him out. It sounded plausible. "Leave it with me, Toby. I'll get one of the divisional DIs on it first thing tomorrow. I'll pop back and let you know how it goes."

"No need, Quince. The slate is clean now. No doubt I'll follow your progress in the Western Mail. Give me your card. If I hear anything between now and my demise, I'll give you or Andy a bell."

Quince shut the front door behind him and stood with Andy Stokes on the front step of the house. The view of the bay really was breath-taking.

"What you reckon, Abe?"

"I wouldn't be at all surprised if it's true. It's a few years ago now, and if they're as cocky as Toby says, they'll be in for a fucking shock."

16

It was just a routine day for retired PC Haydn Stewart, who had spent most of his service, working the Neath valley. Like most of the valleys carved by ice through the south of Wales, the Neath valley had changed considerably during the years of his service, and mostly not for the better. Since the miners' strike of the early eighties, the Neath valley had lost its major employer and the people had suffered the inevitable strife that unemployment brings. Neath town centre had become plagued by drugs and the easy availability of the full range of narcotics had spread into the valleys and those people that had once been fiercely protective of each other.

Haydn retired three years ago and took up a position with the police firearms department. Born and raised on a small sheep farm in Glynneath, he'd been handling guns from a young age. When Haydn joined the Force, it was a natural progression that he would become an armed response officer, and later a firearms trainer. Part of Haydn's new remit was to make sure that firearms, and shotgun owners were complying with the law regarding possession, and storage of their weapons.

Today he only had one call, and that was to an old family friend's farm, situated high above the village of Glynneath. Haydn knew the area like the back of his hand, he'd been stationed and worked the beat for nearly eighteen years. Like all villages and towns in south Wales, Glynneath had grown from the profits of mining and the rugby club was the centre of the community. Home of the legendary Max Boyce, Glynneath had fought against the inevitability of village demise, with small shops reopening and offering the personal touch that cities or superstores couldn't match, but even the most optimistic of commentators would wonder at the longevity of these businesses in the increasingly difficult financial climate.

The sun had begun its decent from its zenith when Haydn made his way along the single-track country road past the Golf Club leading to Glyn Farm, owned by eighty years old Bill Glyndwr, or 'Bill the Ram' as he was known by the locals.

A confirmed bachelor, Bill had never been short of female company and had once thought settling down with a woman was something that would just happen. It never did. He knew that the longer he lived alone, the harder it would become for him to share his life with someone else. Rumours in the village were rife that he had fathered a few children, however, nothing was ever confirmed. The farm had not seen a child since his own early years and had been in the family for over three generations; sheep being the main source of revenue. These days, Bill had downsized, and his main income was now from the rental of outbuildings and barns. Bill was making a tidy living and the farmhouse itself and been given a modern update with all the conveniences. Old Bill didn't want for anything, to be fair, he even had even subscribed to Sky Q and the sports channels.

Haydn pulled up outside the main farmhouse as Bill tottered out with a firm strong handshake.

"How are things, Bill? All well, I hope?"

"Not too bad, Haydn. I'm keeping busy like, you know. Come on in, I just put the kettle on."

"I could do with a nice cuppa, Bill, any chance of a Welsh Cake?"

"I can read you like a book Haydn; you know where the tin is."

"I was telling the wife that you make the best Welsh Cakes."

"That must have gone down well with her," Bill chuckled. "How are the folks doing?"

"All well, Bill. Enjoying the quiet life. Dad's got Alzheimer's and mam is doing what she can for him. It's not easy but they're both in their eighties now."

"I know. I was in school with your dad. Good second row, he was. Could have played for Wales if someone had pushed him."

Haydn nodded. "He's half the size he was. Still, what can we expect? Have you ever thought about packing it all in? You must find it tough these days?"

"Not really. I just plod along. I don't even have to collect the rents each month, it's easier now than ever, it's all done automatic, like. Bank transfer, you know? Those early mornings and late nights were a killer, especially during lambing, this diversity nonsense is far easier."

"How many are you renting to, Bill? I could see driving up it's a hive of activity, much busier than last time I visited."

"Six local businesses on here now. It's like Piccadilly Circus on occasions. I'll show you around later."

"I've seen so many changes over the years, you take our old farm, after mum and dad sold it, it was redeveloped. Must be about twenty to thirty log cabins on the land now."

"Yes, I popped up the other day. I'm thinking of selling a bit of land off here, do the same thing."

"Should make a few shillings, Bill."

"Money's not everything, Haydn. It's no good to you when you're six feet under, is it?"

"What about relatives, Bill? I know you've got a few cousins living down the valley."

"Aye, but they're bloody older than me. I'll outlast the buggers the way things are going."

"What about the old rumours, you know, the old nickname?"

Bill laughed. "I sowed a few wild oats, Haydn, I won't deny it. If I have fathered a few I suppose when I pop off, they'll soon come out of the woodwork. Won't do them any good, cremation for me, so there'll be no DNA." He grinned wickedly. "Now, I'm sure you've not come to chat all day?"

"OK, let's crack on with the firearms paperwork. Any changes from the last visit?"

"No just the two, well used and always locked away."

Bill walked over to what would once have been the kitchen pantry. He unlocked two mortice locks and opened the heavy door to reveal the secure gun cabinet that was bolted to the interior wall. Three padlocks secured the steel door. Once removed, the old man opened the door with reverence. "There they are, Haydn. My two favourite Purdey up-and-over girls, both worth a pretty penny now too."

"They're the best I've ever checked, Bill. I'll sign them off, as normal."

"Can I lock 'em up again?"

"Haydn nodded as he began filling in the form. "When I was growing up, I had some fabulous times here on the farm. The most enjoyable was when us kids were used as beaters on the pheasant shoots."

"Aye, never be allowed today, not with all this health and

safety bollocks."

"Do you still shoot much?"

"Oh aye, yet another source of income. They pay good money these days." Bill peered at the form over Haydn's shoulder. "Shall we have a look around? I think you'll be pleasantly surprised what's going on here."

Directly across the yard from the main farmhouse were two large modern barns, one was being used as an agricultural repair unit by a well-known local business. They were obviously doing well, with several high-end tractors, trailers, quad bikes, and other heavy farming machinery both inside and outside the building.

Outside the second building was a large hand painted sign, which read; 'MONEY FOR CLOTHING-PAYMENT BY WEIGHT.'

This building was secure. A little too secure, Haydn thought for a second-hand clothing business. Two CCTV cameras were affixed to the eaves of the roof and angled to record anyone approaching the doors.

"Who's got that one, Bill?"

"A couple of Polish fellas. They work 24/7. Go out in the morning, come back late at night. They've got a few vans which are always loaded with old clothes. Fair, play they work their bollocks off. Never had a problem with them. On weekends, the locals bring all their old gear up, then weigh it in for cash. Quick cash."

"The one's I know don't shirk work like some of the local lads. But it's usually car washes with them. There's a few down in Neath."

"You're right there. I found that when I needed help with the hay, it was mostly Poles I used. Gave them a tidy hourly rate, fed and watered them, they were happy as Larry. Remember the old cow sheds, and pig pens?"

"Too royal, I do."

"Come around by here and have a look at them now. What do you think?"

The old pens had been repurposed into small industrial units. A wood carver nodded as he assembled what looked like a fancy carved park bench. A roller shutter of the unit next to it was rolled up and Haydn could see several stainless-steel tanks with pipes and bags of malt being emptied into one. "That's the Celt Brewery. Small yield apparently but cracking beer. Selling to all the local pubs, they are."

"It's like a bloody cottage industry, no wonder you don't want to call it a day."

"You can get grants for everything these days. Just tell a few porkies here and there, you know what I mean? Most of it is European and WAG start-up money. These are all local businesses, so at least they keep work in the valley."

"I think that's enough for one day, I'll head off back to file the form for you."

"Well, it's been nice seeing you, Haydn. You should pop up a bit more often. Perhaps a day shooting would tickle your fancy? And don't forget give my regards to your mum and dad."

"That would be great, Bill, and I will."

17

Connor Harrington sipped coffee from a cardboard cup as he walked with purpose through the streets of Swansea. A get-up-and-go kind of police officer, having spent most of his service policing Swansea city and the outlying areas, he was knowledgeable when it came to the community and its needs.

He had joined the Force not long after completing a Geography degree at Chester University. His parents thought he would become a teacher, or do something with the environment, but Connor had always had other ideas and decided to join the police Force.

The offer to join as a graduate entry did not appeal to him. He wanted to start at the bottom. After just eight years, four of those years being on the CID, Connor was loving the job and knew he had made the right career choice.

Having been briefed by Quince about the two bodies recovered from the marina, Connor had begun making enquiries amongst the Swansea Vietnamese community, not an easy task because like all ethnic communities they were very wary of the police, close knit, and protective of each other.

Connor however had one thing going for him, he was straight-talking, honest and well respected. His face even looked like a lie would scar his boyish good looks. On many occasions he had helped ethnic groups throughout the city, including the Vietnamese and tirelessly raised money for local charities through daring stunts that on several occasions had taken their toll on his body. Undeterred, this charitable nature had filtered through to those with influence in the minority communities. If anyone could get information, it would be Connor.

It is not known exactly how many Vietnamese nationals are living in the UK. Many thousands came to our shores in the mid-seventies, they were commonly referred to as the 'boat people.' The vast majority were relocated in the London areas of Lewisham, Southall, and Hackney, all of them fleeing from the brutal Communist regime in their country. Many were businesspeople, academics, and students. As the years have passed, many have moved on to other major cities in the UK, and set up their own businesses, including catering, and the growing nail bar industry.

Connor finished his take-out coffee and pushed through the door of The House of Spice restaurant on John Street. The restaurant was owned by Nadir Huang, a man in his mid-sixties. Nadir was one of the original boat people who landed in 1975. He was located to Hackney where he worked as a waiter in an Indian restaurant. Nadir worked all the hours under the sun, until he had saved enough money to move on.

In 1980 he relocated to Swansea where he opened The House of Spice restaurant. It was only small, but the food was superb, and over the years he gradually extended it, making it one of the most popular restaurants in the city centre.

In 1985 he married Gaynor White, a Swansea girl, and together they had two sons, Tomas and Hadrian. All three worked together in the family business.

Gaynor looked up from polishing a wine glass. She smiled warmly. "How are you Connor? We haven't seen you around here for some time. We thought you'd moved on."

"No, I'm still here on the job, Gaynor. How's the family?"

"They're all well. The boys are out sorting the supplies. Nadir has only yesterday returned from Vietnam, he's upstairs. He'll be glad to see you. I've got a feeling I know what this is about," she frowned. "Is it those lads they found in the marina?"

Nodding, Connor sat on a stool at the bar as Gaynor placed the now sparkling glass on a shelf behind her. "I'd been told that Nadir was away. He's my last resort, truth be told."

"Pop on upstairs. He's probably got his headphones on. He's into classical music now."

"Classical? Prefer a bit of Funeral for a Friend, myself." The confused look on Gaynor's face betrayed her lack of knowledge of the noughties Welsh screamo band.

The lighting in the tastefully decorated restaurant was typically subdued but Connor knew his way around. He had eaten many times there in the past and had always made a point in attending any reports of trouble there. He climbed two flights of stairs to the family living quarters.

Nadir was sitting with his back to Connor, head moving from

side to side, headphones on, waving both arms like a conductor. He sat in the middle of a low-back red sofa. Ahead was the music centre – something that would have been popular in the seventies. A turntable spun at thirty-three and a third revolutions, but Connor could hear nothing other than the rhythmic crack from the needle.

Connor tapped Nadir on the shoulder, he jumped up like an electrocuted cat, and spun around like Bruce Lee. A small man, no more than five-five and slim, his skin had aged beyond his years and his once thick shock of black hair had greyed and thinned to greasy strands combed over his scalp.

"Bloody hell, Connor, you frightened the shit out of me." A sigh of relief and a toothless grin. "Where have you been? Sit down, for God's sake. What is it now, business or pleasure?"

"Purely business I afraid, Nadir." Connor sat on a red leather armchair. "You've heard about the two young men fished out of the Swansea marina?"

Nadir sat too and lit a small cigar. "Yes. We've been watching the news. A very sad state of affairs. Do you know who they are?"

"No, that's why I've come to have a chat with you. We believe they are Vietnamese, and God knows how they got to Swansea. We think they arrived via unscrupulous means. I know you're probably the most respected guy within your community and was wondering if you could put a few feelers out. It's a bit of a long shot."

"Well, I haven't heard anything at the minute, but I will start asking around. But I warn you, our people are very guarded."

"I understand completely, Nadir. We're pulling out all the stops on this one."

A deep inhalation of smoke followed by a perfectly formed ring. "How did they die, Connor?"

"They didn't drown, Nadir, but that's just between me and you, do you understand?"

"Mum's the word. It's a bad business."

"The consensus is that these two lads had been trafficked. Whether or not they were just dumped in Swansea is another question we don't have an answer for just yet."

"Coming to our shores for a better life, Connor? At least when I came to the UK we were welcomed and looked after."

"If they are Vietnamese, surely their families must be worried sick if they haven't heard from them in a while?"

"It would be terrible for their families, even if they were dead, the families will still have to keep paying the traffickers. Life means nothing to them."

"Have you had any dealings with this sort of thing before, Nadir?"

"Oh yes, only the once, many years ago. I had two young Chinese men knocking on my door. It was obvious they were illegals. I took them in, fed them, and put them up for a couple of days. The story they told me was horrific."

"What did you do?"

"What would you have done, Connor?"

"Bloody hell, Nadir, that's a tough one. I'd have probably given them some cash and seen them on their way."

"No, I didn't do that. I spoke to them both and contacted the police who dealt with them compassionately. I knew that these men would be better off with the authorities, they would be looked after, and treated humanely. What would have been their future, on the run, being taken advantage of, and exploited by gang masters, and drug dealers?"

"What was their fate, Nadir?"

"They were two brothers, who went on to seek political asylum, and after years of legal battles, they were granted it. If you pop in to the Go Sing down the road, they own that now, they've done well."

"A nice happy ending, Nadir. Would they remember the people who trafficked them? Perhaps it's the same crew?"

Nadir shook his head. "I doubt it. They were rounded up some months later. I also don't think the lads would talk. Too dangerous for them. Look, I'll start making a few calls for you. If I get something, I'll ring you. Still got the same number?"

"Yes, still the same."

Connor knew that Nadir now had an idea that the two lads were possibly Vietnamese, he would pull out all the stops for him.

As sure as eggs were eggs, later that afternoon Connor had the call from Nadir.

"Connor, I've made a few phone calls, and at the minute, I've only got little snippets. It is like putting a jigsaw together. Even if these lads have gone missing, the families will be scared about reporting anything, I'll have to tread very carefully."

"I understand, Nadir, but you've no leads at all?"

"Nothing concrete, as I say, just rumour and speculation at the minute. I don't want to get your hopes up, but I'm sure something's going to come to light. We're all upset about this."

"Cheers, Nadir, many thanks, keep in touch."

Connor immediately rang Quince with the feedback.

"Nothing concrete, boss, but I've made contact with a good friend of mine, Nadir Huang, a well-respected man within the Vietnamese community. He hasn't heard anything concrete, however, there are rumours going around, he doesn't want to send us off on a wild goose chase, but he's going to keep digging."

"Well, you stick to him like shit to a blanket, Connor. We've struck out at the minute, so it's down to you."

"Not a problem, boss, I've got a feeling Nadir will come up trumps."

"I'll leave it in your capable hands, Connor."

18

Like most cities in the UK, the homeless situation in Swansea has risen over the years. Not as bad as some of the bigger cities in the UK, there had still been a twenty per cent increase in the last four years. It was estimated that at least twenty individuals were now sleeping rough in the nights and begging during the days. A seemingly small number in the grand scheme of things, but a devastating outcome for the affected. Those were just the ones known to the authorities. The council, and other support services were doing their utmost to overcome the problem. However, their initiatives would take years to solve the plight of these poor unfortunate people.

There are many reasons why individuals take to the streets, sleeping rough in shop doorways, unoccupied buildings, sheltering like meat in a cardboard sandwich. The list is long: drink, drugs, money problems, marriage breakdowns, care issues, mental health, PTSD, loneliness. There are some that are not even recognised. The loss of personal security creates a vulnerability that is easily preyed upon. The homeless were victims of a world that seemed not to care.

As a result of the two deaths, Quince had instigated Operation Warsaw, which had been set up to identify the Polish gangmasters. The operation had been going for a couple of days without any success.

DC Snowy Hicks, (Juliet one-zero) an experienced officer who had seen action with the military, had been sleeping rough on the streets since the beginning of the operation. Fitted with a covert radio, Snowy reported back to the Incident Room at regular intervals. Snowy had been drafted in from the Force Drug Squad. He was an experienced 'crop' operative, and it wasn't a problem for him to survive in severe weather conditions. It was common knowledge that he would often dig himself in, building hides in the countryside, from where he could observe and gain photographic intelligence. Snowy had been instrumental in busting major drug suppliers throughout South Wales. He never needed to be asked twice to take part in an operation of this kind, in fact he thrived on it. And if anyone could glean information on the Polish gangmasters it would be him.

Snowy had bedded down for the night in a doorway deep enough to be lost in the shadows. He didn't wear a watch – he wore nothing that could suggest anything other than a man down on his luck, but he checked the time on a cheap and strapless digital watch he kept in his coat pocket. It was just coming up to midnight when Snowy spotted a black VW Caddy van with black tinted windows. The van crawled along Clarence Street, now and again it would stop for a few minutes, this happened on three occasions, arousing Snowy's suspicion.

"Juliet one-zero to control, vehicle check on VW Caddy van, location Clarence Street." He relayed the number and waited just seconds for the reply.

"Juliet one-zero, vehicle registered to Neath Recycling, Main Street, Neath. There are a couple of intel reports on the vehicle, nothing criminal, just routine checks throughout South Wales. It seems they travel far and wide."

"Juliet one-zero, all noted. It's on the move again now. I'll keep you informed. I think it's heading for the Tesco car park."

As the van then disappeared out of sight, Snowy rolled up the old blanket he used at night and hid it beneath the large sheet of cardboard that did little to insulate him from the cold ground. He stepped from the shadows and pulled his filthy beany hat down over his forehead and walked slowly to the rear of the multi-storey car park that led to the short-stay car park, a haunt for a few other rough sleepers, his intention being to join them for the rest of the night.

He'd only been there a few minutes when he noticed the van being driven slowly across the car park towards him.

The van stopped a few metres away. The doors opened and two white men got out and approached him. One of them started talking, it was obvious from his accent that he was eastern European – probably Polish, Snowy guessed.

"Any of you lot looking for work?" he asked.

"What sort you got in mind, and what's the pay?" Snowy asked.

"The usual, collecting clothing to recycle and delivering bags."

"The money?"

"Thirty pounds a day."

"No thanks, mate, I get more than that begging. I'll pass," he nodded to the others in various states of unconsciousness, "as you can see, this lot are out of it, they'd be no use."

The two men scanned the group, the tramp was right. The others were either sleeping or unconscious. They grunted something unintelligible, got back into the van and drove off.

"Juliet one-zero, for your info, I've just been approached by two Polish men offering work. They're the ones in the van I checked. Suggest a follow. They're heading out of the centre towards Oystermouth Road. One male is six-foot, medium build, short cropped dark hair. One male is six-three, very large build and shaved bald. Both wearing jeans and dark bomber jackets. I suggest you put the bike on them for starters, see where they lead us."

"Roger that, Juliet one-zero, the team are on the move."

The van trundled out of the car park onto Clarence Street then onto Albert Row and Oystermouth Road. In under a minute, Snowy saw the surveillance motorcyclist following the van at a safe distance and listened in to the radio transmissions.

"Juliet one-six, I've got eyeball on target vehicle, making its way along Oystermouth Road, speed 30mph, suggest team start plotting up, they're obviously heading out of the city."

DI Charlie John sat in the passenger seat of a grey Audi A3. DC Fred Earl put the car in gear and gunned the engine. "Juliet one-one, look lively ladies and gents," DI John barked into his radio. "You know the drill, keep on your toes. God knows where this will take us."

The team followed the van out of Swansea as it headed towards the M4. The van kept to the speed limit, clearly not wanting to be pulled in by any traffic cops.

"Juliet one-two, we've got the eyeball. Speed forty... stand-by, stand-by... target vehicle pulling into nearside, we're overshooting. Looks like they may be trying it on, team hold back."

"Juliet one-six, they're back on the move. Don't think they've clocked us, looked like one of them got out to secure the rear doors."

"Juliet one-five, target vehicle now slowing near the

roundabout, taking the second exit, can someone pick it up?"

"Juliet one-four, we've got the eyeball, target vehicle has taken the second exit and it's a stop, stop, stop. Target vehicle has pulled over to the offside and stopped outside the old Tenoco service station."

"Juliet one-six, I'm now on foot. I have the eyeball. If you all plot up, I'll relay their movements."

"Juliet one-one, to team, you all heard the man."

"Juliet one-six, this premises has been empty for donkey's years. There's a massive security fence around it. The passenger has got out of the vehicle and opened the double gates." There was a short pause in transmissions. "Target vehicle has been driven in and is now at the rear of the premises. The passenger has secured the gates and run to the rear…" Another pause. "Lights have come on, looks like they're in for the night."

"Juliet one-one, it looks like it's going to be a long night. Juliet one-six, whack a tracker on that van, if you get a chance. It will save us a lot of leg work. When they start moving again, I'll inform the Incident room. They can monitor it for us, the boss can make a decision in the morning. Just keep your eyes peeled. I reckon these blokes are surveillance conscious. So, what are they hiding?"

19

The surveillance team had plotted up around the old filling station perimeter. It was going to be a long night for all involved. Any kind of surveillance is ninety per cent pure boredom. The other ten percent is not much better. Modern day surveillance had changed over the years, vehicles were more adaptable and were fitted with the latest kit - with the constant high terrorism threat, they had to be. Teams were on stand-by 24/7, not like in years past. No force wanted to be caught with their pants down. The same applied to armed response and dedicated search teams.

Due to the seriousness of the case, the matter was now being dealt with as a double murder enquiry, together with possible people trafficking and other associated crimes.

All the official authorities for surveillance during the enquiry had been signed off by the Assistant Chief Constable, hence the approved actions of Juliet one-six in concealing a tracking device on the van. It made more sense. All the surveillance vehicles, plus the Incident room could now monitor the van's movements without causing any suspicion, as it was becoming obvious that the driver of the van was looking for tails.

"What's your take on it, Fred? Are they involved?" DI John said as he munched on a chocolate bar.

"Who knows, boss? They're obviously up to no good. They're into all sorts of crap. Mark my words, they'll show their hand soon enough. Anyway, we're here for the night. Do you fancy a roll?"

"Cut it out, Fred, you're not my type."

Fred laughed. "Cheese and onion or ham?"

"Ham it is, Fred. Fair play, you always come prepared. I've got the coffee."

Charlie poured the coffee into two cardboard cups he'd brought in a small kitbag and devoured the sandwiches. Who knew when they'd have the chance to eat again.

"You know we're losing Karen in a few weeks, Fred? I suppose the team have heard?"

"Yes, boss. Any idea where she's off to?"

"Well, there are a few after her, she's well experienced. I know she's favouring a stint on major crime, once this one is over. I'll have a chat with Quince, see if he's got a vacancy on his team."

"I'll miss her, boss. When I came on the team, I didn't know shit from clay, look at me today. I know what shit is and I know what clay is," he laughed. "It's all down to her."

Charlie nodded in the dark interior of the car.

"Anyway, get your head down, boss, I'll take first watch. What's it to be, Classic or Radio 2."

"Definitely Classic, Fred."

***

The first rays of sun broke through the gloom, an orange glow gaining strength of colour as the sun began to rise in the east when a light came on in the building. Fred checked his watch. Five-twenty-seven. A white man, shaved head, aged about thirty and wearing a black plastic-looking bomber jacket and faded jeans then walked out of the building and opened the padlocked gates. He opened and started the van and drove out and clear of the gate before returning to secure the yard behind him.

"Team, stand-by, stand-by. Target vehicle on the move, Juliet one-one, over." The DI was now on full alert. "Juliet one-six, can you take up the eyeball, keep a safe distance? You'll know where he's heading. The rest of the team, keep your positions. There's at least one male we know of still in the building."

"Juliet one-six, I've got the eyeball, leave him to me."

The driver was definitely surveillance conscious, his manoeuvres at times were out of the normal – pulling over and stopping briefly, circling roundabouts more than once. Driving into dead end roads and pulling back out.

Because the tracker had been secured to the target vehicle, there wasn't any real need for the team to follow so closely, however sometimes things still don't go to plan, and to be in proximity is a must. Finding the balance was the key to success.

The target vehicle was heading north along the Neath valley, but where?

"Juliet one-six, it's a stop, stop at Glyn Farm. I'm now on foot and have eyeball on target vehicle. It's pulled up in front of a large barn. The doors are open and two white males have appeared. The vehicle has been driven in, and doors are closing. Suggest you get Juliet one-zero up here a bit sharpish."

"Juliet one-five... will do. Stay on plot. We'll get Snowy up as soon as possible. I'll get the boss up to speed as well."

***

"Morning, boss. Charlie here. We've got two premises under surveillance."

"I know about the old filling station, Charlie, where's the other one?"

"It's an isolated farm in Glynneath, boss. One of my boys is keeping observations on it, but I've got Snowy on the way up there. He can dig in until this is all resolved. The target vehicle is now located in one of the barns."

"How many targets are we talking about Charlie?"

"At least one in the old filling station, and at least three up at the barn, boss. What's the next move?"

"Seems you've got all ends covered, Charlie. Just sit on it for the time being. I'll call a briefing, get some warrants, and we'll bust the two premises. Hopefully, later this evening, when it gets dark, we'll go full hog, chopper, armed response, the lot. Can't be too careful with this."

"No problem, boss. If there's any change, I'll ring you direct. The Incident Room is monitoring as well."

Quince ended the call and then began arranging a major briefing for mid-day.

***

"This is Juliet one-six... stand-by, stand by. I have movement near the main farmhouse, looks like an IC1 male, late sixties. He's making his way over to the barns. Looks like he's just checking them to make sure they're secure, he doesn't seem all that bothered, he's now returned to the main farmhouse."

20

Quince sat in his office, making calls that would see a major operation unfold. It would involve all the specialised departments. Everything would be co-ordinated. It would begin with another briefing of the team. Operations could succeed or fail on the quality of communication between members of the team. Quince had to know everything to ensure he made the correct decisions. The briefings were crucial to keeping on top of the case.

The coffee was hot, if a little thin on flavour. Quince hated instant coffee, preferring to use a percolator a previous incumbent of his post had set up in his office. Things had been so busy he'd forgotten to buy more beans and was reduced to sipping the dishwater the other detectives seemed happy to drink. Quince remembered the coffee his father used to brew. Dark, full of flavour with no sugar and no milk. Brits had no taste when it came to coffee. It was strange, even though he had lived the best part of his life in the UK, he still thought of himself as American. He winced as he finished the last drops in his mug. He'd buy more beans as soon as the briefing was over. He couldn't think properly without good beans.

"Listen up everybody," he said, loud and clear to gain the attention of the detectives assembled. "Thank you all for turning out at short notice. You've all got briefing notes in front of you, however I'll fill you in. This is the story so far. Operation Warsaw began with the discovery of the bodies of two Asian lads recovered from the marina. Initially it was thought drowning was the cause of death, however the PMs showed they'd been overdosed on methamphetamine and their hands had been tied. Now we don't know whether they were illegals, and their bodies were just dumped or if there's a bigger picture. Clive, perhaps you can go through the timeline?"

DC Clive Purcell stood and stepped to the front. "Cheers, boss. The bodies had been in the water for a very short time, probably dumped sometime late on Thursday night. Unfortunately, the marina CCTV was out of commission, so we drew a blank there. A white Ford Transit van was picked up in the vicinity by the ANPR, suffice to say it was on false plates, so I guess it's involved. We've no idea where the vehicle is now. We also received intel about a Polish team who have been targeting the homeless and using them for cheap labour. So, as a result, the boss set up Operation Warsaw, which looks like it may prove positive. Hence the reason we are all here today. Late Saturday night, Snowy Hicks, who most of you know, was undercover, sleeping with the homeless in the Swansea town centre, when he was approached by two Poles in a Black VW Caddy registered to Neath Recycling. We've done the checks, there's no such premises in Main Street. The Poles asked him if he wanted some work. He obviously refused, never been much work in Snowy," Clive joked. The others laughed along with Quince. "So, they drove off. Since then, our Force surveillance team have been on them like limpets. As a result, two premises have been identified as being of interest. Firstly, the old filling station near Crymlin Bog where the VW initially parked up overnight. Secondly, a remote farm in Glynneath, Glyn farm. We've obtained warrants for both the premises. The premises are still under surveillance. The VW is now in a barn at the farm. There's been no movement for over twelve hours at either property, so let's hope it stays like that."

Chief Inspector Mel Smythe, the Firearms Co-ordinator, stood. "How many suspects at each premises, Clive?"

"Definitely one IC1 at the filling station, Chief. Three IC1s in the barn, a fourth being the owner called Bill Glyndwr in the main farmhouse itself. He rents the properties out."

"Is there any indication that this Bill Glyndwr is involved?"

Clive shook his head. "I'd say no. A few of us know old Bill. I think he's rented the barns to these Polish blokes and they're taking advantage. We're following many lines of enquiry at the minute, also liaising with Customs and Immigration regarding any intelligence they have on people traffickers. This is the first time in South Wales that this sort of incident has occurred, so it would be pure supposition at this moment in time."

"We intend to strike both premises after dark, around ten pm," Quince confirmed. "It will a co-ordinated strike and will be led by our armed response officers. Chief Inspector Smythe will hit the petrol station with his team, and Inspector Seb Crole will hit the farm with his team. The rest of you will be back up. So, when both premises are secured, and the targets are in custody, thorough searches will be carried out by the specialised search units at both premises. All prisoners will be conveyed to Swansea Central, and for God's sake ensure that they're properly searched." Quince paused. "Are there any questions? I trust you know your roles in this operation. If not, speak now. I have no idea what will confront you, the only thing I will say, and I stress, please keep safe and watch your backs. I'll be in the Incident room monitoring all transmissions, so the very best of luck."

***

Time seemed to drag, as if taunting Quince as he waited for ten pm to finally arrive. The moment the minute hand hit ten, Quince gave the order, "Strike, strike, strike." All team leaders responded in the affirmative, then the airwaves fell silent.

Quince felt the nerves, a feeling he knew he shared with everyone else on the operation. Adrenalin would be pumping, more so for the firearms officers who were always first through the doors. Operations like this could be over in minutes, however, now and again they could get violent and messy taking a great deal longer. Quince knew that in Smythe and Crole, he had officers he could rely on.

He checked his watch as the airwaves began to burst into life again. Nine minutes past ten.

"FO-one to control, the farm has been secured. We have four IC1s in custody, including the farm owner. I don't think the owner has got a clue what's going on. We got two other males we found chained in a barn basement, which is being used as a cannabis factory.

"The two chained males..." Quince broke in. "What nationality are they?"

A moment, then the crackle preceding a response. "Their nationalities are not known, but they look Asian..."

Quince punched the air. "Yes!"

"All six are on their way to Swansea Central. None of them are talking, apart from the old man who won't shut up. The Asians are terrified, looks like they could do with a good feed."

"Many thanks, Mel," Quince said. "Pass on my thanks."

"Yes, Abe, all covered."

Seb, a firearms officer with prior military experience was operating as call-sign FO2 and was next to transmit a result. "FO2 to control, petrol station secured. One IC-one in custody, together with two Chinese males who were found concealed in an inspection pit. We've recovered several small arms weapons, with a lot of drug paraphernalia, and equipment." FO2 wanted to say that the Chinese men were in a bad way, that they looked like full-on junkies by the track marks on their arms, but thought it best to keep that off the radio waves. That would become apparent to all.

"Excellent, Seb. Just to confirm, in case you missed the last message, the farm has also been secured, with a number of males in custody, no sign of weapons, just a large cannabis factory. I've got Immigration on stand-by. They can get into the Asians. I just hope that it leads to the ones who killed the two men in the marina. I'll call a de-brief after the Poles have been bedded down for the night. Good job, thank all concerned for me."

"Will do, boss, it's been a pleasure."

DCI Cross tapped Quince on the shoulder. Her smile was reserved but a smile none-the-less. "Well, Abe, that seems to have gone very well. I must admit that I did have my reservations. Do you think that this is the team responsible for the murders?"

"I'll keep an open mind, Ma'am. Let's see what the prisoners say, if they say anything at all."

"No short cuts. Keep it straight and tidy."

This caused a bristling in Quince. He always 'played it straight,' and if Cross bothered to get to know her team, she would know that. She was playing at detective at the moment and either needed to step up to the plate or stand down. "I resent the implication I'd run it any other way than straight, Ma'am."

"Now, Abe, if you're not careful I may pull rank and take the enquiry over. I'll see you tomorrow, just bear it in mind."

Quince took a deep breath as he watched DCI Norma Cross totter out of the office on shoes that were more suitable to a night out than policing and stuck two fingers up as a mock salute. "Up yours!"

21

The next twenty-four hours was so important to solving the deaths of the two Vietnamese men.

It was going to be a long day, so Quince brought in a new team of interviewing officers to relieve those who had been involved in the operation. As always, the briefing would be key to keeping everyone on task.

"We have four Polish traffickers in custody at the minute. We've recovered a cache of small arms and drug making equipment at the old petrol station and an underground cannabis factory at the farm in Glynneath.

It's obvious to me that they've been picking up homeless individuals off the streets and then imprisoning them to keep their factories going. But I want to ensure that you make it obvious to the court further down the line. They've basically been treating them like animals. I'm not speculating at this moment in time as to whether they are involved in the murders of the two Vietnamese. It looks like the two at the farm could in fact be Vietnamese, and the two at the petrol station are Chinese."

A diminutive detective with a name to match stood. Kevin Small was shorter than the average copper, but height restrictions had been removed from entry many years ago. Small was an example of a man who always punched above his weight. Efficient, and as tough as a terrier. "Boss, I've just been down to the custody suite and I can confirm the ones from the farm are definitely Vietnamese. They've all been booked in. Their English is just about passable but the custody sarge has decided to call out a few interpreters, they'll be here by nine."

"Cheers, Kev. I'd like you," Quince pointed to Connor, "to get your mate Nadir here for the same time. You never know, they may open up to him. They must be scared. They've been through a hell of an ordeal."

"I'm on to it, boss. I'm sure Nadir will be all for it," Connor said.

"If we can get into them, Connor, who knows what may develop. I've prepared some briefing notes for the interviewing teams. It's going to be a long day and the clock is ticking. There's another bit of good news, the search teams have found stacks of documentation relating to an address in Neath, which is being searched as I speak. Hopefully, it's the premises they've been keeping these poor bastards before farming them out. Are there any questions? No? Then those who were on the operation get home and have some kip. The rest of you prepare yourselves for the interviews and we'll crack on at nine."

After the briefing, Quince headed down to the custody suite and had a chat with Frank Doyle the custody sergeant.

"Busy Night, Frank. Sorry about all this, you must be rushed off your feet?"

Frank shrugged. "Not a problem. I prefer it busy. Shift goes quicker. Anyway, they're all bedded down. Got to say that the Poles are mean looking bastards. I don't think you'll get much out of them."

"We'll see how they react when we hit them with the murders of the two Vietnamese. That may loosen their tongues. Do we have any names for the men they had chained?"

"Yes. The two Vietnamese are Dahn Lieu and Chi Phan. They're only kids, boss. Not a lot of English between them. They understand me and can make themselves understood. The two Chinese are a bit older…" he checked the paperwork he had completed for them. "…Cheng Tai Shi, and Heng Dong Fang. They speak nearly perfect English. I thought it best to get interpreters for the Vietnamese to ensure we don't get it thrown back in our face further down the line in court. There's no problem with the Chinese. They've been given a clean bill of health by the FMO. All they need is a good feed."

"Cheers, Frank. The interview teams have been sorted and briefed. I'll be back in a couple of hours to oversee it. Hopefully, by the time you come on tonight, it'll all be sorted."

"I have no doubt about that, boss. You get off and grab a few hours."

Quince headed home, he never really switched off. It was the main reason for the failure of his marriage and as much as he was aware of that fact, there was nothing he could do about it. He was determined to clear up the double murders as quickly as possible, however he never put all his eggs in one basket. Experience had taught him that things could change in an instance. The best advice he would give new detectives was to never be blinkered, look at the broader picture. Quince had been on enough murder enquiries where senior detectives had made their mind up who the culprit was, and were later proved wrong. It's so easy to put persons of interest in the frame, having gone off all guns blazing. This was not going to happen in this case.

Quince had a quick shave, changed his shirt, and then had a half hour power nap on the settee.

***

Meanwhile, Connor swilled a Meal Deal sandwich down with a sip of tea before scrolling through his contacts and pressing call. "Good morning, Nadir, sorry to call you so early."

He explained the situation and was impressed by the man's willingness to help.

"I'll be there in twenty minutes," Nadir said.

***

Quince arrived back at the Incident Room at eight on the dot, and the interview teams were also there, eager to start.

Connor was sitting at his desk with an older Vietnamese man Quince guessed was Nadir. Connor stood and nodded to the older man. "Boss, this is Nadir. He's agreed to help out with the interviews of the two Vietnamese lads."

Quince shook Nadir's hand and thanked him for assisting. "Nadir, we'll let the boys have a chat with the interpreters and interview teams first. They must be terrified and depending how that goes we will take the enquiry forward. If we don't get anywhere, for whatever reason and they are afraid to talk, you can speak to them with Connor. Please ensure them that they are not in any trouble, and they are not going to be locked away. They have my word on that. All I want to do is get to the bottom of how the two men were murdered in the marina."

"That will be no problem," Nadir nodded.

Connor and Nadir then headed off to the custody suite as DCI Cross made her appearance.

"Looks like things are taking off, Abe?" She said as she took in the team assembled.

"Morning, Ma'am. Yes, but it's early days at the minute. The team will be getting stuck in shortly, but I'm not holding my breath."

"Think positive," she smiled. "I'll be down the big house all day and I'll be going home from there. It's an all-day job, diversity training," she grimaced.

22

Sky the colour of a battleship, a damp and cloudy August morning and it summed up Nicola Spearman's mood, as she sat quietly on a beautifully carved oak bench in the rose garden at Coychurch Crematorium, Bridgend.

The brass plaque on the bench read "IN LOVING MEMORY OF MY DARLINGS. RYAN and CALVIN.... BOTH TAKEN TOO SOON.... NEVER FORGOTTEN, ALWAYS IN MY HEART, ALL MY LOVE NICOLA"

Head cupped in her hands; she was praying to a God she wasn't sure she believed in anymore. Tears tickled her cheeks. Her whole world had been shattered by circumstances that could never have been foreseen; circumstances that had changed her life forever.

Nicola was only twenty when she married her first, and only love Calvin Spearman.

Calvin was a few years older than Nicola, and was entrepreneur, having made his fortune in the world of computers. He was a multi-millionaire by the time he was fifty, having sold off all his business interests.

Both were blissfully happy. They raised two lovely children, Kelvin, and Ryan, had a holiday home in Madeira, life couldn't have been better. However, this wasn't to last. Their world was turned upside down in early 2016 when Kelvin, their eldest son, was arrested and charged with offences relating to possessing and downloading indecent images of young children on his computer.

Kelvin admitted the offences and was sentenced to five years in prison. From that time on, Kelvin was disowned by Nicola and Calvin. They were ashamed of him. They cut him off, as if he had never existed.

During the months after Kelvin's sentencing, the Spearman family began to get their lives back on track. They couldn't believe that Kelvin could do such a thing. At first they couldn't, and wouldn't believe it, however, Kelvin fully admitted his crimes to the police, so they had no choice.

They refused to visit their son in prison. Their hearts were broken.

More tragedy was to strike the family in the summer of 2017 when Ryan, the youngest son, was found dead in his bed. He was twenty-three years of age at the time.

Nicola had just made him breakfast and had taken it up to his room. Ryan was curled under the blankets and when Nicola began prodding him she got no response. This was nothing unusual with Ryan, he wasn't an early riser, in fact sometimes he wouldn't go to bed at all. He would spend all night on his computer, playing all sorts of games.

Both he and Kelvin had inherited the 'computer' gene from Calvin. They were both brilliant.

Nicola pulled back the bed covers to find Ryan lying on his side – lifeless.

It was later found that Ryan had suffered a massive heart attack. The post-mortem revealed that he had the heart of a seventy-year-old and was a ticking time bomb. He could have died at any time.

From that day on, Nicola and Calvin became very protective of each other, and were very rarely on their own. Every day, they would visit the crematorium, and put fresh flowers in the silver urn on Ryan's headstone. It was a tragedy. They had now lost two sons in totally different circumstances.

This wasn't to be the end of Nicola's heartache, however. There was more to come the following year, and it would leave her totally devastated to the point that she no longer wished to live.

It was nearly twelve months since they had lost Ryan when Calvin broke the news to Nicola that he had been diagnosed with a rare form of cancer, and that the prognosis was far from good. The doctors only gave him a couple of months to live. There was no cure, and the disease had progressed to his liver and kidneys.

As he broke the news to Nicola, Calvin wept, too. His wife had been through so much. He didn't want to leave her alone but knew that was exactly what would happen.

Nicola's world had come to an end. This was the last straw. She would be on her own. What good was money when she had no one to share it with.

Two months later, Calvin passed quietly away at home in his sleep. Nicola had nursed him and never left his side throughout his illness. Unlike many when they lost children, their relationship had grown stronger.

The house had always been filled with energy and laughter. There was always something going on, especially when the boys were growing up and their friends would come around to play music and computer games.

It had all gone. The house was a void, an empty shell.

Nicola checked the answer phone. There was one message. Nicola pressed the play button.

"Mam, this is Kelvin. I'm sorry for everything. I miss you. I should have been there for you. Hopefully you'll let me explain. I want to explain……"

Before another word was said, Nicola picked up the phone and threw it against the kitchen wall, it smashed into pieces on the floor. She screamed.

23

It was obvious from the onset that Dawid was the ringleader, or gangmaster. He was the kind of bloke that Quince would like to double tap on sight. He was arrogant, brutal, and never thought twice about the lives of the poor souls he had kidnapped, starved, and chained up like animals. Dawid was a solid frame. His short, cropped light-brown hair and black bomber jacket was probably carefully designed to make him look tougher. Looking the part seemed to be important to thugs.

Quince was happy with his interview teams. He assigned DS George Brodie, who had just returned from leave to get stuck into Dawid. Brodie was a seasoned detective and first-class interviewer. Tall and thin, he looked like every year had taken its toll on his face. His long face was lined and topped by unruly fair hair and his hands were the biggest Quince had ever seen. He could hide a pint glass in his hand. His dark brown eyes were shrouded in heavy, unruly brows and his very presence was intimidating without him even trying. Brodie could make a villain crack with just a frown.

With all the formalities done, it was now crunch time. Dawid had declined a solicitor.

Brodie sat his big frame on a chair opposite Dawid. "Well, Dawid, it looks like you are up to your neck in bother. Would you like to explain everything to me, bearing in mind you're still under caution?"

"No comment."

"Oh, it's going to be like that, is it?"

Dawid grinned. "No comment."

"Well, let me just tell you, you've got a rude awakening coming. In fact, by the time I finish with you, you'll enjoy talking," Brodie grinned now but the heavy eyebrows made the expression more akin to a demon sizing up its next meal. Yes, I have a couple of surprises in store for you."

The grin slipped from Dawid's face. "No comment."

"How long have you been in the UK, Dawid?"

"No comment." Dawid folded his arms across his chest defensively.

"Your fingerprints have been circulated to all police forces in Europe, including your homeland of Poland."

"No comment."

"OK, let's have a look here now," Brodie scanned a sheet of printed information. "You've been arrested for kidnapping and being concerned in the cultivation and supplying of cannabis. That'll do for starters."

"No comment."

"Now, on top of that, even though you were arrested at the farm, your prints are on firearms and drug making equipment at the old petrol station. For those offences, I am duty bound to arrest you. Now, before you open your mouth, I must caution you again."

Dawid's Adam's apple bobbed up and down like an Otis elevator as George Brodie recited the caution.

"Anything to say about that, Dawid?"

"No Comment."

"There's just one final thing, no... I'm sorry, Dawid... there are two, in fact. The first one is, I'm also arresting you for being concerned in the double murders of two Vietnamese nationals, their bodies being found in the marina after being injected with meth. Before you open your mouth, I must caution you again," Brodie smiled. "Isn't this boring?"

Dawid dropped his head and stared at the floor. "No comment."

"Lift your head, Dawid. Look me in the eyes when I'm talking to you."

Dawid raised his head, the colour had drained from him, it was clear to George that his body language showed he was now scared.

"And now... for the piece de resistance, Dawid. Why didn't you tell me that you were wanted in Krakow for the attempted murder of a prostitute? Also, you escaped from police custody, during which you assaulted an officer who ended up with a fractured skull. You naughty boy." Another grin from Brodie. "They are rubbing their hands in anticipation for your return, so it's up to you... have a little think, because you've got a lot to take in."

Dawid nodded his head. "What do you want?"

"What do I want? The truth, obviously. You play ball and we'll see how things go."

"I've killed no one, do you understand? No one."

"OK." Brodie nodded. "Let's say I believe you. You've got four people imprisoned, two being Vietnamese. Bit of a coincidence that within in a week we've got two dead and two alive. So, this is what I think. You and your associates, and I use that word very loosely, are people smugglers. You collect them off the boat and put them to work in your drug factories under the guise of a legitimate company."

"You're wrong!"

"Then explain it all to me, it's simple… you just move your mouth and let the truth come out."

Dawid sighed. He was breaking, that much was clear. "Will I be sent back to Poland? If I am, I'm dead. You don't know what the police are like. They will have me killed. No trial, just killed." He made a hand gesture of two fingers mimicking a gun pressed against his temple.

"That's above my pay scale, Dawid. I'm just a simple sergeant, but I'm sure if you co-operate, the CPS will view it kindly."

"I need to think, I need to know what the others have said."

"Whatever, Dawid, but that's for me to know. I'll return you to your cell after updating the custody sergeant on your position and of the additional arrests."

Quince was waiting in quiet anticipation when George Brodie walked into the Incident Room.

"How's it going, George?"

"Well, boss, I've hit him with everything. He's not so cocky now. I've arrested him for the murders. He's denied them, of course. He's sweating in the cells now. I think he wants a deal, but there isn't a lot we can offer him. He says he's a dead man if we send him back to Poland."

"That's his bloody problem. If you can't do the time, don't do the crime. Anyway, that's great, George. I think the others are just muscle. They're coughing their guts up but are scared of Dawid. What's your take?"

"What have they said about the murders? Have they implicated Dawid in them?"

"No. Even though they are bubbling him as the gangmaster, they won't have anything to do with the murders. They say all they do is trawl the streets for anyone homeless and basically kidnap them, simple as that."

"What about the guns?"

"Dawid just knocks them out to whoever will pay the cash."

"Bloody hell, they don't give a shit. What's the country coming to, eh? Anyway, I reckon he'll soon be ringing the buzzer."

"Good job, George."

"What about the two Vietnamese, boss?"

"They wouldn't say anything with the interpreters, so I've stopped their interviews, changed tack, and just sent Connor down with Nadir. They can have a chat with them both together. Perhaps Nadir can loosen a tongue or two."

"When murder's afoot, and there's so many who may be implicated, somebody usually cracks. I'm fifty-fifty with Dawid. My next interview may throw more light on it. I don't think they're into the smuggling. I think they just pray on the vulnerable and illegals."

"Just do the business, George."

"Let's hope so, boss. I'll get back down there to see how he's shaping up

.

24

When Connor and Nadir entered the interview room, Lieu and Phan were sat close together, shoulder to shoulder. It was obvious from their body language that they were still scared, even though they were being well looked after by the custody staff. Both had paper cups of a liquid the custody staff called coffee. They must have been wondering what their future was going to be like from here on in and that was a difficult fear to break.

Nadir spoke first. "Hello, I'm Nadir Huang. I live here in Swansea with my family. I am originally from Vietnam too. Do you understand?"

Both Lieu and Phan nodded their heads.

"I understand that you weren't very talkative with the interpreters and other officers. Is there any reason? I'm assured that all they want to know is how you came to be chained at the farm. There's no need to be afraid, I can assure you."

"Will we be locked up forever?" Lieu asked.

"I can't answer things like that, but all you've done is what many others have done and have been exploited."

"What will happen?"

"Look, this is Connor, my very good friend. I have known him for many years. You can trust him, I swear. Just listen to him. Will you please do that?"

Both nodded.

"Like Nadir has said, you're not in trouble. I'm going to ask a few questions about how you got here, that's all. I must ask you, do you know about two other Vietnamese lads, who are sadly now dead? They were discovered in the marina a few days ago."

Lieu and Phan looked at each other, they were startled. It was obvious that Connor had hit a nerve.

"Look, if you know anything, please tell us. It's very important. And if these men who have kept you chained up are responsible, they must pay for it."

"They kill us if we talk," Phan said, shaking his head. His hands trembling.

"No, you're safe. They'll never treat you like that again.

They're all going to prison. I promise you that."

Phan spoke quietly. "What you want to know?"

"The whole story. We know it will be difficult, that's why Nadir is here, he's here to help you. We all are," Connor smiled warmly. "Let's start at the beginning. How long have you been in the country?"

"No idea, ran off, sleeping on streets."

"These men who have been keeping you prisoner, are they the ones who brought you into the country?"

"No, they picked us off street. Offered work, so we went with them."

"So, you've been trafficked halfway around the world. Have you any idea exactly where you are now?"

"In jail?"

"No, you're not in jail. You are in a place of safety. We are going to look after you. You have nothing to worry about. You're in Swansea… on second thoughts, perhaps you do have something to worry about," Connor laughed and both Lieu and Phan managed a smile. Connor knew that he had connected with them and hoped he would be able to get the whole story. It was obvious that the traffickers had smuggled the boys by offloading them on to numerous boats, probably kept in some shithole of a hold and treated badly. "The two young lads in the marina, they didn't drown. They had been drugged, overdosed in fact. Did anything like that happen to you?"

"No, we obeyed commands. Never beaten."

"Do you know the names of the boys? At the moment we have no idea who they are."

"Dinh and Taavi, both beaten and tied up. Would not listen."

"OK, so where in Vietnam have you come from?"

"We from Ha Tinh, they from Nghe AN."

"What are they talking about here, Nadir?"

"They are two impoverished provinces in north central Vietnam. My guess is that their families have paid the money for them to get to the UK. They've probably paid about £10,000 for each one of them, perhaps more. They've had to trek overland through jungle before arriving at a port to be shipped, just like cattle. I have no doubt most of the time they've been blindfolded, and completely disorientated. Once we've finished here, I'll make some calls. Now we have some names, and the area they are from, maybe we can get the full picture. These two are very lucky indeed."

"Thanks, Nadir. Boys can you tell me what happened at the marina. Did you see anything at all?"

Phan nodded but stared at his hands. "We got off boat, then bundled into van. Dinh and Taavi tied up. Thought they were dead."

"So, you were OK, but the other two lads appeared dead? Are you sure about that?"

"Yes."

"How long were you in the van before you got to the marina?"

Phan shrugged, it was obvious he and Lieu had no idea about time.

"What happened at the marina?"

"Men pulled Dinh and Taavi out, then threw them on ground."

"What did you do?"

"We jumped and ran away."

"What about the men, did they chase you?"

"No. Looked back, they were dragging Dinh and Taavi to water."

"What did you do then?"

"We run for our lives."

"The bodies were found early last Friday morning. They hadn't been in the water long. So, I assume you ran away late Thursday night?" Again, the men shrugged. "When did the men who imprisoned you pick you up, have you any idea?"

Lieu now spoke. "Two nights, I think. Helped by other homeless. Sleep on floors in doorways and theatre car park."

"Is that when the Polish men picked you up?"

"Yes. Offered work and food, so we went with them."

"Do you know where they took you? Was it straight to the farm?"

"No, to house, many miles away."

"What happened there?"

"Gave us room to sleep in."

"How long were you there?"

"Put to work in morning."

"I take it you mean on the farm where you were found?"

"Yes. Out of van, then underground. Then chained and left."

"Look boys, that's all for now. I've got the picture, I'll leave you with Nadir for the time being, he'll have a good chat with you. And, like I said, don't be afraid. Is that OK with you, Nadir?"

"Not a problem, Connor. I'll have a chat and see if I can get a bit more for you."

Connor then left the room to bring Quince up to date.

***

"Boss, I've finished the initial interview with the two lads. It doesn't look too promising, but they've calmed down a bit. They were terrified. I've left Nadir with them for the time being. He'll have a good chat with them and make a few calls for us."

"OK, Connor. So, what have we got?"

"We've got the first names of the two boys in the marina. Dinh and Taavi. Both from Ha Tinh province, a poor area in Vietnam. Nadir, like I say, will try to get their full identities for us. He's well connected. This is how I see it, boss. These four poor bastards left Vietnam hoping for a better life. They've been dragged from pillar to post by these traffickers, eventually ending up on numerous boats and finally ending here in South Wales. It looks like Dinh and Taavi were handfuls, so were tied up and later drugged to keep them quiet. The boys say that when they got off the boat they were bundled into a van. Dinh and Taavi were out of it, subsequently arriving at the marina. The two boys managed to run away from them, the traffickers didn't even bother to chase them. They slept rough until the Poles picked them up."

"I take it then that the Poles are not involved in the deaths?"

"I wouldn't think so, boss. These Poles are just predators, and gangsters. The boys say they weren't the smugglers."

"Would they be able to identify them?"

"I wouldn't think so, boss. I'm sorry but that's the way it is. We're no further on with detecting it."

"We need a break, or this will run and run. Look, sort out the illegals with the Immigration. I'll brief the teams then about charging the Poles. I've already spoken to the CPS; we'll throw the book at them. They'll be banged up for a very long time."

"Good enough for the bastards, boss."

It was now mid-afternoon, and Quince was disappointed. However, he never showed his feelings to his team. He gave Cross a ring.

"How is it going, Abe?"

"Not too good. Looks like the Poles are not involved in the murders, so the enquiry has fallen a bit flat. We're at a dead end," he sighed.

"Well, Abe, you and the team have done a cracking job thus far, so don't beat yourself up. I have every confidence in you. I'm a bit tied up at the minute, I'll see you first thing Monday. If anything breaks, give me a bell. You don't need me there, do you?"

"No, Ma'am. You enjoy your weekend."

25

It had been a hard week on the buildings site, harder than usual because they were on a tight deadline. Kelvin was having a deserved lie-in. All the workers had been given Monday off as they had met that deadline and the new job would start on Tuesday. That meant a move to another site some ten miles away on the other side of the city. He thought about ignoring the knocks at the door but thought better of it.

He groaned as he rolled out of bed. He ached like he had never ached before. Every muscle screamed for rest. Gibbs stood in the doorway, grinning.

"Mr Gibbs, what can I do for you? I've never seen you on the weekend before."

"No, that's right, Kelvin," he pushed past him and sauntered into the lounge. "Coffee with two sugars, if you don't mind. And a digestive, if you've got one."

"Yes, I'll make one now. No biscuits, sorry."

"No problem," Gibbs ensconced himself on one of the lounge chairs. Kelvin was trembling as he filled the kettle, he knew that Gibbs wanted something, and if he refused him, it was back to prison.

He didn't want to ask but neither did he want Gibbs in the flat for any longer than necessary. "What can I do for you Mr Gibbs?"

"Come and have a sit down. It's time we put you to work. Bring the coffee in with you."

Kelvin duly obeyed, he was at Gibb's beck and call. He hated it, but what could he do? He couldn't refuse.

"You know the score; we've got you by the bollocks. So, it's entirely up to you. Either you go along with it or it's back to the nick. Now you wouldn't fancy that, would you?"

"No, Mr Gibbs. There's no way I'm going back."

"If you do as your told, there'll be no problem. There'll be a few shillings in it for you as well."

"What do you want me to do, Mr Gibbs?"

"What do you think?"

"You want me to smuggle for you?"

Gibbs laughed.

"Smuggle? You couldn't be further from the truth. No, something a bit more refined."

"Like what?"

"Well, it's your game, Kelvin."

"I don't understand."

"We want your computer skills. You know how to hack. Our last genius had a stroke, he's no use to man or beast, and he had all the passwords, so we're somewhat disadvantaged at the moment. We can't get at the data."

"I don't understand."

"Identity theft, Kelvin, that's what I mean."

"I still don't follow."

"We want you to create new identities for blokes who want to disappear... get my drift?"

"Oh God, give us a break."

"I've got the leash, you're my property and, like a dog, you'll do as I say, got it?"

Kelvin couldn't say a lot, but he was sick to his stomach. "What does it involve, Mr Gibbs?"

"Well, your kind, Kelvin," he spat to emphasise his disgust. "Bloody paedophiles who just want to disappear. They pay good money, especially the ones who are worth a bob or two."

"Why would they want to disappear?"

"You're naïve, or thick, or both? Let me explain. If you hadn't gone to prison, would you be worth a bob or two?"

"Well, yes. But what's that got to do with it?"

"Now I suppose you'd like to start a new life, somewhere in the sun where no one would know you, with a new identity. Don't tell me you haven't thought of it?"

It suddenly dawned on him what Gibbs was getting him involved in and he didn't like it.

"I don't know, Mr Gibbs, if we get caught, it's back to prison. I'm not interested".

"OK. After I've gone, expect a knock on the door. It'll be the boys in blue and it'll be curtains for you. Do not pass go, do not collect two-hundred pounds. Straight to jail."

Gibbs got up and headed for the door.

"OK, I'll do whatever you want."

"That's more like it," Gibbs turned and laughed. "Nice to see you playing ball. Now this is how it works. You create a few false accounts, do a bit of hacking and Bob's your aunt. You'll be using the flat of our last computer geek. All the gear is there for you use. I've got some passwords, but not them all. He was a cunning fella but now it's all set up for you to get cracking."

"How long will it take?"

"How long is a piece of string?" Gibbs handed kelvin a small square of paper with a typed address. "Look this is the address of the flat. We'll meet you there Saturday morning, about eight, and we'll run through it with you. I'll sort work out for you. They won't report your absence."

The address was in Deri Road, Neath.

"You know where that is? It's just a spitting distance from here."

"I'll find it, but who is he?"

"Now, now, Kelvin, the least you know the better. Just do as your told and we'll get on swimmingly. Now don't let me down."

Gibbs left. Kelvin felt helpless. He didn't know where to turn. He was being blackmailed into doing something that was a major criminal act. He couldn't go to the police; they'd never believe him. He just had to go along with it. There must be some other way of getting out of it. Gibbs must be involved with other people of the same ilk. Was there a network, and how far did it reach?

It was then Kelvin remembered the name of a solicitor's runner, a man he had had dealings with - Andy Stokes. He had no one to turn to but he knew he had to tell someone.

***

The telephone rang for what seemed like an eternity before someone answered.

The words were not practiced but conveyed Kelvin's fears and predicament as efficiently as was possible. By the end of the short conversation, Stokes was convinced the caller was genuine. "Blackmailed? By whom? Why don't you go to the police?"

"I can't. They won't believe me. It's a big conspiracy. You've got to help me, please."

"I can't see how I can help you. It's the police you need."

"Surely you know someone in the police? Who would listen to

me? It's all about a paedophile ring."

"You mean to tell me that you, a convicted paedophile, wants to blow the gaff on a paedo ring?"

***

The taxi driver wasn't the talkative type and Kelvin was glad for that little mercy. He wasn't in the mood to talk. He could barely force himself to think.

He had been to airports several times before. He had flown to a handful of airports in Spain, and twice to Amsterdam - either from Cardiff or Bristol - and each time he'd passed through an airport he had been happy. Not today. He was terrified; he couldn't think because he didn't know what to think. He knew that Gibbs had him by the bollocks, and whatever he was getting involved in, he was now up over his neck in it. He knew it would only take a word from Gibbs and he'd be back inside. There would be no point in protesting his innocence, who'd believe a bloke who'd just done a stretch inside and was currently on licence?

The airport was bustling with happy, smiling faces. Kelvin stepped through the large rotating glass door and stopped for a moment to get his bearings. He watched the multitude of smiles wander in all directions, colourful had cases and bags in tow, clearly delighted to be escaping the shitty Welsh weather. He saw the check-in desk he needed and passed through without any problem, even though he was expecting to be nicked at any time.

A large brandy in the lounge made little difference to his mood. He knew they didn't 'call' flights at the airport anymore. As soon as he saw the 'Boarding' message appeared alongside his flight he made his way to the gate.

No turning back, he felt his hands tremble as he stuffed his hand luggage into the locker above his allocated seat. He knew he had to carry out his orders; he had no idea what Gibbs wanted him to carry but he knew it was going to be something that would end his freedom if caught.

Kelvin slithered across two seats to the window and tried to make himself comfortable. He stared out of the window but nothing his eyes set upon registered in his head, not even the man clambering into the seat alongside him could break his self-imposed trance.

"Business or pleasure?" a bright voice asked.

Kelvin turned to see a rotund, forty-something with close-cropped hair and what looked like two-day's growth on his face. A bright blue T-shirt bore a large white printed date; '1969.' Beneath it were the words 'All Original Parts.'

"I'm having a few days break from the Mrs," the man continued. He held out a bulbous hand. "I'm Mike," he smiled.

Kelvin forced a smile in return. Just what he needed – the 'village friendly'.

"Kelvin. Just overnight, a business meeting in the morning," he grumbled unenthusiastically in the hope the 'friendly' would take the hint.

"What you into? Must be something juicy to visit Jersey."

"Not really, I'm in construction."

Kelvin's stomach churned.

"Ah, construction, hard old game, greasing a few palms no doubt?"

"I'm just a runner, exchanging a few contracts for the firm."

"What firm is that? Must be doing well if they're doing business on the island."

"It's a family business, pretty low key, what are you into?" he said, hoping Mike 'the friendly' would be more interested in talking about himself.

"Bit of this and a bit of that, if you get my drift," he winked. "I'm a bit of a 'facilitator'. So, where are you staying?"

"The Apollo"

"Bloody hell, what a coincidence, we can have a snort or two in the bar tonight, have you stayed there before?"

Kelvin felt his bowels begin to protest. "No, this is my first visit."

"You won't be disappointed, cracking food and a tremendous welcome."

"That's good," he had to stop the questions from Mike. "You say you're a facilitator, what exactly do you facilitate then?"

"You name it, I'll facilitate it, you know what I mean? by the way I'm Doug, Doug Greenslade."

"I thought you said your name was Mike?"

The stranger then shook Kelvin's hand again. "Did I?" he

grinned wickedly.

"We can share a taxi to the hotel, you up for that?" Doug offered.

Kelvin knew there was no point in making up some excuse. "Why not?"

"Anyway, I'll let you have a break."

Thank fuck for that, the bloke was a real pain and obviously a bit of a wide boy.

The aircraft touched down with hardly a bump, a textbook touchdown. Both Kelvin and Doug passed quickly through customs and shared a taxi to The Apollo. Doug had seemed to run out of things to say but Kelvin wasn't bothered. He didn't really want to get into conversation.

They both checked in and then went their separate ways with no mention of meeting for drinks, this also suited Kelvin because all he wanted to do was a good night's sleep – not that he imagined he'd have one - collect the package and get home.

Kelvin lay in until about ten in the morning and didn't even think about breakfast choosing instead to straight to reception.

"Morning," he smiled at the young receptionist. "I understand there's a package here for me, Mr Kelvin Spearman?"

The young woman walked over to one of the pigeonholes. "Ah yes, Mr Spearman, here it is, you'll have to sign for it."

"Yes, that's not a problem."

Kelvin signed for the six by three-inch package. It was heavy and well wrapped.

As Kelvin turned around, he was confronted by Doug.

"Good morning, young man, how did the meeting go, what you got there, I hope you're not smuggling?"

"Bloody hell, no, it's a retirement present for one of the bosses, all pre-arranged, you know the score."

"Oh aye, Kelvin, I know the score alright," he smiled.

"Well," Kelvin felt his face blush. "I'd like to chat, but I've got a plane to catch."

"What about your meeting?"

"Like I said, Doug, just some papers to sign, the firm likes the personal touch."

"I hope to meet you again, Kelvin, we can have that drink."

"Yes," Kelvin sighed as he turned and walked toward the exit.

Another meeting with Doug or Mike or whatever his name it was the last thing Kelvin needed.

Outside the hotel, he placed the package in his bag and hailed another taxi to the airport.

He settled into the back seat as his phone began to vibrate in his pocket. He checked the caller ID, it was Gibbs.

"Hi, Kelvin, have you collected the package?"

"Yes, I have."

"Have you opened it?"

"No, of course not," he said tersely.

"What do you reckon is in it?" Kelvin could hear the mocking tone in Gibbs' voice. The bastard was daring him to look.

"I've no idea, I hope it's not drugs or diamonds, for God's sake, if I'm caught, I'll get ten years."

"You won't get caught, Kelvin, I can assure you of that. Now, listen, I'll meet you at the flat tomorrow morning before you go to work, so hide the package and I'll collect it. Do you understand? But don't open it."

"OK, whatever you say, but this is the last time I'm doing this shit."

Gibbs snorted. "In your fucking dreams, Kelvin. In your dreams."

The call ended abruptly.

At least the commuter traffic had eased by the time Kelvin took another taxi from Swansea airport and the sun shone red as is began to slip toward the shimmering orange sea as he turned the key in the door of his flat. Everything had gone like clockwork, like Gibbs had said it would but he felt no sense of relief. He knew he was getting drawn deeper into something that was now out of his control. He stared at the package, tempted to peek inside but, instead, hid it in one of his work boots.

Sleep was impossible, confusing visions of hairy arsed coppers smashing down his door, a police dog snarling on tight leash, the smiling, slapable face of Gibbs watching as he got cuffed and thrown into the back of a police van. He was going to end up back in prison, of that he had no doubt.

True to his word, Gibbs was outside Kelvin's door at seven. Another smug, smiling face appeared from behind Gibbs. Kelvin was shocked to see Doug Greenslade, the guy from the flight.

Gibbs pushed Kelvin inside and strode into the flat. Doug followed and tapped Kelvin on the shoulder as he walked past.

Gibbs stopped inside the doorway. "I believe you've met Doug. Now, where's the fucking package?"

Lost for words, Kelvin retrieved his work boots from a cupboard and tipped the package out into Gibbs' hands.

"I hope it was worth it?" Kelvin grumbled.

Gibbs ripped opened the package and poured the contents over the carpet.

"What the hell are you doing?" Kelvin spluttered, shocked to see the contents of so much worry now piling up on his threadbare carpet.

"Well done, Kelvin, you've proved yourself," Gibbs smirked. "Don't worry, it's only sand. Doug told me that you were cool when he was *questioning* you. We had to be sure. We've got big things planned for you and, there'll be a few shillings in it for you," he wrapped his arm around Kelvin's shoulder.

Kelvin pulled away. "Who are you, Doug, Police, Customs, who the fuck are you?"

"Let's just say I'm your guardian angel, Kelvin, where you go, I go."

"What have you got me into, you pair of bastards?"

"You name it, Kelvin and we'll facilitate it. As Doug says, we've got the connections and now we've got you. The future's bright, mate."

Kelvin shook his head and stepped away. "I can't do this."

"Remember," Gibbs threatened, "either you play ball or it's back inside for you, my son."

Gibbs and Greenslade shut the door quietly behind them and Kelvin could hear them laughing as they walked down the street.

26

The two men sat quietly in a corner of the lounge of Morgan's Hotel. They were in deep conversation and, on occasions, were becoming irate with each other.

"What the hell happened? You told me everything had been sorted. And then what happens? They fish two Vietnamese out of the marina. The place has been buzzing with coppers ever since."

"Don't panic, it will all settle down."

"That's all very well, but where are the other two?"

"I've got it all under control. There's no sweat."

"No sweat? It's alright for you to say that. I've had to put it all on hold because of this debacle. What the hell happened?"

"We've got nothing to worry about. Even if they pick the other two up, there's no way they can tie us in with it."

The older of the two men seethed. "I'll ask you again, what happened?"

"They all got a bit moody on the boat, so I had to keep them quiet. I tied them up and jacked them with some meth. They went out like lights."

"Where this was?"

"Just off the coast, down off Burry Port."

"So how did they end up in the marina?"

The younger man sipped his whiskey before replying. "Well, when we landed, two were dead, and the other two were scared shitless. So, we bundled them into the van, drove to the marina, and dumped the two dead 'uns. While we were sorting that, the other two legged it."

"The two died because you filled them with drugs. Why didn't you top the other two while you were at it?"

"I wish you'd take a chill-pill. They'll think they were smuggled in through the marina, it's a no brainer."

"Can these two on the loose identify you?"

"What do you take me for? We've been doing business for years, making a good living out of it, what's your problem?"

"What's my problem? What's my problem? Nobody's bloody died before, have they?"

The younger man sighed. "Point taken. Look, nobody will give a toss about them. It will all blow over in a few weeks, guaranteed."

"I like your optimism, only I'm not too sure."

"I'm in the loop, one step ahead."

"Oh? How many times have I heard that before? I think we should shut down for a couple of months. Where's the cat now?"

"She's back in France, ready for another shipment."

"Well, get back out there. Don't pick anybody up and just bring her back empty. Berth her in the marina at Porthcawl. Not here. Leave her there for a few weeks until it all dies down."

"There's too much cash at stake. No. I'm not doing that."

"You'll do as I tell you. I set all this up, and if I want to shut it down, you'll do as you're told."

"Whatever!" The young man waved his drink dismissively. "But I've got other irons in the fire. I know all the routes. I'm connected. I see no problems."

"Aye, we'll see what your like when you're nicked and doing a fifteen stretch. Well, you're not taking me down with you."

Now the young man seethed, barely able to keep his voice low. "When I went in with you, you had a pair of balls. I never thought I'd see you chicken out. You've made a fortune from this game. Can you afford to throw it all away?"

The older man paused to drink some of his gin. His hand trembled slightly. "You make it sound all so easy."

"It is easy. The Customs, and Immigration are running around like blue-arsed flies. All the Customs are interested in is drugs. As for the Immigration, well, least said the better. And, like I say, I've got all bases covered. How do you think we've been so successful so far?"

The older man sighed. Tension began to slip from his face. "So, what have you got planned?"

"I got a pickup booked. The biggest so far. Eight in total. They're from all over. I plan to drop them just off the coast around Southerndown."

The older man nodded. "OK."

"Look, these sheep are shitting themselves from the time they get on the boat until we drop them off. Half of them can't speak English anyway, it's not a problem."

"You're so cocky."

"They're blindfolded from the get-go. Even when we take the blindfolds off, we're all hooded up. It's no sweat."

"Whatever, but I'm still mindful of the ones fished out of the marina. What if they pick the other two up. You should have done them as well."

"Look who's talking. You want to shut it down on one hand, on the other you want blokes topped. Make your mind up."

Shrugging his shoulders, the older man drained his gin. "Do you fancy another whiskey?" He sighed, resigned to playing the hand dealt.

"No, I'm sound. Anyway, how's your other businesses going? I see you're branching out and rubbing shoulders with the big wigs."

"Got to keep in. I'm sussing out a nice property development at the minute, but I'll have to grease a few palms to get planning permission. I tell you; nothing is sacred these days, they're all at it."

"Tell me about it. I'm shelling out on both sides of the channel. A few have even tried to put the arm on me for more cash. I soon put a stop to that. When I show them the pictures of the envelopes being handed over. You've always got to have a plan B. Have you got one?"

"Oh aye, for sure."

"Anyway, it's been nice chewing the fat with you, but I've got to be somewhere. Promised the missus that I'd treat her to a night at the theatre and a slap-up meal. She moans she doesn't see much of me these days," the younger man laughed. "She has no idea what I get up to keep her in the lifestyle she's accustomed to."

27

Kelvin arrived at the flat as instructed. All he could think of was how to release himself from the Gibbs stranglehold. He rang the bell, the door opened, it was Doug Greenslade - the bloke he had met on the plane.

"Come on in, son. Perhaps you can sort this mess out for us?"

The flat was on the ground floor; one bedroom, one small lounge, very compact with a kitchen diner and a small bathroom. Kelvin got the impression that it hadn't been lived in for some time.

Gibbs was sprawled on the settee and was smiling. All Kelvin was thinking about was smacking the smile off his face. He's never been a violent man, but he would make an exception for Gibbs.

"Welcome to our little domain. Make yourself at home. You'll be spending quite a bit of time here, that's if you can get into that thing," Gibbs pointed to a top of the range Apple Mac computer on a desk in the corner of the lounge.

"Well, get on with it," Greenslade snapped. "I understand that you're a whizz kid when it comes to this type of thing, shouldn't be too difficult."

Kelvin switched on the computer; it only took a couple of seconds to come to life. He pressed the keyboard and up it came…'Password.'

"It's locked."

"We fucking know that that's why you're here." Greenslade said.

"I need more information. The last bloke who used this wasn't an idiot. He password protected it, obviously bearing in mind the information he's stored on it, which is probably encrypted. I need his details, invariably the password will be connected to him in some way." Kelvin began feeling a little bit more confident, he knew Gibbs, and Greenslade were desperate to get the computer open, for once he held the upper hand.

"What sort of information are you talking about?"

"His full name, date of birth, you know, anything that he may have used to make it password protected."

"For fuck's sake, Kelvin, why didn't you tell us that before?"

"You never asked. You said you had passwords, I just assumed you had this one. Anyway, you're always telling me what to do."

"Doug, have you got the info he wants?"

"Only his name... Spencer Oldman."

"Look I'll have to go back to the office and get his file."

"Mr. Gibbs, I'll need some equipment as well from my mother's house if I'm going to do this properly. I'd imagine the police have returned most of what they took when I was arrested. It's not discs or anything, just a few monitors, bits and bobs all compatible with this computer."

Kelvin knew he didn't need these items, he just wanted to know how his mother was.

"I'm telling you now, you better not be messing us about."

"I'm not, Mr. Gibbs, I promise you."

"Watch him, Doug. I'll go back to the office. I'll get cracking and sort this mess out."

Gibbs stormed out of the flat. Kelvin was sure he saw steam coming from his ears.

Kelvin sat on the settee.

"Hey, what are you playing at? Get back there and crack on."

"It's no good. I need the details and some equipment. To hit on the password by just playing about with it, would be like winning the lottery. I assume you and Mr. Gibbs are not computer literate, probably old school, pen and paper?"

"Watch your mouth, son, and don't take the piss. You blokes are two-a-penny these days. You'd be 'Rule forty-three as soon as you hit the nick.'"

As soon as Kelvin heard this, he knew Greenslade was, or had been a prison officer. How else would he know the rule applying to sex offenders in prison? It wasn't common knowledge. A probation officer and a prison officer, what was going on? How many were involved? Kelvin had to get more information, perhaps the data on the computer would throw more light on it.

**

Gibbs knocked on the front door, and Nicola Spearman answered. She looked tired and pale - far older than her years.

"Mrs. Spearman, my name is Russell Gibbs. I'm Kelvin's probation officer. I'm supervising him after his release. There's no problem, he's OK," he assured her, thinking she would be concerned.

"Mr. Gibbs, I've nothing to do with my son. He's ruined my family. If I never see him again it'll be too soon. Now tell me what you want."

"I understand some of Kelvin's computer equipment is still here?"

"Yes, a couple of small boxes. The police confiscated the rest, but you obviously know that I suppose. Do you want what's left?"

"Well, yes if possible?"

"Stay here. I'll get it for you. I'll be glad to get rid of it. Then there's nothing left in the house to remind me of him."

A few minutes later, she returned and gave Gibbs two small boxes of computer equipment.

"That's all there is Mr. Gibbs. You're welcome to it."

Mrs. Spearman handed it over and closed the door in Gibb's face.

***

Gibbs arrived back at the flat a couple of hours later with the file and a large box of assorted equipment.

"Right, Kelvin, there's all your gear. Here's all the relevant information on Spencer Oldman, chapter and verse. Now get on with it."

Kelvin rummaged through the boxes and pulled out a few pieces of equipment which he plugged in to the computer, knowing full well that they were useless.

"OK then, let's see how we go then. What exactly is on here, Mr. Gibbs?"

"You'll know soon enough when you get into the thing."

This pair has no idea what I'm doing, Kelvin thought. This was a shift in the power dynamic. He was going to keep them on a string for a couple of hours, but it was less than thirty minutes later that Greenslade seemed to guess what was happening and grabbed him around the neck and banged his head on the keyboard.

"Stop fucking about!" he screamed. "If you don't sort it in five minutes, I swear I'll top you and dump your sick body into the marina. They'll think you topped yourself, no one will give a shit, got it?"

"Yes, I got it." Kelvin gasped. "I'm no use to you if I'm dead, am I?"

Gibbs must have agreed and pulled Greenslade off him.

"For crying out loud, Doug, leave him alone. We need this. Kelvin, shape up. I'm giving you ten minutes. If you don't come up trumps, I'll take you straight to the cop shop and leave you there. And no one will miss you. Even your mother hates you. I'd say she's heartbroken and that's down to you."

Kelvin didn't reply and kept tapping away at the keyboard. His guts were churning, all he could think of was his mam and what she must be going through.

28

Quince had left the de-brief as late as possible.

There were many loose ends to tie. The Polish nationals had to be charged, and the illegals had to be processed by Immigration, and then safely housed. At least they now had the names of the victims but nothing else was known about them.

Frustrated and angry that the Poles were not responsible, Quince was happy that his team had put paid to their gangmaster activities.

"Listen up everybody, I'm not going to keep you late, you've had a long, tiring day and I appreciate what's been achieved," he smiled and checked out the faces staring back at him. They were a good bunch, a team he had helped to forge into an efficient unit that he knew would enter hell for him if he asked. He felt a stab of pain deep in his soul as he thought of the Bride of Frankenstein taking the helm. Cross really wasn't good for this team. "This is where we're at," he sighed and sat facing the gathered group. "It looks like the Poles are out of it. They are certainly not the ones who dumped the bodies in the marina. The two young Vietnamese guys at the farm have confirmed that." There were some words that still betrayed Quince's roots and 'guys' was one of them. The American accent had changed over the years, replaced by a strange mix of North American and South Walian. "To say I'm disappointed is an understatement. However, that's not down to you, that's just the way it goes. We know the names of the victims, and what province in Vietnam they are from, so hopefully it won't be long before we can identify them and give their families closure. The two boys from the farm have been taken in by Nadir, this has all been done with Immigration approval, and Connor will be liaising with Nadir. No doubt there'll be an asylum process. We've still got a mountain of actions to sift through. There are a few POIs in amongst them, so whoever's got them, don't go in heavy, if anything, play a little dull, so that if they are involved they may think they're in the clear." POIs were Persons of Interest. They were usually persons who were suspected of being involved but without evidence to elevate them to suspects.

DS George Brodie raised a hand. Brodie had a habit of producing the goods when it mattered and already had had a breakthrough with Dawid. "Do you think locals are involved, boss? Like you say, the Poles are in the clear. If we accept what the young lads have told us."

"Who knows, George? I believe these kids were meant to be dropped off the coast of South Wales. I'm pretty sure of that. So, yes, I would say there's got to be some connection. But as you all know, people smuggling is worldwide. We've never had it so open in our Force area before, so it may be the first and, for some reason, went tits up. I'm sure this isn't the end; they're making too much money. All they'll do is change the dumping point. When the two guys ran from the van, the smugglers didn't bat an eyelid, just dumped the bodies and buggered off," Quince nodded to Clive, "How are we doing with boat movements during the timeline?"

Clive always cut a dash in the office. He took pride in his appearance. He seemed to have more suits than the rest of the team put together and sported a gold watch on a chain across his matching waistcoat. "Well, I can tell you, boss, nothing came into the marina during that time. As for stuff off the coast? There were over a hundred yachts or ships either anchored or on the move. The Coast Guard are trying to narrow things down for us."

"Clive take Fiona and Hugh, with you and put your heads together to see if we can narrow things down." Quince nodded and pointed to the two DCs. "Fiona and Hugh, you do all the leg work and anything you find feed it into Clive. Doesn't matter how insignificant you may think it is, you got that?"

DCs Fiona Short and Hugh Munro nodded their understanding.

"Are there any other questions, team? At this moment in time, I'm open to any suggestions."

DC Robin Lewis, a six-five behemoth, had slumped in his chair to match the height of the others. He raised a meaty mitt to speak, "Boss, I reckon these young lads could have been dropped off along the coast," his voice was deep and sonorous. "There's lots of ideal places. Perhaps a scout along the coast may give us some information on any previous activity."

"Good shout, Rob. Tomorrow evening, take a run along the coast, make a few enquiries. I'm sure there are always a few nosey bastards about late at night."

Robin grinned, "I'm on it, boss."

"Now, all of you go home, have a good night's kip. I want you back here fresh as daisies. I know it will be Sunday and it'll interfere with your Sunday worship," he grinned, "but the enquiry needs a bit of a kick-start. Thank you all."

After the team left, Quince returned to his office and started updating his policy book with a mug of black coffee laced with a small shot of whiskey. The SIO or Senior Investigating Officer was responsible for the investigation policy – the extensive list of enquiries that were carried out to solve the case and all of this had to be meticulously recorded in the policy book.

"How are you, Abe?"

He looked up, standing in the doorway was Cross.

Being an old-school copper, Quince stood, though he had no time for Cross, he still respected her rank.

"Don't get up, Abe. Have you got another mug of what you're drinking?" She grinned. "Give me an update," she added as she threw herself into a chair opposite the desk.

Quince opened his desk draw, produced a paper cup, and poured Cross two fingers of whiskey. No point in hiding it in coffee. The coffee Quince had bought on his way into the office had cost more than the cheap blend of booze one of his junior detectives had given him after Quince got him off a disciplinary charge.

"Well, Ma'am, we've hit the buffers. We had a nice pinch with the Poles, but they're not involved in the murders."

"You sure of that, Abe?"

"As sure as I can be, Ma'am. We need a break at the minute." He took a sip of his laced coffee and wiped his mouth with the back of his hand. "I thought you were off for the weekend," he added, eyebrows raised, curiosity outranking dislike. "Are you OK? You look a bit pale."

Cross shifted awkwardly on her chair. "I'm heading off for the night tonight. So, I thought, as I was at a loose end for an hour, I'd pop in on the off chance."

That was nice of her, he thought sarcastically. Perhaps she needed to re-think her priorities? "Well, like I say, that's where we are at the minute," he sipped another shot from his mug. "How did your conference go yesterday?"

"So much bullshit and diversity crap. I swear I dropped off a few times in the afternoon."

Quince nodded. "Well, that's what comes with the rank, Ma'am."

Cross sighed and crossed her legs. "Do me a favour, Abe, there's no one about, call me Norma. I'd feel a lot more comfortable."

That was something Quince would never be comfortable with. "I'd rather not, Ma'am. I'm a bit old school for things like that."

She raised her eyebrows and took a sip of her whiskey.

Quince poured another – without the coffee additive - and raised his mug. Cross reciprocated. She sank her whiskey, placed the empty cup on the desk and winked before she left.

He smiled as he watched her leave. Cross hadn't attended any conference, Quince knew that. He had checked. She was up to something. He'd let it play out, for the time being anyway.

29

Cross drove her hired Vauxhall Mokka out of Swansea and headed west to The Cliff Hotel in Cardigan. Cross was heading for a meet-up with Pat.

As a result of a restoration and upgrade, The Cliff had become a go-to hotel overlooking Cardigan Bay, with stunning views of the rugged coast and the Teifi estuary. The whole area teamed with wildlife, but it was the view of the sea that most guests loved.

Passing a row of houses and crossing a cattle grid, Cross arrived and parked up in the furthermost corner of the car park and headed in through large glass doors into reception.

"Good afternoon, I'm here to meet a friend of mine. My name is Cross, Norma Cross."

"Oh yes, we've been expecting you. Your friend is already here, she's having a drink in the lounge, will you be staying with us?"

"I doubt it, but you never know. I've brought an overnight bag, just in case I have one too many."

"Well, your friend has ordered an evening meal for you both, so I hope you enjoy."

Cross made her way into the lounge and was immediately beckoned over by Pat who was sitting in the corner with two glasses and a bottle of champagne chilling in an ice bucket.

"How are you my darling, so glad you could make it. We're going to have a fabulous time; you mark my words."

Pat leaned forward, pecked Cross on the cheek, and poured her a glass of champagne.

"There we are, get that down you, it will take the edge off, you look really uptight, what in heaven's name is wrong with you?"

"What's wrong with me? I've got a double murder on the go. I'm supposed to be in a conference, and here I am with you. If you were in my shoes, you'd be bloody uptight."

"Norma my darling, what have you got to worry about, that copper Quince will sort it all out. You should be in my shoes if Ted ever gets wind of our relationship… it's a good job he's more concerned about making millions than he is of me."

Cross picked up her glass and wolfed down the champagne in one go. "I bloody needed that."

"Look, I've booked a suite, you'll love it, fabulous views, and a jacuzzi on the balcony, what more could we ask for."

"Sounds great," she forced a smile that lacked conviction.

"Oh, come on, Norma, get with it, I hope you're not going to be miserable for the duration?"

"I'm sorry, Pat, I'm just worried, that's all." She sipped her Champagne and smiled. "OK. I'm all yours."

Pat leaned across and planted a tender kiss on Norma's cheek.

***

Karl Hatcher looked like he had just finished a disappointing round of eighteen holes. But his solemn expression had formed many years before and was now part of his everyday appearance. He had just finished his pint, and made his way out onto the hotel patio, and made a call.

"Mr Howe, this is Hatcher. I'm at The Cliff Hotel. The pair of them are in the lounge, all lovey-dovey, sipping glasses of champagne. Your missus seems elated, but Cross looks a bit stressed. I've got some pictures. I'll download them to you. Where are you?"

"I'm in Dublin at the minute. I'll be home late this evening. Great work. Stay there and keep a watching brief. Let me know if they stay the night. If they do, watch them leave, then call it a day. I think I've got what I need. I'll pop into the office on Monday and settle my account with you."

"Not a problem, what with all the other surveillance evidence I've given you, I think you got them both by the short and curlies."

"Cheers, Hatcher!"

***

Pat and Cross polished off the champagne in double quick time and headed for the suite. Hatcher followed them at a respectable distance and watched them both enter. Hatcher knew what they would be getting up to, this wasn't the first time he'd kept them under surveillance. When he was hired by Pat's husband, it was initially thought she was having an affair with some male bit of rough, however, when he knew it was another woman, Pat's husband didn't really seem that bothered. Perhaps it was because the other woman was a high-ranking detective? Hatcher knew the score. Howe was ruthless, and no doubt would use the information to his benefit.

30

Edward *Ted* Howe liked to think he was a man about town. Dressed in labels that were clear for all to see, eyebrows plucked and shaped, gold chains hanging from neck and wrists. He preferred to be called Ted because he believed it made him appear more approachable – more like the plebs he wanted nothing to do with. Appearance was everything to Ted, but the manicured appearance hid a mean streak, which kept him high in the standings of his fellow football fanatics back in the day. He was the antithesis of his gene pool. His grandparents had emigrated from Ireland and set up home in Swansea. Never afraid of work, they opened a small fruit and veg shop and, over the years, built it up into a successful and popular business.

That business was handed down to Ted's Parents. However, Ted had never really involved himself. He did anything and everything to avoid the work he despised. Living on his wits and making a fair bit of cash on the side, his parents would always write the cheques if ever he got into dire financial straits. Risks were easy to take when the loss wasn't your own.

Ted's life changed at the age of forty-three after an affray at The Vetch football ground. His love of the beautiful game, and the inevitable argy-bargy that went with it, resulted in a charge of Section 18 - Wounding with Intent. Ted had no option but to plead guilty. He was captured on ITV Sport coverage in full flow putting the boot in to an already unconscious victim dressed in opposing team colours, and as a result pulled a five stretch. His only saving grace was that he served his time in Swansea nick, just within spitting distance of his home.

2009 had been a turning point and when Ted was released, he vowed that he'd never go back inside. That didn't mean Ted would change his lifestyle and his attitude. He saw his incarceration as his apprenticeship. He'd shared a cell with some real hard cases, con men, and drug dealers. It had led to some tasty connections. Since his release, Ted used those contacts to make a hefty wad of cash. Property development, flats for rent, dodgy deals, but his dream was to purchase the now dilapidated Vetch field and turn it into a high-end restaurant and casino that would be frequented by celebrities and sportspersons.

In 1990, he married the love of his life, Patricia, someone he actually loved more than himself. To all intents and purposes, they were blissfully happy. Patricia was the natural hostess and would entertain business clients. The lack of children was the only blight on their relationship and began to eat away at them both.

Spending a lot of time away from home on business suited Patricia. Their sprawling six-bedroom mansion on The Gower came with all the trappings of success. A brace of his and her Porsches and Mercedes sat on the drive, headlights always facing the main gate – guarding the property from unwelcome visitors. The love of fine furniture, finer wine, expensive ornaments, and quality paintings screamed ostentatiousness.

***

A silver tray rattled as Ted climbed the marble staircase to the first floor. He pushed the bedroom door open with his foot. "Morning darling. Breakfast in bed. I haven't spoilt you for a while, and there's a little present to go with your boiled eggs and toast."

"Oh, Ted, you are an old romantic. What are you after?" she said with a grin.

Pat opened the small box that he had tied with a pink ribbon.

She gasped, bringing a well-manicured hand to her chest. Her eyes popped at the sight of the platinum eternity ring nestled in the blue cushioned box.

Pat removed it reverently, like an ancient, priceless relic, and slipped it on her finger.

"I thought we'd renew our vows next weekend," Ted grinned back. "I've booked it all up. What do you say?"

Pat said nothing. She bounced out of bed and plastered her husband with kisses.

"By the way," Ted said, extricating himself from the expected show of love, "there's another surprise there, open the envelope."

"Don't tell me," She giggled. "Tickets to the Caribbean, where we spent our honeymoon?"

The smile slipped from Ted's face. "I don't think so." He

feigned a pained expression. "You may be disappointed."

Pat was still excited. It had to be something really special to top the ring. She opened the envelope and pulled out the contents. The smile slipped from her face too as she saw four A4 pictures.

"Lay them out on the bed, and you can explain it all to me. Not that I actually need an explanation," Ted growled.

Pat's mouth made shapes, attempts to say something but no words came out. She looked to her husband. She expected fury, raging anger, but there was nothing. No expression that could be read. "I... I c-can explain T... Ted," she finally spluttered. "It's not what you think."

"Oh? Not what I think? How long has it been going on?"

"What can I say? It's nothing she's a good friend."

"Good friend? She's a top cop. And you're having an affair with her."

"It's not like that Ted, I swear."

Ted snorted and stepped to the French doors leading to a Juliet balcony overlooking the patio below. "I don't really give a fuck. I'm only glad it's a woman. If it was a man, I'd have the two of you topped. You know that, don't you?"

"I'm sorry. I can't explain, not now but it's not what you're thinking. It's true that she wanted me to leave you. Not because we're having an affair. But I'd never do that, you know that." Now Pat was sobbing. She knew only too well what Ted was capable of. The weekend had been a mistake. She loved her time with Norma, but it wasn't what Ted thought, and she just couldn't tell him the truth. The truth would hurt him even more.

"Look, this affair with this tart may suit me, but that's another thing," Ted said. His voice was calm. He wasn't reacting the way Pat would have expected and that worried her even more than a beating. "What do you mean?"

"You don't see or speak to her again, do you understand? If you do, you know what will happen?"

Pat said nothing.

"Every meeting you've had with her, every hotel. I've got the lot. There are plenty more like that," he said, nodding briefly to the photos now spread on the bed. The photos were innocent enough, but she could see how they could be misinterpreted. "Now get dressed and get out of my sight. I can't bear to look at you."

Ted spun on his heel and shoved Pat onto the bed as he marched out.

The large brandy in the morning was out of character for him, but Ted had achieved what he set out to do, and he deserved the drink. Now he had the means to put the squeeze on a very senior police officer. Ted made a call.

"It's me, got a bit of news, do you know a Detective Chief Inspector by the name of Norma Cross, works out of Swansea Central?"

"No, the name doesn't mean anything to me."

"I've got her by the bollocks, I'll keep you informed."

"So, what's the score with her then?"

"I'll tell you when I see you next."

31

The sun had cast a deep red glow over the stone patio slabs, the limestone had magically become sandstone and Ted watched the descent of the blood-red globe as it slipped behind The Gower Peninsula. He had watched it hundreds of times and it never failed to ease the tension of the day. He stubbed out the last inch of his cigar into a crystal ashtray he had balanced on the stone wall that bordered his property and a steeply sloping field of tress that snaked down towards the bay a hundred feet below the patio. He was glad he'd sorted the issue with Pat. She now had no doubts where she stood in their relationship. Pat was easy. But he wanted Cross to pay dearly for daring to steal from him. Pat was his property, and no one ever stole from him without paying a price. And he knew the value of that property.

He tapped in the number Pat had reluctantly given him and waited for the call to be answered. "Is that Detective Chief Inspector Norma Cross?"

"It is. Who am I speaking to?"

"We haven't met, Chief. However, I'm in possession of something that may be of great interest to you."

"You're calling on my private number. How did you get it?"

Ted could hear the simmering anger in her voice. She was probably wondering which of her minions had supplied the number and would be keen to roast the person responsible for the indiscretion. She was clearly more interested in the release of her number than the information he said he had for her. "That's the least of your worries."

"What the hell are you talking about? Tell me what you want. I'm busy."

Ted laughed. "For how much longer, I wonder?"

Now Cross was boiling. Her voice had raised an octave." "Look, stop messing me about. If it's important, get on worth it."

"Important? Well, it will definitely play a part in your future career. I wouldn't say there was promotion in it for you. But, on the other hand, it could very well get you demoted, or even dismissed. Who knows?"

"Look, I don't know who you are, or what your game is, but I don't give a shit."

"Are you a lesbian, Chief?"

"What?"

"Are you a lesbian?"

"What the hell has that got to do with you?"

Ted could sense Cross was about to end the call, so spat out the next words quickly, "Because my better half clearly is. You may know her, Pat Howe?"

Silence.

"Have you lost your voice, Chief?"

"Yes, I know your wife, we're very close friends," Cross finally admitted, her voice dropping two octaves.

"I think it's a bit more than that, Chief. I've got pictures. Numbers of the hire cars you've been using. In fact, the last time you met my wife was Saturday evening at the Cliff Hotel. I've had her followed by a private detective."

Up an octave, "What you want, just spell it out."

"I don't want money. I don't want revenge. But I think you could be helpful to me, a woman in your position?"

Another octave up, with a substantial gain in volume too, "You bastard!"

"I'll meet you down on Mumbles Pier in half an hour. We'll have a chat then. No funny stuff, like bringing the boys in blue. I've got some pics for you, just to let you know I mean business, get my drift?"

A pause to think, then, "How will I know you?"

"Don't worry, I'll know you."

Ted ended the call and grinned to himself.

Cross on the other hand was furious, and threw her telephone in anger, smashing it against the lounge wall.

***

Cross arrived at the Pier, as Howe had instructed. She sat on one of the weather-beaten benches for what seemed like an eternity before she felt the presence behind her.

"Ah, Chief, punctual as ever, like a good honest copper," he scoffed.

"What do you want, Mr Howe?"

"Well Chief, it seems my wife is having a good living off the back of me, and you haven't done too bad. You haven't dipped your hand in your purse since you've been having it off with her, you're nothing but a slag."

"Look, there's no point in me arguing. You won't believe me. So, what are you going to do?"

Ted handed Cross an envelope containing copies of the same photographs he'd given Pat.

"Those are for you, Chief, I've got more. Call them a sample. So, what are *you* going to do about it?"

"This is blackmail."

"Blackmail? I don't think so. I haven't asked for anything really, money or anything like that. Anyway, why would I ask for money? I'm a millionaire. I've got everything I need, even a lesbian wife."

Cross shook her head and sighed. She wanted to put him straight, to tell him the truth but she had promised Pat that she wouldn't. "So, what's it all about then?"

"I hope you're not wired, Chief?"

"No, I'm not. Can we get to the point?"

"Since you've been seeing my missus, I've had chapter and verse on you, Chief. You're not very well liked, and rumour is that you've been over promoted and you're not too fussy who you bed, be it a bloke or my missus."

"And the point is?"

"The point is, Chief, your career is in my hands. This is my proposition… you work for me."

Cross shook her head, "No way."

"Let's say the odd bit of information here and there. I'll duly reward you of course."

"What about the pictures?"

"Well, that's my insurance. I could post them to the Chief Constable tomorrow, it's your call. You and Patricia have got the originals, the negatives are in a safe deposit box. Should anything happen to me, my solicitor has been instructed to follow my instructions to drop you from a great height… metaphorically speaking of course," he laughed.

"Looks like you're holding all the cards?"

"Definitely, Chief. Here's five grand for you, call it a little retainer. Feel free to refuse it if you like, but I think it would be a big mistake. If you're co-operative I may even let you see my missus again."

"I don't want your money."

"Take it, Chief, or you're finished."

Cross hesitated, she didn't have a choice. She needed him off her back. She didn't need the money. She could keep it and hand back if things got messy. She took the envelope off Ted, placing it in her bag. She knew Ted would think she was sunk but there had to be a way out of this. Now she knew what Pat was facing too. She had to sort him, or her career was over, one way or another.

"I hear Abe Quince has been a busy boy," Ted said as he turned to leave. A light rain began to sweeping across the bay, vertical columns of precipitation dancing like celebrities on Strictly.

"You know Quince then?"

"Oh aye, gave me a five stretch years ago. Haven't seen him for a while."

"Where's this going?"

"Are you working on these bodies in the marina? How's that one going? it's the talk of the city. Nasty business, two youngsters like that, it's a tragedy."

"It is, but no, I'm not. Quince is the SIO."

"Oh, they can look out then," Ted grinned. "Whoever's responsible will be in for a hard time. He's like a bulldog chewing a wasp."

"I think you've mixed your metaphors."

Ted looked confused.

"Never mind," Cross sighed. He was a lost cause. "Now, is that it, or is there something else I can do for you?"

"Don't be aggressive, Chief. You're not talking to the lower ranks now. Today is the first day of the rest of your life. Expect a phone call in the next few days, got my drift?"

Ted Howe walked off towards the ice cream parlour, leaving Cross in a state of flux.

She had to make a call.

"Abe, this is the DCI."

"What can I do for you, Ma'am, is everything OK?"

"Yes, no problem," she lied. "Just to let you know that I'll be in first thing tomorrow. I'll want a full update on the marina murders, and I'll be running the enquiry from now on."

"Whatever, Ma'am. I'll look forward, see you in the morning," Quince lied.

32

Quince smiled at his reflection in the toilet wall mirror. He checked his watch. Cross would be swooping in soon. She was like a thief in the night, a hit-and-run driver. He could think of lots of analogies but none of them really described the parasite she had become. Indeed, he wondered if she had always been this way.

His second cup of coffee had begun to cool when Cross breezed into his office. She smiled and closed the door behind her.

"Don't get up, Abe," Cross said, as she pulled a chair from the wall and sat alongside the desk – he had no intention of standing for her. Now she was too close to Abe for his comfort.

"Right, can you bring me up to speed on the marina murders?" The words spat out in a machine gun stream. "I've got a conference with the ACC Crime at mid-day, he's having a lot of pressure from above and wants it all wrapped up as soon as."

Quince rolled his chair away from Cross, putting distance between them before replying. "Well, he's going to have a bit of a wait, Ma'am."

She sighed and leaned an elbow on the desk and stared out the window over her right shoulder. This time, the words were more measured, and he guessed they were well rehearsed. "I'll be taking the enquiry over from here on in, and I'll be setting policy for the way forward," she turned back to Quince and pulled a fake smile – brief and condescending.

"Whatever you say, Ma'am," Quince said, not rising to the bait. "I'm barely keeping my head above water at the minute. Thought we'd cracked it with the Polish lot. It was a good operation, but they had no links to the young lads found in the marina."

Cross sat back. "Are we any nearer to actually identifying them?"

"There's no problem with the two guys at the farm, they're co-operating with us, but they don't know the victims and I believe them. They've given us two first names and details of how they were trafficked. But as for where they were off loaded, they've no idea. All they can say is that they were dropped then bundled into a van with the other two who then turned up dead."

"Were they dead in the van, before being dumped in the marina?"

"Well, they didn't drown, so it's very likely that they had been overdosed on the boat. The other two lads said they were handfuls, hence the drugging."

"What drug?"

"That would be methamphetamine, Ma'am."

"So, what are we doing to identify the two dead men?"

"As I said, we've got their first names and we now also know the province they hail from in Vietnam. The Vietnamese authorities are doing their best, together with Nadir Huang, a local Vietnamese restauranteur who's putting some feelers out. He's probably going to be our best bet."

"Good. And the two lads from the farm, where are they now?"

"Nadir Huang and his family are looking after them."

"That's unusual, isn't it?"

"Well, it was sorted with the Immigration, and I've got Connor liaising," Quince shrugged and finished the dregs of his cold coffee. He grimaced. "It keeps them local if we need to have further chats with them."

"OK. But what if they do a runner?"

"I don't believe they will. They have no reason to. They've been assured they'll be treated fairly and that promise seems to outweigh the idea of life on the run."

"So, what's next, Abe?"

"The coastguard is trying to identify boats that were off the coast during the relevant timeline. Enquiries are being made along the coast during the evenings and throughout the night with local fisherman to see if they saw anything suspicious. There are virtually hundreds of other actions that the team are sifting through and prioritizing."

Cross sighed, again it looked rehearsed. "And what's your take on it?"

He shrugged again, his eyebrows matching the gesture. "Dumping them locally could be a red herring. They could have come ashore anywhere. I'd guess they came in down west. The last thing they want to do is give away their access point."

"West would make sense. The quieter the better. And some of

the coves down there rarely see visitors. Any idea who may be involved?"

"Not a clue. Plenty of intelligence on individuals who are suspected traffickers, but no one local to Swansea."

"You don't think there's a local connection?"

"Personally, I think there is. I think all four lads were destined for Swansea. But the two dying would have messed it all up. They weren't concerned when the two lads escaped, they were more concerned with dumping the dead bodies," he paused, picked up his mug and stepped over to the coffee percolator perched on the top of a filing cabinet. He filled his mug with fresh coffee. "No, there's a connection, I can feel it in my gut."

"Gut feeling won't solve this, Abe. Like I say, I'll brief the ACC for Crime later. Is there anything else you'd like to add?"

"Not really, Ma'am," He took a sip. "But I'd like to know what my role in the enquiry will be from now on?"

"You'll still be involved, obviously, but I'll take the pressure off you," that fake smile again. "Don't mind, do you?"

Her eyes bore into Quince, looking for signs that she could exploit, an opportunity to say what she really wanted to say but Quince wasn't going to make it easy. "Not at all, Ma'am," Quince slipped back behind his desk. "You're fully up to speed, and fresh eyes may give us the break we need."

"That's exactly my thoughts, Abe. A fresh take on it."

Quince knew he and his team had covered all the bases in the enquiry. What Cross would bring to the table was at best a rehash of what had already been done, but sometimes that worked. "Will you let the team know, Ma'am?"

"No, you can tell them, Abe. Fix up a conference for this evening and I'll outline the way forward. This is no reflection on you or the team, I just want to be on top of it all."

The insincerity was barely disguised. Quince knew managers like Cross would say and do whatever the ACC wanted because everything had become political. The appointment of politically motivated Police and Crime Commissioners had done nothing but accelerate the decline towards a service more politicised than effective. Cross would see this appointment as another step up the ladder and Quince would bet she'd be off up another rung before this case was detected, leaving everyone, including himself, to take the flack and clear up whatever crap she stirred up in the meantime."

"Well, Abe, I'm off to the big house for my meeting with the ACC. Keep up the good work. I'll see you later."

This was his chance. "Oh, Ma'am, seeing as you're taking over, I take it I'm released to concentrate on other pending matters?"

"Yes Abe. We can't ignore other serious crime. If I need any input from you, I'll make it known in the briefings. By the way, they won't be too regular, unless something really important crops up."

"And if I get any information, you'll be first to know, Ma'am," he smiled. He had what he wanted. There was a growing pile of files that needed work and at least now he was free to get stuck into them. He leaned back in his chair, both hands behind his head, grinning as Cross marched out. Something was afoot with her and he felt the urge to find out what.

Connor Harrington answered his call on the first ring. "Morning, boss, what can I do for you?"

"Where are you, Connor?"

"I'm with Nadir, down at the restaurant, boss. He's waiting for a call that may take the enquiry forward for us."

"How are the two lads?"

"Happy as pigs in shit, boss. They think Nadir and his family are the dog's bollocks."

"Excellent. Just to let you know, DCI Cross is now heading the enquiry, so you'll be seeing more of her in the future."

"What's the reason for that, boss?"

"Politics. But do me a favour… whatever information Nadir gets, feed it to me first, just keep me in the loop."

"I understand, boss."

***

The team had assembled, waiting in anticipation for Cross to arrive. Some of the old heads were wondering why Cross would be heading the enquiry.

Cross bounded into the Incident Room, accompanied by Quince, following in her wake.

"Good evening, team. I understand DI Quince has brought you up to speed. As from today I will be heading the enquiry. This is not a reflection on the way you have been performing, I just feel that fresh eyes may take us forward more quickly. DI Quince will have an input, however, he has enough on his plate now, so this change will take pressure off him."

Quince raised his eyebrows, there was definitely a hidden agenda, and he had all the time in the world to expose it.

33

He had better listen to them, especially in view of Greenslade's threats. Within a few minutes Kelvin was in. He leaned back and placed his hands behind his head.

There we are, Mr. Gibbs, I'm in. What else do you want me to do?"

"Just open the fucking files and make sure that all the information is still there."

Kelvin tapped a few keys.

"Well, there are eight closed files on here, Mr. Gibbs. Nothing to show what they relate to. I'll try to open the first one." But whatever he tried he couldn't open the file. "He's encrypted them, as I thought, Mr. Gibbs. This could take some time."

Kelvin stood up to stretch his rapidly cramping legs. Greenslade, in temper, grabbed him by the lapels.

"You're fucking us about, I warned you."

"I need more time. The last bloke who did this for you was no mug. You must know what the files contain, surely? For all I know he may have deleted everything."

"And why would he do that? He was one of you."

"Look" Gibbs said. "We'll come back tomorrow. He can have another crack. Now, clear off and be back here at nine in the morning and don't keep us waiting, or I'll send Doug to drag you here, do you understand?"

"Yes, Mr. Gibbs, but what about work?"

"I told you, I'll sort it."

"Kelvin hurried out of the flat, giving Gibbs, and Greenslade the impression he was going home, however Kelvin had a different idea.

***

"Doug, I hope this turd can get into the files, we've only got a week to sort Jackson out bearing in mind he's being released next Saturday. I'll be registering him straight away. He'll be out of the country the following week if things go to plan. Everything's sorted, passport the lot, but we need the files to continue as before."

"Oh aye. He'll be our best payer so far. Just hope things go to plan. How much is he into us for."

"Fifty big ones. He's got plenty stashed."

***

Kelvin kept an eye on the flat from a short distance and watched Gibbs and Greenslade drive off. He gave them ten minutes, then made his way to the rear of the flat.

He took off his hoody, picked up half a house brick, wrapped it in the hoody then smashed the bathroom window. Kelvin climbed in and crept to the lounge, switched the computer on, entered the password then brought up the files. He opened the first one and was gob smacked. It was a full and comprehensive list of convicted pedophiles, from all over UK, names, dates of birth, addresses everything.

He opened the second. This contained copies of birth certificates, death certificates, photographs, P.O. Box numbers, and all that sorts of other stuff.

Each file he opened contained similar information, it was obvious what Gibbs and Greenslade were up to.

Kelvin quickly rummaged through the two boxes that contained a couple of pen drives, he checked them on the computer but there was no data on them. He then downloaded all the files onto the drives before shutting it all down.

He had to think fast to cover his tracks. He upturned the furniture to make the break in look the work of a genuine burglar. He unplugged the computer and placed it in the bath beneath the window, so that when the dynamic duo turned up, they would think the culprit had been disturbed and dropped it.

Kelvin left the flat via the front door and headed home.

On the way, he rang the office of Andy Stokes, who he had earlier contacted with his suspicion of corruption.

'Hello, can I help you?"

"Can I speak to Mr. Stokes, it's Kelvin Spearman again. Tell him I've got all the evidence. He'll know what it's about."

A short pause, then a voice. "Mr. Spearman, Andy Stokes

here. Now what exactly have you got?"

"I've got the information. I spoke to you about it. I may be in danger if you don't help me," a pause, then, "No, I *am* in danger."

"OK, where are you now?"

"In the Adam and Eve."

"Stay there, wait outside. I'll bring my mate with me."

"No police!"

"Whatever," Stokes said. "I'll see you in twenty minutes."

Stokes thought it sounded unlikely; a pedophile grassing, but there again, nothing surprised him. He made a call.

"Abe, what are you up to? have you got five minutes?"

"What now, Andy?"

"This bloke Spearman has rung me again, about this corruption nonsense. If what he's saying is true, and it sounds like he's got the evidence, this could be big. I'm meeting him outside the Adam in twenty minutes. I'll pick you up, where are you?"

"OK pick me up."

Stokes picked up Quince and drove to the Adam. They spotted a worried looking man standing outside. His head was darting left and right, clearly checking the street in all directions. Stokes stopped the car and opened the window.

"Are you Kelvin?"

The man approached nervously. "I remember you, even if you don't remember me. You came to see me once when I was arrested."

"Sorry, Stokes said. Long time ago. Now jump in the back, let's have a chat. It had better be worth it."

"It will be, Mr. Stokes, it will."

"Kelvin this is my mate Detective Inspector Abe Quince…"

"I told you, no cops."

"…He's sound. If what you say is on the up and up, I guarantee Abe will get it sorted. Anyway, you can't get out, the child locks are on. Now spit it out."

"I'm out on license, and under the supervision of a probation officer by the name of Russell Gibbs, he's running a false identity scam for pedophile's and he's blackmailing me."

"In what way?"

"Well, it's all to do with false identities on a computer. If I don't do what he says he'll turn me into the police for breaching my license."

"How's he going to do that then?"

"He planted a mobile with images of kids on it. He said he found it in my flat. He's a bastard, he's been stringing me along, him and another bloke called Doug Greenslade. I think he's a prison officer."

"What are they up to?"

"Like I said, getting new identities for recently released pedophiles like me, and then getting them out of the country. Sounds like they're making a lot of money."

"And what evidence have we got, other than your word?"

"I've downloaded files from their computer on to pen drives. I've got it all. They've no idea. I've fobbed them off so far by saying the files are encrypted, but I can't keep them off my back for long. That bastard Greenslade has already threatened to kill me."

"When are you seeing them next?"

"Tomorrow at nine. They've got a flat which they obviously use to run their operation."

Quince chirped in. Listen, Kelvin, I'll sort this for you, but you've got to trust me. Give me the pen drives. I'll keep them safe and call out our cyber-crime unit to download them and see exactly what's on them. We can see for ourselves what this information is, have you got that?"

"How do I know I can trust you?"

"You don't, but you trusted Andy, and he trusts me, enough said. Now, what's the address and are this pair tooled up?"

"I don't think so. I've never seen any weapons." Kelvin gave Quince the address of the flat in Neath. "I broke in there earlier to download the files; will I get into trouble for that?"

"Kelvin, if this is on the up, you can forget about that. Now, off you go and don't say a word. Try to stall them for a few hours tomorrow. Don't worry, we'll have your back."

Kelvin gave Quince the pen drives and got out of the car.

"What do you think, Andy?"

"I believe him Abe. These blokes need nailing. Kelvin's a bit naïve and to be fair I'd never place him as a paedo."

"Yes, I think he's either trying to smear the probation officer because he's been caught with the pictures or he's on the up.

Whichever, it's worth checking. I'll get the pen drives sorted and brief the ACC. They can get an OP on the flat and raid it in the morning. I'll make sure Kelvin is nicked as well, to make him look innocent of involvement with us and then we'll sort him."

"Will your team deal with it, Abe?"

"No, my lot are up to their necks. The paedo unit can sort the pair of bastards out."

34

Quince had already given the cyber-crime unit a call and was waiting at the nick for Adrian, the unit supervisor. He told Adrian he had to keep this close between them and what he needed to know from the drives and handed him the devices. Perhaps he could crack the paedophile case now he had some time.

Adrian pulled a laptop from a soft case and opened it on Quince's desk. "Shouldn't be a problem, boss. Give me a few minutes. Got to be careful with these. One mistake and you can delete all the data."

Quince stared at the computer screen, not knowing what to expect.

"There we are, boss, file number one. No name on it, but very interesting."

Whistling, Quince leaned closer to the screen, "Wow! the boy's spot on. A full list of convicted sex offenders. We've got to action this sooner rather than later."

"Will you check the other files, Adrian, before I make a decision?"

Adrian opened them one by one; their content was exactly what Kelvin had described.

"That's enough for me," Quince sighed, sickened by the vast list before him.

"No Problem, boss. I take it you'll authorise my overtime?"

"Goes without saying. You're worth your weight in gold," Quince teased.

The ACC listened to Quince's call without interrupting and was in total agreement that the paedophile unit would deal with the matter. He would call a briefing for six in the morning. Quince would attend to brief the officers involved and an observation point would be set up. As soon as Kelvin, Gibbs, and Greenslade were in the flat, the team would strike.

***

Kelvin appeared, as promised, but he had no idea what sort of shit storm was about to fall.

Greenslade snarled like a rabid dog and dragged him into the lounge.

"Look we've been burgled. I told Russ that you weren't to be trusted. You've grassed us up, you little bastard. Probably one of your paedo mates."

"I haven't. It's nothing to do with me. You've got to believe me." This was Kelvin's worst nightmare playing out. Why the hell did he think it would be anything other than a disaster?

Greenslade's hand appeared at Kelvin's throat, a cutthroat razor pushed into the skin far enough to draw a single drop of blood. The thug manhandled Kelvin to the desk and sat him down at the computer. "Now switch it on and you'd better open the files straight away or I'll open you up like I'm gutting a fish."

"Cool down, Doug, for God's sake put it away. Can't you see he's shitting himself?" Gibbs pleaded. "Cool down, he'll do it, won't you Kelvin? Now you'd better start shaping up or I won't try to stop him next time."

Greenslade closed the razor but was still hovering over Kelvin, breathing down his neck.

Pretending to struggle with the file coding, Kelvin finally relented. He couldn't hold out any longer. "There we are, Mr Gibbs. I've opened the first one. Is that what you want?"

"That's my boy, Kelvin," Gibbs patted him on the shoulder and grinned like a shark about to strike. "Now let's see the others, eh?"

Before Kelvin could tap another key, the front door exploded inwards, large chunks of wooden frame and door spun through the air and crashed down into the hallway. Before the last piece of airborne timber hit the floor, the lounge was swarming with police. "Keep your hands where I can see them and get down on the floor now." A voice shouted. "DO IT NOW!" the voice louder this time, leaving no doubt what had to be done. Kelvin and Gibbs did as they were told, but not Greenslade. As Kelvin slid off the seat, heading for the floor, Greenslade slashed out at Kelvin with the razor, catching him across the throat. A line of claret appeared like a necklace and then burst open, spraying the room with blood.

The barbs of a Taser struck the man in the back and the crackling sound of the disabling charge sent Greenslade into spasms as he collapsed to the floor alongside Kelvin, blood spouting from his throat.

Gibbs and Greenwood were hurriedly cuffed and dragged from the flat.

One of the officers had acted quickly and thrust his gloved hands pressed firmly on Kelvin's throat to try and slow down the blood loss. Kelvin was going in and out of consciousness, the officer kept talking to him, trying to keep him awake.

Within minutes, the paramedics arrived and did what they could to staunch the flow while Kelvin was rushed to Morriston Hospital with a police vehicle leading the urgent race to save Kelvin's life.

***

Quince was in the Divisional Chief Super's office when the ACC rang. He watched as the smile slipped from the Chief's face as he listened intently to whoever was on the other end of the call. The Chief ended the call with a single word. "Thanks." He looked at Quince, his dark brown eyes impossible to read.

"Look, Abe, the operation was a success. Two in custody, but this Kelvin fella has received a serious injury to the throat. It looks like Greenslade slashed him with a cutthroat razor."

"Bollocks, how is he, boss?"

"He's being operated on as we speak."

"I'll get up there right away."

"Keep me updated."

Stopping at the door, Quince turned back to his boss. "What about his family, are they aware?"

"They've informed his mother, but she wants nothing to do with him, probably because of his conviction."

This was a can of worms. Why would they want to injure the lad? There must be a lot at stake. Probation officer, prison officer, God knows who else might be involved. A cold shiver ran down his spine. He hoped there were no names of police officers in that list but knew he would never bet on the odds.

Mr Michael Sweeney, the Accident and Emergency consultant was short, less than five-three, and resembled a bearded character from the imagination of Tolkien. Sweeney spoke softly in an octave that would have been more appropriate for a pre-pubescent schoolboy. "Kelvin has lost a tremendous amount of blood," he squeaked to Quince. "He's in a critical condition and he'll be in the operating theatre for many hours. There's nothing anyone can do at this time. It's all in the hands of the surgeons."

Quince thanked the doctor and gave him his mobile number before heading for the car park and calling Andy Stokes.

"We've let this lad down, big time," he said, before Stokes could speak. "Greenslade has made a mess of Kelvin's throat. They're operating on him now. I hope to God he recovers, but it doesn't look too good."

"All I can say is, he must have been desperate.

"He's got to pull through."

***

Detective Inspector Meirion Jessop was heading the Kelvin enquiry and Quince had known Jessop for years. They had come through training school together and while Quince had found the academic aspect of the initial course a breeze, Jessop had locked himself away each night to ensure he retained the information imparted each day. So, while Quince and two of his friends hit the police club for a few beers each night, Jessop hit the law books. It paid off. At the end of the course, Jessop snatched second place on the course, beaten only by Quince.

It had been a while since they last met, and Quince was glad to see him. "What's the score?"

"How's the young lad?" Jessop asked, keen for an update before saying anything else, the actions they had to take would be the same whatever the lad's condition.

Quince shrugged, hands now in pockets and impressed yet again by Jessop's single-mindedness. "Pretty rough. Still operating on him. I've had an armed bobby assigned to him."

"Good idea, Abe. If what he said is true, there might be others wanting to get a piece of him or see him in little pieces in a bin liner somewhere."

"My thoughts exactly. So, any progress?"

"Well, early days yet," Jessop said as he walked to the percolator sitting atop a filing cabinet in the CID office. He nodded to a spare cup and Quince nodded back. "Looks like Gibbs may roll over. He wants nothing to do with the attempted murder. Crapped himself when he was arrested for it."

"What about Greenslade?"

Jessop poured the brace of beans. "Different kettle of fish, that bastard." He handed Quince a mug and nodded to the milk jug and sachets of sugar. "He's spent too much time inside. Knows the score. Bat-shit crazy, that one."

"So, what's your take?"

Jessop walked back to his desk, a small, partitioned office section at the far end of the open plan office. Quince followed, grimacing at his first taste of the coffee.

"Not a bad scam," Jessop said as he sat and nodded to a chair opposite. "New identities for sex offenders for cash. Not bad, is it? The only problem is that the last bloke they had on the computer kept his own file, naming names, positions, the lot. Must be about eighteen altogether, nationwide."

"Please tell me there are no bobbies involved."

"I don't know yet, Abe. There's so many of them. Makes my flesh crawl. Looks like the probation and prison service, and a couple of names from the Customs so far. We reckon at least ten paedophiles have gone missing from the UK in the last twelve months, all organised by these two twats."

"Look Mei, leave Kelvin to me. I've got a gut feeling about him."

"No problem, Abe. I hope he pulls through."

***

After an hour of reminiscing about old times, talking about the merits of rugby over American football, Quince left Jessop to get on with the enquiry. The work wouldn't get done if they kept chewing the fat. A short walk took him to Enzo's front door - a local greasy spoon served a far better cup of coffee, more like the good stuff he remembered from his youth back in the States. The café always had a rack of local newspapers. Quince rarely bought a paper, preferring to catch the latest events on the websites. He had worked through two nationals and a local rag when the hospital A and E consultant rang him.

"Kelvin is out of theatre. He's just coming out of the anaesthetic. He can't talk because of the throat injury. If you pop in about an hour, I'm sure you can see him."

"Thanks, Mr Sweeney, very much appreciated."

35

Two further cups of Enzo's coffee and a slice of carrot cake later, Quince was feeling alive again, when he parked the pool car in the multi-storey car park serving the hospital. It took fifteen minutes to find the ward Kelvin had been moved to. The uniform constable was sitting in an armchair facing the door. He stood as Quince entered.

"How is he?"

"He's barely awake, boss. He can gesture with his hands. He's had a nasty injury and he's lucky to be alive. I overhead one of the doctors say another five minutes and he'd have snuffed it. Do you want me to stand outside while you talk to him, boss?"

"No, stay where you are."

Kelvin's skin had begun to recover some colour, but his lips were still blue. Quince leaned close to his right ear. "Kelvin, it's Abe Quince. I'm so sorry about all this."

A bloodshot eye flickered open and a hint of a smile appeared on Kelvin's face as he slowly lifted his hand.

Quince grabbed it tightly.

"You did well. Gibbs, and Greenslade are locked up. You don't have to worry about them anymore. No more blackmailing for them. You just concentrate on getting well."

Kelvin squeezed Quince's hand and rolled his eyes.

"I won't tire you, get some rest. Is there anything you need?"

Kelvin nodded his head and gestured for a pen and paper.

Quince gave him his notepad and pen and Kelvin began scribbling.

Letter with Mr Sr, for my mother.

"Mr Senior, who is he?"

More scribbles - *Solicitor.*

"Where is his office?"

Court Road, Bridgend, letter for my mother.

"David Senior? I know him. No problem. I'll get in contact and make sure your
mother gets the letter. Now, get some rest."

Kelvin closed his eyes and drifted off within seconds, mouth open and drooling.

"You keep an eye on him, make sure you keep him safe," Quince told the uniform.

Quince knew David Senior. The man was a first-class criminal advocate, until the bottom dropped out of the legal aid system. Senior saw the change coming and diversified by going into family law and child protection.

It was getting late, but Quince gave Senior's office a ring, hoping that he may still be in work. He was in luck. A receptionist put him through.

"Dave Senior, how can I help you, Inspector?"

After a few moments of pleasantries, Quince got down to business. "Do you know a young man named Kelvin Spearman?"

"I certainly do. He's a client of mine. Just released from prison."

"Yes, I know all about his background and circumstances of his conviction. I'm calling to tell you he's critically ill in Morriston Hospital at the moment."

"Good God, what the hell's happened?"

"He was helping the police when things turned nasty. He was slashed across the throat. It was touch and go whether he'd make it. I'm hoping he'll pull through, but it's a serious injury."

"Thanks for letting me know, but that's not the only reason you called, is it?"

"No, it's not," Quince admitted.

"So, how can I help?"

"Well, he said something about a letter that you're in possession of. I believe it's for his mother?"

"Yes, that's correct. I was instructed to deliver it personally should anything untoward happen to him."

"That's an odd request."

"Not really. Not under his particular circumstances. Someone like him will always be a target."

"Do you know the content of the letter?"

"No, Inspector I don't."

"Well, I think now is the time to deliver it. He wants you to."

"OK. Our firm represented him in the criminal case and my colleague always thought there was more to it than Kelvin was letting on. He pleaded guilty against our advice."

"Would it be possible to meet you at his mother's house?"

"Of course. I'll be there in about an hour with the letter."

What the hell was in the letter that was so important to Kelvin? He'd soon find out.

Michael Sweeney's name popped up on Quince's phone as it began to vibrate in his hand.

"Inspector, I've some bad news. Kelvin has taken a turn for the worse. He's been rushed back to theatre. It doesn't look good. He's fighting for his life. I think his next of kin should be informed, and if possible, they need to come to the hospital."

"It's that bad?"

"Yes, I'm sorry to say. Can you sort that for me, Inspector?"

"Leave it with me Mr Sweeney. I was already sorting something out."

Quince knew it had turned to rat shit. Kelvin's mum didn't want anything all to do with him, which was understandable under the circumstances. But Kelvin had been let down by police and now the poor soul was fighting for his life.

The Spearman family home was a neat and tidy semi in an estate of identical properties. Probably built in the seventies, each house wore a render of pebble dash that had been replaced at least once since they were built. Some bragged new trendy pastel shades but the Spearman home was grey and seemed to be appropriate for the situation the family found themselves in. David Senior was waiting in his Mercedes saloon when Quince arrived.

"You got the letter?"

"Yes, but I'll leave all the talking to you."

Quince knocked the front door, not knowing what sort of reception they'd get but expecting the worse.

Mrs Spearman answered, the woman looked drained of substance, a husk of the woman she had probably once been. Frail, hunched, and dressed in a grey cardigan that matched the colour of the house. It was clear that she'd been crying.

"Mrs Spearman, I'm Detective Inspector Quince and this is David Senior, Kelvin's solicitor. May we have a word with you?"

"Is he dead?" her eyes remained fixed on the doorframe, not once had she made eye contact with either of her visitors.

"No, but he's not very well. May we come in?" Said Quince softly.

"I've got no son," she answered as she stepped aside and shuffled into the dark hallway. "He brought shame on my family. I have no one. I've lost my husband, and my youngest boy. I've nothing to live for. Look at me," now she stopped, turned and her eyes searched Quince's. "I'm a wreck. It's destroyed me. My neighbours blame me for his..." she paused as she thought of an appropriate word then spat it out. "Perversion."

David Senior stepped closer. "Mrs Spearman, I have a letter that Kelvin deposited with me. He gave me strict instructions to give it to you should anything happen to him. It must be important. Will you read it?"

Senior handed her the envelope; she hesitated and then slowly opened it. Unfolding it like an unwanted bill, she stepped into an equally grey and depressing living room – a room that had not seen a loving touch in many years – and quietly read the typed page.

The two visitors watched her baleful eyes fill, the tears run down her cheeks, and then she grasped the letter to her chest.

"Oh my God!"

She reluctantly handed Quince the letter, and he read it. He too felt shocked. If what it contained was true, Kelvin had gone to prison for something he claimed in the letter that he never did. All to protect his brother. "Mrs Spearman, is this possible? Can you believe it?"

"Kelvin worshipped his brother; I don't know what to believe."

"Well, I think the only way we can sort this, is if you speak with Kelvin. Will you come with us to the hospital?"

"Yes, I will. God forgive me if this is true. For years I've hated Kelvin. For years I've been tormented, feeling guilty. Was it all my fault?"

"No, Mrs Spearman. Kelvin thought he was protecting you all, especially his brother. Circumstances have changed all that. He's probably felt as much pain as you over the years, and recently he's been through another kind of hell. Look, let's get to the hospital, eh?"

"Yes. Yes, I must see... my boy," she finally whispered and now the tear taps were set to flood.

Mrs Spearman travelled with Quince but all three of them headed to Morriston Hospital as quickly as the speed limits would allow.

Parking was easier than the last time Senior had been there. "This is a useful addition," he said after he followed Quince's pool car into the multi-storey car park.

"Been here a few years now," Quince said.

"I guess I'm lucky not to have had to come before."

The solicitor followed Quince once more, this time on foot, to the ward. A maze of corridors led to a first-floor complex of six bedrooms, but Kelvin had been allocated a private room in the middle of the ward reserved for gravely ill patients. The room was empty, and Quince feared the worst.

They waited at the ward desk until Mr Sweeney arrived. Quince introduced Mrs Spearman to the Consultant.

"Mrs Spearman, your son Kelvin is gravely ill. We had a bit of a scare earlier, but we've got things under control, at least as much as we can. He'll be brought back to the ward in a few minutes. Don't be distressed, but the next twenty-four hours is critical. Would you like to stay with him?"

"Yes, I would. Thank you. Thank you so much," she blubbered as she tried to control her emotions but failed.

The ward door opened and a gurney, surrounded by a team of medical staff, was wheeled in. Kelvin was unconscious. His mother followed the team into the private room and waited for them to finish the necessary checks before she took hold of her son's hand.

"I'm sorry, please don't die. I'm sorry," she whispered into his ear.

36

Gibbs and Greenslade were stewing in the cells, having been arrested for the attempted murder of Kelvin Spearman. For a man used to supervising those released from prison, and a prison warder more accustomed to being on the other side of the heavy grey, steel door, the sudden and dramatic change in their circumstances hadn't yet sunk in. Neither showed any remorse or fear for their detention.

Big Mei, or Detective Inspector Meirion Jessop to all but his closest friends and colleagues, organised the interview teams before calling a conference. A former South Wales Police second row forward, Mei was six-five and carried no unwanted padding in his scale weight of seventeen stones. A jaw like Desperate Dan, he oozed menace without even trying.

"Listen up, team," he shouted above the raised voices of half a dozen detectives. Mei had never had to tell anyone to be quiet more than once. "This is going to be a long, and busy enquiry. We have two real turds in custody. Gibbs is a probation officer, and Greenslade a prison officer. They are a disgrace to their professions. They've both been arrested for attempted murder. We know Greenslade caused the injuries but as far as we are concerned, they were both in it together.

"In addition to that, it would appear they have been running an identity scam. They have been arranging new identities for convicted paedophiles and relocating them abroad, mostly to countries with no extradition. We do not know if it's just the two of them, or whether it's an international setup. It looks like they have been making a fortune. There is a list of about thirty names at the minute who were released, placed on the register, and then disappeared off the face of the earth."

He took a deep breath before continuing, his already massive chest filling and straining at the buttons of his oversized shirt. "I do not assume anything, but there must be more of their ilk involved in this. The paedophiles are from all over the country, so they must have had help. The tech unit have already furnished us with a great deal of information, at least enough to get stuck into the pair of bastards.

"I have organised the interview teams. Ivor, you and I will do Gibbs. Adam and Hazel, you get stuck into Greenslade. The rest of you can liaise with the tech boys. If anything, new crops up, just let us know. They've both got briefs, so I doubt they'll be very forthcoming; they've got too much to lose. We have got to find a way to get into them."

A walk to the custody suite followed a fresh cup of coffee and a pastry donated by a new detective constable. Buying snacks to keep the team going was a rite of passage for new detectives on Quince's team and one that evolved rather than was implicit. Nonetheless, it was a welcome break, a chance to think through the plan of attack.

Prepared for the interviews, the game was on. Gibbs was represented by Dylan Squires, and Greenslade's brief was Frances Carter, a young but slick solicitor making a name for herself in the area. She was as smart as any Jessop had met. Short, a little over four feet and as wide as she was tall, Carter seemed to glide into the interview room on two small but rapidly moving legs. Her charcoal grey suit was tailored but still looked out of place on her. Jessop imagined she was happier lounging in sweatpants and comfortable shoes. But then again, so was he.

Gibbs led Squires into the interview room, the solicitor frowning, a large black covered diary, and notebook tucked under his left arm and a matching black briefcase dangling from his right. They duly took up their positions at a bare, square table bolted to the concrete floor, facing the heavy wood door.

A chest like a barrel of Best Bitter and arms thicker than most men's legs, Mei had worked hard to keep in shape. A committed anti-drug sportsman, Mei had made it clear to all those in his local gym that if he even heard a rumour that any of those sharing the dumbbells with him were using steroids, he'd hit them harder than a severe dose of Covid 19. Cheating at anything in life was alien to Mei and whilst he didn't expect everyone to share his views on life and keeping fit in particular, he did expect them to respect his position as a police officer. Only once in those twenty years had he had to follow through on his threat and arrest a gym monkey for possessing and dealing in the shit. Just like his attitude on training, Mei was equally transparent in his dealings with the criminal element. He had no time for anyone who broke the law – any kind of law – and no quarter was asked from him, nor was it ever given.

After all the formalities, Mei sat his massive frame on a chair designed for lesser mortals and began the interview with Gibbs.

"Mr Gibbs," he smiled to set the scene, his expression appeared out of place on his face. "Is it OK if I call you Russ?" Mei had developed a non-confrontational style of interviewing that he rarely had to change. Few men had ever wanted to get physical with him, but he was never short of those of the opposite sex who were keen to do so. A smooth and fluent speaker, Mei rarely had to resort to strong words to get suspects to talk. If they were set on no comment, Mei was OK with that. He believed that the interview was the icing on a cake. If the rest of the cake of evidence wasn't supporting the icing, then the likelihood of getting a confession was remote.

"Don't see why not," Gibbs shrugged.

Squires looked at Gibbs, and raised his eyebrows, a clear sign that he had advised Gibbs to make no comment.

"You've been arrested for the attempted murder of Kelvin Spearman, who I understand you've been monitoring since he was released from prison? Have you anything to say, bearing in mind you are still under caution?"

"That was fuck all to do with me. That's down to Doug," Gibbs spat. "He's off it. He had the cutthroat," Gibbs folded his arms across his chest and sat back. "Nothing to do with me."

"But *it is* something to do with you, Russ," Mei's words were slow and measured. "You were there, and you had Kelvin there against his will, didn't you?"

Now Gibbs looked to his brief. The expression on Squires' face didn't need verbal elaboration. "No comment," Gibbs said.

"Look, Russ, we all know what you've been up to. Not a bad little scam," Mei said as he too sat back and matched Gibbs' posture, his huge slabs of muscular arms barely meeting. "You must have pulled in a fair few grand? I'm curious. How did it all start, and who else is involved?"

"No comment."

"We've already got the names of thirty paedophiles who have, in fact, disappeared into the woodwork. There could be more. Our tech boys are getting stuck into the files, fair play to Kelvin he came up, trumps."

Gibbs turned to his solicitor and whispered into Squires ear. Mei watched and waited.

"Can I do a deal with you?" Gibbs finally said after an almost imperceptible nod from Squires. "I'm no murderer. I'll give you everything about my part in it all. But I'll need reassurances, and protection. You lot don't know who you're dealing with. How do you think I got involved, eh?" Gibbs sniffed and wiped his nose on his sleeve.

He had cracked. Mei was shocked at how easy it had been. Was this all going to be bullshit?

"My family were threatened. I had no option. Doug is well connected," Gibbs added.

"Do yourself a favour, Russ, and pull the other one. You mean to tell me that you're a victim in all this? If that's true, tell me who's running you?"

"That's it," he shook his head. "I've no fucking idea. Doug does all the dealing. He gets the names and we go from there."

"My unit have trawled the South Wales Sex Offender's Register, and at least eight sex offenders have disappeared in the last two years, when did it all start?"

Gibbs began to rub his knees. Nerves evident now. "Look, I need assurances before I say anything else."

"Russ, what's with the computer files, Kelvin's statement, and whatever other dirt we can dig up, you're not in any position to ask for a deal," he paused and made a play of thinking about what to say next. "Look, I'll put a word in for you., that's all I can promise, you scratch my back, and we'll see how it goes."

DS Nelson, a man half the size of Mei but still bigger than Gibbs, spoke, "I think you'd better listen to the boss, Russ. He's being fair with you. Have a little think before you dig a hole for yourself. All we want to know is, if you're not the top man, who is?"

"Like I'm saying, I don't know. Ask Doug. He roped me in to all this."

"How did that happen, Russ?" Nelson continued.

"In the nick."

"I take it you mean Swansea Prison?"

"Yes. He approached me a couple of years ago. He ran the scam by me. At first, I didn't want anything to do with it, but like I said, my family were threatened, and they just sucked me in."

"Just like you sucked in Kelvin. Did he ever tell you he was innocent?" Meirion said.

"Aye loads of times, but they're all the same... they always plead innocence. You should know that."

"Well on this occasion, he was."

"What do you mean, he was innocent?"

Mei leaned forward. The table shook as he rested his arms on the top. "He took the fall for his younger brother. Spent four years in nick for something he never even did. The only good thing to come out of this shit storm is that he's re-united with his mother. Fair play, Russ, you've caused some damage."

Gibbs eyes darted to the floor, no longer able to look at the behemoth opposite.

"Let's get back to the nitty gritty, Russ, let us have it all... chapter and verse."

"Like I said, Doug approached me. He told me about the scam. Said it was easy money, and that all we needed was a computer whizz to do the business for us in South Wales."

"The files that we've retrieved show offenders from all over," Nelson chipped in.

"Yes, but we only deal with the South Wales scrotes. When I say we, I really mean me. Doug sorts the rest."

"Well, who does he deal with? There must be someone he answers to," Mei said.

"If there is, I don't know who he, or who they are. I just sorted out the whizz kids."

"How many have there been?"

"Just the two. I wouldn't say the first one was a kid, he had a stroke and fucked it all up. That's why I did the business on Spearman, he was an easy touch, opened his heart to me, he did."

"Who was the first one?"

"A guy by the name of Olson, Simon Olson, an old lag but a whizz on the computer. I put the arm on him when he was released a couple of years ago. It was all going great until he had the stroke. That fucked it all up, he's like a cabbage now."

"So that's when Kelvin Spearman came into the equation?"

"Yes, he fitted the bill. A right bleeding heart, he was. I reeled him in a treat. He didn't see it coming," a hint of a smile as Gibbs recalled what he clearly still thought was a clever operation on his part.

"How could you go along with all this crap, Russ? You've been relocating paedophiles, giving them new identities, knowing they would probably re-offend in third world countries where children don't mean anything and are just prey for these perverts."

"I'm sorry, what can I say?"

"Bit late for sorry, don't you think, Russ?" Mei sighed and sat back, the chair creaking under his weight. "We'll call a halt for now. We've got a load of enquiries to carry out and at this moment in time your home is being searched. Will we find anything incriminating there?" Gibbs shook his head, but his expression betrayed his doubt in his own conviction. "Well, I hope we do," Mei continued. "Now, you have a chat with Mr. Squires and perhaps we can find some common ground, beneficial to all parties."

"Where's Doug?" Gibbs asked.

"Being interviewed next door, probably blaming you, Russ. Never mind, whatever the outcome, you'll both be doing a fair bit of bird."

"I've said too much, no more. That's it."

Nelson stopped the recording. "Interview suspended."

***

"OK, team. We just interviewed Gibbs," Meirion said to the assembled detectives. "He's shitting himself and is putting it all onto Greenslade. He doesn't want anything to do with the attempted murder but has given us a bit on the scam. He spouted some cock and bull about his family being threatened. We'll take that with a pinch of salt. He also says he is low down the food chain and that Greenwood has got the ear of whoever is behind it all," he turned to the other pair of interviewers. "Adam, Hazel, what's Greenwood saying?"

"Not a bloody dickie bird, boss," Adam said. "He went no comment all through the interview. Twitched a few times, when we hit a nerve, but that's about it."

"Well at least tech have gleaned all the information off the pen drives," Hazel said. "We've got dates, bank details, false passports, birth certificates, we've even got the countries these perverts have been relocated to."

"So, we've got a lot of work," Meirion smiled. "The custody clock is ticking. The search teams are still doing their house. Let's keep our fingers crossed we'll get something. Now, let's crack on and make sure we bin these two."

37

Russell Gibbs paced the very limited floor space of his cell. He felt as if he was on death row. He knew that he was in deep water with nowhere to swim. His career was over, and he was facing jail time. He'd been involved in the justice system for over thirty years, dealing with all sorts of offenders. He never trusted any of them. His adage was, once a bad apple, always a bad apple. Now he had joined their ranks. He was corrupt to the core.

In the past couple of years, he had seen his once beloved probation service bomb into decline. Two years ago, Greenslade made Gibbs an offer that he couldn't really refuse. It was supposed to be a one off, an easy ten-grand. However, it spiralled out of control. Greenslade had reeled him in, much like Gibbs had hooked the unsuspecting Kelvin Spearman.

As Gibbs placed his finger on the cell buzzer, he'd made his decision. He was going to come clean and spill the beans.

***

"Well, Russell, I understand you want to talk to us," Mei said. "I must remind you, that you're still under caution."

"Yes, I understand."

"Since your last interview, my team have been delving deep into your background, bank accounts, mobile phone records. I must say that they make very interesting reading, as does Greenslade's. A veritable can of worms. I'm not surprised Greenslade has kept his trap shut."

"Look, do you want me to tell you or not?"

Mei raised his eyebrows and sat back, getting as comfortable as he possibly could on the chair.

"I'll tell you all I know, as long as the attempted murder is off the table?"

"Well Russell, you're a lucky man there. Spearman tells us that Greenslade was the violent one in this despicable partnership. I've spoken to the CPS and, as long as you co-operate, you'll have your wish."

"Yes, I had to stop him a few times from going nuts. The man's a fucking psycho."

"Tell us when it all started, Russell. When did Greenslade approach you?"

"I've only been involved with Greenslade, nobody else. He's the go-between in all this. I've just cultivated the whiz kids, like I said earlier."

"OK, Russell. Let's go back to when it all started, chapter and verse. Who approached who?"

"Greenslade made the first approach. I was in Swansea nick interviewing a client. He was there as a relief. His normal nick is Cardiff, as you probably already know."

"So how did the conversation go?"

"He just mentioned that he had a proposition that would benefit us both. Then he hooked me with the ten-grand sweetener."

"Did you ask him what you had to do for ten-grand?"

"No, he left it at that. Then I met him later for a coffee, that's when he ran the scam by me."

"Your bank account details show that, during the last two years, you've deposited in excess of one hundred and fifty thousand into your account. That's a bit more than ten grand, if my limited knowledge of maths serves me well."

"It's the money that I've had off Greenslade. He'd give me cash each time we did the business."

"Tell me about Olsen. Who is he, and where is he?"

"I recruited him from the offset. He'd just been released from the nick. I was his supervisor. I did the usual for him, you know, somewhere to live, a job, the usual crap. He was a paedo on licence, like Spearman. It was easy to set him up with a few planted pictures."

"So, what role did he play?"

"He set the whole computer system up for us. He hacked into everything, you know, births, deaths, marriages, DVLA, passports, the lot. He was a real sharp cookie."

"So where is he now?"

"He went and had a stroke. He's no use to anyone now. Still in the Princess of Wales hospital, last I heard."

"So, how did it work?"

"Simple," he grinned. "Greenslade would trawl the release

dates for paedophiles. Invariably, they'd be individuals who were worth a few quid, who wanted to get out of the country with new identities, no questions asked. Nearly always single men."

"Did you meet any of these men?"

"No, I just recruited Olsen, and Spearman. I then had a cut for every new identity. Like I said, Greenslade was the main man. I honestly have no idea who they are."

"Are you sure about that, Russell? Because at this moment in time, there are four other individuals in custody, all as a result of Greenslade, who I must say for a prison officer, must be thick as two small planks, or arrogant. He's left a trail the Three Blind mice could find."

"I don't know who they are, I swear. The money was good, and as you know, these paedos go missing in the UK all the time, at the drop of a hat. The police and probation service haven't the resources to keep track on them. Truth be told, nobody really cares."

"I care, Russell." The menace in Mei's tone was not lost on Gibbs. "You stated that Olsen would be of no use to us, well that's where you were wrong. He did the business on you all. He hacked all your personal details and held them on an encrypted file, which Spearman hacked before Greenslade tried to kill him. Our tech department did the rest and pulled it all up for us."

Gibbs sniffed. "Never trusted the twat."

"I'll mention these names to you, Russell. Tell me if you recognise any of them?"

"Gordon Coleville, a probation officer from Liverpool?"

"Never heard of him," Gibbs said with conviction.

"Harrison Thompson, prison officer from Worcester?"

"No."

"Stefan Owen, Customs officer, Fishguard?"

"No."

"Finally, and this one is very interesting... Vincent Garcia, a commercial pilot from Lincoln?"

"Never heard of any of them."

"Well, they're all in custody, and I must say they all lead back to Greenslade. I'll tell you straight, none of them are linked to you. So, I'll take it that you're on the up with me."

Gibbs nodded. He sighed with relief.

"Their operation has been well and truly blown wide open."

"What do you think I'll get? I reckon I'm looking at a ten stretch," Gibbs said. "I'll end up like half the fuckers I've been supervising for years."

"Hard to say these days. As you know, our justice system is not fit for purpose. Your only plus is that there's no attempted murder charge."

38

Cross had only carried out a handful of briefings since taking charge of the enquiry. Quince felt she looked like she was a fish out of water. The investigation hadn't moved forward, in fact it had stalled and whilst the motor was turning over there was no sign of it starting again.

Quince kept a low profile in the briefings, and when they were over, he carried on quietly with his own work. Cross was out of her depth. She could either sink or swim, and the way it was going he could see she was struggling to keep her head above water. If it were anyone else, he'd step in to help, but Cross was not the type of character who would accept his help. She had a misplaced belief that she was better than the reality of her abilities. It wasn't a gender thing. Quince had worked with many excellent women coppers. Cross had climbed the promotion ladder on the backs of others who were overlooked in her favour. Now she was in a position where delegation would get her only so far. The ladder had broken rungs and she was about to step on one and fall back down to earth.

"How do you think it's all going, Abe? Do you think there's anything more we can do? I know the team is working hard, but as you can see, we've lost a bit of impetus." Cross fiddled with some sheets of notepaper. Very little was written on any of it.

Quince bit his lip. He wanted to say a lot but knew he had to be tactful. "I don't think we can do more than we're doing already, Ma'am. The team are ploughing through the actions at a fair rate of knots."

"I feel we should be doing more. Is there anything you would do differently? You see, I'm having a bit of pressure from the big house, they want it sorted."

Cross actually asking for his help? Quince had a fleeting feeling of sympathy for her. "Well, they would, wouldn't they? Sat up there in their political ivory tower, they haven't a clue. No, we are doing all we can. We'll sort it."

"I know I've asked you before, but do you think it's local?"

"I did initially, but the more it's gone on, I'm moving away from that now, Ma'am."

"My thoughts exactly, Abe. I believe it's outsiders."

"Is that all, Ma'am? I've got a fair bit on."

Before Cross could reply, her mobile rang.

"Hello, who's speaking?"

Quince could see the colour drain from her face.

She held the phone tight to her ear. "Abe, that'll be all. I've got to take this. Can you excuse us please?"

"Not a problem, Ma'am."

Quince made a quick exit. Something wasn't right.

***

"What do you want? Why are you ringing me at work, are you mad?"

"Those who know me say I am, Chief."

"Look, I'm up to my eyes…"

"Don't stress yourself, just checking in, you know, making sure we're on the same page. I hope you haven't spent all the cash? Pat sends her best. Well… she doesn't really."

"I can't handle this shit, what do you want?"

"Let's just say, it's time you started earning your money, Chief. No, let's cut the crap and be less formal… Norma, you don't mind me calling you Norma, do you?"

"Fuck you! What do you want?"

"Meet me in the Sea View in an hour. I've got a room booked, just ask for me. I've a bit of business to discuss. There's a few quid in it for you."

A pause before Cross answered. She knew she had no choice. "I'll be there, you bastard."

Cross ended the call. This was turning into a nightmare.

She grabbed her coat and stormed out of the office, hurrying after Quince. "Abe I've got some urgent business to sort. I'll see you in a couple of hours." There was no explanation.

Quince's suspicions were rapidly growing. Cross was distracted. Something was wrong and he was going to get to the bottom of it.

***

"You're very punctual, Norma. Come and sit down on the bed. I've ordered some champagne. I thought we'd make an afternoon of it."

Cross removed her coat and threw it onto a chair at the bottom of the bed. "Fuck you and your champagne," she seethed. "Let's just get on with it."

The man grinned and poured two glasses of champagne and offered one to Cross.

"Here, Norma, I know you're on duty, but hey, you are the boss, or so I've been led to believe."

"It's right what your wife says about you," Cross seethed.

The grin slipped quickly from the man's face. "And what was that, Norma?"

Cross stopped herself. Howe was a dangerous man. She had to be careful. "I won't waste my breath."

"I've often wondered what you and Pat got up to. Would you like to talk me through it?" The grin returned.

"You don't deserve her. You don't love her, and she doesn't love you."

"Pat loves the money, Norma. Don't you think I know that? You're right, I don't love her. She's just a smart bit of stuff on my arm, a bit of window dressing," he waved a hand dismissively. "Anyway, we're digressing. I suppose you want to know what I want?"

"Just spit it out."

"Well, I want you, Norma. You know what I mean. I know all about you, how you've risen up the ranks, or should I say, slept your way up the ranks? You've put the arm on your conquests, a little bit like me..." the grin broadened, "...with you. How does it feel? The boot is on the other foot."

"Do you really think I'd sleep with a scumbag like you?" she scoffed. "You must be joking." Cross snatched at her coat and turned to leave.

"Think of it this way, Norma, it'll be like keeping it in the family. Come on, have some champagne, it'll put you in the mood. We can have a bit of nonsense and then perhaps a bit of room service. Of course, it's your choice." The grin slipped from his face again; replaced by a sneer. "Otherwise, I make the pictures public and end your career." Now he laughed and took a sip of champagne. "It's your choice, but I've got it all on tape, the five grand, everything. But I'm no animal. Let's get a drink first, eh? You go down to the bar and I'll join you after a quick shower."

Cross glared at Howe in disgust, she had no option.

39

Cross had finished briefing the team then hurriedly left the Incident Room like a scalded cat to go to her 'other business,' whatever the hell that was. Quince had been watching Cross throughout the briefing. He knew there was something up, her body language, her delivery was more inept than usual. He was determined to get to the bottom of it all, come hell or high water.

Most good detectives possess 'a nose for crime,' often called 'a gut instinct.' It frequently pays off and Quince always felt it was a shame it couldn't be used in evidence. On this occasion Quince's gut was working overtime. He was going to spy on his boss. He had to be discreet because if his suspicions were off beam he would end up in deep trouble. If Cross had any inkling that he was watching her, she would take him to the cleaners, have him demoted, or even booted out of the job. No, Quince had to watch his back. He had followed her to Morgan's Hotel. He needed to know who she was meeting. She was bound to see him but perhaps he could bullshit a reason for being there? Morgan's Hotel was a perfect place to do some thinking. The four-star hotel, once a nineteenth century port building, was unusually quiet. There was no sign of Cross. Ordering a pint of lager, he had choice of stools and sat at the bar with his back to the front entrance. Quince could see exactly what was going on behind in the large bar mirror. He hadn't been there ten minutes, when Cross sidled up to the bar. Initially, Cross was completely unaware of Quince's presence.

"I'll get that, Ma'am, put your purse away."

Shocked, Cross glanced at Quince, briefly dumfounded. "Abe, what are you doing here?"

"Just chilling. I find the ambiance here very soothing after a shit day. What you up to, meeting somebody?" Cross blushed. Quince knew he'd hit caught her off guard.

"No, Abe. Like you, I just fancied a drink."

"Didn't know you used this place."

"No, I haven't been in here for a few years," she forced a smile.

"Shall we have a sit down on one of those sofas?"

"No, I'd prefer it by the bar, Abe."

Cross was distracted. She kept looking up at the mirror. Cross was either there to meet or hide from someone. Quince was sure he knew who as soon as he saw a man in the mirror enter the bar.

She jumped in her stool as Quince said, "Well now, there's a rave from the grave. Ted Howe. I put him away for a five-stretch when I was a young DC. He's done well for himself since he came out. You must have heard of him? He's well connected these days."

"Sorry, Abe, but he doesn't ring a bell," Cross mumbled nervously.

Quince turned around, "I'll introduce you." He rose from his stool and heard a gasp of dread from Cross. Approaching Howe, Quince could see that the man was as surprised as Cross, at seeing him.

"Good God... Ted Howe! How's it going? Long time, no see," Quince said in a mock welcome.

"Oh, Quince. What do you want?" No hint of pretence from Howe.

"Fancy a drink for old time's sake, Ted? And let me introduce you to my boss."

Quince Beckoned Cross over to join them.

"Ted, this is my boss, Detective Chief Inspector Norma Cross," he said.

Cross shook Howe's hand and her face flushed red. Quince was sure she was here to meet him but why?

"Let's grab a seat. What you are drinking, Ted?'

"I'll have a Scotch on the rocks, if you're paying?"

"Of course. My round. I can afford it. Still got some overtime money saved up from the time I put you away. Earned a nice wedge from you, I did," Quince grinned as he headed to the bar, leaving the pair to stew.

"What the hell is he doing here, Norma?"

"No idea. The twat was here when I came in. Just play it cool. I'll handle him."

"You'd better. Keep him on a short leash. I don't want him sniffing into my business."

Quince returned with Howe's drink.

"There you go, Ted. Bottoms up." Quince took a sip of his

own drink then placed it on the low table between him and Howe. "I've been watching your progress these past years. A real pillar of society, or is it pillock? What are you into these days?"

Howe didn't take the bait. He smiled. "Bit of this, bit of that, you know what it's like, eh?"

"Nope. No idea," Quince smiled back. "Nothing dodgy, I hope?"

"Abe, I don't think Mr Howe needs that kind of provocation."

"Call me Ted, please," Howe said to Cross in a poor attempt to hide what was now obvious from their expressions that they knew each other. Quince just wanted to know how and why. "I don't mind. I know Quince is a straight shooter. I'm not fazed by him."

"Glad to hear it, Ted. Hard feelings, I hope?" He said sarcastically.

"No. I paid my debt to society. I have to say that you treated me tidy. I swore I'd never spend another day in nick. I'm doing well now. Plenty to keep me occupied."

Quince said nothing for a brief moment, eyes darting between Howe and Cross. They were doing well, but not well enough. They were here to meet up. "How's your wife?" Quince said.

"She's OK. I'll pass on your regards."

"Yeah, you do that. Got a good 'un there, Ted. She stuck by you. Many wouldn't have."

"Yes. Pat's stuck by me through the bad times and we're now enjoying the fruits of our labour. Unlike your missus, by all accounts. At least that's what I've heard?"

Quince shrugged. "Shit happens," He seethed at the dig but kept his rising anger in check. "But I'm interested in you, Ted. Anything in the pipeline at the minute? I know your casino is opening shortly. Swansea expanding at a rate of knots. I have no doubt that you'll make a killing."

"Yeah. All on track on that front. Got a few irons in the fire. I've been keeping an eye on your career too, Abe. You're doing well for a Yank in the South Wales Police. I understand you're on the marina murders case?"

"I do alright. But you're wrong on the Marina job. That one's down to the boss here."

"Never?" Howe feigned surprise. "How's it moving along? A nasty business by all account. There's too much of this type of thing going on at the minute, what with that and drugs. There's no need to rob or burgle these days," he grinned. "Norma, you're very quiet. Cat got your tongue? What's it like lording it over the likes of Abe here? Must be very satisfying."

"Not really. We all work as a team. It's very stressful at times but Abe's what you might call my right-hand man. We work well together."

Quince winced. The woman was delusional.

"Funny that, I always thought of Abe as a bit of a lone wolf. He certainly was when he did me up like a kipper."

'Look, Ted, I'd love to chew the fat a bit longer, but I've got a little bit of business to sort out. I'll leave you in the boss' capable hands." He finished his beer and stood. He was now more certain than ever that Cross was involved in some way with Ted Howe.

"Well Norma, now it's just the two of us," his smile shark-like, a predator moving in for the kill.

"What do you want? If he gets a sniff, he'll hound us. You know what he's like."

"Well, he's one of your lapdogs, Norma. You sort him. If I had my way, I'd like him to be found face down in the marina, like them two poor foreign bastards."

"I'll pretend I didn't hear that."

"Look, there are a few business associates that I'd like you to meet. They're all above board, you understand," that smile again. "They have no idea that you're in my pocket, so I'll be discreet."

Cross scoffed. "You discreet?"

Howe laughed.

"Where and when?"

"Pat and I are having a bit of a house party. It's all to do with one of her charities, well you'd know all about those wouldn't you? I'd like you to come along and do a bit of circulating, an ideal cover for you. Get there early, say mid-day next Wednesday?"

"I don't want to go to your home."

"I don't think you're in a position to refuse, Norma. And anyway, you and Pat can have a nice catch up. I haven't told her about our little liaison, which I enjoyed immensely. Do you think Pat would be jealous if she ever found out?" He laughed but there was no humour intended.

"You're a nasty piece of work. How the hell did she end up

with a piece of shit like you?"

"It's all about money and power, Norma, I've got both. Pat knows which side her bread is buttered."

"You're pure fucking evil, and your time will come."

"I don't think so. Not any time soon." Howe handed Cross a small piece of paper.

"There are a few names and car registrations on there. Check them out for me."

"You must be joking. It's not possible. Maybe years ago, but not today. Everything is checked."

"Well, I'll leave you to work that one out. Let's call it a good faith gesture."

"I'll lose my job."

Howe snarled, "Do it!"

Cross sighed and stuffed the paper into her purse.

"I expect you to be at the party and bring the information with you."

"What choice do I have?"

"You've no choice."

Cross remained seated as Howe left the bar. She felt like she's been hit by a demolition ball. Howe had left her no option but to do his dirty business.

40

Cross sat at the front of the assembled detectives, legs and arms crossed and silent. Indeed, Quince was sure she wasn't even listening as detective after detective stood up to brief the others.

The bodies in the marina enquiry had fallen flat, the team were working hard but information was as rare as hens' teeth. They didn't have a single lead on who was responsible for the deaths, and time was racing on. They needed a break, and they needed it sooner rather than later.

A call from DI Rowan Dylan pinged on Quince's phone as the briefing was ending. He slipped into his office and shut the door.

"Result, Abe. That pair of bastards have been at it big time. We hit them this morning. Your information was spot on."

"Have you recovered the sawn-offs?"

"Oh aye, and plenty more. Looks like they're into everything; drugs, antiques, vehicles, firearms, the whole nine yards. It's going to take a bit of sorting, that's a fact."

"Excellent news. Did they give you any trouble?"

"No. Like two pussy cats. They shit themselves when ARTs, give them the spiel. Even I shit myself," he laughed. The Armed Response Teams were intimidating without even trying. The fact they carried guns had a lot to do with that.

"Did you find anything that may involve people trafficking?"

"No, nothing that stands out, Abe. But this pair are involved in so much shit, who knows what they've been up to. Look, I'll make sure the team go through everything with a fine-tooth comb. If anything crops up, I'll ring you straight away. Have you got any leads at all?"

"Nothing. And, as you've probably heard, Cross is running it now. I'm now officially lurking in the shadows."

"Aye, I had heard. But it should be water off a duck's back to you, Abe."

"Look, I'll leave you to it, Rowan. I'm glad you got a result."

Quince needed fresh air. He opened the office window and pressed call for Toby Walters.

"Hi, Toby. Quince here. Just to let you know that those two

scumbags have been nicked, and your information was spot on."

At first, Toby could barely make a sound other than the rasping noise of his breathing. Quince gave him time.

"Good... that's good, Abe. Glad... to be of... help," another pause before Toby found the strength to continue. "Did they... get... the shooters?"

"Yeah, all sorted. They'll get a fair bit of bird, guaranteed."

"The marina... any... news?"

"No, it's gone flat. Why, have you got anything?"

"Just... a rumour that... it's local."

"Any names?"

"Nothing... I'll call... if I hear... but I haven't got long... now."

"I'm sorry about that, Toby, anything I can do?"

"Toby junior... is sorting me... he's a... good lad."

"OK, look I'll get you a few quid for the information."

"Don't insult me... now do me... a favour..."

"Of course."

"Fuck off... I've got to go... for a run."

Quince laughed. "You haven't lost your sense of humour. You look after yourself, do you hear me?"

"I hear... it's my lungs, not... my bloody ears... that's... buggered."

No sooner had Quince ended the call, he received an incoming off DI Charlie John.

"Just ringing to ask a favour, if possible?"

"What do you want?"

"Have you any vacancies on the team for a DS?"

"Well, now you come to mention it, Charlie, I'm about to lose one on promotion. So, yes, I'll have one going. Who have you got in mind?"

"A real cracker, Abe, and I'll be sorry to lose her."

"I take it you're talking about Karen?"

"You got it in one, Abe. I guarantee she'll be an asset to your team. She's been brilliant for me over the last four or five years."

"Any particular reason why she wants to come off your team, Charlie?"

"I've had a long chat with her, Abe. She's talking about going back into uniform, but it would be a waste. I mentioned your team to her, and I think she may have taken the bait."

"I'll be guided by you, Charlie. I know her track record and she'd definitely be an asset. When can she start?"

"You can have her whenever you like, Abe. We're quiet at the minute."

"Tell her to come and see me in the next few days. I'll have a chat with her and take it from there."

"That'll be cracking, Abe. My loss is your gain, my friend. You know if you need my team again, just give us a bell."

Quince thought about Karen as he walked into the Incident room to see if there was any progress being made. He had worked with her briefly when she joined and had made an impact straight out of training school. She was keen and could look after herself.

His thoughts were broken by Clive the office manager. "How's it hanging, boss?"

Quince smiled. "Not too good. How's it with you, Clive, any news?"

"It's slow, boss. Loads of actions, but nothing forthcoming that may give us a lead. We're at the mercy of the Vietnamese authorities and I reckon they're on a fucking go slow. Plenty of e-mails but nothing as to the identity of the two lads. The British consulate in Hanoi is doing its best, but you know what it's like. I ask myself, does anyone over there really care?"

"Getting you down is it Clive?"

"No, boss, but it's so frustrating. You know how hard the team are working and, between you and me, the DCI is notable by her absence. She breezes in, gives a ten-minute briefing, and then does a vanishing act. Why doesn't she let you run it?"

"OK, Clive, enough of that. I can see what's going on. You just carry on as per normal. It'll sort itself out. Anything from the Coast Guard, and Immigration?"

"Nothing concrete, boss, still got dozens of vessels to eliminate, and as for POI's, they're coming out of the woodwork. The routes the traffickers are using are common knowledge, but without real intelligence it's like looking for a needle in a haystack."

"I've studied all the routes. But these traffickers are smart and I've no doubt they pay good money to corrupt officials in countries like Vietnam."

"What about over here, boss?"

"Probably exactly the same, Clive, if the money's right. God knows what people will do."

"If only we could identify the poor bastards, boss. At least it would be a start."

"Keep plugging away, Clive. When's the next briefing?"

"Who knows, boss? Later on today, I would imagine."

"Look, I'll give the DCI a bell, see how the land lies. I'll get back to you," Quince punched Colin's shoulder and headed back to his office with a fresh coffee and gave Cross a ring.

"Afternoon, Ma'am"

"Abe, is there anything wrong?"

"No, nothing at all. I was wondering will there be a briefing later today?"

"Has anything out of the ordinary cropped up, Abe?"

"No, nothing, Ma'am. The team are still ripping through the actions but keep coming up empty."

"OK. I'm a bit busy at the minute. You take the briefing. I'm sure there's no need for me to be there. Obviously, if something materialises, I'll be straight there."

"Leave it to me, Ma'am.

41

Quince was under no illusion that the team was disillusioned with the lack of input from Cross. He knew she was having pressure from upon high – all senior investigating officers had pressure for results, but she seemed to be ignoring it. Was she perversely enjoying it? Was it some strange way for her to hog the limelight? Whatever the reason, she was leaving herself wide open.

He knew exactly what information was going into the room and could have taken over the SIO's role in a heartbeat. But politics had to be played.

It took an hour to get everyone back in the room for the next conference. "OK, ladies and gents, unfortunately the DCI is otherwise engaged," he said ironically, "so here I am. I know you have all been working your nuts off for the last couple of weeks, and this is probably one of the most frustratingly complex murder enquiries that we've ever had. Our hands are tied with all the political crap, dealing with consulates, and there is so much corruption involved with people trafficking. I guarantee that half the enquiries in Vietnam are probably shredded. The only thing I'll say is just keep plugging away. I'm confident we'll get a result. Now I'll throw it open to you all. If you've any fresh ideas just spit them out, don't be afraid, let's clear the air."

Ken Lewis raised a meaty arm, his jacket straining under the pressure of his beer-modified bulk. "Boss, why don't you take over the enquiry, give us back a bit of impetus?"

"Ken, you know that's a no-no at the minute. The DCI makes policy, I'm just giving you all a pep talk," he smiled. "Look, are there any lines of enquiry we can pursue that may throw up something?"

Clive Purcell sat opposite Ken in the circle of seats that Quince had set up. He had seen Terry McGuire use the circle – the idea that all officers were equal and valued in a team meeting. Not only was Purcell opposite Ken in the circle, but he was also the opposite of his neighbour in every possible way. Slim, fit from running more marathons than Mo Farrar and sharp as Angela Rayner's tongue. "Boss, I reckon the answer is definitely local. There's nothing coming from any other agencies, no concrete information, the majority of it is pure speculation."

With that the office phone rang and Purcell was nearest. "Excuse me, boss," he said as he reached behind to a desk, picked up the phone and spoke. "Incident room DC Purcell speaking."

"Good evening, this is Alistair Baines, British Embassy, Hanoi. Is it possible to speak with DCI Cross regarding her double murder enquiry?"

"Ah, Mr Baines... DCI Cross is not here at the minute, but I'll hand you over to DI Quince."

Purcell put the receiver to his chest.

"Boss, it's the British Embassy, Hanoi again. A Mr Baines."

Quince took the handset.

"Detective Inspector, I know it's been a while; however, we've managed to confirm who the two unfortunate men were. As you can appreciate, it is very difficult to glean information from villagers for fear of reprisals."

"I totally understand, Mr Baines."

"Anyway, these are the names, and they are both from Ha Tinh village, as was first thought. The first is Dinh Chien, born 11.8.2003... that makes him..."

Quince helped, "Seventeen."

"Yes, thank you. Then we have Taavi Dong, born 7.8.2002, aged 18. Neither of them has been reported missing. As you can appreciate, once families get involved with these traffickers, they are constantly under threat, and what you must bear in mind is that lives mean nothing over here. The number of youngsters that go missing every year is shocking. The majority end up being used as slave labour. Personally, I'll be glad to get back home after my stint."

"Well, this is good news in a bad situation, Mr Baines. At least we've now identified the poor bastards. Have you any pictures?"

"Luckily, yes, Inspector. I'll get them to you forthwith."

"Mr Baines, how the hell do the Vietnamese authorities allow this to happen?"

"Inspector, there's so much corruption. We obviously look after Brits entering Vietnam, we supply them with all necessary information on how to keep safe, but many are tourists and back packers, and once they put themselves in any danger that's usually the end of them. As for the trafficking, it's a multimillion-pound business, and for every gang of traffickers locked up I guarantee that there are ten others ready to take their place. They have a network that spreads worldwide. It can never be policed, and that's a fact. I take it you are aware of all the routes, and nationalities involved Inspector?"

"Yes, Mr Baines. We have regular conferences with Customs and Immigration, but there again, it's like throwing a pebble into the ocean. Is there information you can give us to take the enquiry forward?"

"No, nothing really, I'm sorry."

"What about the families of these deceased lads, have they given any information?"

"Nothing of any relevance. Like I say, they are very tight lipped, and in fear for their lives."

"What about the bodies, Mr Baines? What do the families want done with them?"

"Nothing, Inspector. May they rest in peace, that is all I can say."

Quince sighed. It was a dreadful thought that two young lads could travel all that distance, end up dead and no-one seemed to be able to even give them a decent send off. "Well thank you Mr Baines. I'm very much obliged for this information."

"By the way, give my regards to DCI Cross."

"I will, Mr Baines. When did you speak to her last?"

"Just a few days ago, Inspector."

"Excellent, Mr Baines. I'll tell her."

Now they were moving again. "Well, team, it looks like we've got a positive ID on the two victims, which is something."

Quince then shared all the details with the team, adding a rider. "I can't see us getting any direct information from the Vietnamese authorities. I believe whoever dumped these two lads has local connections. I'm not saying for a minute that a yacht from the marina was used, but I think a concerted effort must now be made because time is running out. I'll brief Clive, and you can get stuck into it tomorrow. Now all go home and have a good night's kip."

Clive stayed behind and waved Ken to stay with him as he approached Quince. "Can I have a word?"

"Of course, you can, Clive."

"In private, if possible, and perhaps Ken can join us?"

All three headed for coffee in Quince's office.

"OK, Clive, spit it out," Quince said as he handed steaming mugs to the two detectives. "I can see there's something on your mind."

"Well, boss, as you know, since the DCI has been guiding the ship, so to speak, I believe the direction she's going in is totally wrong. She's very brief and very guarded. Did you know that she'd spoken to that bloke in the embassy?"

"Well, I did. No one else was to deal with the embassy, on her instructions. She also trimmed down the team on the yacht enquiries, which I believe is where the answer lies."

"Boss she's a nightmare," Ken said. "The team don't know where they are, they're like mushrooms in the dark."

"Boys, I appreciate where you're coming from, but leave it to me. I'll sort it. Keep this between ourselves. I'll have a word with her in the morning and we'll see what develops. Now get home and get some kip. I'll see you in the morning."

42

Ted Howe vowed that he would never spend another night in prison. The three years, four months and one day that he had served inside had taught him a stiff lesson. From the day of his release, Howe started wheeling and dealing, but nothing criminal. He never stepped over the mark again. A shrewd businessman, Howe could sell sand to the Arabs. He had built up an impressive property portfolio and was now worth millions. But his latest investment was the biggest to date. He'd noticed that there was a niche market for a high-end restaurant and casino in his home city of Swansea. Howe had invested over two million in the business and had appropriately named it The Vetch, as it had been built on the site of The Vetch football field that seen its last game in 2005.

The land had been earmarked by the council for a housing development and community centre, however that never came to fruition. Demolition of the ground began in January 2011 and was completed within six months. The land was then left to vegetate until Howe put forward his proposal.

Howe had a vision, but to get the necessary planning permission and gaming licences, he had to grease a few palms along the way. This was his first taste of criminality since his release.

"Tonight's the night. Our grand opening. I want you to doll yourself up for the occasion. I don't want people thinking I'm married to a frump," he said casually; no care for the cutting words that struck Pat like a kick in the ribs. He was dressed in a threadbare pair of tan shorts and an equally worn grey t-shirt that brough thoughts of pot and kettle to Pat's mind. "I reckon we'll knock it out of the park with The Vetch. I can feel it in my water."

"I've no doubt it will be a success," Pat said through gritted teeth, the earlier remark still stinging. "You're a little bit like King Midas, everything you touch turns to…" she wanted to say 'shit!' but said what she knew he wanted to hear "…gold."

Howe liked that; to be compared to the King with the golden touch. "By the way, Pat, have you been in touch with Norma, lately?" The slyness in his voice was not missed.

"You know I haven't," Pat snapped. "I can't take a piss without you knowing about it."

Howe smiled but his eyes betrayed a calculating mind. "Look, let's put it all behind us shall we? I don't mind you speaking to her, or even the odd dalliance, but nothing heavy, OK? And definitely nothing to cause me any embarrassment, do you get my drift?"

"You've changed your tune, haven't you? What's your game?"

"No game, darling. Let's just call it one of those open marriages, you OK with that?"

Pat sighed. She knew when her husband was lying. "Ted, you're the boss."

"And don't you ever forget it," he nodded. The edge in his voice returning. "I'm off to the casino to make sure everything's on track. I'll expect you there about mid-day to do a bit of meet and greet," he paused, Pat could almost hear the cogs turning in his head. "And why don't you give Norma a ring?" he added. "Tell her I've had a change of heart about you two. I bet she'll love that."

"I know you won't believe me, but there isn't anything sexual going on between us. I'm not gay, Ted."

Ted snorted and headed for the door.

***

Quince had arrived early and didn't bother going into the Incident room because he knew what was coming. He knew that Detective Chief Inspector Norma Cross wouldn't be a happy bunny, not that he really gave a toss.

As sure as eggs were eggs, Cross bounded into his office less than half an hour later and slammed the door shut behind her. He was in a bit of a tirade.

"Morning, Ma'am. Is there a problem?"

Cross didn't bother with a chair. She placed both hands on Quince's desk and leaned towards him, teeth bared.

"What the fuck are you playing at, Abe?"

"I beg your pardon, Ma'am?"

"I've just been told that you've changed my policy. Why didn't you discuss it with me?"

"Well, I thought you'd be pleased, bearing in mind you were nowhere in sight."

"Don't be fucking sarcastic, Abe."

"Is there something bothering you, Ma'am? I've noticed a change in you the last week or so."

Cross stood up, surprised. "What makes you say that?"

"There's something going on. You've taken your eye off the ball. This murder enquiry is dying on its feet, and the squad are demoralised. Truth be told, Ma'am I don't think you're up to it."

"Don't you dare speak to me like that. I'm your senior officer. Have some respect."

"Have some respect, Ma'am? Your reputation has gone before you. You've got no respect here."

"Abe, you're treading on thin ice. Choose your next words carefully."

Quince pondered a few seconds.

"I take it you know we've had the two young lads identified by the Vietnamese authorities?"

"When was this?"

"Last night, when I briefed the team on the new policy. I had a nice chat with a bloke by the name of Baines from the British Embassy. I understand that you've spoken to him before, but I couldn't find anything in the embassy action to that effect."

"Oh, him," she waved a dismissive hand. "It must have slipped my mind."

It was time to go for her throat, to get it all out on the table, if there was any chance of moving on. Quince knew he was taking a risk with his own career, but he had had enough of shoddy leadership. Something had to be said. "Look, Ma'am, what's the problem?"

"You seem to be my problem."

"Well, I think you're out of your depth, Ma'am. This isn't a straightforward investigation. Most of the avenues of enquiry have petered out. I think you're under pressure because let's be fair you've never really had to investigate. You've always hung onto the shirt tails of officers who would leave you for dead. So that's it. There, I've said it. Now you can lump it or leave it. I'm not really concerned. So do your worst. However, be mindful, because even though I say it myself, my reputation with the top brass outweighs yours." Quince knew he had hit a raw nerve. He felt bad, now he'd said what he thought. It was sounding very personal, bitter even, but something had to be said before the team unravelled.

Cross nodded in the affirmative, she was seething. She knew he was right, but it still hurt to hear it. She wanted to smash his oversized coffee mug into his face and put him on the book for insubordination, but Quince was one of the best in the department and she knew the rest of the team would back him before her. She took a deep breath. "So, what do you suggest?"

"I'll make the policy calls, you just hover in the background, as per normal. If you're having problems, take a few days off. I'll watch the fort."

Before Cross could answer Quince, her mobile rang, it was Pat.

"Excuse me Abe, I've got to take this."

"Shall I go and sort the Incident room, Ma'am?"

"Yes, Abe. Whatever. Close the door behind you, please."

She watched Quince until he left the office then answered the call. "Pat, what the hell are you playing at? If Ted finds out you're talking to me, God knows what he'll do. My career will be finished."

"Don't panic, Norma, truth be told, Ted's easing up. We don't have to avoid each other, as long as we're discreet. There'll be no problem."

"I don't trust him, Pat, he such a devious bastard."

"You don't have to tell me…" she paused, a tense moment of silence. "Pease tell me that you'll not let him get to you. You're the only one who keeps me sane."

"It's been great to meet you after all these years. I just wish you'd married someone nicer."

"Yes, Norma," now a brighter tone to her voice, "so when can I see you again?"

"I'm up to my eyes in work at the minute, so I don't know."

"Look, we've got a charity house party on Wednesday, will you come? I can't see Ted making a fuss, he'll be too busy showing off his art collection."

Another pause as Cross considered the offer. Perhaps it was a setup, Ted playing games. But it would be nice to rub the bastard's nose in it too. "What time?"

"Mid-day. I've got to go. See you Wednesday?"

Cross gathered her thoughts and made her way to the Incident room.

Quince was talking to Ken and Clive when she walked in. Conversations ended abruptly. "Thank you, Abe. Have you got everything sorted? If so, I'll leave you to it, just keep me in the loop."

"Not a problem, Ma'am."

As soon as Cross left the room, Quince winked at Ken and Clive. "Carry on as normal, gents. Just ratch it up a few cogs. Any news, I'll be in my office."

Quince headed back to the silence of his office and sat back in his chair. He grinned to himself. He was now back in control.

He pressed the play button of his small Sony Dictaphone and sat there a moment = stunned.

43

"I've sorted the next run out, I'll be leaving for Calais next week, it should be a dawdle, I was over there last week, and it's all sorted, the palms have been greased, and the wheels are in motion."

"How many?"

"Eight, like I told you. It's the most we've had on one run. It'll be worth over a hundred grand."

"And I told you to curb it. The heat is still on. I'm telling you now, you're pushing our luck."

"What's wrong with you?" his mate sniped. "Have you lost your bottle completely? You used to be all for it, and don't tell me the cash doesn't come in handy. Trouble with you is you've lost your focus since you went legal."

"OK, where are you going to land them this time?"

"Put it this way, it isn't going to be anywhere near Burry Port. I think that bridge has been well and truly burned," he laughed. "No, we'll drop them off down by Southerndown. What happens to them then will be nothing to do with us. Have you been listening at all to anything I told you? I forgot to mention, there'll be a little bonus this time. I'm bringing in a few kilos of coke, so there'll be a couple of grand on top."

His mate groaned "Drugs? It gets worse by the minute with you. You're doing my head in."

"In for a penny, eh? So, how's the cat looking?"

"Sound. She's had a good overhaul and spring clean. She's good to go."

"OK, so don't come anywhere near the marina. The police are still sniffing around, things have quietened down a lot and I think they're looking elsewhere, but better safe than sorry."

"Whatever you say. You're the one with ear to the ground there."

***

Quince believed that Cross was up to her neck in something smelly - whatever it was. If Ted Howe was somehow involved with her, it would be something criminal. It was obvious to Quince that Cross's mind wasn't on the job in hand. If anything, she was a bit like a rabbit caught in the headlights, and as much as he had always believed she was not up to her job, this was an even greater decline in her performance profile.

He knew that he had two options. The first was to report his concerns, possibly to the Assistant Chief Constable for Crime, or he could go it alone and investigate Cross on the QT. Whatever he decided, Quince had a gut feeling that it would all end in tears. He had to tread carefully, otherwise he could end up with a load of grief, not that he cared for himself, he'd been there and done it before. But if he was wrong, he'd be causing a whole load of grief for Cross when perhaps she didn't deserve it – at least not this much.

The sun was ready for bed, dropping to the grey-blue quilt of the Bristol Channel and the Incident room was as quiet as a house with a napping new-born. Calls had dried up and the team were still out trawling through actions.

Clive was reclined in his seat, feet up on his desk and hands knitted behind his head. He yawned as Quince approached. "How are you doing, boss?" he smiled tiredly and dropped his feet quickly to the carpet-tiled floor. "It's dead at the minute, truth be told. I think we may have lost this one."

"Don't be such a killjoy, Clive," Quince punched him lightly on his shoulder. "Never say never." He pulled up a chair and sat facing his junior detective. "I've run murders enquiries for months. Something will turn up; you mark my words. I'm off for a pint so don't hang about. Get yourself home."

"Will do, boss, see you in the morning."

Clive stood slowly and moaned as his knees cracked with the effort. "Jesus! Hear that? Even my bones have had enough." The phone rang before Quince could reply. Clive answered and pressed the loudspeaker button for Quince to hear. "Good evening, Incident room... DC Purcell. How can I help you?"

"My name is Lewis Gardener, I'm a retired navy Captain. I've been away for a few weeks cruising the Med in my yacht..." Clive made the universal sign of the wanker. Quince grinned. "...I'm only just learning about these two unfortunates who were fished out of the Swansea marina," the captain continued. "I think I may very well have some information for you. Whether or not you feel it's relevant, I'll let you decide."

"How do I address you? Captain, or Mr Gardener?" Clive said.

"Dispense with formalities, officer, just call me Lewis."

"Okay, Lewis. You're on loudspeaker so that Detective Inspector Quince, the Senior Investigating Officer can listen in. I'm sure he'd like to hear what the information is?"

"That's fine. I just hope I'm not wasting your time."

"So, what can you tell us, Lewis?"

"Well, from what I understand, these two unfortunates were discovered during the early hours of a Friday morning, just over a fortnight ago. Would that be correct?"

"Yes, that's correct."

"OK. So, I live in Burry Port. I've got a cottage overlooking the bay, and as you can imagine, I spend most of my time on the water. I've got my own little yacht, which I moor a short distance away. I don't know if this is of any significance, but I did notice something a little strange during the early hours of that morning."

"What would that be, Lewis?"

"That's the morning I left for my little cruise around the Med. As I made my way out into open water, I noticed a very pale blue catamaran. The cat, I believe, was anchored, because I saw a small dingy heading towards the shore, I assumed it was from the cat, there was nothing else around there that it could have come from."

"And you are sure about the dingy?"

"Oh, most definitely. Neither the dingy nor the cat had a light on. I had to blast the old foghorn and put the spots on to alert them of my presence."

"Did you see any people?"

"Well, that's it, I didn't notice anybody on the cat. But there were four or five in the dingy."

"Could you describe them, Lewis?"

"Not really, as you can imagine, it was very dark." He thought for a moment before continuing. "If my memory serves me right, there was a bit of sea mist as well. Look, I hope I'm not wasting your time."

"Lewis, this is DI Abe Quince. First thing, your call is very much appreciated, and we're very much obliged. You say it was dark, however, was there anything significant about the catamaran?"

"I can definitely say that it didn't have sails, but that's not unusual."

"No?"

Lewis shook his head and grinned. "Some of these cats are like gin palaces. Big Volvo diesel engines and owner-skippers with no real interest in sailing. So, no sail, just luxurious bedrooms, heads like hotel suits…"

"Heads?" Quince asked.

"Sorry. Yeah, it's what we call the conveniences on board. The toilet," he added for clarity.

"What about colour?"

"It had two tone hulls. Black and white, I think."

"Any name?"

"Not that I could see, Mr Quince. I wasn't taking all that much notice."

"Would it be unusual to see such a craft in that area during the early hours, Lewis?"

"It would be very rare indeed. It's the first I've seen, since retiring five years ago."

"If we do trace this catamaran, do you think you'll be able to identify it?"

"I'm pretty sure I could. It looked a unique. Worth a few shillings, no doubt. I'd say it was best part of half-a-million-plus. The dingy was dark orange with a white, fluorescent stripe."

"Well thank you, Lewis. I'll get a couple of my boys down to see you in the morning to take a statement, is that alright with you?"

"Not a problem. I'll even take them to the very spot I saw the cat. I hope they won't get seasick?"

Quince laughed. He was glad he wasn't going. He had never been good on water. "I'll hand you back to Clive, and he can take all your details. Again, I can't thank you enough."

"My pleasure. Anything to help."

Clive jotted the relevant information from Lewis whilst Quince poured a brace of coffees from the team percolator. He listened to Clive finish the call and dropped two cubes of sugar in Clive's mug.

"What do you reckon, boss? Could this be the break we've

been praying for?"

"Put it this way, Clive, this Lewis fella sounds as if he knows what he's talking about. Action his statement out to someone. Also, I want all relevant organisations issued with a description of the catamaran. It may ring a bell with someone. I also want an action for all marinas within a twenty-mile radius to be visited. I want this fucking catamaran. It shouldn't be too difficult to find."

"I'm on it, boss."

44

Occupying nearly half of the footprint of the former football ground, The Vetch Casino looked out of place amongst the neat rows of terraced houses of Swansea's Sandfields area. It looked like no expense had been spared. Black marble and glass front elevation gave the building an opulent appearance but, just like Howe, it was all show and no substance. The marble was the cheapest veneer he could source, and the large, tinted windows were reclaimed from a cancelled job his builder had found through contacts. The inside was a little better, but not by much. Everything appeared to be better than it was, like a Disneyland version of a Vegas gambling den. None of that matter to Howe. It was the day that he had been waiting for. His dream had come true after years of wheeling and dealing. His high-end restaurant-casino was finally opening, and it would elevate him to heights that he never ever thought he'd realise.

Howe stood in the reception area with his Pat, who was putting on such a happy devoted appearance, as fake as the building itself. Her stomach was churned. She didn't want to be there.

There were all shapes and sizes of suited and finely dressed punters at the reception. Councillors, actors and sportspersons, the whole shooting match, not forgetting a few well-greased palms of members of the council planning committee. Ted had sent out the invites personally, he was on a mission, and nothing was going to spoil his day.

***

Quince needed to unwind after what was quite an eventful day, what with Cross' antics and the new information that may or may not give him a lead as to who killed the two Vietnamese lads.

"Andy? Abe here, how do you fancy a pint?"

"Why not?" Andy sighed. "I've had a grim day, truth be told. All I've had is guilty twats pleading their innocence. If you listen to them, all bobbies are vindictive fascists, and all detectives are bent, whilst butter wouldn't melt in their granny-kissing mouths."

"Well, my day hasn't been as bad as that, but I still need a break. So, say... twenty minutes in the Adam? I'll get the beers in."

"You're on, Abe, I'll see you there."

Quince strolled the half mile or so to The Adam and Eve, got a round in and ensconced himself in the lounge. No sooner had he settled, he was joined by Andy.

"Cheers, Abe. I've been looking forward to this all day. Your very good health, my son."

Quince raised his glass and took what he felt was a well-deserved slug of his beer. He had bought two pints of real ale. Something he had fallen in love with when he was first able to legally drink. That was one of the great things about his adopted country, not only could he drink at eighteen, as opposed to twenty-one in the States, but the UK brewed proper beer. On the few occasions he had travelled back to the country of his birth, he had never found anything that came close to British real ale.

"So, tell me what's cooking in your kitchen?" Andy said, wiping dregs from his lips with the back of his hand.

"At the minute, it's like pushing shit uphill, Andy. We seem to be getting nowhere. What about you?"

"Like I said," he shrugged. "Spent most of the day down the nick, Abe. Two real rippers who the firm have taken on. I'd give them the boot, . Two pieces of shit. Been on the rampage down Bridgend and the Vale, befriending old people and then taking them to the cleaners under the guise of roofers. They've made a fortune and ruined lives. Couldn't roof a doll's house, none of 'em."

"Oh, I've put a few of them away in my time, Andy."

"No doubt, Abe. Always some useless scum willing to screw the elderly and the vulnerable. I think the only thing to stop them is take them down a dark alley and smash their kneecaps. That would at least stop 'em running away."

Quince grinned. "You haven't change then?"

Andy snorted, "Nope. Never will, either. Anyway, tell me what's screwing up the murder case and twisting your sack."

"Just hit a brick wall, if truth be told."

"Really?" he grimaced, then nodded. "Foreigners, see. I guess it must be difficult dealing with foreign types?"

"Nightmare," Quince agreed. "Everything is corrupt and dealing with the Foreign Office is hard work."

"Did I tell you our office is representing one of the Poles you got locked up?"

"No. Which one?"

"Dawid," he said, pronouncing the w as a w and not a v. "What a piece of shit that man is. Can't even spell his name properly."

"He's screwed. Has he told you he's wanted back in Poland?"

"Aye. Mentioned something about it," Andy finished his beer and thumped the empty down on the table. "Get it down you, I'll get another couple in."

Quince sank his pint and Andy headed to the bar.

"There we are, Abe. Bottoms up."

"Cheers, Andy." Another long gulp of ale. "So, what about you? How's Nick Mason behaving? He cost me some serious money. Took me to the cleaners with the divorce. Good job I syphoned a few bob away, otherwise I wouldn't have had a pot to piss in."

"He's head honcho since his old man called it a day."

"Let's be fair, he's not in the same league as his old man."

"You got that in one, Abe. He's not really concerned with the practice," gulp of beer, lips wiped dry again. "Pops in for a few hours a day. He's a bit of a useless gambler."

"Speaking of gambling, have you had anything to do with Ted Howe?"

Andy nodded. "He's big mates with Nick. In fact, Nick is down at The Vetch as we speak, quaffing free champers, and probably losing a bundle."

"What do you make of him?"

"Nick, he's not that bad"

"No, not him, Ted Howe, I mean."

"Well, what can I say? He's done well for himself. Got all the trappings of success. Fabulous pile down the Gower coast with views to die for. A property portfolio worth a couple of million. Anyway, he's into everything. How he had planning permission for The Vetch I have no idea, wink, wink," he mimicked the action with the words.

"I don't know what's happening in the city anymore. Planning seems cock-eyed and the shopping centre seems to move around so often even the shopkeepers lose track of their gaffs. Bloody clueless."

"Gaffs?" Andy laughed. "You been watching too many Jason Statham films."

Quince grinned.

"How are you getting on with Cross, by the way?"

"Awkward, Andy. She's ambitions and God help anyone who gets in her way. Anyway, I've cleared the air with her, so I'm back in charge. I think she's on a different planet at the minute."

"In what way?"

"Well, she took the double murder over after a few days. She's distracted and has no interest. So, I'm back as the SIO, and I'm telling you now, I'll detect it."

"I've no doubt you will, Abe. Do you think it's local?"

"Who knows, Andy. All I know is that people are making a fortune out of misery."

"All this people trafficking, Abe, it's big business but it must take some organising?"

"I was talking to the British Embassy in Vietnam earlier. As useful as a peg-leg with bloody woodworm," Quince said. He finished his second pint and held out an empty hand. "Drink up, let's get hammered."

"Your wish is my command, Abe,"

Another couple of pints arrived at the table, courtesy of Quince.

"Fuck tomorrow!" Andy said as a toast.

"I'll drink to that, Andy, cheers."

Quince watched a middle-aged couple walk to the bar, holding hands. He felt a sudden pang of loss. When he married, he thought they'd be like that; holding hands and enjoyed each other's company, but life decided otherwise.

"Abe, I know you said I wouldn't have made a copper, but knowing what you know about me, what do you really reckon?"

The interruption was timely. Quince had stood on the edge of an instant fall into despair and Andy had pulled him back. Good old Andy. "Put it this way, Andy, I reckon if you had joined, you could have blagged your way to the top. They're pro diversity these days."

Andy looked shocked. "What do you mean?"

Quince thumped Andy on his arm. "Andy, I know you're gay. I knew it when we were in school. It made no difference to me then and it makes no difference at all to me now."

Stunned, Andy had always put on a front for his friend, believing he'd walk away if he knew the truth. "Only you could say that, Abe. Anyone else, I'd rip their head off."

45

Ted Howe nursed the hangover from hell.

Pat, like a devoted and loving wife - which she was not - kept supplying him with copious cups of black coffee, together with occasional pairs of Paracetamol tablets.

"My head is hurting, Pat."

"I'm not surprised, the amount you put away yesterday."

"Did I make a fool of myself?"

"Not more than usual," she said acidly. "Nobody really cared. The majority were as pissed as you. I've never seen so many hangers on, especially those council no-marks."

"Not no-marks, Pat, friends in high places, I call them."

"The way you're carrying on, Ted, you'll end up back inside, and where would that leave you?"

"It will never come to that. I've got all bases covered."

"I'd hate to estimate the amount of cash you've paid out over the years to corrupt officials."

"Like I said, I've covered all bases. My hands are clean. Nobody's got anything on me, except you, my darling," he laughed dismissively.

"As if I'd shop you," Pat said, thinking that was exactly what she would like to do.

"Exactly. Look at the life I'm providing for you. You wouldn't want this to go to rat shit, would you?"

"No, of course not." The arrogant idiot believed he was her saviour, that she couldn't survive without him. She was just a stupid housewife, and he was the great conquering hero. What an arsehole, she thought.

"Oh, and talking of no-marks, how are things going with that no-mark fucking son of yours? I notice that he hasn't been around for a while. What's he up to these days?"

"I've no idea, the last I heard from him he was working abroad."

"Doing what? There's no work in him. Like you asked me how much cash I've laid out to corrupt officials, I could ask the same about your useless son."

"You never gave him a chance," Pat seethed, barely able to reign in her temper. "You're the reason he doesn't bother with us."

"Truth be told, if I never hear or see him again, it will be too soon. How you spawned him I have no idea."

Truth was, there were a lot of things Ted had no idea about. "Thanks very much!" Ted had hurt Pat so many times that not much got through her hardened skin these days but that did. Jason was her little boy, and even Ted had no right to say things like that. "You can be a right sod sometimes, Ted, you know that?"

"Look, what more do you want? The restaurant and casino are in your name, you'll be running it. I won't interfere. If I should croak, you'll have it all. You'll be a rich woman in your own right. Let's be fair, you'd be in the gutter somewhere now if not for me. I saved you, remember, from that life. Don't I have the right to tell some home truths now and again?"

"I suppose you are comparing it to the baby you could never give me. And anyway, you wouldn't know the truth if it were a dog and it bit you on your fat arse."

Ted twisted and looked at his rear. He'd put a bit of weight on but that was to be expected at his time of life. How dare she? Ted grabbed Pat by the throat and raised his hand to hit her.

"Go on, I am daring you. You haven't got the guts," Pat goaded.

Ted paused. That was the closest he had ever come to actually hitting her. Hitting women was not Ted Howe's game. He let her go.

"I'm sorry. You know I'd never hit you; I know it doesn't seem like it sometimes, but I love you."

"Funny way of showing it though."

Ted slumped, as if the stopper had been pulled from a hot water bottle. Pat was shocked. She had never seen him like this – upset. It must be the booze.

"I'm going to the study. I've got a few calls to make."

Pat shrugged. "Well, I'm off to the restaurant, to make sure that everything's running smooth after yesterday's celebrations."

***

Quince, even though he'd had one over the odds with his mate Andy the night before, was feeling optimistic, as he gave the morning briefing to the troops. Quince never let alcohol interfere with his work, period. He'd been in a few scrapes when in beer, but they were always confined to outside work.

"Well, team, I've no doubt that you've all had a browse through the actions for today, so you'll know that we had a call from a retired Navy Captain, Lewis Gardener last night, who may very well have seen the vessel that transported the four Vietnamese lads to our shores. He's given us a rough description of a catamaran that was anchored off Burry Port, and he saw a dingy making its way to the shore. Now the catamaran, according to the captain, had no sails, suffice to say it was a motorised gin palace. Bearing in mind that the investigation has hit a brick wall, I've decided that we'll put all our efforts into tracing the catamaran, unless something else more concrete transpires. George, you and Kevin get stuck into the captain. By the sounds of things, he'll take you to the exact location. The rest of you split up into pairs and visit any marinas or other sites where this catamaran could be moored. If anyone does come upon one of a similar description, get right back to Clive, with location etc. Don't make any enquiries, just sit on it. The first place I want checked is our own marina, however my gut instinct tells me that they haven't moored it there. Any questions?"

"Boss, do you think these traffickers would be dull enough to keep carrying on, even after these two deaths?"

"George, you and the team have read all the information on these scumbags, the routes, the millions they are making. They don't give two shits about any of these poor sods dying in transit, they treat them like garbage. So, a few of them die, they've had their cash up front, it means nothing to them. Look at the Polish blokes we just locked up, and the conditions they held those poor fuckers in. Oh, they'll be at it again, there's no doubt about that, I'll put money on it. By the way, George, don't forget your life jackets, and don't spew in front of the captain. Now chop-chop, all of you, let's get cracking."

No sooner had Quince finished the briefing when his mobile rang. He looked at the caller ID, it was Cross.

"Morning, Ma'am. I thought you'd be in for the briefing this morning. There's been a development. It may be something or nothing, but I've put the team on it, full bore."

"Excellent, Abe. I'm sure that you're doing the right thing."

What the hell would she know? She didn't even ask what was afoot. Cross had no interest whatsoever in the enquiry. Not that it worried him, it was better that she kept out of the way; less seen the better.

"Abe, just to let you know, I'm taking a week off. I've got some personal business to take care of. I've had the OK from the ACC. He's more than happy with you running the enquiry. All he asks is that you brief him daily, either by phone or personally."

"That's no problem, Ma'am. I hope it's nothing serious. If I can help in any way, just give me a bell."

"I don't know whether you're taking the piss or being sincere, Abe?"

Quince grinned. "Look at this innocent face, Ma'am."

"Yeah, right," Cross said, a brief smile appeared and faded just as quickly. "It's something I have to sort myself."

"Will you want any updates on the enquiry, Ma'am?"

"No, Abe. Just keep the ACC in the loop, that's all I ask."

"Of course. See you next week."

The air of confidence and superiority was missing from Cross. Yes, there was something afoot.

46

Pat was busy as a bee as she rushed around organising the restaurant. She wanted nothing to do with the casino, that was Ted's baby.

After sorting the menus and checking the bookings, Pat retired to the office. After the earlier confrontation with Ted, all she could think of was her past, and Jason, her wayward son.

Pat was seventeen when she became pregnant with Jason. The father wanted nothing to do with the child. Pat managed as best she could but struggled to cope. When Jason was a year old, Pat gave him up for adoption. At the time, Pat thought it was for the best, believing that Jason would have a better life. Little did she know that many years later Jason would in fact come looking for her, much to Ted Howe's dismay. But it wasn't the first time Pat had felt forced to give away a child. It hadn't got any easier with Jason. If Ted knew she had given away another child, that would be the end of their marriage. She had too much to lose.

Ted couldn't stand Jason, he once described him as a bloodsucking leech, always on the cadge, for the last five years. Jason was a free spirit, not unlike his father who he had never even met, and whose identity Pat had never revealed.

The trill beeps of the desk phone had Pat reaching for the handset.

"Mrs Howe, there's a lady asking for you, says her name is Norma. She hasn't an appointment. Will you see her?"

"Yes, I'll see her. Please send her through, and we don't want to be disturbed."

Pat got up and opened the office door, and beckoned Norma in, closing the door behind her, then locking it."

The women embraced.

"For God's sake Norma what are you doing here? if Ted finds out, there'll be bloody murders."

"Fuck Ted, look Pat I'm at my wit's end, Ted's blackmailing me, and I've accepted money off him."

"He threatened to hit me this morning. He's never before raised his hand to me, but this morning I thought he was going to throttle me or something. I'm going to have to tell him."

"No. He's holding the pictures over my head, if I don't do as he says, he's going to send them to the Chief Constable. He forced me to have sex with him too."

Pat's face flushed red, the anger building like a steam kettle about to blow. "The bastard."

"I can't sleep, I can't concentrate. I have no idea what I'm going to do. If you tell him, he'll have more to screw me with."

"Then we'll have to stop him, one way or another." The expression on Pat's face scared Norma.

"Don't joke, Pat. When I met him down the Mumbles, if I'd had a gun, I swear to God, I would have topped him there and then."

"So, what can we do about it? He doesn't mind me seeing you, so he says, but he thinks we're lovers," she laughed. "I should have told him the truth, but I guess I enjoyed seeing him squirm and I know he'd use it against me. I'd lose everything."

"Aren't I worth it?" Norma said, sounding hurt.

Pat pulled her into an embrace. "Of course you are, but I never told him about you because I was only thirteen when I had you. Can you imagine how scared I was? I was just a kid."

"No, I can't imagine. It must have been tough. What about my father?"

"You really don't want to know. Just leave it, please."

Being Pat's daughter would be a black mark as far as the police was concerned – Ted was not a shining example of decency. But her father's identity would make thing very awkward indeed. She pulled away and turned to look out the window. "Well, Ted wants me at the party on Wednesday, no doubt to mingle with his cronies, probably wants me to get the dirty on them so he can probably blackmail them for his own good."

"Sound like him, look for the time being do as he says, just play along with him, in fact nothing's changed as far as we are concerned, we'll carry on as normal."

"Norma, I don't think you understand, this is my career, my life we're talking about, I can't go on like this, we've got to get the memory cards with the photos, where would he keep them?"

"God knows Norma, he's got a safe at home, probably got a safe deposit box, who knows?"

"Look, I've taken a week off to try and sort this shit out, so you've got to find those memory cards."

"I'll try my best, love. Now you've got to go, just in case he decides to call in. Mind you, the state he was in this morning, I doubt it very much."

"Please be careful, if anything happens to you, it will break my heart. I've lived my whole life wishing I could find you. Now I have, I don't want to lose you."

"It'll all work out in the end, you'll see," Pat smiled."

They embraced, Norma kissed and Pat on the cheek and left the restaurant.

Pat was so pleased that Norma had called in out of the blue, however, an hour later she had a surprise that would make her day even more memorable.

There was a knock on the office door.

"Come in, it's not locked."

"Hello, mum, long time no see, I see you're doing well for yourself."

Pat looked up, and to her amazement, her son Jason was there, grinning. She didn't know what to say.

"Well, I've never seen you lost for words, mum."

Pat hurried to her son and pulled him to her.

"Bloody hell, Jason, where have you been? It's been ages, I've been worried about you."

"There's no need to be. Look, I'm here, I'm well, what more could you ask for?"

"Oh, it's so good to see you, where have you been? What have you been up to?"

"I've spent the last four or five years travelling around Europe and the Far East."

"Doing what exactly?"

"Working for a Spanish property development company. I suppose you could say I'm a bit of a fixer for them."

"I hope you're not involved in anything illegal Jason?"

Jason laughed. "As if someone in this family being involved in crime would be a first. But, no, mum, you can put your mind at rest on that front. I'm making a cracking living. I've got a fabulous apartment in Malaga, which I use as a base."

"Why haven't you been in touch?"

"You have to ask me that? I see that twat Ted is doing alright for himself. How's he treating you, well I hope?" The last words were loaded with menace.

"You know Ted, he hasn't changed."

"Bet he still thinks I'm a leech, especially after you gave me the twenty grand? Well, fuck him. Just give me your bank details and I'll have the money in your account, quicker than you can say, do you fancy a bit of lunch Jason."

"Lunch sounds good but don't be so silly, the money means nothing to me. I gave you that so you could get a fresh start, and by the looks of you, you've done just that. If only Ted could see you now."

Jason shook his head. "I don't want anything to do with that bastard, he's never accepted me, he always assumed that I wanted to sponge off you both."

"So, what brings you back to Swansea, Jason, is it business or pleasure?"

"A bit of both, truth be told. I've been back a few times since I last saw you, but this time I thought, no I've got to see my mum."

"I'm so glad, Jason. You don't know what this means to me. You've come at the right time. I'm at a bit of a low ebb, but I'll explain everything over lunch."

"Is it Ted, what's the bastard done?"

"Like I say, it's a long story, some of which you may not like to listen to."

"Look, mum, I don't really give a shit about anything really. Nothing surprises me these days, but when I look in your eyes, I can see that you're troubled, and if I can ease them. I'm here for you, no matter how long it takes."

The tears welled in Pat's eyes. Jason put both his arms around her.

"Don't worry, mum, we'll sort it."

47

Quince had already arranged with the ACC Crime to attend a briefing. The ACC had assured Quince that there was no problem, all he wanted was an up-to-date overview on the progress of the investigation.

On his arrival Quince was shown into the ACC's office by his secretary. The ACC sat behind his desk and a young woman sat on a chair off to the left of the desk.

"Good morning, Abe, take a seat, do you fancy a coffee?"

"No thanks, boss. I'm OK."

"Before you bring me up to speed, I'd like to introduce you to Francine."

"Pleased to meet you, Francine."

Francine stood and they shook hands.

"Abe, I know the marina murders are in good hands, and I've every confidence that you'll detect it, I also know that DCI Cross handed you the reigns," the ACC said. "No bad thing in my opinion. So let me explain why Francine is here. Perhaps you'd like to bring Abe up to speed Francine?"

"No problem, boss. I've been working undercover operations for many years Inspector. My current assignment is to get the goods on an individual by the name of Ted Howe, who I believe may be a friend of yours?"

"Ah Ted. A friend? I don't think so. Call him more of an acquaintance. I put him away for a five stretch a few years ago, but a friend... I don't fucking think so."

Francine smiled. "Well, you seemed pretty cosy with him a few days ago in Morgan's?"

Now Quince smiled. "More of a coincidence. I normally wouldn't give the guy the time of day. So, obviously you were there and I'm sure you saw everything?"

"And a little bit more I can assure you," Francine nodded.

"Perhaps you can explain, Francine. Let's not beat about the bush. Then we can move this forward."

"Ted Howe is being targeted by the National Crime Squad. Information has come to light that he's involved in a money laundering operation and dealing in fake art sales throughout the UK. He's recently opened a restaurant and casino in Swansea, which we understand he's going to use to up the money laundering side of the business. Howe has put the business in his wife's name, but it's only a front."

"So, who's your informant?"

"Obviously, I can't divulge that. My brief is to get close to Howe and see how the land lies."

"And how exactly are you doing that?"

"I'm managing the casino security for him… you know, keeping an eye on the dealers, that sort of thing. I had an interview with him a few months ago and got the job. We opened last night. He was pissed. It was a good job his Mrs was looking after him."

"Pat? She's stuck to him like shit to a blanket."

"What do you think of Pat?"

Quince shrugged. "She's OK. I suppose you could call her a modern-day gangster's moll."

"I think she's a little bit more than that. The night you met Howe in Morgan's, what was your take on all that. Do you think it was a coincidence?"

"What are you getting at?"

"Well, I know that you were joined by DCI Cross. Was that arranged?"

"No, but I know where this is going. Put it this way, I know there's something going on with Cross. This past couple of weeks, her behaviour has been somewhat off the wall. That's why she's handed the marina murders back over to me."

"I've been sticking to Howe like a limpet for months. He's definitely at it, and I'm going to bring him down, you can bet on it. If Cross is involved, so be it. I've got her receiving a package off Howe down at the Mumbles Pier, God knows what was in it but I suspect cash."

This was a shock to Quince. He knew she was up to something, but he would never have suspected Cross to be bent. "This art nonsense, what's in that?"

"Forgeries. He's got a local artist by the name of Chris Richards doing the business for him, the usual crap forging and selling off as originals. Most are going to greedy collectors. They buy a painting and keep it hidden away from all preying eyes. Ted and his gang are making a fortune."

"OK, I get the picture."

"I was also wondering if you know Howe's accountant, a bloke by the name of Theo Stead? I've only recently met him at the casino. He's fiddling the books for Howe. He's got no form and I find him a bit strange and distant."

"Yes, I know Theo. I dealt with a bad assault a few years ago in one of the town's clubs, Theo was a witness, and in fairness a real good one. Anyway, I made a few enquiries about him like you do, found out he liked doing a bit of coke, nothing major, a user but nothing regarding dealing."

"Good to now, I'll bear it in mind."

The ACC held up his hand to stop the conversation. "OK, Abe, now let's get back to DCI Cross. She's off for a week, so she can go on the back burner, for now. So, what's the way forward Francine?"

"Howe is holding a charity party at their house down on the Gower tomorrow. I've been invited. I'll keep you in the loop. I just want to see who turns up and see if I can put two and two together."

"I've got no problem with that Francine," Quince said. "Apart from a tenuous connection with my boss, I don't see how this will hinder my enquiries. I knew there was something up with the DCI, and knowing now that Howe is involved, God knows where it will all end."

"And you didn't tell me?" the ACC said with a hard edge.

Quince shrugged. "What did I have to tell you? That I suspected my boss, the woman who got my job, was up to something I had no clue about? I can see that being taken seriously."

Now the ACC shrugged. "Fair point."

"Are you working alone, because I don't want my team stepping on your toes," Quince said to Francine.

"Yes, I'm flying solo on this one. I just meet my handler once a week for a de-brief."

"OK, both," the ACC said. "I take it now that we're singing off the same hymn sheet here, and let's hope that we get a result on both fronts."

"I'll stick with the double murder enquiry and give Francine a free run. Perhaps Howe can be put in the frame for people smuggling, now that would be a bonus," he laughed.

"If I think anything I glean may overlap into your enquiry, you'll be the first to know, Inspector."

"Call me Abe. I'm sure our paths will cross in the future, Francine," Quince smiled. "You just keep safe."

48

The sun had burned a haze onto the road as Norma Cross drove along the coast towards the Howe's house on the Gower. It was late afternoon, but the heat had only just begun to ease. Even without the heat, Norma would have been sweating. By accepting the money off Howe, Cross knew that the line had been traversed and from now on things would become very tricky. The only thing that was keeping Cross on an even keel was her need to keep her mother, Pat safe. Cross was resigned that Pat would never leave Howe, and that was a fact. So, somehow, she had to find a way to get Ted Howe out of pat's life without costing Pat everything she had.

The house was enormous, not quite a sprawling Southfork ranch type of spread but clearly the architect had been a fan of Dallas and designed a half-size version for Ted. Cross guessed it was worth millions, especially being situated on some of the most desirable real estate in south Wales. A balcony on the front elevation boasted views of Three Cliffs Bay to the east and a partial view of Worm's Head to the west.

As she pulled up at a stone gate pillar, a camera moved to track the car as the wrought iron gates parted slowly on runners buried in the stone driveway. She rumbled along the cobbles for almost a hundred metres before pulling up outside the portico. A young man dressed in a cheap and ill-fitting black uniform opened her door and held out his hand for the keys. Norma Cross dropped the keys into his small hand and smiled nervously before heading in through the tall double doors that were open into a cavernous marble hallway decorated by paintings and sculptures she had only seen in art galleries. Dressed in a black pants suit with a white, silk blouse, Norma felt as false as the impression Ted was trying to make with his property and art collection.

"Good afternoon, Norma."

She spun to see a grinning Ted Howe standing behind one of the large doors. Ted had slicked back his hair with gel and wore a powder-blue golf sweater over a matching pair of slacks and loafers. He held two glasses of champagne and offered one to her.

"I'm glad you could make it. Have you got the information for me?"

"You're a piece of work, Ted. How Pat lives with you is beyond me."

Cross handed Howe an envelope.

"Here, but that's the last."

"Now Norma, that's not the way it works, you know that. As for Pat leaving, look around," he waved a hand around the hall. "Would you give this all up for a skank, bent copper who won't have a career or a pot to piss in. Wait until you see the rest of it. Who knows, we may be able to have an hour in the sauna together, what do you reckon?"

Cross didn't reply but swallowed back the taste of vomit in her mouth as she thought of Ted Howe touching her again. She followed as Howe escorted her into a capacious lounge with several large picture windows facing west. The sun had already moved into view, on its decent towards the horizon and Cross could see the attraction of the location, even if she detested Ted's taste.

"Pat is out on the patio, mingling with guests. I'll be introducing you to a few of my business associates during the afternoon."

Cross knew that the situation was getting more dire by the minute, and it was obvious what Howe had in mind. She made her way out on to where Pat was playing host. A waitresses offered her a glass of Buck's Fizz. Cross needed something to ease her tension. She downed the glass and snatched another before the waitress could move on.

Pat waved and smiled and excused herself from a middle-aged couple dressed in designer labels and dripping in gold chains. On this occasion there was no hugging, just a polite peck on the cheek.

"I'm so glad you've come, Norma. I'm at my wits end, there's so much going on today. It's overwhelming me."

"I'm only here because of that bastard in there. He's playing me like a fiddle, God knows where this is all going to end."

"Just go along with him for now. It'll sort itself out, I promise you." She stopped talking as she saw Ted approach.

"Ladies. I take it all is well and you're enjoying the Champers? I hope you haven't been running me down," he said, faking a pout.

"Not at all darling."

"Norma, there's someone I'd like you to meet, if you're not too busy with Pat?"

"No, not a problem," Cross lied.

She followed Howe through another pair of enormous doors into a snooker room.

"Norma, this is my casino head of security Fran. Fran, this is DCI Norma Cross. She works from Swansea Central. I thought maybe the two of you could chew the fat for half an hour, you know, a few security tips and all that. I'll see you both later."

Francine wore a black dress that Norma had seen on a rack in Next but it suited Fran far better than it would have her. Fran looked smart and business-like but not really a part of the crowd. Her glass of Champagne had not been sipped.

"Ted doesn't let the grass grow under his feet does he," Fran said. "How long have you known him?"

"Not long," Cross said through gritted teeth. "I met him in a charity do a few months ago. He invited me to this today and that's about it."

"Well, like he said, he's brought me up to speed with your relationship."

"There is no relationship. And let me give you a bit of advice, keep your distance. He's bad news."

"I'll bear that in mind, but we both know why we're here. I'm head of security at the casino and I'll be hiring and firing. Ted told me that you could help with background checks and all that kind of thing. You never know who you're employing, especially in the gambling game."

"I don't think so, Fran. I can't help you."

"I've been around the block a bit," Francine said. "I've worked in casinos all over the world and know how things work between local cops and casino owners. It's just business."

"I don't know what you're talking about. This is Swansea, not Monte Carlo."

"Don't be so naïve, Norma. You're, a senior police officer, here on a Wednesday afternoon, rubbing shoulders with a casino boss. It doesn't take a brain surgeon to know what's going on does it?"

"I think you've got me wrong."

"Like I say, I've been around a bit, and I've seen it in every casino I've ever worked. A little cooperation keeps things nicely oiled."

Cross didn't like the way this was going. Had Ted got Fran to wear a wire to dig an even deeper hole for her? "I don't know what he's told you, but whatever it is, it's a pack of lies."

"So, what exactly are you doing here?"

"I'm wondering that too. He's a scheming, conniving clown. He makes my skin crawl."

Pat broke the tension as she shouted from the doorway. "Here you both are. Ted said you were in here. Come on, you're missing the fun. The auction is in half an hour." Pat took her arm and led Cross away from Francine. "Can I have a quiet word?" She whispered.

"Of, course."

"Before Ted comes sniffing, there's something I've got to tell you."

They walked back out to a quiet corner of the patio. At least thirty couples were now enjoying the evening, chatting loudly over the sound of eighties pop music playing through discreet speakers built into the low patio wall.

"I've been meaning to tell you for ages. I know this might come as a bit of a shock but I've got a grown-up son too. You have a half-brother. His name is Jason. I hadn't seen him for a while, but he turned up yesterday." Pat smiled but it was a hopeful smile – unsure of Norma's reaction.

"I didn't think you and Ted had any kids."

"We haven't. I had Jason when I was seventeen. I gave him up for adoption."

"So, what's the problem? I don't care. It's in the past. You were young, I can understand that. Does Ted know about Jason?"

"Oh, he knows alright. Jason found me when he was old enough. Ted can't stand him, thinks he's a scrounger and is only out for what he can get. But he's a good boy. I think you'll like him." Now Pat's smile was more assured.

"Is he here?"

"No. I saw him at the restaurant yesterday, not long after you left. We had lunch together."

"What does he do for a living, Pat?"

"A few years ago, I gave him some cash to help set him up and he left. He had to get away from Ted. Ted was glad to see the back of him."

"What's he doing back here?"

Pat shrugged. "Said he's here to see me before he goes back to Malaga in a few days."

"So, you've got us both now. Why don't you just dump Ted?"

"I can't, Norma, I'm sorry. But that's just the way it is. I've invited Jason today. I don't know what Ted will say when he sees him, but I wanted you to know before he arrives. Ted will probably go nuts."

49

As far as Ted Howe was concerned the day had gone well. A large amount of money had been raised for local charities. It was Howe's way of making himself appear respectable. The only hiccup was that Pat's son Jason had turned up unannounced, and a few harsh words had been exchanged between them both. A timely intervention by Pat had smoothed things over. At least temporarily.

All the guests had left by early evening, leaving just the three of them and Pat thought she could make use of the time to clear the air. It would have to be managed carefully. Both Ted and Jason were liable to flying off the handle when together, but something had to be done.

They sat in the lounge. Pat had ensured both men were far enough away from each other to prevent any physical altercation.

"So, what are you up to these days, Jason? Your mother tells me that you're actually doing a bit of work over in Spain?"

"I'm getting by, no thanks to you. You're still at it I see."

"I do a bit of business here and there. The casino is going to be a winner."

Jason nodded. "I know what you're into. You don't go from clink to this without greasing a few palms."

Howe shrugged and nodded his head in agreement. It was true. He saw nothing wrong in that. It was how the world worked. "Think what you like, but I've never lived off my mother."

"That's not true though, is it Ted? You had the family business. You're not the self-made man you like everyone to think you are."

"Will you two please stop all this bickering, I've had enough," Pat said. "I'm at the end of my tether with you. I'm off to bed. Jason, I've sorted your room. You'll be staying the night?"

"Yes, mum."

"Is it safe to leave you together?"

"Don't worry about us, it's only a bit of banter," Jason said. "We're used to it, aren't we Ted?"

Ted nodded. "Anything to keep the peace."

"Well, you both make sure you keep it civil. I'll see you both in the morning."

Ted kept a fixed smile until Pat closed the door behind her. "OK. Why are you here after all this time?"

"I know the score."

"What score?"

"Mum's filled me in on your business. She tells me you're into art these days. I see you've got some nice paintings…Impressionists? Never saw you as an art collector, Ted."

"Now I can afford it, I like to buy the odd piece. It's an investment I can enjoy."

Jason stood and walked to a large colourful landscape and peered closely at the signature. "Cezanne?" He whistled – impressed. "Is the paint dry?"

Ted barked, "What do you mean?"

"I had a drink or two with your artist friend. He can't hold his drink. But he's a cracking painter, I'll say that for him."

"What are you on about, you little shite?"

Jason wanted Ted to know he had the inside line on his forging number but didn't want to push it, just yet. "I know for a fact that mum has had a gutful of you, the way you've been treating her lately."

"I've no idea what you're on about."

Ted rose and poured himself a tumbler of whiskey.

"Did you actually have my mother by the throat, Ted?"

Howe said nothing.

"Guilty by silence, I would say. But mum has told me everything."

"What has she told you?"

"You were going to hit her after giving her a tongue lashing about me. She said you didn't go the distance and follow through and just skulked off to the study with your hangover."

"I didn't hurt her and it's nothing to do with you."

"You lay a hand on her again and it'll have everything to do with me. I'm not the kid you used to push around anymore."

"Listen now, tread carefully."

"Is that a threat, Ted? You may have scared me a few years ago, but today, truth be told I don't care about you. You're a blackmailing forger. But I do care about my mother."

"She's been cheating on me, you imbecile."

"You really are thick, aren't you? She's not cheating on you."

"You have no idea what you're talking about."

"Even if she was, could you really blame her?"

"Blame her? I took her in when she had nothing. She couldn't even keep you."

Ted could see he had hit a nerve.

"Ted, I've been back a few days, and I've a good idea what you're up to, so I've got a proposition for you."

"Here goes, what sort of proposition?"

"You never, ever lay another hand on my mother. If you do, you will suffer the consequences. Secondly, you cut me in. All I'm asking is a few grand in the old skyrocket each month. What do you say?"

"Are you demented or what? You must be having a laugh. Look at you, a real mammy's boy," Ted spat. "You can get stuffed. You'll get nothing off me."

"Ted, if truth be told, we are not unalike in many ways, the only difference being I don't mind dishing out a bit of pain these days?"

Ted laughed. "Are you threatening me?"

"Take it whichever way you like. I'm off to bed. Have a little think about our chat and let me now in the morning."

"The first day you came back into your mother's life, I couldn't stand you. You've done nothing to change my mind. If you think you can threaten me, you're badly mistaken. Look around you, this is what success gets you. I've only got to say the word, and you'll end up in a ditch somewhere."

"Ted, I know all about you. Property magnate, a bit of money laundering, fake art, you're no bloody Goodfella. But I think you've underestimate me. I'm connected both here and abroad. I've only got to say the word too."

"You're bluffing?"

"There's only one way to find out. I suggest you sleep on it. All I'm asking is my mother's happiness, and a few grand as a way of impressing the need to stick to keeping her happy. Sleep on it."

50

"Morning, Abe. Just to bring you up to speed on my meeting with Dawid. He's hard work. The usual crap from him, but I can see he's shitting himself. He doesn't want to be deported back to Poland after he's done his time. He comes over all hard, but I can read him like a book."

"Was he forthcoming?"

"Not really. He's going to plead, I think. I tried to wheedle information out of him, you know, like if he knew anyone local who may be involved in smuggling in these illegals."

"And does he?"

"I don't think so, Abe. Him and his thugs just trawl the streets. He can give chapter and verse about routes to the UK, but as for smuggling them in, I don't think so."

"So, top and bottom Andy, he was no use at all, is that what you're saying?"

"I think he's looking for a deal, Abe."

"Well, when you visit him next, tell him that he isn't having one off me, he can rot, as far as I'm concerned." Quince squeezed his phone, frustrated at the news.

So, how's it going your end, Abe? Are you anywhere nearer to clearing it up? It's getting on a bit now."

"Very slow, Andy. Probably the most frustrating murder enquiry I've ever been involved in."

"I'm sure you'll crack it, Abe. I'll keep chipping away at Dawid. You never know, he may open up nearer his trial date. If he does, perhaps you could have a word in the CPS's ear and work something."

"Well, if he does, Andy, I'll want names, the whole nine yards."

"So, what's your next move Abe? I noticed you haven't locked anyone up since Dawid and his crew."

"Like I say, we're really struggling at the minute, but keep in touch and we'll have a couple of sherbets one evening."

As soon as Quince ended the call, he headed into the Incident room and conferred with Clive Purcell for an update. He hoped something positive had developed.

"How's it going, Clive, has anything interesting come in?"

"Not really, boss, mind you, Captain Birdseye has been a great help in trying to locate the cat."

"In what respect?"

"He's been sailing in his yacht, searching local coves and possible places where the cat could be moored."

"That's not a bad thing I suppose?"

"The team have also been sending him pictures of any catamarans that might fit the bill, but we've had no luck at the minute."

Quince's mobile rang.

"Boss, it's George. I'm down the Porthcawl marina with Connor. It looks like we've found the cat. I've forwarded a few pictures to Lewis Gardener, he's had a look at them, he's hundred per cent sure it's the one, even down to the dingy at the back."

"Excellent, George. Have you made any enquiries?"

"No, boss, thought it would be best to play it low key and check with you first."

"Excellent. Just keep an eye on it for now. What's the name of the boat?"

"The Dolphin, boss."

"OK. I'll start the ball rolling this end. We've got to find out who owns it and then sort out some surveillance. It might move again."

Quince ended the call and dialled the office of the ACC.

"It looks like we may have located the catamaran that may have been involved in the trafficking murders. It's called The Dolphin."

"Excellent news, Abe, so where is it?"

"It's moored at the Porthcawl marina. It's been positively identified, and two of the boys are keeping an eye on it."

"So, what's your next move, Abe?"

"I think the priority is to keep it under surveillance, boss, but for how long I have no idea."

"OK. I know this has been a problem enquiry, and I guess you want all the necessary authorities, tracking, audio, the works?"

"Yes please."

"Abe, you've got it. I'll sort it, just keep me updated at each stage. If things get out of hand, I'll take the flack. You and the team just put it to bed."

"I'm much obliged, boss."

Clive was still looking at Quince, waiting for the next move.

"Clive, I want to know who owns the cat. Can you action it out for me please?"

"Already sorted, boss, The Dolphin is actually owned by a bloke by the name of Roy Percival Evans."

"The only Roy Percival Evans I know was a local brief, but he died a few years ago. He was in his sixties at the time. I knew him well. He was a good brief. He left a widow. I think her name was Violet. Anyway, what the hell is going on here, Clive?"

Clive shrugged his shoulders and raised his eyebrows. "Well, that's who owns it, boss."

"OK, action that enquiry to me, and call the team back. George and Connor can keep an eyeball on the cat until the surveillance team are on the ground."

"Leave it to me."

***

Next was a call to Charlie. He was a tech genius and had access to the support technology available to the force. Charlie answered after the third attempt. "Charlie? Abe Quince here. Are you and the team free for the foreseeable future?"

"Don't tell me, you've got a lead on the murders?"

"Well, it looks promising, Charlie. There's a catamaran called The Dolphin, which is at present moored at the Porthcawl marina. We've got a reliable witness, who has identified it as being present off Burry Port during the early hours before the bodies were dumped."

"So, what do you want, Abe?"

"I want the works, Charlie. The ACC has signed all the authorities, so do what you like."

"Your wish is our command, Abe. Leave it with me. I'll have the team on plot within the hour. You'll be able to hear most of the conversations, and if she's on the move you'll be able to track it. I suppose you'll want to monitor it from the station there?"

"Yes, Charlie, if it's no problem?"

"I'll get one of the boys straight to you with the gear. He can set it all up for you."

"Cracking, Charlie. I don't know how long it will last though."

"Not a problem, what with drone technology, manpower has been reduced greatly, but it'll be a walk in the park. What's the name of the op for my requisition order?"

"Operation Finale."

"Very apt, Abe."

51

The Incident room was buzzing with activity. After three weeks to the day since the two Vietnamese boys had been found, the team were now speaking in positive tones. However, Quince had an old head on his shoulders, he knew that leads in murders could fizzle out rapidly.

"OK, Ladies and gents, I've got to thank you all for the effort that you've put in on this enquiry during the last three weeks. I know your families have taken the brunt. It's not easy being married or having a relationship with a dedicated detective, which you all are. So, thanks! As you are all aware, it appears that we have located the catamaran called The Dolphin. That may or may not have been involved in the trafficking of these poor lads. Our witness, retired Captain Lewis Gardener has positively identified it and I have no reason to doubt his powers of observation and recall at this stage. We have a surveillance team keeping observations on the catamaran moored at the Porthcawl marina. The team has already topped and tailed it with listening devices and a GPS tracker, in fact I believe it's now a floating GCHQ." The detectives laughed before Quince handed over the briefing. "Now, Clive has a few things to add."

"I've made some discreet enquiries, and The Dolphin ordinarily has a mooring birth at our marina here in Swansea. But, we've been told it's been having maintenance carried out at Porthcawl. As you may know, these catamarans, yachts and small boats are in and out like yo-yos and keeping track on them is nigh on impossible, so God knows where The Dolphin has been in the last four weeks. At the minute, there has been no movement near the cat. What the boss has decided to do today is that we concentrate all our resources down at our marina, and yacht club. By doing this, we may give the impression that the marina is the answer to the murders, it's a long shot. However, our main priority is The Dolphin, because we believe that's where the answers lie. 'Operation Finale' is the code word, and it will be co-ordinated from the Incident Room. The Dolphin is registered to one Roy Percival Evans, a retired local solicitor. From what the boss says,

Evans is dead but survived by his widow. The boss will interview Mrs Evans to see if she can throw some light on who is using The Dolphin, or if it's been sold on. Has anybody got any questions? If not, let's all get cracking."

Quince stepped forward again. "Before you all go, I must emphasise that not a word of this operation is to be uttered to anyone. This is to be confined to this room. So, please no loose lips, not even to your loved ones or uniform colleagues. I don't care if the Chief Constable questions you. If he does, refer him to me. If this operation comes to fruition, it will be a remarkable achievement."

***

Quince and Fiona made their way to the home of the late Roy Percival Evans.

Fiona drove as Quince read through his notes.

"I take it you know the family then, boss?"

"Yup. I first met Roy Evans when I was a young bobby on the beat. It was the first time I'd actually given evidence. I'd nicked a scrote for shoplifting. I thought it was going to be pretty straight forward case and that he'd plead guilty, how wrong I was."

"Don't tell me, he was the bloke's solicitor, and he gave you a hard time."

"Well not so much a hard time. Roy tried his best for the lad, but back in the day not many walked, no matter how good your brief was."

"Was he a good brief, boss?"

"Oh yes, without a shadow of a doubt. He'd built up a cracking practice in town and made a lot of money. He was very pro police too, and as in my case, if he were ever defending and the bobby in the case was a newbie, he'd put them through the ringer, nothing too overbearing though, and he knew when to pull back. I think it was his way of hardening us up for the future. I've known a few solicitors like that. Salt of the earth."

"He sounded half tidy, boss. When did he pass away?"

"It's a few years ago now. I went to his funeral. There was quite a big police presence, he was that well respected."

"What about family?"

"I met his wife Violet a few times in social functions. They never had children. She was a few years younger than him."

"So, surely his Mrs isn't using the cat?"

"I wouldn't think so, Fiona, perhaps she's flogged it to someone?"

It only took Fiona fifteen minutes to reach the home of Mrs Evans on a small but well-kept estate in Sketty.

A bungalow, the red roof tiles looked new, and the white render looked fresh from the paint pot. The small front garden was laid to lawn and the grass seemed un unnatural green. Quince thought it might be Astroturf but as he got closer, he could see it was just very well cared for grass.

Fiona rang the bell, and the door was answered by Violet Evans. She had shrunk since the last time Quince had seen her. He remembered her as a slim, smiling, vibrant woman. Confident, attractive and comfortable with her life. Now she looked as if someone had pulled the air stopper out of her, and she was slowly deflating like a redundant Lilo.

"Good morning, Mrs Evans I presume?" Fiona said. Quince stood behind, just out of sight.

"Yes, that's correct, how can I help you?"

Quince stepped towards the door.

"I'm DC Fiona Short, and this is…"

"There's no need to introduce this gentleman," she smiled. "How are you, Mr Quince? It's been a few years since we last met."

"It has, Mrs Evans, but that was under sadder circumstances."

"Come on in, both of you. It must be something very important for you to be calling on me. I don't get many visitors these days. When Roy was alive it was like a circus here. Would you both like a cup of tea?"

"No, don't trouble yourself, Mrs Evans."

"Roy always spoke fondly of you, Mr Quince."

"Call me Abe. Yes, Roy was a fine man and very well respected by the police in Swansea."

"He was a workaholic and it killed him in the end."

"I thought he retired, Mrs Evans?"

"That was a bit of a joke, Abe. He sold his practice but couldn't leave it alone. He was doing a fair amount of consulting work. In fact, he was even busier than when actually practicing."

"Mrs Evans, the reason we've called is about Roy's catamaran, The Dolphin."

"What about it, Abe?"

"What can you tell us about it?" Fiona asked.

"Oh, I called it his mid-life crisis purchase. He bought it to cruise the oceans in his retirement. Fat chance, I used to tell him. He'd get seasick in a jacuzzi."

"Did he ever sail The Dolphin?"

"Sail it?" she laughed. "No, Roy never sailed it. As far as I know, he birthed it down at the marina, and I know this sounds daft, but I've never actually seen it."

"Well, as far as we know, Roy still owns it, Mrs Evans."

"I don't know about that. I was always under the impression that he'd sold it on. Or, knowing Roy, given it away."

"Have you any documentation for the boat?"

"No, nothing at all. After Roy died there were so many papers here for various things. I got rid of the majority of it. Just holding on to a few that were required. So, as far as The Dolphin is concerned, it means nothing to me. Never did."

"What about close friends and associates? Would any of them have access to The Dolphin?"

"It's quite possible, Abe. Roy had so many friends. Perhaps the firm can help you? Anyway, what's this all about? It must be very important for a senior officer like you to be asking questions."

"It's a major fraud enquiry regarding yachts being stolen from the UK and then sold abroad," Quince lied. "There are hundreds of boats named The Dolphin, it just so happens that Roy's has been birthed at the marina. All we need to know is who's now in possession of it. It could be sailing in The Aegean as we speak."

"Lucky them, Abe, I say." She smiled.

"You mentioned the firm earlier? I take it you're talking about, R.P. Evans Solicitors?"

"Yes. They kept Roy's name. He was proud of that. I think it was all in the negotiations when he sold out."

"That I can understand. Roy had a great reputation. They would have been fools not to keep the name."

"Look, Abe, the more I think about the firm, it could very well be that The Dolphin was part of the sale. It's just a thought. I know that Roy paid a pretty penny for it, and he was a shrewd old fox."

"That's worth thinking about, Mrs Evans. I'll sort that end out. It's been a pleasure having a chat. We'll leave you in peace now, and please look after yourself."

"I certainly will, Abe, and you make sure you look after this young lady as well."

"Always, Mrs Evans," Abe smiled and winked at Fiona. "Have no fear about that."

52

"OK, team, just to bring you all up to date. Fiona and I have interviewed Mrs Evans regarding The Dolphin, and she's intimated that her husband was suffering a bit of a mid-life crisis when he purchased it, and in fact never set foot on it. As far as she's concerned, it's moored down at the marina. Mrs Evans hasn't got any documentation for it, so we are no further on as to who owns it, or who has access to it. One thing she did mention was that it could have been part of the deal when he sold his law practice, R.P. Evans Solicitors, which as you all probably know is local."

George raised a hand and spoke. "Boss, your mate Andy Stokes works for a local solicitor, perhaps he can do a bit of sniffing around for us? He may be able to find out if the cat was being used by the firm."

"No, George, nobody, and I mean nobody is to know about us looking into The Dolphin, and that also means Andy. You've all been down to the marina most of the day, what's the consensus amongst our sea faring friends?"

Clive's turn to chip in. "From what the team are saying, boss, the majority down at the marina don't think the answer lies locally, and they should know. Mind you, nothing's come out about The Dolphin."

"Clive, is there no control over these boats? I always thought they had to plot their course and all that shit."

"So did I, boss, until this enquiry. Seems there's not enough resources to deal with it all. You could sail out of the marina tonight, and nobody would know any different, and it's probably the same from any marina. The Dolphin could be just one of them, specifically being used as and when needed. Most of the time it could just be moored at any marina, like now at Porthcawl. Nobody really gives a monkey's until the shit hits the fan. Even with this enquiry, most of the agencies I've liaised with have downed tools, however I've an idea that If the Dolphin comes up trumps, they'll all want a piece of the action."

"Probably, Clive. I think the surveillance team is our only hope of pushing this on. I know it may be a long job, but I don' t want anyone knowing about this operation, not even other agencies. The first they'll be aware of it is at the last minute, have you got that?"

***

"It's me," the voice declared over the phone. "The marina here has been swarming all day with murder squad detectives. Looks like they're concentrating here in Swansea, sort of putting all their eggs in one basket."

"That'll suit us down to the ground. I've arranged a pickup for tomorrow. It was supposed to be eight, but now it's down to six, courtesy of a slight accident in transit coming across France."

"What about the money?"

"Keep your hair on, we'll get our full share."

"So, what's the plan?"

"The cat is fuelled, and the boys are ready for the off first thing in the morning."

"Have you any idea where you'll land them?"

"Not at the minute. I'll play it by ear, and keep you informed. And for God sake don't panic. You'd swear you were taking all the risks. I'll pop down the marina later, and get things squared off on the cat. The next time we speak will probably be late tomorrow."

"Sound, but let's not have a repeat of the last fuck up."

***

It was a time often described as dusk, but all Quince knew was it was getting darker, and the blue sky had turned red. 'Red sky at night, shepherd's delight.' It would be a nice day tomorrow.

Juliet-one-zero broke radio silence. "Stand-by, stand-by. Black Porsche Carrera with personalised number plate has just pulled up and parked by the marina. An ICI male has alighted and is making his way towards the moorings. I've got the eyeball."

Juliet-one-one wanted more. "Any description?"

"Juliet-one-zero here. Male at six feet plus. Dark, curly hair with a full beard, wearing a black donkey jacket. He's a big bugger, boss, fair play. I've taken a few snaps of him and the car. He's just boarding The Dolphin."

"Juliet-one-zero to team, the vehicle is registered to a Darryl Hayes, in Porthcawl. He's got form for possession, burglary and ABH, so he looks like a player. As soon as he's off the cat, do the follow and bed him down for the night."

Ten minutes passed. "Juliet 1 zero to all units. Stand-by, stand-by. Target off the cat and making his way back to his vehicle. He's in and it's an off, off, off."

"Juliet-one-one to all units, start doing the business."

The surveillance team was off and running.

"Abe, this is Charlie, are you listening to this?"

"I certainly am, Charlie. There's only me, George, and Clive here. I've sent the rest of the team home."

"Abe, have you heard of this Darryl Hayes? Snowy says he's a big bastard. Wouldn't be at all surprised if he's in charge of the cat. As you can hear, the team are on him, they'll house him for the night and then we'll see what develops tomorrow."

"Great, Charlie."

"You don't need anyone manning the kit all night, Abe. I'll get the feedback and if there's anything out of the ordinary, I'll ring you, how does that sound?"

"I'll be guided by you, Charlie."

"Just authorise the overtime, Abe. I've got a feeling this might pay for my new stereo."

"Stereo, Charlie? Don't think they call them stereo's these days."

"Don't care what others call them, Abe. I know what I mean."

Quince was buoyed as he ended the call.

"Well gents, this could be the start of something big, or it could be a load of bollocks. Hopefully it'll be the former, so let's all get home and get some kip. I reckon tomorrow is going to be a long day."

"Do you think they'd be stupid enough to pull the same stunt, boss?" George asked.

"George, the money's too good not to, my friend. And once they've had a taste, well you know what it's like, it's like a drug to them and they don't care who lives or dies. That's been proved. If this guy Hayes is involved, he'll get his come-uppance, one way or another, guaranteed."

53

It was six in the morning and Hayes was off and running. He was straight into the car and heading towards Porthcawl, stopping as he approached the Dan-y-Graig roundabout, where he pulled into the kerb and picked up two white men, both carrying holdalls. One squashed into the tight rear of the sports car.

The surveillance team followed at a discreet distance. Hayes at no stage carried out any manoeuvres that gave the team reason to suspect he was surveillance conscious.

The Porsche, as expected, ended up at the marina where the OP took over the static surveillance.

All three targets then strolled laughing on to The Dolphin and disappeared out of sight. This made no difference because the cat had already been bugged and within seconds the surveillance team picked up a call made from inside the boat's cabin.

"We're down at the marina, and good to go."

"Are you positive it's all clear?"

"For God sake, how many times have I done this run?"

"Too many, if truth be told, this is the last one, I'm telling you now!"

"Eight times, and how much have we made? I'll tell you, over half a million. If you can cock your nose up at money like that for doing nothing, you're a bigger fucking fool than I thought."

"Where are you landing them this time?"

"Down Llantwit way. It's all sorted, the van will be there around midnight. We'll get them ashore, and the lads will drop them off at the nail bar as arranged. We've got to shove off, so just chill before you have a pull."

Charlie had already rung Quince bringing him up to speed, and he immediately made his way straight to the Incident room and conferred with George and Clive, where they earnestly listened in to the conversation on The Dolphin.

"OK, let's set course for Rosslare. We'll do the usual when we get there, anchor up a couple of miles offshore, do a spot of deep-sea fishing, and then meet up with the French, load the cargo as usual, then fuck off out of it."

"I just hope they don't start cutting up rough."

"There'll be no problem this time, they're all women, so it should be a cake walk. Stick three in each pod and give them some water and a bit of grub. Now, the two of you get up top, and keep your eyes peeled. No phone calls, you got it. In fact, as per usual, give me your mobiles and I'll keep them in the safe."

"Where are we landing them Dar?"

"Off Llantwit Major, but that could be subject to change."

***

"Well lads, it looks like it's going to be a bit quiet for a while. I'd say they've got it off to a fine art. They sound confident that they've got things nailed in place. They must have officials on the take and Hayes sounds like an asshole."

George grinned. He often chuckled at Quince's use of words that had hung over from his past and the distinct differences in American pronunciation of words that Quince often didn't notice himself. "What about the other two, have we any ideas who they are? They must have a bit of form. You don't get involved in this shit as a first timer."

"Charlie's sorting that out, he's had his man download the film to tech to see if they get anything from facial recognition. We'll probably have something around nine, I reckon."

"It'll be a bonus if we can identify them. We can start the ball rolling then on their houses."

"No, George. We'll hold off with all that until we round them up, and I can't see that happening until the early hours. It's now a waiting game. We'll assume there'll be firearms involved, so I'll start the ball rolling to get a firearms team on stand-by."

Quince was now satisfied that The Dolphin was the catamaran that brought the illegals in via Burry Port.

"ACC update time, I think," Quince said as he checked his watch.

As usual, the ACC answered immediately. "Boss, just to let you know that Operation Finale is up and running. The Dolphin has left Porthcawl and is heading for Rosslare to pick up six illegals. It looks like they're going to off load them near Llantwit Major, but the location may very well change. We have ears inside the boat, so the info is from the horse's mouth."

"That's excellent news, Abe. Sounds like his could all be wrapped up by Monday with a bit of luck?"

"If things work out as planned, boss and I reckon that a minimum of five will be nicked, three on The Dolphin and probably two in the van that will collect them when brought to shore. We also know the illegals are all women this time around."

"Is there anything else you need from me, Abe?"

"There's no evidence of firearms, boss, but with this type of job, who knows what's up their sleeve."

"Leave that all to me, and when the time comes, I'll get you the chopper as well."

"I'll have to play it by ear, boss. Whatever is said on The Dolphin is driving this at present and will give me some idea of what strategy to take."

"I'll leave it with you, Abe. And before I go, between you and me, don't worry about Norma, I'm seeing her first thing Monday at HQ. I've got a little job for her, which should keep her out of your hair for a while."

***

"Anything on the facial recognition, Clive?"

"Yes, boss. We've identified them both. Two brothers living locally in Porthcawl. Frankie Noble with previous convictions for Burglary, Possession of cannabis and taking without consent. Never been inside. And Brett Noble, his younger brother by a year with previous convictions for Possession of Amphetamines, Indecent Exposure, and Criminal Deception. He's not done any time either. Last known address in a flat in the Woodlands, Porthcawl."

"This sounds a bit out of their league, boys, but there again, if the money's right who knows what these guys will do. Look, let's not get ahead of ourselves, but I've had a change of heart. Let's pull an action for search warrants on the Noble's flat and Haye's house too. We may not need them once they're arrested, but let's be ready."

George nodded. "When we bring them in for charge, can we add Poor Choice of Music on to the sheet too and Singing whilst

Tone Deaf? They have shit taste in music."

Quince laughed. "I'd love to know who this Hayes is talking to on the phone. Whoever it is seems to be a bit of a fixer but is now getting cold feet. We'll have to be careful how we play this. We have no idea who the fixer is, however, he has access to The Dolphin, and he could be connected to the solicitors, that's if what Mrs Evans says is right. It's obvious Hayes and the Noble brothers are the facilitators, bring illegals in, and there are at least two unidentified who pick the illegals up in a van, which is probably stolen or has false plates. Once we know exactly where they're landing, it's logical to say that the van will not be too far away."

"Who do you reckon injected the two lads with meth, boss?"

"From the little I've heard; I would say Hayes. I think the brothers are just doers. Hayes has them by the nuts, and perhaps we can use that to our advantage. I think we'll be arresting a minimum of six, George. Can you organise the interview and search teams for me? This is all going to depend on what we hear on The Dolphin, in the next few hours, so keep everything crossed."

54

Chris Richards was relaxing on the settee with a G and T when the intercom buzzed a couple of times, Richards didn't rush, he never rushed anything, it was why he was so good at what he did. He let the intercom buzz a few more times before he loped off to check the CCTV monitor. It was Ted Howe. He pressed the button to let him in.

It took just seconds for Howe to trot up the stairs and reach his door.

Howe looked impressed as he took in Richards' apartment for the first time. "Very nice, Chris."

"What are you doing here, Ted? I thought we had an agreement?"

"There's no problem, Chris. I just want to run a job past you that's all."

"And this couldn't be done by phone? Anyway, Ted, you haven't paid me for the last one yet. That's what I wanted to talk with you about on Wednesday, but you were jabbing all day, I couldn't get near you. I thought you were trying to avoid me," Richards returned to his couch and G and T. "So, when am I getting my money?"

Howe followed him into the lounge and sat in an armchair opposite. "I had my hand's full, what with the auction," he smiled. "A few of the masterpieces brought a pretty penny."

Howe fished a thick brown envelope out of his jacket and tossed it onto the coffee table. "There you are, Chris, five grand. I never ever renege on a deal."

"Five grand, you owe me ten times that, and I want it all."

"Fifty K? Let's get serious. We're a team. Like Laurel and Hardy or Cole and Williams."

"I want my money or no deal, do you understand?"

"You'll get all your money when I get it and the next job is done."

"You're a twat, Ted. If I don't get it you can look out."

"Pipe down, will you? Have I ever let you down?"

Richards sighed. "I suppose not, but I've had enough. I'm

knocking it on the head after this one."

"This will be an easy job. Just trust me."

Richards finished his drink and nodded. "OK. But this is the last time, OK?"

Howe smiled and slapped his knee. "Fair enough, whatever you say. So, what about pouring me one of whatever you're drinking?"

55

Quince knew that the operation was going to be a runner, and that he would have to all bases covered. One of his main dilemmas being who should he share the current information with.

"I'm not counting chickens, boss, but I believe that we're on a winner," George had obviously been thinking the same thing. "It's just a matter of time, but there's hardly any talking on the cat. I suppose that will come when they make the pickup, unless they've twigged us."

"I don't think so, but I've been racking my brains, George, about who to update."

"You mean Customs and the rest of them?"

"Yes. You've been out there throughout, so what do you reckon?

"We've had hardly any information from the other agencies. Immigration and every other Tom, Dick and Harry has been piss poor in feeding any scraps to us. If you listen to them, they're so short of manpower they can't cope. It's not a wonder they haven't come up with anything concrete."

Nodding, Quince headed to the coffee pot and poured himself another as he pondered the question. "Well, I've decided, none of this information will be passed to any of them. I know there'll be flack, if it all goes tits up, but I can't take a chance that there are people on the take. If that Hayes gets a sniff, he'll be back to port like a horny sailor and we'll have nothing. No, this stays in-house."

"I've got to agree with you."

"Where's The Dolphin now, George?"

"According to the GPS tracker, halfway across to Rosslare, boss"

"Clive, what's the score with the solicitor? Have we found out who the top man is?"

"Yes, boss. Just had a message as you were filling up your umpteenth cup of Joe. Bloke by the name of Roy A'Hern. He's the senior partner. Doesn't practice anymore though. He was the money man when Evans sold the firm."

"Have we got all his details, home address, that sort of thing?"

"Not exactly had time yet but I was thinking he'd be down to you. Too big a deal to mess this one up."

"Well, I'm convinced more than ever now that someone within that firm is involved, and they probably have access to The Dolphin, but are letting these scrotes use it. We can't rule A'Hern out at the moment from being up to his neck in it either. However, I think it's someone lower down the food chain. When we've got all this scum banged up and bedded down, I'll pay him a visit. The answer will hopefully be found in Haye's mobile."

"That would be nice and convenient."

"Well, they were blabbing enough on the cat to make me think they aren't that smart."

"True."

"Also, action out the interview teams for me, Clive. I reckon a minimum of six teams to start with. If we need anymore, I'll draft them in from division."

"What about search teams?"

"Obviously The Dolphin will be our priority, bearing in mind our two young lads were probably brought in on it. I want Bill and Ted on that with a search team. They can have a Big Adventure," he laughed at his own joke. "I don't care how long they take, but they've got to go through it with a fine-tooth comb. In relation to house, there'll be a minimum of three., Haye's house being the most important, as it looks like he's the main man. There's a fair bit to sort out, Clive, but we must be prepared for any eventuality."

"I've already got Darren and his team from tech on stand-by, they can examine mobiles, computers and any other electronic devices that the search teams take possession of."

"Excellent, Clive. That should be enough to go on with. At least we have plenty of time to organise things. I've got a few things to sort and I'll be in the office. If you have anything significant from The Dolphin, give me a shout."

"I'll let you know straight away, boss."

As Quince turned to leave, he stopped and called to George.

"Can I have a quick word in the office? Bring the marina actions in with you."

George looked concerned. "Will do, boss."

***

"Is there a problem, boss?"

"No, I wouldn't say a problem, George, there's just one thing niggling me."

"What's that?"

"How many yachts, catamarans and vessels moored at the marina are actually capable of making long trips like The Dolphin?"

There was an audible release of air as George realised he wasn't in trouble for something. "Too many to count, boss, They're in and out like yo-yos. You're probably talking in excess of two hundred, that's without visitors from all over mooring overnight and all that."

"So, what's the story about The Dolphin?"

"Well, as far as we know, it hasn't been moored at the marina for over a month, and let's be fair it's been like looking for a needle in a haystack. Once the mooring fees are paid, nobody at the marina really cares. If it weren't for the captain, we'd still be chasing our tails, and we wouldn't have had a clue about The Dolphin."

"What I've noticed throughout this enquiry, is that our seas and oceans are a free for all, and nobody's keeping tabs."

"It's not like there's an ANPR for boats, boss. The authorities take a lot on trust, and as you know most of the maritime arrests are intelligence led. I bet if you told them about this operation, they'd be all over it like a rash."

"That's the problem with it, George, once this is all over, there'll have to be guidelines, most certainly in relation to marinas. I want this knocked on the head over the weekend so there'll be no repeat in South Wales waters."

***

Pat ended a tearful call with Jason and flicked through her contacts for Norma's number. Jason had left the house without saying goodbye and was in Cardiff airport waiting for a flight back to Malaga. He sounded angry but assured her that Ted wouldn't bother her again. She hoped nothing bad had happened between them the previous night. She pressed the hyperlink to connect the call to Norma.

"Hi, Norma, I'm so sorry to bother you on a Saturday, but I'm a bit concerned about my Jason."

"What's the problem? I thought that everything had been sorted."

"He's on his way back to Spain later. He's still very angry with Ted. I just hope that his anger doesn't fester. I don't want him doing something silly."

"I know he and Ted had that bit of a barny, but I thought you said it had cleared the air, that's why Jason spent a few days there with you both?"

"I thought so too," there was a pause as Pat pondered things a while longer. "Anyway, there's nothing I can do, I suppose. Not with him in bloody Malaga."

"Exactly. Just don't go thinking the worse. It'll be OK, I'm sure. Perhaps next time he comes over I'll be able to spend some time with him. He is my half-brother, after all."

"Yes! That would be nice."

"So, how's the restaurant business going?"

"Very well, fully booked today as a matter of fact."

"I'll have to pop in one lunchtime, we can have a natter over lunch."

"I'll make sure Ted's out of the way. Just give me a warning. I don't want him making a scene. He already thinks we're lovers," Pat laughed. "I should put him out of his misery but that would make things really awkward for us all. If he dug into your father, he'd really have some heavy stuff he could use against us."

"So, tell me who he is," Norma felt aggrieved her mother still hadn't confided that information with her. "Don't you think I should be forewarned? Ted's certainly got me on a bit of a leash at the minute, and truth be told I can't see him letting me off it any time soon, so it makes no real bloody difference, even if my dad was Jack the bloody Ripper."

Silence.

"Pat?..."

"Pat, tell me it's not some serial killer, is it?"

Silence.

"Pat?
"No, don't worry. Best you don't know."
"Now I am worried."

56

Quince had the call from George as he was about to tuck into his afternoon sandwich.

"Boss, looks like The Dolphin is on stop about five miles west of Rosslare. Up until now, there's been hardly any conversation of note between the three of them, but now they won't shut up. Looks like they're doing a bit of deep-sea fishing. They've got all the gear on board by the sound of things."

"Deep sea fishing?" Quince scoffed. "Sounds like it's a goer, George. I'll call a briefing for about ten. You make sure the team are all here, and the interview teams are sorted. I'll sort out the firearms and search teams."

***

"Well boys, we'll have a few hours here before those fucking froggies decide to turn up," Darryl Hayes barked to his cronies. "They never turn up on time. I just hope the fishes are biting, we could be here a while."

Brett, who liked to think he was Hayes' number two, stood in the doorway of the galley. Chomping on a Flake chocolate bar, most of which was littering his T-shirt. "I hate this waiting about," he said through a mouthful of the treat.

"Stop grizzling and keep your eyes peeled. The last thing we want is our Froggy or Paddy pals fucking it all up."

"Dar, how many more trips have we got in the tank? After the last debacle, I thought we would have cooled it a bit."

"And what would you and the snorter have done then?"

"He's been wired since the last time. I've had to watch him like a hawk. He's off his tits most of the time."

"Just keep an eye on him, that's all I ask. As long as he does his bit this time around… that's all I'm concerned with. I'm going below. Let me know if and when the others decide to turn up."

"I've got a feeling about this, Brett said."

"Jesus, Frankie, just go with the flow. Not a problem. We'll be home before we know it, and then we'll get you help, you can't go on like this."

"I know that Brett, but I can see those two, they're there in my head."

"Just forget about them. I have. Nobody gives a shit about them."

"I'm telling you now, the quicker we ditch that lunatic the better," Brett nodded towards the galley.

"Cool it! We'll do this run and that'll be it. Just keep an eye out."

"What time are we picking them up?"

"The rendezvous is just after dark, so just chill."

***

"Listen up. At this moment in time, we are running Operation Finale. It began late last night at the marina in Porthcawl. As you all know, we are investigating the double murder of two Vietnamese who were found floating in the Swansea marina." The briefing room was full. Most of the officers he knew but there were some he had never seen before, young, old, experienced and newbie detectives, but they all had to know what they faced. "All you need to know about how they died can be found in the briefing notes. We believe that the two victims, along with two other youths, were trafficked in a catamaran called The Dolphin, via Burry Port. The Dolphin is now anchored offshore west of Rosslare. There are three IC1 males on the cat, again all their details are in the briefing notes.

"The Dolphin has been bugged as best we can in the time we had available to do it, and there's a GPS tracker on board. It's not perfect but better than nothing. What we've gleaned so far is that they are due to pick up six illegal females from a French boat, and then drop them off the coast of Llantwit Major, however the location could be changed at the drop of a hat. From what we've heard, there is no doubt Darryl Hayes is the main man, together with the brothers Grimm, Brett and Frank or Frankie Noble. However, from what we've heard so far, Frankie seems to be on the edge, possibly as a result of the murders. The plan this evening is as follows; once the illegals have been transferred to The

Dolphin, we'll track her all the way. The initial information is that Llantwit Major beach is the drop off location, so there'll be an armed response unit under the command of Chief Inspector Smythe, together with a search team on stand-by in that area. It's more than likely that a van, possibly a Transit, will be used to collect the illegals. Should the drop off location be changed by Hayes at the last minute, Inspector Crole will take command of the second armed response and search unit and will make their way to that location and secure it. It's believed that The Dolphin will be returned to the Porthcawl marina. If that's the case, whichever firearms unit is not deployed at the drop off, can do the business at the marina. I must stress that at this moment in time, we have no idea who this Darryl Hayes is dealing with at this end. We believe it to be someone working for a local solicitor's firm who own The Dolphin, so I want all the mobile phones of those arrested confiscated before they can use them. Are there any questions?"

Chief Inspector Mel Smythe stood. "Abe, are there any other agencies involved in the op?"

Behind closed doors, Quince knew the chief by his first name but when gathered with other ranks he was always sure to respect the rank. "No, sir. We've been on this enquiry for weeks. It's only by luck that we've connected The Dolphin with it. We've had no solid evidence from any other agencies, and truth be told they've given us nothing. It's obvious by what Haye's has been saying on the cat, he's greasing a few palms along the way."

"So, if things go to plan, what about the French side of it?"

"The ACC will start the ball rolling there. He'll get eyes in the sky, and hopefully the traffickers will be intercepted. But the truth is that I don't really care, as long as my double murder is cleared up and we save six vulnerable females. International politics is not something I'm eager to get involved with."

Mel nodded, knowingly. "That sounds good to me, Abe. The least interference the better. But what about firearms, any intelligence there?"

"Nothing, sir. So, take it as read that they may well be tooled up. I've no doubt once you hit them, they'll shit themselves.

"Anyone else with questions?"

Nothing. Everyone began to rise, eager to get stuck into Hayes and his crew.

"OK, then I think that's about it. Now we could be waiting for a while, but as soon as we have the relevant information, we'll get it straight to you and you can act accordingly. Now get out there, do the business and keep safe."

57

The evening light was just fading, there was a thin veil of mist like a scene from a James Herbert novel, and the waters were beginning to get choppy.

Brett Noble pointed excitedly towards a large buoy moored over a hundred metres away. "Darryl, I can see them, I can see the dingy, they're here."

"Well chuck the rope ladder over the side, give them something to grab hold of." Hayes squinted in the direction Brett was pointing. Sure enough, a large black dingy was powering slowly towards them out of the mist.

As the small inflatable neared the cat, Brett did as he was told and grabbed a rope that one of the heavies on the dingy had thrown to him.

Hayes peered over Brett's shoulder. "Brett, Frankie, get them on board quick sharp and lock them up below. You know the score, tie their hands and if they make any noise just gag the bastards.

The Noble brothers did as they were ordered and bundled the six young Vietnamese women into the galley and then pulled a fixed bench from the hull to reveal a small hatch into the port hull. "Right, you three," he pointed to the three nearest to him, "Get your arses in there and keep fucking quiet. You understand?" The women clearly didn't understand his words but knew they had to go where he was pointing. The space was low and narrow and a tight fit for one, let alone three. When that hatch was secure and the bench replaced, Brett did the same on the starboard side. All that was left was for Hayes to collect payment.

Hayes stood confidently on deck, facing off against the three heavies that looked keen for a fight. "Have you got my money and the drugs?"

Luckily for Hayes, the trafficker handed over two holdalls, one containing thirty thousand in cash, and the other had five kilos of cocaine."

Hayes checked the contents and the traffickers got back into the dingy.

Hayes shouted to Frankie. "Lift the anchor, and let's get the fuck out of here before anyone comes sniffing around. This bit of mist will do us proud. I'll set course for home."

"Where are we landing them, Dar?"

"Don't you worry your little head about that, Brett. You'll find out soon enough. Just keep your eyes peeled, that's all."

***

Quince was sitting in the incident room, reading his notes. The last four or five hours had melded into one long and tense blur. It had been boring, and he knew that everyone involved was on tenterhooks.

Clive broke the tension. "Boss, The Dolphin's on the move."

Quince punched the air and whooped. "Yee haaa!" He laughed at his own stereotype. "Any idea what course she's on, Clive?"

"Look for yourself, boss. Looks like she's heading our way."

"And how long before you think she'll hit our shores?"

"The early hours, boss. Say… about three or four in the morning."

"Just keep an eye on it. We've got plenty of time then."

"I just hope the bastards don't change course and try to off-load at some other place."

"No, I reckon South Wales will be the destination. We'll nick the lot of them."

***

Hayes set the automatic pilot, and then set about giving the Noble's their cut.

"Here we are, boys. Five grand apiece, as agreed, and don't spend it all at once," he smiled. Whatever you do, don't bring attention to yourselves when we get back to dry land."

Brett peeked inside the holdall containing the drugs. "What sort of weight you got here, Dar?"

"About five kilos. Should bring us a pretty penny. I've got a buyer lined up, so as soon as I knock it out, you'll both get a little extra wedge." Hayes nodded to Frankie. "Go check on the cargo, give them something to eat, and some water. We don't want them starving to death, do we?"

"I hope not, Dar. Not more bloody deaths."

Frankie was beginning to worry Hayes. He had become a weak link. "Go check on them and be careful. It was down to you that I had to jack up the other two."

Frankie didn't reply and he scurried off and Hayes grabbed Brett by the throat. "You'd better keep a tight rein on your brother because he's getting on my wick, and if I ever find out that he's been opening his trap about it, I promise you he'll never talk again. There's too much at stake."

Holding his hands up in surrender, Brett needed Hayes to cool down before he choked the life out of him. "Look, Dar," he gasped, "when we got involved in this lark, we both saw it as easy money..." Hayes released the pressure. "But after the last time, things have changed. It took all that I had to persuade him to come along on this job. I can't see him doing another run, his nerves are shot to pieces."

Now Hayes let go and stepped back. "When I jacked them up I made the call, OK? Anyway, who gives a toss? The police are running around like chickens without heads and we're in the clear. There's no problem, alright?"

"Whatever you say, Dar." Brett was just relieved to be still breathing. After what Hayes had done to the two illegals, Brett believed he was capable of doing it again. "I'm going up top to get some fresh air, and make sure everything is sound."

"I'll just check how the cargo is doing."

"How are they Frankie?"

"Fed and watered, Dar. Quiet as mice. They're scared, all cuddled up together."

Hayes crossed his arms and stood in the aisle between the benches. "How are you doing?" He asked.

Frankie was surprised. Hayes had never shown any kind of concern for him before. "Truth be told Dar, not too good."

"When did you have a hit last?"

"Been clean for a few weeks."

"I bet this is the longest you've gone for a while?"

"Oh aye," Frankie said quietly, not wanting his brother to hear. "But I need something. This is too much. Can you sort me out? I'm on the edge here?"

Hayes snorted. He knew this was coming and he was happy to keep Frankie subdued. He was a liability. "Your brother would go ape shit."

"Please, Dar, I can't see me making it home. You've got the gear. I just want something to take the edge off, that's all."

Pretending to weigh up the circumstances of giving coke to one of his crew, Hayes wanted Frankie to think he was doing him a favour, one Brett was not to know about, not that he wouldn't know as soon as Frankie took a hit. Still, Brett could be handled. Hayes would blame it on Frankie and swear he knew nothing of it. "OK. But I had nothing to do with this, OK?"

"God's truth Dar, I won't say a word to anyone, not even Brett."

Hayes pulled up a false panel in one of the steps to the upper deck and held out a small plastic bag of coke and gave it to Frankie.

"Don't go overboard. I don't want you off your box when we off-load this lot."

"Cheers, Dar, I won't forget this."

Hayes left Frankie to his business and headed back up onto deck.

Brett was feeding coordinates into the autopilot. "How are they down there?"

"All sound. Frankie's fed and watered them."

"Where is he?"

"He said he was going to grab an hour. I told him to chill and join us for a beer when he's sorted."

"He's worrying me."

"Well, when we get home, get him in to rehab or something." Hayes cracked open a can of chilled beer from the ice box under the seat. "I'll help you sort it and perhaps in a few weeks we can get him back on track. We can all chip in a bit of our shares to pay for it."

"It's worth a shot, cheers, Dar."

"I know he means the world to you Brett, and I'll help you both, as best I can," he lied. He had no intention of wasting another penny on either of them.

58

Brett wanted to check on Frankie, but Hayes had told him to leave him get some sleep, that he'd be better when he awoke. A couple of hours had now passed, and Brett was even more worried. Frankie only slept a few hours when he wasn't on the juice. Hayes was now at the helm and swigging his third can of beer. "I'll go and check on Frankie."

"Check on the cargo as well while you're down there." Brett was just as soft as his brother.

Within seconds of Brett dropping down into the cabin, Hayes heard him scream.

"Darryl, get down here, somethings happened to Frankie, I think he's dead."

Hayes wasn't surprised but rushed below and. Frankie was on the floor, lying on his back with Brett squatting over him.

"Brett, what the hell's happened? Get out of the way."

Hayes pulled Brett away from his brother and checked for a pulse. None. Haye's rolled Frankie over on to his side but knew he was a goner.

"What's he done, Frankie?" Hayes turned on his best Oscar performance. "He's dead."

"But he can't be. How?"

"He is, and what's this?"

Under Frankie's body was a small plastic bag containing a white powder, which Hayes knew was the coke he'd given him.

"Where did he get that shit from? he was clean when he got on the cat, I swear."

"The problem we've got now is what do we do with him?"

"What do you mean?"

"Exactly what I say. What do we do with him? This could cock everything up." Hayes stood and paced, pretending to ponder the pressing problem. "Think," he said as he tapped himself on the forehead. Then he stopped and looked at Brett. "We've got to get rid of him."

"No way, Dar," Brett shouted. "You're not tossing him overboard; no way are we doing that."

"Well, what do you suggest?"

"Keep him on the cat. We can sort something when we get back to Porthcawl. I don't mind where he's found, but he's not going overboard, do you understand?"

It would have been easier to just smash Brett in the face and dump Frankie anyway, but he had to let Brett think Frankie's death was a case of stupid misadventure. "OK, get some tarpaulin. Wrap him up and stow him in the engine compartment. We'll sort it all out later. We're only a couple of hours away from home and I've got to make a few calls. Now get on with it."

***

"It's me. I've made the call. I've changed the drop off rendezvous. It's not Llantwit Major, it's Dunraven Beach, Southerndown. We'll be there in a couple of hours."

"Any trouble?"

"Could have gone been better," Hayes admitted. "The pickup went smooth enough. The girls and coke are safely on board, but we've got a problem."

"What is it this time?"

"It looks like Frankie has overdosed on coke. He's dead as a dodo. We've wrapped him up in tarp and stowed him in the engine room."

"What are you going to do with him? Why didn't you just dump him overboard?"

"I'll sort it, so no more jabbing. The longer we're on the phone the more risk there is of being intercepted. I'll ring you later this afternoon. I've got a shit load on my plate right now."

The was a moment of silence. "Where did he get the coke from?"

"I'll explain it all when I see you. Everything is sorted for the pickup. That's all you need to know."

Hayes ended the call and shouted down through the hatch to Brett. "I've changed the drop off point. We'll be heading for Dunraven Bay. The boys and the van will be there waiting for you, so get the dingy sorted."

"Are you coming with me? Now that Frankie's dead I'll need help."

"No, you'll be OK. Just get them in to the dingy and drop them off. Simple! Now go and get them prepared for the off-load, and make sure that their hands are still tied. I don't want a repetition of last time."

"OK, but what are we going to do with Frankie?"

"We'll sort it when we get to Porthcawl. I think the best thing we can do is get him home. We'll make it look like he overdosed in the house. The locals know he's a druggie, so hopefully when you report finding him dead in bed, the police will put it down to an overdose at home. You'll have to lay it on thick and tell them he'd lost the plot, do you understand?"

Brett nodded. "I never thought it would end like this. It's a nightmare."

"It sure is, Brett. As they say, life's a bitch.

***

"Boss, The Dolphin is about an hour away. I don't think she's heading for Llantwit; she seems to have changed course and now she's heading more towards Southerndown and Porthcawl."

"Cheers, Clive. I'll alert both firearm teams and deploy them to Southerndown and Porthcawl. Let me know when The Dolphin stops. We'll have a better idea then as to where the offloading will be. My guess is Southerndown is as good a bet as any. I can't see them bringing the women into Porthcawl. It's too busy there."

Quince began making the calls. "Mel, we're on," Quince updated the new location. "Are you ready?"

"We sure are, Abe. We'll be there in twenty minutes. It will give us plenty of time to plot up and we'll strike once the women have been off-loaded into the van. What about the dingy? Do you want us to take it out as well?"

"No, Mel, leave it go back to The Dolphin. I've already briefed Seb and his team will do the business in Porthcawl."

"Sounds as if it's all coming together, Abe?"

"We'll soon know in a few hours Mel. You and the team keep safe."

59

A few hours had elapsed before Clive said the magic words.

"Boss, The Dolphin is on stop, about a mile off the Southerndown coast. It looks like you've called it right."

"Cheers, Clive," Quince picked up a handset. "OK, everyone, this is it, this is what we've all been waiting for. Chief Inspector Smythe will call the strike and all units will be on this talk-through channel," a talk-through was a channel on which everyone tuned in could hear all transmissions by the rest of the team. "We'll know exactly what's going on at all times. Just keep everything crossed, and let's hope for a result. God knows you all deserve it after the graft you've put into the last few weeks."

Mel Smythe had already plotted his firearms officers in two positions. Half were concealed in undergrowth, where they had a clear view of the beach, the rest of the team were parked up in a pub car park with unrestricted view of the road leading down to the beach.

"F.O-one to control, Black Ford Transit van just passed us. Driver and passenger both IC-one. They came from the direction of St Brides and has made a left and is now travelling along Beach Road. I've deployed a footman. F.O-three, keep your eyes peeled, and be careful not to show."

"F.O-four here, I have eyeball on target vehicle. It's definitely making its way down to the beach."

"All units from F.O-three, I've now got the eyeball. Vehicle now at the bottom of Beach Road and is driving into the car park. All lights have been knocked off and two male IC-ones have alighted. There are no other vehicles about and they're having a good look around."

"F.O-one, we'll make sure you don't get any company."

"F.O-one from F.O-three, all noted. One of them has just opened the rear doors. There's nobody in the van, he's just left them open. The other one has jumped back into the driver's side and is flashing the headlights. Looks like they're expecting company."

"F.O-three from F.O-one, Keep a watching brief. Wait until

they've loaded the women up. As they're making their way out of the car park, we'll strike, understood?"

"F.O-three, noted."

***

Brett Noble had loaded the women into the dingy and started the small outboard motor to propel them to the beach. Brett had blindfolded the women and bound their hands. They had no idea where they were or where they were going.

"Don't make a sound, any of you, or I'll dump you overboard," he hissed at them. It had been the worse day of Brett's life. He'd lost his brother and if it hadn't been for this run Frankie would probably still be alive.

Within five minutes, Noble had the dingy in shallow water and the women wading through knee-high water. Brett led the way, dragging the first in line while the others followed like baby elephants holding onto the tails of their mothers.

As soon as they hit the dry beach, Brett flashed his torch to signal the van, then ran back to the dingy. It was easier to move now it was empty. He turned it around and headed back to The Dolphin.

***

"F.O-three to all units, the women have been dropped off, and are just standing blindfolded on the beach. The target who dropped them off is back in the dingy and heading back to the cat."

"F.O-one to three, any movement near the van?"

"No, nothing. Stand-by," a moment's silence, just a crackle on the radio, then another message. "They've got the women and are manhandling them into the back of the van," another short pause. "They're all loaded, and the back doors have been locked. Both men now back in the cab, lights on and making a U-turn."

"F.O-one to all units, strike! Strike! Strike!"

Black-clad officers, fully armed and in body armour, popped out of the shadows and within seconds the van was blocked in and surrounded by the Armed Response Team.

A loud voice left the occupants of the van in no doubt about what they must do next. "Armed police put your hands on the steering wheel and dashboard so we can see them if you don't want to get shot. Do as your told and get out of the vehicle slowly."

Both men did as they were told, neither clearly wanting to test the armed officers.

"Get on the ground. Face down and hands behind your backs, don't make any sudden moves or it may be your last."

Both men duly obliged.

S.O-one stepped forward and nodded to one of his team. "Cuff them, search them and take them straight back to Swansea Central. Someone check on the women."

***

"Did everything go smoothly?"

"Yeah, no problem," Brett grunted as he pulled himself onto the catamaran. "I just dropped them in the shallows, signalled to the boys and high-tailed it back. I wasn't going to hang about but it was dead quiet."

"Well done." Hayes took a thick envelope from his pocket. "Here's Frankie's five thousand. It's no good to him now. You did good, under the circumstances."

"How are we going to play it, you know, with Frankie's body?"

"We'll get him home and do what we agreed. Once we've done that you can kip at mine for a few days and then you can come home and find him. We'll knock the heating off and open a few windows. Then if there's any query about time of death, we'll play it by ear and tell them you've been staying at mine. Have you got it?"

"I got it, Dar. I'll go below and tidy it up any evidence. Make sure there's nothing left to tie us to the merchandise."

"Aye, you do that, Brett. Can I rely on you for any further jobs?"

"Not any time soon. This has shaken me up, you know, with Frankie. I've always looked after him."

Hayes wanted to say, "You didn't do a very good job then, did you?" But didn't. He felt a smile begin to break but fought it back.

"He was a fool to himself, but he didn't deserve to die like this. I was always fearful that he would overdose, but I kept a close eye on him."

"Don't guilt trip yourself. It was bound to happen sooner or later. When it's sorted, we'll give him a good send off. I'll see to that. Now you go and crack on below."

Hayes set course for Porthcawl with a self-satisfied grin he was proud to display. A job well done. The weather had stayed good, but little did he know about the shitstorm that was brewing on the horizon.

***

"They are petrified, boss," S.O-three said as he peered into the dark interior of the van. "They're like rabbits in the headlights. We've taken blindfolds off them, and cut the cable ties from their hands, but I think they'll need some counselling too."

"OK. We'll take them and the van back to central as well. This will make Quince's night. Well done, lads. A cracking job, and not a shot in anger. We'll have a de-brief back at central."

60

"A cracking result," Quince smiled. "However, we've got a long road ahead of us. It looks like The Dolphin is heading for Porthcawl. So, like earlier, let's keep our fingers crossed that we could do the double. It should be docking in about half an hour, so sit back and enjoy the show.

Quince's radio crackled. "F.O-two to control, my team is in position. We have eyes on the marina and the Porsche. I'll call the strike as and when I see fit."

Quince smiled. "Control to F.O-two, we are in your hands, take care."

***

"All sorted below, Dar. I just need a hand to carry Frankie up on deck. He's a fair old weight."

"I'll be there now. I'll put her on stop. We're only a few minutes from the marina."

The catamaran had begun to roll on choppy water as the craft neared the port. Neither man were natural sailors, but neither were bothered by the conditions.

Hayes dropped down below and helped Brett carry Frankie up on to the deck, handling him like a sack of spuds. Frankie was trussed in a yellow tarpaulin tied with thick rope.

"OK, let's get to the marina, park this thing, and get home," Hayes panted. When this was over, he'd spend a little money on a gym subscription. He was out of shape.

***

"F.O-two, Target in sight, manoeuvring slowly into the marina. Confirmed. It's The Dolphin. I can see Darryl Hayes and Brett Noble but no sign of Frankie."

Several minutes passed, then another message. "Brett has just tied off. The running lights have been switched off and Brett has gone back on board. He and Hayes are now manhandling what looks like a heavy tarpaulin off the cat. They've laid it on the walkway. Hayes also has a holdall, there's still no sign of Frankie. Christ, I don't know what they're up to…" A pause then another transmission. "Now they're carrying the tarpaulin together. They have no idea whatsoever what's about to go down."

"This is it. All units. Strike! "Strike! Strike!"

A grin had spread across Crole's face too. "What's in the tarpaulin and the holdall lads?"

Neither replied. Hayes tried to stare him out, but Brett stared at his feet, resigned to his fate.

Crole opened the holdall. It was jam-packed with blocks of white powder. "Oh, what have we got here then? Importing flour, boys, are you?" He laughed. Then Crole untied the ropes binding the tarpaulin, and there was poor Frankie. Dead eyes stared out of the folds of thick plastic.

"Jesus!" Crole said, shocked by this new twist. "What have you got to say about this?"

Again, neither replied.

"OK. I don't give a shit! You're both under arrest for people trafficking and possessing what I believe are class A drugs. As for Frankie, perhaps we have a murder to add to the list? A PM will give us the answers, so I don't care if you make no reply," he turned to the officers surrounding the prisoners. "Take them both up to central and bed them down with their mates."

"Crole contacted Quince and brought him up to speed on developments. "Looks like we have more than we bargained for, Abe."

"Not a problem, Seb. Just secure the scene and I'll get in touch with Terry McGuire, he covers Porthcawl, in fact he lives nearby. Leave it to me."

Quince didn't relish ringing McGuire. The fact that the op was concentrated mainly on his patch might have got his goat, and now he'd landed McGuire with a corpse too.

"McGuire, who is it? It had better be good?" McGuire growled as he answered the call.

"Terry, it's Abe Quince. Sorry to bother you, and don't blow your top."

"Depends on what you're going to tell me. I guess it's not a social call at this ungodly hour."

"You know I've been dealing with a double murder, some Vietnamese kids that were dumped in our marina…"

"Of course. Haven't you sorted them yet? You're slipping, Abe," McGuire teased.

"Well, here's the rub. I've been running a covert operation and it's overlapped on to your patch."

McGuire groaned. "Go on…"

"The Dolphin, a catamaran has been used to bring illegals into the country and tonight we've made our arrests. Which is great, of course."

"I think I know what's coming," McGuire sighed. "Where and when were they arrested?"

"Two down at Southerndown, and two at the Porthcawl marina. All four are on their way to Swansea Central with six female illegals as we speak."

"I'm pleased for you, Abe, but you could have told me this in the morning, surely? Molly will not be best pleased with you waking us up."

"You live near the marina, don't you?" Quince said, knowing full well the answer.

"Two minutes away, why? What do you want?"

"Well, we've got a dead body wrapped in a tarpaulin on the marina walkway. It came off The Dolphin."

"Well, Abe, thanks a bunch. Do we know who it is?"

"Yes, a local by the name of Frankie Noble."

"Young Frankie? No doubt his brother Brett is involved. Is anyone else?"

"For sure. A guy called Darryl Hayes. Do you know him? He lives in Porthcawl."

"I know the *Noble brothers*," McGuire's sarcasm at the pronunciation of the name wasn't lost on Quince. "So, you want me to pop over and sort it for you, hence the call?"

"Well, if you could, Terry? I'm in Swansea Central now but I'm going to be a bit tied up."

"Leave it to me, Abe."

"Bill Daniels and Ted Farmer are there. I want them to do the cat and Haye's Porsche."

"Who else is there at the scene?"

"Seb Crole with his firearms team, and a search unit."

"I'll sort it, Abe. I'll get the PM organised for later today. You'll have a cause of death this evening, with a bit of luck."

"You're taking it quite calmly, Terry, what are you not telling me?"

"It's a good job," McGuire said. "I get a possible detected murder without even opening a room up and you get a boat load of assorted crimes. What's not to be calm about?"

He knew? The realisation hit Quince. Someone had tipped McGuire off. "Did you know about it?"

"I'm saying nothing, and don't go thinking it was one of your team. You can't go all Wyatt Earp on a mate's patch."

"Point taken." Quince smiled to himself. He should have known McGuire would have had a tip-off. Well-liked by his team, they looked after each other and that included giving McGuire the heads-up when something secret squirrel was happening on his patch. At least Quince knew those secrets were safe with McGuire. Now he felt bad for not cutting him in from the start.

"I'll keep you updated, now don't stress yourself, and just sort your stuff out."

Quince and McGuire went back a long way, they were cut from the same cloth. The job was their life, and they were on the same wavelength. They were also like the adage of opposites attract. Two different personalities, but both totally motivated by the job.

61

Quince was delighted with the operation, but there was one final piece of the jigsaw to complete. They had to arrest the inside man responsible for The Dolphin and God only knew what else.

"Right, pipe down everybody. I know you're all on a high, and the first thing I want to do is thank you all, especially the firearms units. I was listening to the way you took down the scum and that was a pleasure." He nodded to the team leaders in amongst the others gathered for what Quince hoped would be the last case conference for these dealers in death. "Mel and Seb, they did you proud. At this moment in time there are four men in custody, and the fifth one called Frankie Noble is dead. It's my guess his death occurred on The Dolphin, but we have no idea what the cause of death is yet. I've spoken with Detective Superintendent Terry McGuire, and his team will be dealing with the death. So that'll leave us clear to deal with this lot. Bill and Ted are on one of their *amazing adventures* on The Dolphin as I speak," the others laughed at Quince's reference to the film. His Bill and Ted were known to do some odd things too, from time to time. "They'll go through the boat with a fine-tooth comb, and hopefully they'll find evidence that our two victims had been on board. I have no doubt in my mind that they had been. The two men arrested with the Transit van are Owen Palmer and Ralph Bayer. They've got a stack of form and are both local guys. All four prisoners' houses are being turned over as we speak. As for the women, well they are being well looked after. The Immigration lot will be heavily involved. Luckily, Connor's mate, Nadir Huang will be helping with any translating. We've got all their mobile phones, and tech will be trawling through them, with any other devices that may be recovered from their houses. This mobile was taken off Hayes," Quince held up a phone in a clear evidence bag, "and there is no doubt that he's been communicating with whoever's in charge of The Dolphin. We know it's now owned by a local law firm. As soon as I finish this briefing, I will be interviewing the senior partner, and hopefully get the identity of this other twat involved. Any questions?"

Seb Crole spoke. "What do you reckon with Frankie, Abe?"

"Who knows?" Quince shrugged. "We'll have to wait for the PM for that one, and I'm sure McGuire and his team will do the business for us."

"And the holdall?"

"Yes, a result. The boys have done a quick test, it's coke, and not far off hundred per cent pure. Quite a few bucks, I'd imagine."

A mobile phone began to ring, and Quince checked the one in the evidence bag. No luck. It was his own, behind him on the table he was sat on. It was the ACC.

"Abe, good job. The donor boat has been intercepted. Four in custody. The French authorities will keep me informed."

"Thanks, boss. A good op, but one little hiccup. One of the brother's has croaked. Terry McGuire is sorting out that end."

"I know, Abe, he's been on the blower. Just liaise with him. I'm sure the end will justify the means. I'll pop down in the morning. So, get the coffee on."

"Will do."

"And none of that Yank shit you usually drink."

Quince grinned. "One mug of instant dishwater will be waiting, sir." He ended the call and dropped his phone back onto the table.

"Another bit of good luck," he said to the team. "The donor boat has been picked up with four in custody, probably on its way back to France, so we'll leave them to it and top and tail at our end. There's nothing more to do at the minute, so I suggest you all go home, get a good night's kip, and be back at eight tomorrow to get stuck into the bastards. George and I will sort this other twat with the catamaran, tout suite."

"Let's get this over with, George. You got the address?"

"No problem, boss. It's only ten minutes away."

***

George knocked on the gloss-black front door of a city centre townhouse, probably built during the early part of the twentieth century. Grand but chipped portico and enormous bay windows leaded with coloured glass in geometric patterns hinted at the building's former glory. After a few seconds a middle-aged man with the salt and pepper evidence of his age answered. Dressed in knee length shorts and a baggy cardigan over a paint-specked lime green T-shirt, the man looked more like a commune artist than a solicitor. The man frowned at the visitors.

"Yes?" he said abruptly.

"Mr A'hern?"

"Yes, and you are?"

Quince stepped forward. "I'm DI Abe Quince and this is DS George Brodie. May we have five minutes of your time? It's very important, and time is of the essence."

"What could be so important at this early hour Inspector?"

"We wouldn't be here unless it was very important, sir."

A'hern sighed and seemed conflicted for a brief moment, before opening the door and stepping aside. "You'd both better come in. I hope it won't take too long?"

"I'll be as quick as possible."

"Good." A'hern ushered the two detectives into a parlour off the hallway.

Quince was impressed by the patterned tiled hall floor and the high ceilings with picture rail supporting numerous framed watercolours and oil paintings he recognised as a collection of Welsh art. "Nice collection of paintings, Mr A'hern."

A'hern stopped and smiled briefly. "You an art lover, Inspector?" It was said almost mockingly.

"Lover but not collector. Can't afford a Kyffin Williams or Will Roberts but I like to look at them."

A'hern nodded. "That Kyffin Williams is one of four I have." He pointed to an enormous palette knife painting above the fireplace. It was a darkly painted vision of a cottage high in the mountains of North Wales with what looked to Quince like a farmer and his sheep dog at heel. "This is one I bought about twenty years ago. A few years before Kyffin died. Got in at the right time. It wasn't cheap back then, but the prices have gone through the roof now."

"A wise investment."

"I like to think so, but the money doesn't mean anything to me. I just love it."

Then he pointed to an abstract that Quince didn't recognise. "Who painted that?"

A'hern seemed happy to talk about art. "That's a Ceri Richards and that one," he said, pointing to a portrait, "is an Augustus John."

"John I've heard of," Quince said, suitably impressed.

"As I say, it's not the monetary value that matters. I buy art because it's good for the soul."

Yeah, right, Quince thought. "I'm led to believe that your firm also owns a catamaran called The Dolphin, which is moored down at the marina?"

"Yes, has it been damaged?"

"No, nothing like that. Do you sail her?"

"Good God, no, Inspector. In fact, I've never seen it let alone sailed it. No, it was basically part of the deal when Roy sold out to us. I'm sure you know Roy?"

Quince smiled and nodded. "Well, the cat is still registered in Roy's name. Can you explain that?"

"Inspector, I'm a solicitor. I wouldn't know a main sail from a boom. Now, please tell me what's going on."

"But you'd understand the requirement to register the vessel."

A'hern snorted. "Is this all because I haven't registered it? Bit of over-kill, don't you think?"

"Well, we have information that The Dolphin has been used in criminal activities."

"What are you talking about?" A'hern seemed genuinely shocked. "To my knowledge, it's only used on rare occasions and never by me. It's a resource, a company asset. That's how I view it."

"Well, it's been linked directly to a murder, and if you don't know anything about it, sure as eggs is eggs, somebody in your firm does. Now have a good think. Is it one of your partners, perhaps?"

Another dismissive snort. "I've known them for years. They wouldn't get involved in anything nefarious, I assure you." But now A'hern didn't sound so confident.

"I repeat, Mr A'hern, time is at a premium, so please think."

"Inspector, the only person in our practice who has access to that boat is Ray Doyle."

"Who is he?"

"He's my office manager. He's been with the firm for years, but he can't be involved." Now A'hern sounded like he wasn't so sure of his opinion.

"Tell me about him?"

"He's been with us for about ten years. Started as a legal rep, you know, police stations and all that out of hours stuff. Then we promoted him to office manager. He's worth his weight in gold. We'd be lost without him."

"What's his connection with The Dolphin?"

"I think he uses it for deep sea fishing."

"Have you got a mobile number for him?"

"Yes, he's always on-call. Never lets us down. He runs the office like clockwork."

"And the number, Mr A'hern?"

"Here it is, Inspector. Shall I ring him?"

"I don't think so, sir."

Quince pulled out Haye's mobile from the evidence bag he had stuffed into his jacket pocket and scrolled through recent calls. He found what he was looking for, nodded at George and held the screen to him for him to see the number of Doyle in the list of recent calls.

"Tell us more about Doyle, is he married?"

"No. He's single and lives in a flat not far from the marina."

"Just give us the address. We'll give him a knock and I'll leave a couple of uniforms just to keep you company until we sort him. You don't mind that do you?"

"I understand, Inspector."

***

"How are we going to play it, boss?"

"Off the cuff, George, I don't expect him to cough it when confronted. That would be too neat. Give the nick a ring, tell them to get a search team down to the address, but tell them to hang fire until we bring the guy out."

Five minutes later, they were outside an apartment block on the fringe of the newly developed marina. Six floors of faux wood clad flats of one, two and three bedrooms aimed at the rising stars of local business. The two detectives took the stairs, mainly because George wasn't keen on lifts or any enclosed spaces. Apartment four B was on the marina side of the corridor and would probably be the more expensive option for buyers.

Quince knocked this time and shouted when he heard movement, but no one came to the door. A shadow behind the peephole. "Ray Doyle?"

"Yes, who are you?"

George tried to look through the hole. "DS Brodie."

"And who is he?"

"I'm Abe Quince, and I'm investigating a double murder. Now, can we come in please?"

A brief pause and then the sound of several locks being thrown open.

"These locks are a bit of overkill for Swansea, boss." George observed.

"Yup. Why is that do you think?"

The door opened and Ray Doyle stood there in a pair of underpants and a string vest.

"Jesus, Rab C Nesbitt lives," George cracked quietly.

Quince kept the smile from his face. "Ray Doyle? Can I call you Ray?"

"Whatever, Inspector, whatever floats your boat."

"Well, talking about a boat, what can you tell me about The Dolphin?"

"The Dolphin, I don't understand?"

"It's owned by the firm you work for and it's moored in the marina. What's to understand?"

"OK."

"When did you see The Dolphin last, or an even better question, when were you on board last?"

"Not for a while," Doyle shrugged. He turned and walked towards a modern, sleek kitchen with pastel colour doors. He flicked on the kettle switch as the two detectives followed him close behind. "Want a cuppa?"

George was about to say yes but Quince got in first. "No thanks. So, it's moored at the marina, as far as you know?"

Doyle dropped a teabag into a mug with a logo of a golden dolphin. "Not for a while," he said as he poured boiling water over the bag.

"I suppose you've heard about the two bodies found in the marina a few weeks ago?"

He nodded as he stirred the contents and tipped a splash of milk from a plastic bottle. "I did read something about it. A terrible business, but what has that to do with me?"

"Do you know Darryl Hayes?"

Quince saw a hint of a tremor in Doyle's hand as he fished the bag from the mug and dropped it into a swing bin. "No, name doesn't mean anything."

"What if I told you that he's in custody on suspicion of murder and people trafficking?"

"Inspector, I have no idea what you're talking about. Now, if there's anything else I can help you with?"

"I'm sure there is, Ray. Can I use the loo?"

"Of course, second on the left."

Quince found the bathroom. Tiled from floor to ceiling in tiles that he guessed cost more than two months of a DI's salary. He closed the door and found Doyle's number on Hayes' phone. He pressed call.

"Sorry sergeant, but I've got to take this," Doyle said as his phone began to ring.

"You carry on, don't mind me."

Doyle made his way into bedroom before speaking in hushed but frantic tones. "What the fuck is going on? I've got the CID here asking about murders, and The Dolphin..." but there was no answer. The phone went dead.

Doyle walked back into the lounge where Quince and George were now sitting with smug expressions.

"Everything alright, Ray? you look a little flushed."

"Yes, just a client who's in a bit of a crisis, nothing unusual."

"A little bit like you then?" Quince said.

"I'm sorry?"

"Roy, excuse me. I've got to make a quick call."

The colour drained from Doyle's face as he realised what was happening.

Quince rang the number again.

George feigned concern as Doyle's phone began to ring. "Aren't you going to answer it, Ray?

Quince shook his head. "I think not. George cuff the lying bastard, caution him, and get the search team in here. But get some clothes on him first. I had a greasy bacon sandwich this morning and I can feel it begin to repeat on me." Quince stood. "Oh, and by the way, Ray, young Frankie is dead, so just have a good think before you decide to lie to us anymore."

"I haven't done anything, this is unlawful. I'll sue you for false arrest."

"Fuck off you piece of garbage," George muttered loud enough to be heard.

62

"OK, ladies and gents, as you know we've got five individuals in custody. From the information we've gleaned, it looks like Ray Doyle is the one who has had access to The Dolphin. He works for Evan's solicitors in town as their office manager. We also believe that Darryl Hayes is the one who actually uses the cat to pick up illegals, together with his muscle, Owen Palmer, Ralph Bayer, Brett Noble and Frankie Noble now deceased. In relation to Frankie, the PM is being carried out as we speak. At the minute, we have no cause of death. All we can say is that he definitely met his maker on The Dolphin. In relation to the double murder, I would say that Hayes did the organising, and we can pick out any one from four for depositing the bodies in the marina. With regard to the origin of the six illegal women, who we have saved by the way, the French authorities have arrested three individuals who no doubt rendezvoused with The Dolphin. That one's down to the ACC, in all fairness to him. I've spoken to the custody officer, and all five now have legal representation, and by fuck they're going to need it.

"You've got your briefing notes, and who's interviewing who. I know it's going to be a long day, so get cracking, and do your best. Any questions?"

Ken Lewis chirped in "Fiona and I are interviewing Brett Noble, boss, are there any specific instructions as to how you want to play it with him boss?"

"Lay it on thick, Ken, something must have gone on for Frankie to snuff it on board. Tie him down, then perhaps we can hit him with the PM findings."

63

"Good morning, Ray. I don't think we need any introduction, bearing in mind we arrested you last night for conspiracy to murder and people trafficking," Quince grinned and nodded to the suit sitting beside the accused. "I see you've now got legal representation, so DS Brodie will go through all the formalities, and then we'll get down to brass tacks."

Quince watched Ray carefully. He wanted to establish his normal demeanour. This might be important later in the interview to determine if he was lying. Many people have heard stories of cops being able to analyse the behaviour of suspects and know whether they are lying or not. The truth is, most don't and can't. Quince, however, was different. He had always been fascinated by body language, non-verbal communication, and linguistics. He had even persuaded his previous boss to send him on further courses at the police college to improve his skills. But Quince also believed in instinct, and nothing was quite as reliable for him that the little voice in the back of his head that would scream out innocence or guilt.

"OK, Ray, now all that's out of the way, what can you tell me about The Dolphin catamaran that's owned by the firm you work for?"

Doyle leaned across and whispered to his brief before returning to his previous position, arms crossed and leaning back in his chair.

"I've been using it for fishing trips," he said smugly.

Quince nodded. "When did you use it last?"

"I can't remember, truth be told," Ray shrugged.

"You've heard about the two dead bodies found dumped in the marina a few weeks ago?"

"I think everyone has, what's it to do with me?"

"Well, I think it's quite obvious. The Dolphin is being used to traffic people into the UK."

Ray tightened his arms. It was barely noticeable, but Quince had seen it. "No comment."

"Okay, let's move on to Darryl Hayes. What's your connection with him?"

The arms relaxed infinitesimally. "I let him use The Dolphin from time to time."

"How often do you speak with Hayes?"

"From time to time."

"Our tech team have examined your mobile, Ray, and it would appear that you talk on a regular basis, and coincidently most of the time around when there are illegal activities going on. Something of a coincidence, wouldn't you say?"

Ray unfolded his arms and wiped invisible fluff from his trousers before resuming his previous defensive position. "No comment."

"Now this is the way I see it, Ray... Hayes is the organiser, and you get a substantial cut for allowing The Dolphin to be used. Yes, I know you don't get your hands dirty," Quince added before any chance for a reply. "However, it all went tits up a few weeks ago, because he had to dump a couple of innocent Vietnamese lads in the dock."

Now Ray's right hand began to scratch at his side. "No comment."

"Look, Ray, you're guilty by association. My advice to you is, just come clean. At the minute, murder is still on the table and we're going through your bank accounts as we speak. I have no doubt that substantial deposits will have been made and you'll have to explain them away. We both know you'll not be able to do that, don't we?"

His face had drained of colour. "No comment."

"When did you first meet Hayes?"

"No comment."

"He's got a bit of form. Why is a bloke like you, an important cog in a thriving legal firm, associating with him?"

"No comment."

"I understand that before you became office manager a few years ago, you were a legal representative. I reckon you met him in the nick, and that's where all this got off the ground."

Ray snorted. "You couldn't be further from the truth."

"Then enlighten us."

"No, that's for you to find out. You think you're so clever, you haven't got a clue what's going on under your nose."

"Whatever?" Quince shrugged. "Now let's get on to the Noble brothers. They were arrested with Hayes last night," he paused as he studied Ray's face. "No, sorry, only Brett was arrested. Poor old Frankie died on The Dolphin, but you knew that, didn't you?"

"No comment."

"I notice that all these 'no comments,'" Quince made exclamation marks in the air with his finger, "are when we hit a nerve, Ray. Look, you may as well come clean, I'm sure that the truth will come out. Surely you know that?"

"No comment."

"Ray, I have four other people in custody. All have been arrested for conspiracy to murder, and people trafficking. I'm sure one of them will crack, so where will that leave you?"

"No comment."

"So, you loaned the cat out to Hayes, and took a cut. But two murders? Come on, that's not you. You shat yourself when I rang your mobile, and that was all on record."

"No comment."

"OK, Ray, have it your own way. I'll ask you once again, are you going to come clean?"

"No comment."

"So be it, Ray. Whatever happens from here on in is down to you and nobody else. You've been given the opportunity to come clean, I can't do any more."

"No comment."

64

In interview room two, Ken Lewis sat back on his hard chair and stared at the man opposite. He thought for a moment about the key questions he needed to ask. It was likely he'd get no comment throughout, but it was vital to ask the questions anyway. Saying nothing meant the accused had something to hide. There was no other reason for someone to clam up, as far as Ken was concerned. Solicitors could dress it up in a whole wardrobe of reasons but if someone had nothing to hide then there'd be no reason to stay silent. He cleared his throat with a sharp cough and began. "Brett, now we've got the introductions out of the way, as you are aware you've been arrested for conspiracy to murder and people trafficking, bearing in mind you're still under caution, have you anything to say?"

"I haven't murdered anyone. What's happened to my brother?"

"We're waiting for the results of the post-mortem and we'll probably get them later today."

"I don't understand it, one minute he was right as rain, the next he's fucking dead."

"I can see you're upset, Brett, however there are more pressing things to get on with, like the murder of two Vietnamese boys a few weeks ago."

"Fuck all to do with me, or my brother. You're not pinning those on us."

"Okay, so I take it you weren't involved in the murders?"

"I'm telling you. Look, I'll cough to last night, but murder? You must be having a laugh."

"Okay, Brett, so say we believe you and you weren't involved in the murders. I find it a strange coincidence that The Dolphin, the cat you were on, was exactly the same boat that the two Vietnamese lads were smuggled in on a few weeks ago. We have a witness to that fact."

"It wasn't me or Frankie, I'm telling you. We weren't involved in that. I know I'm going down for a long time, but not for fucking murders."

"Do you want to tell us all about it, Brett?"

"Look, I want a deal. I'm not getting fitted up for something I haven't done. I'm no killer."

"I don't know about a deal, Brett, what will you bring to the table? From where I'm sitting, you've had your chips. So, I think you'd better come clean about it, your full involvement."

Brett folded his arms and shook his head. "I'm saying nothing until I find out how Frankie died."

"How do you think he died, Brett?"

"It looked like he'd been snorting coke. I don't know, perhaps it was a bad batch? But I can't understand it. He's been clean for ages."

"So, did he have any gear when you left Porthcawl?"

"Not as far as I know."

"What about the coke we recovered, could he have had a crack at that without you knowing?"

"No. No way, Darryl stowed that away."

"Look, Brett, if we connect The Dolphin with the murders of the Vietnamese lads, you'll be right in the frame for it. So, think on it. You've lost your brother, and I reckon it's every man for himself."

"I don't know."

"OK, let's go back a little bit. What's the score with you, Hayes, Palmer, Bayer, and Doyle?"

"Doyle? Who the fuck is he? I don't know any bloke called Doyle."

"Ray Doyle, he works for a local solicitor's firm, and it looks like he's the custodian of The Dolphin. Have you ever met him?"

"No. The name means nothing to me."

"Well, if that's the case I'd say you, Frankie, Palmer and Bayer are the muscle in this little enterprise."

"Look, if you know so fucking much just charge me."

"It's early days yet, Brett. There's no rush. I'm sure somebody will eventually see a bit of sense and come clean. Like I say, a double murder charge could mean life in prison. Could you handle that?"

"Look, here's the deal, find out how my brother died. I've got an idea what happened to him, but I'm not saying anymore, that's it."

65

The initial interviews had been completed, and as was expected, there were no admissions forthcoming. However, as far as Quince was concerned, it was early days. Hayes, Palmer, and Bayer had made no comment all the way through their interviews.

A heavy rain played a rhythm on the windows of the CID office as Quince sat on the edge of a desk to debrief the troops. "I don't know about you, but this is how I see it at the minute. The brains behind all this are Doyle and Hayes, I believe they organise, and call the shots. As for the other four, they are the muscle at the beck and call of Hayes."

Ken Lewis appeared confused. "So, how do you see the overdosing and the dumping of the Vietnamese lads?"

"I reckon it's down to Hayes. I think he's the killer, and the others do the dumping."

"Well, Brett is adamant that him and Frankie weren't involved in any murders," Fiona said. "He's resigned himself to a long stretch for the trafficking, but he'll have nothing to do with the murders. He also says that Frankie was clean. If that's the case, where did he get the cocaine from, if in fact he did overdose?"

"So, what do you think, Fiona? Palmer and Bayer have gone no comment all the way through."

"I reckon that something went wrong on the cat, and I believe Brett thinks so as well. He's really spooked over his brother's death."

"Well, we should shortly have the cause of death. We've got to have some tangible evidence to put to these bastards later. We've got them by the bollocks for trafficking, but that's not enough, I want them for murder," Quince said with passion.

A knock on the Incident room door preceded the unexpected arrival of Terry McGuire.

"Good afternoon, Abe," McGuire smiled warmly. "I thought I'd pop down and give you the PM results. I think you'll be pleased."

"Bloody hell, boss, nice to see you. Ladies and gents, for those who don't know who this is, this is Detective Superintendent Terry McGuire." The team stood in respect but McGuire waved them to sit.

"Afternoon team, I've heard you've worked your socks off on this one. Am I right in saying you've got five in the hole? That's a cracking result. So, how's it progressing now, Abe?"

"Slow at the minute, boss. We've done the initial interviews, but no admissions for the murders."

McGuire walked to the large white board covered in photos and scribbled names and dates and places. At a hair over six feet, McGuire was pushing the limits of his service and had already taken steps to ensure his career after the police service. A case earlier in the year had him teaming up with a private investigator and investing in his business. Sharp and quick witted, McGuire had become something of a legend in the South Wales force but had mainly worked serious crime in the Bridgend and Cardiff city and valleys areas. It was rare for him to venture down west to Swansea. "Well, the PM on Frankie has been done, and fair play they rushed the tox samples through for me, you've handed me a cut and dried murder, with only two suspects, Brett who I believe is Frankie's brother, and Darryl Hayes."

"Don't keep us in suspense, boss? just spit it out," Quince said.

"OK. The pathologist didn't find any bruising or defence marks on the body, and when he opened him up and examined all the internal organs, he couldn't find any definitive cause of death. Obviously, what with Frankie's previous drug history, it was all down to the tox report. I can tell you that Frankie hadn't ingested any cocaine, however his body contained a massive overdose of methamphetamine. As a result, his body was re-examined, and a small needle puncture - barely visible - was found near the carotid artery. I'm reliably informed that death would have been almost instantaneous."

"That's the same type of drug that was found in the systems of our two Vietnamese victims, boss."

"I'll go one better, Abe, it probably is the same. I've had all the samples compared, and it's highly likely that whoever jacked up poor Frankie also did your two boys."

"That will give us some leverage," Quince nodded.

"Well, I'll leave it in your capable hands, Abe."

"I reckon when Brett hears this, boss, he'll soon change his tune," Fiona offered.

"Well, don't just stand there, get downstairs and get stuck into him," Quince said.

"We're on it, boss."

"Abe, would it be alright if I hang about for a while? I'd like to see what Frankie's brother comes up with."

"Not a problem, boss, let's get a coffee."

***

Ken Lewis stopped outside the interview room and spoke with Fiona. "You can take the lead on this one. I reckon a bit of empathy from you may very well open Brett up."

"Cheers, Sarge," Fiona nodded seriously. She was a capable detective but still got a feeling of nervousness whenever she took the lead in an interview in front of a more senior detective. She knew that was only to be expected but wished she could be as confident as some of the other less experienced colleagues.

"Well, Brett, I don't suppose you've changed your mind about co-operating with us?" Fiona said gently, as if he would be the one to lose out if he maintained his intransigence.

"No. All I'll say is that Frankie and I had nothing to do with any murders."

"OK, well we've had the post-mortem results, and I must say they are very interesting."

"In what way?" Brett was clearly keen to know more. He leaned forward and grabbed the edge of the table.

"It seems you were right. Frankie hadn't been using. There was no coke in his bloodstream."

"So, how the fuck did he die? He was as strong as an ox."

"His heart packed in after been given a massive overdose of methamphetamine."

"What?" Brett was clearly shocked by those words. This was not what he was expecting. "No! You're lying."

Fiona shook her head and sighed. "It looks like Frankie had been injected in the neck with the overdose."

Brett leapt to his feet and thumped the table with his fists. This is bullshit!"

Fiona stood and snapped, "Sit down!" She waited for Brett to calm himself and sit before continuing. "Put it this way, Brett, you are now a suspect in the murder of your brother, what have you got to say about that?"

"When we found Frankie, there was no fucking needles anywhere, just a little bag of what I thought was coke."

"It doesn't look too clever for you though. Did you kill Frankie?"

"No, I loved him," his voice cracked. "I looked after him. He was my brother for God's sake. If he was murdered, it must have been Darryl."

"That's easy to say, Brett, blame it on Darryl."

"Look, I've got to get my head around this"

"It's quite simple Brett, if Darryl did kill Frankie, he's got to pay for it, surely you can understand that?"

"Of course, I do."

"So, just come clean. Tell us about your involvement with Darryl. Tell us when all this business started and how it ended in Frankie's death. As you said earlier, you're knackered on the trafficking, but thankfully all the women are safe and well."

Fiona saw a tear briefly appear at the corner of Brett's left eye before it was brushed away. "Fuck, fuck, fuck, OK. OK." Brett took a deep breath and slumped back in his chair. "I'll tell you everything."

Fiona resisted the urge to use Del Boy's famous line of, 'You know it makes sense' and restricted herself to a grateful nod. "How long have you known Darryl?"

"We met him about eighteen months ago in one of the local pubs. We had a drink with him. He obviously knew who we were and propositioned us. At first, we were doing a bit of smuggling, you know, fags, wine, and drugs. We were doing OK. The money was good. He had it all sorted."

"So, when did the people trafficking start?"

"About a year ago. We went across to France as normal, and it went from there. We brought a couple of Chinese blokes back, dropped them off down the docks in Cardiff, and left them to it. It seemed so simple."

"So how many trips have you done?"

"Not many with people. Three or four, perhaps?"

"And always in The Dolphin?"

"Yes. Darryl had it all sorted."

"Now let's get back to the two Vietnamese lads dumped in the Swansea marina. Were you and Frankie involved?"

Brett hung his head and now couldn't hold back the tears. "Yes, but we didn't kill them. I think they were already dead."

"So, Brett, tell us all about that from start to finish."

He wiped his nose on the back of his sleeve and sniffed. "Me and Frankie weren't on the boat. It was Owen and Ralph that time. We'd take it in turns, see. This time, me and Frankie had to pick four up and drop them anywhere in Swansea, but it all went tits up."

"What happened?"

"Well, we parked up down Burry Port, and just waited for the dingy, once it arrived, we bundled them all into the back of the van and got from there as quickly as possible."

"Were they all alive?"

"Well two were but the other two were dead. I checked for pulses. They were definitely dead. That's when I decided to dump them in the marina. I couldn't very well drop 'em at the nick but I wanted them to be found, you know, by dropping them in a busy marina they were bound to be found and then they'd get a burial. You know?"

"Very charitable of you," Fiona said with no attempt to hide her sarcasm.

"Well Frankie shit himself, so I put him in the back of the van with them."

"Were their hands tied?"

"I can't remember, I think they were. We may have cut the ties. I think we did. Like I say, we panicked."

"What happened when you got to the marina?"

"Me and Frankie got the two dead ones out, put them on the floor and that's when the other two legged it."

"Didn't you think of chasing them?"

"Not really, we were more concerned with the other two. So, we just dumped them, and pissed off back to Porthcawl."

"What about the van?"

"The same one the other two were using last night, we just changed the plates. The ones we use relate to genuine hire vans so if they're checked they don't show up as stolen."

"OK. I can tell you that both the lads were in fact dead before they entered the water, and in fact, they'd been injected with the exact substance as Frankie. So, what does that tell you?"

"What does it tell me? It tells me that Darryl is a murdering bastard, that's what."

"I'll ask you again, do you know Ray Doyle?"

"I've never heard of him. But he could be the bloke Darryl's always on the mobile to."

"Will you be willing to give evidence against Darryl?"

"If you charge him with Frankie's murder, then too fucking royal."

"Tell us what happened before you found Frankie dead?"

"Well, we'd picked up the women and drugs, stowed the women away, and Frankie fed and watered them. I went back on deck to keep an eye out."

"So, only Darryl and Frankie were down below?"

"Yes."

"What happened then?"

"Darryl came up on deck, and I asked him where Frankie was. He said Frankie was having a couple of hours kip because he was a bit stressed."

"What happened then?"

"Well, a while later I went down to check on Frankie and that's when I found him, dead on the floor. I called for Darryl, but I knew Frankie had gone, and when I saw the bag of powder, I knew he'd overdosed."

"What did Darryl want to do?"

"The callous bastard wanted to dump him overboard, but I wasn't having any of it"

"So, what did you decide?"

"Wrap him in the tarpaulin and get him home to our place. I was going to leave it a couple of days, and then call the police, knowing as far as they'd be concerned it was just another druggie overdose death."

"Well, that wouldn't have worked, knowing what we know now about the methamphetamine."

"I know that now. Look, that's all I can say. I've told you everything. These murders are down to Darryl, nobody else. I'm fucked, I know that. All I ask is that you nail the bastard."

"Did you ever see Darryl with any syringes, Brett, especially before Frankie's death?

"No, I've never ever seen him with syringes. Coke and dope, but not syringes."

Fiona had what they needed. This would crack things wide open. "We'll keep you informed, as to how it goes."

***

Fiona looked like she had nicked the cat's cream. Things were looking brighter. Even the rain had stopped, and bright shafts of light pierced the windows of the CID office. "Well boss, we've re-interviewed Brett and he's come clean on everything. Both he and Frankie picked up the four Vietnamese boys at Burry Port, as we believed. He says that two were already dead. They had been instructed by Hayes to drop them in Swansea, hence the marina. While they were dumping them, the other two legged it, but they weren't concerned about that, they just wanted to get out of town and head back to Porthcawl."

"What about the van?"

"It's the same one as Palmer and Bayer were in when they were arrested. The four of them use it and keep changing the plates."

"What did he say when you told him the cause of Frankie's death?"

"He's not happy, boss. He knows now that Darryl Hayes overdosed him, and he'll give evidence."

"What about Palmer and Bayer?"

"They brought the four ashore at Burry Port. It looks like they alternate for each run. Brett and his brother have been doing it for about a year and that's all."

Quince beamed as brightly as the sunlight. "I think Bill and Ted's Big Adventure is going to play a big part in this," he paused whilst Fiona giggled at his film reference, even though she had heard it before. "Certainly, as far as physical evidence is concerned. So, the DNA will be important. I think we've enough to charge them all, but I'll run it past the CPS. The fuckers are not going anywhere anytime soon so we've got a fair bit of leeway."

McGuire patted Quince on the shoulder. "Well, Abe, looks as if you've got a bit of a result, so I'll leave you all to it. I'll have my

team tie everything up at my end and get the paperwork to you."
"Sounds like a plan, boss."

66

"OK, Ray, just to bring you up to speed," Quince said brightly. He was struggling to keep a smug expression from forming on his face. "I now have evidence that Darryl Hayes is responsible for three murders, the two Vietnamese lads found in the marina, and Frankie Noble. Now, there's no doubt that you are connected to Hayes, and most certainly you are complicit in all three by association. So, is there anything you'd like to say, bearing in mind you're still under caution?"

"Look, Inspector, I had nothing to do with any murders, I swear."

"Ray, we've got all your bank records," Quince opened a file for effect. "I must say you're worth a few bob. In fact, not far off two hundred grand in the last twelve months," he whistled. "Can you explain all the deposits?"

"Investments," Ray shrugged. "I speculate on the stock market."

"Pull the other one, Ray. The money is your share for the use of The Dolphin. You'd better start shaping up, because you're looking at a life sentence if convicted. You understand that of course?"

"Of, course I do, I know the score."

"Well, I must say, I think you're being incredibly stupid for an intelligent man. The whole gang are in custody and one of them is singing like a canary on Britain's Got Talent. We know exactly what's been going on for the last twelve months, and you are slap bang in the middle of it." Quince looked for tell-tale signs of a breakthrough in Ray's face. There was a slight raising on the eyebrows – barely noticeable - and Ray began wringing his hands. It was working. "You'll pull a fair bit of bird for the trafficking, but the murders? That's a life sentence without parole. So, just think on mate."

Now Ray's face began to drain of colour. He was worried. If he was guilty or not, Quince knew the threat of appearing before a jury on a charge of murder was serious business and not something anyone would want to face if they were in their right mind. "Can I speak with my solicitor in private?" Ray asked.

"Of course, you can. We'll wait outside. Interview suspended at the request of Mr Doyle," Quince said for the benefit of the recording.

Outside the interview room, Quince led the way to the nearest coffee machine. It was a poor instant bean, but it was also better than nothing.

"What do you reckon, boss?"

"What do I reckon, George? I reckon he's just filled his nappy. He's weighing it up and wondering if there's enough shit in it to justify getting the wet wipes out. Does he try and bluff it out, pretend there's no shit in there and possibly go down with Hayes, or does he reach for those wet wipes and come clean? There's nothing worse than a shitty arse."

"What do you think? Shit or wipes?" George grinned.

"It'll be the wipes. I'll put money on it. No one likes to wallow in shit, especially if it's not their own."

Now George laughed. "I like your confidence, boss."

A few minutes later, the door opened, and the solicitor's weasel face poked through the crack. "Officers, my client is ready to co-operate, but he wants assurances."

"Let's hear what he has to say first."

The interview resumed with George running through the introductions and a reminder that Ray was still under caution.

"Ray, I understand you may have had a change of heart?" Quince said.

"Look, if I tell you everything I know, are the murder charges off the table? I'll plead to the trafficking."

"I think that can be sorted, Ray. Now give it to me chapter and verse, how did it all begin?"

Ray sighed, nodded, and took a long swig from a plastic bottle of water. "It was about eighteen months ago; Darryl had been arrested in town on an alleged possession charge. It was only a bit of blow. I attended at the nick as his legal rep and I got him a caution."

"OK, go on."

"Well, one thing led to another, and it came up in conversation that I had access to a boat, and he pitched a deal to bring in cigarettes and wine. I was gambling a lot at the time, and I needed quick cash. I was in heavy, and my wife had no idea. I had promised her I wouldn't bet again but… I just couldn't let it go." Ray thumped the water bottle onto the table. "So, I went along with it. I gave him access to The Dolphin and it just escalated from there. Before I knew it, I was up to my ears in it and was finding it increasingly difficult to keep my head afloat."

"You must have been really in the hole to go along with that?"

"Oh aye, as I said, up to my fucking neck. I owed thousands."

"How many thousands?" George asked, scribbling in his notebook.

"Over thirty-five at the last count. Too much for me to find from elsewhere. It was only a matter of time before Jasmine rumbled me." He paused and wiped his eyes. "You've got to understand, I love her. She's my world but I know if she finds out what I've done she'll be off… and I don't blame her. The thought that she'll think less of me breaks my heart. I've only ever wanted her to be proud of me…" his voice broke. Tears now streamed down his face. "I've been a fucking fool. Now she'll know anyway, and I'll do time."

Quince gave him a moment to compose himself before continuing. "So, when did the trafficking start?"

"Well, that was about twelve months ago. I had no idea about the first lot. Darryl just gave me a tremendous wedge; he only told me after I took the cash."

"So, how many times has The Dolphin been used for trafficking?"

"I reckon… about eight times in total."

"I must say, Ray, you're one stupid individual."

"Tell me about it," he nodded.

"OK, tell me about the two Vietnamese lads found in the marina."

"That was a tremendous fuck up. I knew nothing about it until Darryl told me. I told him to knock it all on the head and take The Dolphin to the Porthcawl marina and if anyone asked, it was there for an overhaul."

"So, why this last trip?"

"Well, I knew you were concentrating on the marina, so I told Darryl, and he just took it from there. I told him it was suicidal, but he wasn't having any of it. He's a real mean bastard."

"We've got Darryl, Brett Noble, Owen Palmer and Ralph Bayer in custody, all linked to trafficking, is there anybody else involved?"

"No, that's the lot, apart from Frankie."

"Ah yes, poor Frankie."

"Can you tell me how he died?"

"The same way as the two Vietnamese boys. Overdosed on methamphetamine, by the looks of it, administered by Darryl."

"Oh, it was him alright. I'm not taking the rap for him. Look, that's all I can tell you about it, I swear."

"So, basically, you gave Darryl access to The Dolphin and let him run riot with these innocent victims?"

"Yes, I've never met, or been in contact with any of them."

"Is there anything else, Ray?"

"No way am I taking the rap for murder."

67

He needed a drink. The meeting had been a waste of time. His font of luck with Swansea Council had apparently run dry and he fumed at their incompetence. They were stupid. None of them had a vision. None of them could see what could be achieved if they just let him run with his plans. The casino had been a battle to get through planning, but Ted Howe's plan to add a nightclub on the old Vetch site had gone down like a lead balloon. 'Too much noise for the neighbours,' one woman, who had probably not set foot on a dance floor in fifty years, had said. Ted had assured them that the sound proofing was now so efficient that they could stand outside the front door and not hear a sound. They dug their heels in and refused to budge. He was angry but not finished yet.

Ted clicked the locks on his X6 which he had parked on the first level of the NCP multi-story in the city centre. He could have parked it in the council car park outside the enormous monstrosity of a grey concrete building that sat brooding on the sea front. The not-so-great white elephant that occupied the most valuable real estate in the city. Only the prison on the other side of the Mumbles Road spoiled the land's potential. What sodding idiot thought it would be a good idea to build a prison on the seafront? It wasn't like the prisoners would benefit from the sea air and a walk on the bloody beach. But Ted had parked in the centre to buy a present for Pat. He felt bad about the way he had treated her of late. What had happened to them? Why had he pushed her away? He had married her because he loved her. She was the only woman he had ever loved but now she was screwing another woman. Had he been so bad that she could only find the love she needed from another woman? He pulled the bottle of Channel perfume from his pocket. Did she still like Channel? Truth was, he had no idea anymore. They had drifted apart. Perhaps he could still save their marriage? Pat was a part of him and if he lost her, it would be like cutting both his arms off. Ted tucked the bottle back in his pocket and sat behind the wheel. He slipped the key into the ignition just as the passenger door opened and a man in a ski mask brandished an automatic pistol in Ted's face.

"Don't make a fucking move, or I'll blow your fucking head off, do you understand?"

Ted struggled to keep his bowels and bladder from evacuating before him. "Whatever," he said as he held his hands up like he had seen in the movies. "Take my wallet, take the fucking car, do what you like."

"I don't want your fucking wallet," the gunman spat as he got into the passenger seat. "Just drive out of the city, do you understand?"

"What do you want? Do you know who I am?"

"Of course, I know who you are. I don't want anything off you. I've already been paid, you fucking arsehole. Now drive, like I told you to."

Ted pressed the start button on the dash and the car roared into life. "Look, I'll double what they paid you."

The gunman laughed. "It doesn't work like that. They told me that you'd try all that kind of shit. Just do as you're told and follow my instructions. If you try anything, I'll top you, have you got that?"

Ted didn't argue. "Where are we going?"

"Just drive, and keep your mouth shut. Once we get out of the city, I'll tell you."

Howe followed the gunman's instructions for about five minutes.

"Do you know Penllergaer woods?"

"Er, yes," Ted said, now even more worried than before. This didn't sound like it would end well for him.

"Well let's go, and no funny business. Stick to the speed limits, we don't want the fucking filth pulling us over, do we?" the gunman laughed.

"For fuck sake, what's going on?"

"Have you ever wondered what it would be like to be buried alive?"

"You must be fucking joking? You can't be serious. Who's paying you to do this?"

"Put it this way, Ted, you've upset a lot of people over the years, and truth be told there are a few who'd like you to disappear, end of. I'm just going to do what I've been paid for."

"What the fuck is that?"

"You'll find out shortly. Just head for the woods. I've got a nice surprise for you."

About ten minutes later Howe arrived at the car park near Penllergaer woods.

"Park the car here, lock it and just start walking towards the woods."

Howe didn't argue. What else could he do? He was powerless to resist but there was no way he was going to let some hood take his life without a fight. First chance he got, he'd tear the man apart and shove the gun where the sun don't shine. Even just the thought of resisting, of fighting back, buoyed his spirits. For now, he could do nothing but comply.

"OK, just walk towards the tree line. If you look behind, I'll just waste you here and now. It's your choice."

Ted led his abductor along the forestry road for what seemed like an eternity. Ted heard the birds, the rustling of the wind in the trees and felt its cold breath on his face. He had walked here many times over the years and yet had never experienced the heightened senses of this day before. Perhaps it was something to do with the fact he was probably going to die? He was getting to appreciate the things he had ignored all his life. If only he had more time. After what was probably no more than a quarter of a mile, the gunman spoke again.

"Now walk left into the trees. There's a clearing about fifty yards in. When you get there just stop. There's a little surprise there for you. I think you'll like it; I know the people who hired me will."

"Listen, I don't know what the fuck's going on, but you're in big trouble."

"Ted, I don't think so."

Ted stepped through a wall of newly planted saplings into the clearing, and his stomach churned. This was it. There before him was a hole that looked like a half-dug grave. The light was fading fast and so was Ted's bottle.

"Oh, for fuck sake, whoever you are, please don't put me in there."

"Ted, it's only half finished. I wouldn't expect you to lie in a half-finished grave. I know you're a man of standards," he laughed then snapped, "Now get fucking digging. I haven't got all day. The shovel is there, and don't fucking try anything or I'll double tap you and bury you myself.

It took ten minutes to finish the grisly job. He had tried to look for something, anything to give him a chance of escape but the gunman stayed far enough away to make it impossible for Ted to take a chance.

"OK, that's enough. Now lie down."

"You can't do this surely? I beg you, please don't do this?"

"Ted, just do as you're told," he waved the gun at him. From where I'm standing, you don't have a choice."

Howe dropped to his knees as he began to sob. How the hell had this happened? This was not how he saw his final moments of his life playing out.

"No, Ted, face down. I never like looking into the eyes of my victims," the gunman said calmly.

Howe lay face down, and a few seconds later felt the soil on his back. The bastard was burying him alive.

"What's going through your mind Ted? Let me think now, 'who the fuck wants to do this to me and why,'" he said in a mock girlie voice. "My theory would be you need to perm any one of a dozen. That's what comes from being a bit of a twat."

Soil continued to pile on to Howe's back until it got to the crucial stage where he could hardly breathe. Then it stopped.

Howe stayed silent; he had now accepted his fate. What would come next? The bullet? The spade through his head? But nothing came. There was no sound of movement above him, just the wind in the trees and the happy birds mocking his predicament. Ted slowly got to his knees, the soil falling from his back. His kidnapper was nowhere to be seen. He craned his neck, looking for the muzzle of the gun pointing at him from behind a tree. The guy had gone. Ted slowly made his way back to where his car was parked. On the bonnet he found the ignition keys and mobile the kidnapper had snatched from him. Now the tears that streamed down his face were of relief. He was in a terrible state, he had not only wet himself, but he'd also soiled himself. The only good thing was that he was alive.

He fumbled numbers into his phone and pressed the call button.

"Pat, it's me."

"Where are you, Ted?"

"Pat, I'm up Penllergaer woods, I've just been kidnapped, and threatened with a gun."

"Jesus, Ted, have you been drinking?"

"Pat, I'm serious. I'd been at a meeting and some fucking raving lunatic got in my car, threatened to kill me, and then brought me up here." His voice broke as he continued. "He had me dig my own grave and started burying me. I'm on my way home, give the casino a ring, tell Francine I won't be in tonight. Tell her I'm not well and I'll see her tomorrow."

"Shall I ring the police, Ted?"

"No, no police. I'll have to sort this myself, whoever did this is going to pay. I swear. I'll be home in half an hour."

***

"Hi Norma"

"Pat, how are you? Everything alright?"

"I don't know, Norma. Ted just rang me, says he's been kidnapped, and somebody tried to bury him alive up Penllergaer woods."

"Is he OK?"

"Sounds OK now, Norma, but he's fuming. He's on his way home."

"Have you rung the police?"

"He doesn't want the police involved."

"Does he have any idea who's responsible?"

"Norma, it could be anybody. He's not exactly popular, is he?"

"Do you think Jason could be involved?"

"God no. Ted's got so many enemies, it could be anybody," she sighed. "Truth be told I wish they had bloody buried him."

"Perhaps this will change his attitude, who knows? Just keep me updated."

68

"OK, everybody, the enquiry has certainly progressed since the interviews." The team was gathered for another of the regular briefings. Quince walked slowly around the outside as he spoke, fingers intertwined, tapping slowly at his chin. "Brett Noble and Ray Doyle, have basically spilled their guts, and have admitted their full involvement in the trafficking of these poor unfortunates. The other three are still going no comment, but I've spoken with the CPS, and they are quite happy for them all to be charged. Hayes will carry three counts of murder, and the rest will be dumped with the trafficking. We've still got plenty of time on the clock, so there's no real urgency." Quince stopped and leaned on the back of a chair. "I intend putting them before a special court on Wednesday morning. Hopefully, the lab will come up with something that will make the case watertight. Bill, perhaps you can bring us up to speed with regard to the examination of The Dolphin, Hayes's Porsche, the Transit van and all their houses?"

"Sure, boss." Bill sat directly where Quince was standing. "The first obvious item is the five kilos of cocaine recovered on the marina walkway. We did a quick sample test and it's fifty per cent pure and has been cut with glucose.

"The Dolphin had been recently cleaned, you could smell the bleach," he frowned at the memory. "However, whoever cleaned it forgot to get rid of the hoover. So, all the contents have been bagged and tagged. We may get lucky there with hair samples. The women had been kept in a confined space within the cat's pod. We also found minute traces of blood splatter on one of the walls. As far as the vehicles and houses are concerned, we didn't get much. We found some drug paraphernalia, but nothing worth writing home about. With regard to prints, we can put the Noble brothers, Palmer and Bayer in the Transit, and also The Dolphin, together with Hayes, of course. All the exhibits are with the lab, and they've all been fast tracked because of the seriousness of the case. Hopefully, we'll have something tomorrow afternoon."

"Any sign of syringes or methamphetamine, Bill?"

"A few syringes in the Porsche, boss, but no meth."

"Thank you, Bill. Well, everybody, you're all up to speed. So, I suggest you all get home, get some kip, and be back early in the morning. Thank you all for your efforts. You've stuck at it and done a remarkable job."

***

Quince left his car in the station car park and walked the mile or so through the shopping centre towards Morgan's Hotel on the marina. Once a thriving shopping town, since becoming a city, Swansea had been on a steady decline in popularity. Many observers blamed this on the planners. There had never been a clear- and forward-thinking plan for the city since it was bombed during the Second World War. The shopping centre seemed to move focus every decade. Areas were revived, thrived, and then died as a new area became the darling of the planners thinking.

Morgan's Hotel occupied an old red brick shipping building on what had become the most recent focus of the city's thinking. Developed by a millionaire who had made his fortune in the holiday travel business, its four-star status made it one of the most popular hotels in the city. Quince liked it for its history. The building retained much of its previous architectural beauty from a time when even utilitarian buildings were designed to show off the wealth of the proprietors. Quince walked past several bars that sold beer and whiskey cheaper than Morgan's, it was, after all, a hotel and hotels were always more expensive, but Quince liked the place. There was always a place to sit quietly and think without being disturbed, except when there was a wedding party or some other celebration filling the bar. Tonight, it was quiet.

The young barman poured Quince a large whiskey just as Ted was pouring his own several miles away.

***

"Ted, what the hell happened, tell me?"

"Pat, the bloke was a raving lunatic. He had a gun, threatened to kill me. I thought I'd had my chips."

"What did he want, was it money?"

"No, he never asked for anything. I think he just wanted to

frighten me, and he certainly did that."

"Did you recognise him?"

"No, he had a ski mask on. I'm telling you he had it all planned, right down to the grave. He had me lie in it, he'd obviously half dug it himself and the spade was already there," Ted visibly shivered at the memory.

"So, who have you upset that much?"

"You know me, Pat, I upset somebody every day," he forced a smile. "No, this was different."

"You'll have to be careful, perhaps you should get a minder or something."

"Maybe. I'm going to have a shower, clean up, and then go to the casino."

"Ted, for God's sake, after what happened to you..."

"Look, I'll be about ten minutes tops."

The sound of the shower running was drowned out by Ted's mobile ringing on the coffee table.

Pat picked it up and answered it. No caller ID.

"Hello, can I help you?"

"Oh, sorry I must have got the wrong number."

"Who do you want?"

"Ted, Ted Howe."

"Yes, this is Ted's mobile, he's in the shower at the minute, who shall I say is calling?"

"Tell him it's Phillipe. He'll know what it's about."

"Hold on, I'll get him."

Pat carried the phone into the ground floor wet room where Ted was just stepping out of the shower, towel wrapped around his increasing waistline. "Phillipe for you," she said as she handed him the phone.

"Phillipe? I don't know any Phillipe. Give me the phone?" Ted snatched the handset from his wife. "Ted Howe here, who the hell are you?"

"Forgotten me already, Ted? Perhaps I should have fucking buried you, eh?"

A mixture of anger and fear gripped Ted. "Who the fuck are you, and what's your game?"

"Money, Ted. You know all about that and how to make it. You're into everything. I want a hundred grand, otherwise I'll blow the gaff on you, big time."

"You can get stuffed; you're having nothing off me."

"Just have a little think, Ted. I got to you once, I can get to you again and next time, I promise you, I *will* bury you."

"You've got nothing on me, Phillipe, or whatever your name is."

"Fair enough, Ted, we'll just let it take its course then. I know you're blackmailing a senior police officer, and you've got your fingers in a few other pies like money laundering."

"You've got nothing," Ted laughed but he was worried. How did this man know all this?

"I'll send you a few pics through the post within the next couple of days, perhaps then you'll change your tune?" The call ended.

"The twat's hung up," Ted threw the phone on to a basket of dirty washing.

"What did he want, Ted?"

"The bastard is trying to blackmail me, Pat. He wants a hundred grand."

Ted's mobile beeped; he rescued it from the dirty clothes. It was a picture of him with Norma Cross handing her the package of cash.

The mobile rang again.

"There we are, Ted, and that's just for starters. There's plenty more where that came from. I'll be in touch, say in about a week or so? I've got some other business to take care of, so keep safe."

"Pat, whoever it is, they're fucking dead. When I find them, they'll wish they'd never been born."

69

It was late when Howe arrived at the casino. The games area was busy and Fran as usual was overseeing everything, making sure that there were no shenanigans going on. Normally she would have been in the security office scanning the CCTV monitors, but due to the fact that Howe hadn't turned up she took it on herself to make sure things were running smoothly.

"How are things going, Fran?"

"Evening, Mr Howe, everything's going smooth, as you can see. We're very busy. Is everything alright? you look a bit flushed."

"Got a lot on my mind, Fran, so thanks for covering."

"If you need to talk, I'm a good listener?"

"No, there's nothing you can do."

"Try me, is it anything to do with the casino?"

"No, nothing like that."

"Well, it must be serious. I've never seen you like this before. You look like you've seen a ghost."

"Let's go into the office, I need a drink."

Fran followed Howe into the office where he poured two tumblers of Scotch.

"There we are, Fran, get that down you." Ted took a long gulp of his drink and wiped his mouth with the back of his hand. "To tell you the truth, I've no fucking idea what's going on."

"What do you mean, what's happened?"

"Look, if I tell you, don't breathe a word. Have you got that?"

"Your secrets are safe with me, Mr Howe. I won't let you down."

"Fran, I was fucking kidnapped earlier, some arse wipe got in my car with a gun, and threatened me."

"What do you mean, kidnapped you? Have you reported it to the police?"

"No. Only you and Pat know about it. I don't want the police involved."

"Did he get money?"

"No, that's it, I had to drive to Penllergaer woods where he'd half dug a grave for me."

"Good God, I can't believe what you're telling me. You've got to report this."

"No, Fran. No police. I'd end up a fucking laughingstock."

"So, what happened up at the woods?"

"He ordered me to finish digging the grave, and then had me lie face down in it. I shit myself."

"So, how did you get away from him?"

"Well, this is it, he started covering me over with soil, then all of a sudden stopped, and disappeared."

"What did he want? He must have wanted something, for God's sake. No one does something like that without wanting something."

"This is it, Fran, when I got home, he rang me. It's all about blackmail now. He wants a hundred grand."

"What's it all about?"

"It's complicated, Fran, that's all I can say at the minute."

"Are you going to pay him?"

"No chance. Do I look like I came up the channel in a bloody coracle?

"I've been about a bit, I know what goes at casinos," Fran said. "Where there's money there's trouble. You haven't got where you are without upsetting a few along the way, I've no doubt."

"You're not far wrong there," Ted poured himself another. He took another slug. Fran could see his hand shaking. "But this is different."

"What about that policewoman friend of yours? Why don't you have a chat with her about it? Perhaps she can do something, unofficial like?"

"No, I've got to sort this myself. Whoever it is, if I get my hands on them, they won't live to regret it. I'm telling you now."

"It must be someone you've had a run in with recently."

"Not really. The only one I've had a barney with lately is Pat's boy, Jason. But he's flown back to Malaga, and he wouldn't go this far."

"You'd be surprised what lengths people got to if they need quick cash. I know a few people, they could keep an eye on you, a bit of protection."

"Pat suggested that, but no, I don't want it. I'll sort it. You get back on the floor, but cheers for listening, and like I said, tell no one."

"It's not a problem, and if you want a chat just call."

***

Inside her 'bijou' flat, Fran felt safe but still couldn't lose her fake persona and become herself. She had to remain within her cover at all times to ensure she didn't slip. Many years of being someone else had often blurred the lines for her but as long as she stayed in character, she would be OK. When she got home, she called her handler, DCI Trudi Lancaster, using a handset hidden in a box of cereal.

"Sorry to bother you so late, boss, but I've made a bit of progress with Howe."

"In what way, Fran?"

"He's come into the casino tonight shitting himself. Somebody kidnapped him earlier, and partially buried him in some local woods."

"Jesus! Is he OK?"

"Like I say, bit shaken."

"That's a bit serious. Has he reported it?"

"No, that's it, the kidnapper was armed with a gun but didn't steal anything. Could have buried him alive but let him live."

"Are you sure he's not making it all up? A bit of insurance for something in the future, perhaps?"

"No, boss, he's genuine. I'm positive."

"So, what's it all about?"

"He says it's blackmail. Whoever it was got in touch with him later on and demanded a hundred grand."

"If Howe's not reporting it, there must be something in it."

"Definitely. He says that he's got no idea who it is, but as you know, he's as fly as a cartload of monkeys, and into everything. He did mention his stepson Jason Corbett. But he's back in Malaga, perhaps you can confirm that?"

"We will. So, what's your next move, Fran?"

"We know about his association with Chris Richards, and the art forgery, but I reckon we ought to let this little drama run and see where it leads us."

"Yes, we've got Howe and Richards by the nuts. Plenty of audio and video evidence of their forgery activities, and that's all down to you. I don't want you putting yourself in danger, God knows who this blackmailer is, but he sounds ruthless to me."

"It's the first time Howe has confided in me. I'll keep an eye on him, and keep you updated."

"Has he made a pass at you, because from what you've told me, he's a bit of a lady's man."

"No, he's never tried anything. Perhaps now is the time to make the first move?"

"You be careful, and don't overstep the boundaries. When Howe is finally nicked, we don't want everything to go tits up, do you understand?"

"Loud and clear, boss, I know the score. I've been doing it long enough."

"Concentrate on Howe from here on in, forget about Richards, we've got him covered."

70

Quince had kept the morning briefing short, everyone knew what they had to do throughout the day. As far as he was concerned all the interviews had been completed, he was just awaiting the results from the forensic lab. If any substantive evidence were forthcoming, whichever defendant it related to would have to be interviewed for their side of the story. It was a question of topping and tailing, ready for charging.

Quince was downing his second mug of coffee when his mobile rang. It was Andy Stokes.

After the usual pleasantries, Stokes got down to business. "I'm ringing because it's common knowledge now that you've got Ray Doyle on toast there. Just thought I might give you a bit of background, for what it's worth."

"That's damned decent of you, Andy. I'm all ears."

"Well, I met him a few years ago, the usual thing, a social meeting of offices. At the time he was doing the same as me, and in fairness, he was good at it."

"I've never had any dealings with him before."

"He's got a fair bit of baggage, truth be told. That's why they've got him in the office, so they can keep an eye on him. He's a terrible gambler, and at one time had a bit of a coke habit. He's gone through tens of thousands, allegedly, over the years."

"So, what's his preferred vice, Andy?"

"The whole nine yards, Abe, you name it he'll have a crack at it."

"Did you have any inkling at all about his involvement with the trafficking?"

"No, I was surprised at that. I know his firm are fucking devastated about it all."

"Well, he's going to pull a fair bit of bird, even on a plea."

"Deserves it, Abe, and all the others with him."

"I must admit I half expected you to turn up as their legal rep."

"Nah, I dodged that one, Abe."

***

"Well, if it isn't the chuckle brothers. I hope you've got some good news for me," Quince said to Bill Daniels.

"Boss, ye of little faith, I think you'll be pleasantly surprised." Daniels replied.

"Well don't keep me in suspense."

"OK, I'll take it from the top... two syringes recovered from the Porsche... positive traces for methamphetamine solution. Blood splatter found on the walls of The Dolphin... Positive DNA match on the two bodies recovered from the marina."

"Anything else, Bill?"

"Boss, what more do you want?"

"Well, I suppose we shouldn't be greedy," Quince laughed. "At least it ties Hayes in with the methamphetamine, and with Brett Noble filling in the blanks. I think he's fucked, don't you? Three counts of murder, possessing with intent to supply, and the trafficking. He isn't going to see the light of day. As for the others, they've been caught in the act, end of. I must say gents, a job well done. Me and George will have a chat with Hayes and put the scenario to him to see what he says. After that, they can all be charged. Bill, will you bring the team up to speed for me? I'll crack on with George. Let's see what the murdering twat has to say."

***

"Well, Darryl, before we start this interview, I'm notionally arresting you on suspicion of the murders of Frankie Noble, Dinh Chien, and Taavi Dong, the latter two being the young Vietnamese lads that were dumped in the maria. I must caution you. Do you understand the gravity of those allegations?"

"Like I've said all along, no fucking comment," he snarled.

"That's your prerogative, Darryl, but I'm obliged to put a few other things to you."

"No comment."

"Our CSI officers went through The Dolphin with a fine-tooth comb, and you may have thought the bleach you cleaned it with did the job, but it didn't. They found blood splatter which contained the DNA of Chien and Dong, so it's safe to assume that something happened in that confined space. Perhaps you gave them a few slaps? No, I don't think you did, I know you did."

"No comment."

"They also found two syringes in your Porsche, they've been examined, and traces of methamphetamine have been found, the same drug found in Chien's, Dong's, and Frankie Noble's systems, so I put it to you that you were responsible for their deaths. Would you like to tell me the full story?"

"No comment."

"Look, Darryl, it's quite obvious that you and Ray Doyle are behind it all, but you've got a big problem. Both Doyle and Brett Noble have seen the light and admitted their full involvement in the whole operation."

"No comment."

"I put it to you that Chien and Dong became a bit of a handful on the cat' and you gave them a massive dose of methamphetamine to quieten them down. However, it went straight to their hearts and saw them off pretty quickly."

"No comment."

"Now we come to young Frankie. I believe the motive for killing him was that he was getting cold feet after the bodies in the marina cock up and wanted out. But him being a junkie, you didn't want that because you were afraid he'd open his mouth when he was high. You'd have probably got away with that if you hadn't been nicked."

"No comment."

"Well, I think that's just about it, Darryl. You'll be charged, held in custody, taken to court and remanded. What have you got to say about that?"

Hayes leaned back in his chair and grinned. "No fucking comment."

"Interview terminated. George, put Darryl before the custody officer and explained the grounds for charging and remand."

Quince headed back to the Incident room.

"Well team, George and I just did a quick interview with Hayes. He went the usual way with no comment, but we've got enough evidence to put him away for life. I suggest you sort all the charges out for the five of them. Do the business, and once I tie up a few loose ends, I'll meet you all in the Adam and Eve about six. Open a tab, I'll sort it," he said to a chorus of cheers.

71

"It's all going to plan I put the fear of God into him, but you know what he's like, he's a stubborn conniving bastard. Perhaps I should have fucking buried him in the grave?"

"Cool down, we'll play the long game here. We've got plenty of time. I can read him like a book. We'll get the money out of him, no problem. And once he pays up, we'll have him on the hook. He's a ruthless bastard, but this time he's bitten off more than he can chew. He treats people like shit, so it's time he had a bit of pay back."

"What's the score with this copper then?"

"He's got the black on her, and I know he's been seeing to her, left himself wide open he has."

"So, what's the next move?"

"We'll let things cool down for a week or two, and then go for the jugular. He'll pay, make no bones about that."

"So, what's the problem with you and Howe?"

"He owes me a few shillings. I've just been biding my time, and the time has come, it's been on the cards for a few years, but I've never really had the opportunity to really stick it to him. Now's the time."

***

Fran had been copying pages from the casino accounts when Ted Howe arrived. She quickly clicked off the accounting software and ejected the pen drive. "Evening, Mr Howe. How are things going? Have you heard anything from the blackmailer yet?"

"No, Fran, nothing. But I'll sort it."

"There's a Mr Hatcher in your office. He said that he had an appointment with you."

"Ah yes, Karl. He's a business associate. Everything alright here?"

"Yes Mr Howe, all going swimmingly," Fran smiled as she slipped the pen drive into the spine of her diary.

"Good, Fran. I'll see you on the floor once I've finished with Karl."

Fran watched as Howe entered his office.

"Evening. Ted. What's the problem? You sounded a bit hyper earlier. What's going on?"

"You're not going to believe me when I tell you, Karl. I was kidnapped last night. Some piece of scum hijacked me and buried me in a grave."

"Didn't do a very good job then did he? Not with you standing here," Karl laughed.

"I'm telling you he shoved a fucking gun in my face and made me drive to Penllergare woods."

"Did he rob you?"

"No, that's just it. He didn't take anything. It had obviously been pre-planned, there was a half dug grave waiting for me."

"Any idea who he was, Ted?"

"He was wearing a ski mask and that's about all I can say."

"Are you sure it was a bloke?"

"Of course, it was a bloke."

"You don't know these days Ted, some of these women today are like blokes."

"Karl, I know the fucking difference. Anyway, the scum rang me up later, and wants a hundred grand. He knows I'm blackmailing that Cross bint."

"The one your Mrs is carrying on with?"

"Aye, that's the one. Says he's got pictures of me handing her cash."

"Well, who do you reckon is behind it? How does he know all this? Is your Mrs behind it all? Let's be fair, Ted, you've really done a job on her and Cross."

"No, Pat wouldn't have set this up. Mind you, I'm beginning to think that boy of hers might have put someone up to it."

"Well. It's obviously someone who knows all about you, Ted."

"Could be anybody."

"So, what do you want me to do, Ted?"

"I want you to find out who it is, that's what I want, Karl."

"Leave it to me, Ted. Do you want me to shadow you for a couple of days, see how the land lies?"

"No, I'll just carry on as normal. I'm waiting for another call from the bastard."

"OK, I'll get on it first thing in the morning. If he does contact you, let me know straight away. I reckon it's someone local, probably someone who may be working for you."

72

The celebratory drink after a murder has been detected is something of a well-established tradition.

The murder of the two Vietnamese lads was a difficult and frustrating enquiry and Quince's team deserved to celebrate their success. But it had cost Quince a considerable sum. Quince had stayed for a few hours and swallowed his fair share of Guinness and whiskey. The rest of the team had made the most of the free bar and none were looking too good the next morning.

Quince had the water boiler ready for the copious mugs of coffee that would be needed as the detectives rolled in. "You look a bit worse for wear, swear you'd been on the piss all night," he said to George. "Now let's get down to the job in hand. I take it that all the charges are sorted, along with the special court?"

"Boss, my head is in a bucket, but aye, they're all sorted. Are you going to do the business?"

"No, George. You can have that pleasure after you've downed a couple of strong coffees. I've got to be down the big house by twelve."

"What about the remand, boss?"

"I've briefed the CPS, there'll be no problem. I understand there'll be no bail applications on this occasion. You know all the facts, so if anything untoward crops up, I'm sure you'll cope. As for you lot, haven't you got some actions to knock on the head," he said to the other sickly-looking troops.

***

Quince rolled up to the ACC's office as instructed. Gloria, a fifty-something, overweight lady who had recently taken the job as the ACC's PA smiled and told him to enter the inner sanctum.

"Afternoon, Abe. You look a bit green around the gills. Heavy night?"

"You know what it's like, boss. Too much grog and an empty wallet."

"The joys of leadership, eh?" he smiled. "You and your team

did a great job on the marina killings. I think all loose ends have been tied, mind you, I've had flak from every department under the sun; Immigration, Customs, the whole nine yards."

"Only to be expected, boss. Through the whole enquiry, they were as much use as fleas in a tramp's vest. Useless, truth be told. As for the Foreign Office, well they were even worse."

"Totally agree, Abe, but that's all been sorted. Don't worry about that. I've got something nice for you, and I'll think you'll be pleased."

"What's that, boss?"

"I've got Norma on toast at the minute. I suppose you could say she's treading water, so to speak. Anyway, as from today, you are the new DCI at Swansea Central."

"Well, I'm flattered, boss, but what about promotion boards and all that crap?"

"Boards, what boards, Abe? The job is yours. Do you want it or not?"

"Of course, I do, boss. But what about Cross?"

The ACC slumped back in his high-back leather chair and stared at the ceiling. "What's your opinion on her, Abe? Don't pull any punches."

"I'm not sure I should go there, boss."

"This is off the record, between you and me."

Quince nodded. OK, well I've always thought she's over promoted for a start, but you know that. But I also think she's corrupt. Anyone involved with Ted Howe is corrupt. Howe is into everything."

"Well, don't worry about Cross and Howe for the minute. I have no doubt Francine will bring them to book."

"How is it going with Francine?"

"Things are progressing slowly, Abe. Time will tell. Getting back to your promotion, have you anyone in mind to fill your position?"

"I don't think there's any need to ask. I want George Brodie. He's doing my job as we speak."

"You got him, Abe. Will you break it to him?"

"It'll be my pleasure, boss. He'll be over the moon. I suppose it's another night on the piss. The way it's going, I'll be bloody bankrupt."

"Like I said, it's called the perks of rank, Abe. Now I'm sorry, I've got a diversity meeting with the Chief and about twelve boring councillors."

"Good luck with that one, boss. Perks of the job, eh?" Quince sniggered.

"Guess I had that one coming."

***

Quince arrived back at the Incident room as the BBC evening news theme blasted out from a small flat screen television on the wall of the office.

"Ignore the telly," Quince said. "I've got a little bit of news for everybody, but first I need a quiet word with George."

George looked nervous and Quince could see the little birds fluttering in his head, panicking, and struggling to think of what he might have done wrong. He followed Quince into the office and close the door behind them.

"How did the remands go, George?" Quince said as he fished his whiskey from his desk drawer. "Want a hair of the dog?"

No, thanks, boss. Think I'll spew if I drink anything."

Quince felt the same and slipped the bottle back in the drawer. "OK. So, fill me in."

"It's all sweet as a nut, boss. All done and dusted, no problems. But I must admit the team all looked knackered."

"Excellent George, and it's understandable. They've worked a lot of hours. Now the other good news is that you are the new DI. I've had it straight from the horse's mouth."

"I might need that drink after all," George said, stunned by the news.

"Before you ask, forget about promotion boards" – interviews for senior promotions were always referred to as 'boards' – "It's a bit like promotion in the field during the war."

"Does that mean I'm working for DCI Cross, boss?"

"Nope, it doesn't, George. You'll be working for me. I'm your new DCI."

It took a few minutes for it to soak in before George told the rest of the team.

The whole room erupted, cheering and clapping promotions

they clearly agreed with.

"OK, everybody," Quince said, raising his hands to quiet the room. "I know you had a heavy night last night, but I think you'd better give your loved ones a bell and tell them you'll be working late again. So, let's hit the Adam at six, and George will foot half the fucking tab this time."

"Chief, it will be my pleasure."

***

Francine knew only too well that being an undercover officer was a very dangerous business, and you had to be on your guard at all times. In many cases officers had become too familiar with their targets. Crossing the line by becoming emotionally and physically involved could ruin months of painstaking work, with cases collapsing at the crown court, usually alleging agent provocateur or honey trap. Francine knew that she had no chance with Howe. Ever since she began working for him, he'd never once made a move on her, and she knew full well that he was a player. The only piece of the jigsaw that was missing as far as Francine was concerned was the money laundering scams. Howe would now be cleaning his dirty money through the casino.

To do this Howe needed an accountant that was up to the task, and Theo Stead was just the man.

Francine had only met Stead a couple of times since starting at the casino, he was a very difficult man to pin down. He wasn't what she'd call anti-social, but he kept his own counsel. Stead enjoyed playing the tables and the machines, losing more than he ever won. Quince had brought Francine up to speed on Stead and his habit, thinking there may be an opening there. On occasions, things had to be done for the greater good, and if it meant bending the rules, so be it.

Francine made a few calls, and then got ready for work. She had done the business. All she had to do was bide her time, and then she could hook Stead.

When Francine took over the security at the casino, one of the first policies that she made was, no drugs on the premises.

Howe was in total agreement with this. Francine knew full well that Howe was also making a fair few quid backing a local drug dealer, but Howe had bases covered and completely distanced himself from it all.

It was just before midnight, when Stead turned up at the casino, making a beeline for the blackjack table. Francine watched him like a hawk on the CCTV. Little did Stead know that his whole world would soon come crumbling down before him.

73

Quince and George Brodie sat in the office discussing the way forward, and the replacement for DS now George had been promoted.

"Right, let's get down to the nitty gritty, George and decide who's going to replace you. Have you anyone in mind?"

"I've never really thought about it, truth be told, boss. This promotion has come a bit on top, and taken me a bit by surprise."

"Charlie John is losing one of his DS's, Karen Covey, and he approached me when the enquiry began whether I could use her or not. Do you know Karen?"

"Not personally, boss, only by reputation. I know she's well respected, so why not."

"I think she could bring a bit of experience, more so around the surveillance area." Karen had spent several years within a team specialising in surveillance and had even taught the dark arts for several months to officers from other forces. She was good at her job and Quince believed her skills would complement those of the team he already trusted with his life.

"I have no doubt, boss and of course we'll have another female, which will be a good thing. You can't beat a good female detective, worth their weight in gold, they are."

"Well then, that's decided. Karen it is. I'll give her a bell. I understand from Charlie she can join the team as soon as we want. Any other areas that you could improve on George?"

"Not really, boss, you saw how they all performed. The only time their heads dropped was when Cross intervened."

"I don't think we'll see her again, George. Look at the office here, there's hardly anything of hers here. In fact, it's all in that box on the desk."

"One minute she didn't give a toss about the enquiry, when it was going smooth, then she gives you the elbow and is full on, like a headless chicken. Then she's gone again, never to be seen."

"Such is life, George. Anyway, we're back on track. As for Cross, there is definitely something in the wind. Get all the team assembled after lunch and we'll give them a good pep talk. These are exciting times."

***

The dust had barely settled after George left Quince's new office when Quince looked up from his case notes to see Norma Cross standing in the doorway.

"Morning, Abe," she smiled but there was nothing genuine about the expression. No warmth, just a hint of malice. "They tell me congratulations are in order."

"How are you doing, Norma?" Equal rank now. No need for formality. "Nice to see you," he lied. "I suppose you've come to collect your bits, and pieces? I've put them in that box over there."

"Didn't take you long to move into my office, Abe?"

"Well, let's be fair Norma, you didn't spend a lot of time in here. So, what are you up to these days?"

"Pastures greener, Abe," this time her smile appeared authentic, although she clearly had no intention of elaborating.

"I hope it's not at the sharp end, Norma?"

"Still the same old Abe, shooting straight from the hip, not giving a toss about anyone."

"That's not true, actually. I do care. It's just I care more about some than I do others."

That must have hurt.

"Whatever!" Norma snapped dismissively.

"At least you seem a little bit more relaxed than the last time I saw you. I was getting a little bit worried about you."

"What do you mean?"

"Well, your character changed. One minute you were full of confidence, like I'm taking over the enquiry, and then the next handing it back. There must have been something going on, something personal. I couldn't quite put my finger on it."

"What do you mean by personal?"

"It couldn't have been work related, because let's be fair, you didn't seem too bothered about the work, so it must be personal. You know what they say, a trouble shared is a trouble halved…" Quince thought he'd throw it out there, just to see what reaction he'd get from Cross, knowing full well that Ted and Pat Howe were involved somewhere along the line.

"Why would I want to share my troubles with you, Abe?"

"I'm a good listener," he smiled. "So, if you'd like to off-load, now's as good a time as any, what do you say Norma?"

"There's nothing to discuss, Abe. End of."

Cross picked up her box of nick-knacks and was about to leave.

"Nothing to do with that twat Ted Howe is it, Norma? I hope you're not banging him, if you are it's a big no-no and it will ruin your career. Perhaps I should never have introduced you."

"Abe... fuck you!"

Cross stormed out of the office, slamming the door behind her with a crash. He was going to give Cross a wide berth. He'd leave her to Francine.

***

Cross was really pissed with Quince. She now knew for sure that he had suspicions about her relationship with Ted Howe. But there was no way he could know the truth. No one knew the truth, not even her. Well, Pat knew, of course, but she wasn't telling anyone. She had to speak to Pat. If there was any chance of her surviving this, she had to know why 'her father' was such a hot potato – a potato that Pat seemed to think would more than just burn her fingers.

"Pat, I've just been speaking to Abe Quince. He believes there's something going on between me and Ted."

"What makes him think that?"

"He was in Morgans when Ted arranged to meet me. You know Quince put Ted away years ago but it was as if they were big pals. Quince left me with Ted after they'd had a chat. I could see he suspected something, but I wasn't sure what he was thinking."

"So, he thinks you're having it off with Ted? So what?"

"So what? Quince is like a bear trap. Once he's got you, there's no escape. But be honest with me. Ted is not the big secret here, is he?"

Silence. Pat said nothing and turned away.

"Pat... mam?"

Cross could hear a sharp intake of breath and the hint of a sob.

"That's the first time you've called me that."

"No big deal, is it?" Cross said dismissively.

"It is to me, Pat said softly.

"Then tell me who my father is and why I'd lose my job if anyone found out."

"The less who know the better. Even you. You can't say what you don't know. I'm protecting you; can't you see? I was just a bloody kid when I fell pregnant with you. That was shocking enough but no good will come from knowing who your dad is."

Cross fumed but knew Pat was stubborn. She had tried to establish her dad's identity before, with no luck. All efforts had drawn a blank and she knew Pat was not going to give way. "OK. But we'll have to be careful from here on in, I'd better tell Ted, because I don't think he'd want Quince sniffing around his business."

"Leave Ted to me, Norma. He's got a lot on his plate at the minute, what with his own kidnapping and blackmail," Pat couldn't stifle a wicked grin. "You should have seen his bloody face." Now she laughed.

"No more than he deserved," Cross agreed.

"Don't worry about it and don't blow it out of all proportion. We'll get together on the weekend."

"Sounds like a plan," Cross finally had reason to smile, albeit briefly.

74

Theo Stead sipped from a glass of sparkling Ty Nant water with his feet up on his antique oak desk when the phone rang. He stretched for his mobile sitting atop a pile of client files. Stead liked to work on paper, even though the company had switched to digital accounting a decade ago.

"TS accountants, Theo Stead speaking."

"Mr Stead, my name is Justin Fellows. I wonder if you can spare me some time?"

"In respect of what, Mr Fellows?"

"Well, I understand from a friend of mine that you may be interested in a new product that I'm selling?"

"Product, what are you talking about, Mr Fellows? I deal in accounts, business accounts, tax, and that sort of thing. I don't deal in products."

"Let's not be so formal, call me Justin. All my friends do."

"I'm sorry, I don't know you. Am I missing something here?" Stead was beginning to lose patience. He kicked his feet off the table and stood. Somehow, standing when speaking into a phone seemed to make him feel just a little more confident.

"I've clocked you at the club," Fellows continued. "I know you like to do a few lines. I'm setting up on my own, so I thought maybe you'd like to try a little sample."

Stead now felt enraged. Who the hell would call someone about things like this? "I don't know who you are, and I have no idea what you're talking about. Goodbye!"

"Hang on a minute, you were in the club last night, weren't you?"

Stead bristled. "I may have been," he said, cautiously.

"Oh, you were, Mr Stead. That bloke you were with, I say a bloke, more of a boy I'd say, naughty, naughty. I've got a lovey pic of you together in one of the traps having a snort. I suppose you'd like to see it?"

"I don't know what you want, but this is sounding too much like blackmail."

"Would you like me to pop around, or shall we meet

somewhere a bit more public? It's up to you. It will be beneficial to you."

Stead felt a hot flush of angry frustration. He wanted to grab this Fellows fella by the throat and strangle him or beat him with the signed cricket bat he had hanging on his office wall. "I'll meet you at the casino at seven o'clock tonight. I'll feel more comfortable there."

"I'll see you at seven. I'll bring some product. Call it a freebie."

***

"It's on." Fellows said. "I'm meeting him in the casino at seven. I hope you'll have everything sorted. Perhaps you can fix us up in one of the booths?"

"It'll all be sorted. What did he say when you mentioned the picture?"

"He knew the score. He fell for it hook, line and sinker. He was off his tits at the time I took it, didn't know what day it was."

"What about the coke?"

"I photographed him doing a deal. Then I gave our boy the nod and the rest is history."

"OK, cracking job. Just leave the rest to me."

***

Stead arrived at the casino just before seven. He parked his grey Mercedes in one of the empty spaces marked for disabled patrons. It was too early for anyone to be bothered with parking transgressions. Anyway, how many disabled slots did they need? He had never seen anyone in a wheelchair in the bloody casino. And anyone else claiming the perks was probably just slinging the lead anyway. Fuck 'em, he thought. He entered the foyer as the automatic doors opened in, inviting him into the inner sanctum. Francine stopped wiping the marble top reception with a bright yellow cloth and smiled at him.

"How are you tonight, Theo? Bit early for you, isn't it?"

"Purely business this evening, Fran. Meeting a client over a few drinks."

"It's early, the lounge is quiet at the minute, so take booth one."

"Cheers, Fran."

The sound of a big engine SUV turned their heads towards the car park. A bright red big-wheeled Toyota swung in quickly and pulled up alongside Stead's Mercedes.

"Is that your business acquaintance? Francine asked.

"To be honest, I have never met him. If it is, could you just point him in my direction?" Stead said as he hurried into the lounge.

Fellows switched off the engine of the Toyota and studied the new Mercedes alongside. He knew all about Stead and his love of flash cars. An idea formed and he grinned. He opened the door into the side of the Merc, leaving a noticeable dent in the gleaming paintwork. The rubber bugger strip on his truck protected his door but he wouldn't bothered if it had been damaged. Cars were tools to him. Nothing more. Fellows headed inside the building and Francine smiled as she greeted him. "Is Mr Stead here?"

"He's expecting you. He's in booth one," she said.

Fellows sauntered confidently into the lounge. Stead sat with his back to the wall and frowned as their eyes met.

"Theo Stead. It's a pleasure to meet you. now let's get down to business, shall we?"

"Business, what business?"

"The product of course. I assumed you'd be interested," Fellows smiled. A glint of light from a gold tooth. "I'll knock twenty-five per cent off what your dealer's charging, and I guarantee it's pure quality, it's not cut with crap."

Stead's eyes darted around the room. "How do I know you've got pictures of me? you could be bull shitting."

Fellows sighed. "No bullshit, Theo. I've got you buying and using at the club, have a look?" Fellows showed Stead the two pictures on his mobile phone. There had been no searching through albums. He had clearly had the images primed ready for such a challenge. "There we are Theo, time and dated. Are you trying to deny it?"

"It looks like me."

"To be fair, you were off your face," Fellows leaned on the table. "Look, this is the deal, Theo. I know the score with you. You have plenty of clients. I'm sure you can knock a fair bit of product out to them. I'll give you fifty per cent. That'll see you right for the old tables. What do you say?"

Stead knew he was left with no option. "Have I got any choice?"

"Not really. If you don't agree, I'll go public. That'll be the end of you, and your lucrative career."

"You bastard!"

"Open your briefcase, Theo. Here's a little sample," Stead pulled a plastic packet from his pocket and slid it across the table. "There are fifty packets in there. Knock them out for fifty quid a pop, and you keep half. I'm sure, in a short period of time you'll build up a nice little fan base. Don't worry about any interference. I'll handle that end of the partnership."

Stead quickly snatched the packet from the table, opened his briefcase, and dropped the drugs inside.

"Well, I think that concludes our business. I'll leave you to finish your drink, and I'll be in touch." Fellows stood and grinned. That gold tooth reminded Stead of a shark or rabid animal sizing up its next meal.

Francine watched Fellows leave then approached Stead's booth.

"Was that your business client?"

"Yes, do you know him?"

"I've seen him in here once or twice. What's his name?"

"Justin Fellows."

"What did he give you, Theo? I couldn't help but watch the pair of you on the CCTV."

The colour drained from Stead's face. "Nothing, Fran. God's honest truth."

"Then give me the case," Francine said firmly, "and follow me to the security office."

"What for, Fran?"

"I think you know what for, Theo. You know the protocol for drugs in the casino."

"It wasn't drugs, Fran. It was my fee."

"Pull the other one. It's got bells on." Francine would have none of it. "Now follow me or I'll have to get the security boys to carry you in there."

Stead visibly shook as he stood and followed her. Once they got to the office Fran locked the door.

"We don't want to be disturbed, do we, Theo?"

"You're not a police officer. You've no right..." he said as Fran opened the case and there it was in all its glory.

"What's it all about, Theo? Is this what I think it is?"

"Y-yes!" He stammered. "He's blackmailing me. He's got pictures..." He stopped his futile attempt at explanation when he saw Francine take a pack from a locked box. "What are you doing?"

"I'm going to do a test on this crap, just to make sure, he's not having you on."

She placed some of the powder into a pre-prepared test tube and whistled as she saw it change colour.

"This is cracking stuff. You could be looking at five years for this my friend. I'll have to let Ted know first and then the police."

Stead began to shake like he was sitting on a washing machine on fast spin. "Please, Fran, don't turn me in. I didn't realise what I was getting into. Ted will finish me."

Francine sat on the edge of the desk. "How did you allow yourself to get into this mess?"

"It's the coke," he sobbed. Tears raced down his cheeks onto his shirt. "I've got a habit, and the gambling. I'm in a mess."

Seeing an opportunity to play Stead, Fran leaned forward and squeezed his shoulder. "Look, Theo, I like you, but I can't let this slide. If it was a bit for personal use, yes it would be no sweat. I'd flush it away, end of story. But I can't ignore this amount. Ted would have my guts for garters, and I'd be gone."

"He won't have to know."

"I'd like to help you. I like you but..."

"Please, Fran. I'll do anything. You name it, I'll do it..." he paused as something dawned on him. But what about Fellows?"

"Leave Fellows to me. I'll get him sorted."

"Thank you, Fran. I'll do anything if you can make this go away."

"I'll have to think about this," she said, as if caught in a personal dilemma. "It's all on CCTV, even in here. But leave it with me."

Francine stood and walked to the large safe behind the desk.

Ted had seen no need to hide it. He was sure no one would ever try to turn him over. She tapped in a number on the keypad and the lock clicked open. Fran opened the door and placed the package inside then locked it.

"Don't worry. I'm the only one with the combination. Ted never uses it and I changed the default to something not even he knows. Now go and unlock the door, and just fuck off out of here, I've got to think."

Stead hurried to the door, eager to escape. He turned the key but before he could pull it open Ted Howe saved him the effort.

"What's going on here? My accountant and head of security. You're not tucking me up, are you?"

"No, Ted," Francine said. "Theo's just giving me a few pointers on my tax returns. I've got my return to file. He's given me sound advice, and he's not even billing me," she smiled.

"Bloody hell. He's never done that for me. Screws me for every bloody penny," Ted complained.

"I've got to split," Stead said, quickly wiping tears from his eyes before Howe noticed. "I've got another client waiting."

***

The apartment was better than the last one. Her previous job had taken over eighteen months to resolve; building trust, getting to understand the complexity of the case she had worked on. Her handler had provided a one-bedroom flat that wouldn't be fit for habitation but was in keeping with the character she had played. This time, the apartment was on the top floor of a block overlooking Swansea Marina. Two bedrooms and tastefully decorated, it was certainly in keeping with her role at the casino. It was the early hours of the morning when Francine got home, and the first thing she did was contact her handler, Trudy Lancaster.

"Just to bring you up to speed, I've got Stead on toast. He fell for it hook, line and sinker. He's terrified. I'd give him a couple of days if I were you, then you can make the pitch. Once he's on board just let me know, and I'll make my exit."

"What's your thoughts on him?"

"He'll roll over, no problem. I reckon he'll sell Howe down

the river once the team take him to one side."

"So, how do you want to play it?"

"Like I said, I'll just split. There's no CCTV of Stead meeting anyone, and the half kilo of sugar is down the pan. So, if he starts carping on about it they'll think he's a Walter Mitty."

"OK. I'll be in touch. I think we've covered all bases. I'll start the ball rolling. The quicker we put this one to bed the better. Once Stead has given up Howe, I'll have teams on stand-by to arrest the rest of the conspirators. I'll give you a ring and you can do your disappearing act. Until then, Francine, you keep safe, and don't drop your guard."

"Don't worry about me, boss." Francine was confident things would go to plan. She wondered what impact this job would have on the grand scheme of things. Trudy Lancaster would get some mileage out of it, no doubt. Lancaster was an odd fish. Francine knew little of her, not even her rank. She had met her a few times but always somewhere dark and very briefly. She had never got a good look at her face – something Lancaster had said was for the best. Francine wondered what kind of person would do Lancaster's job. Was she married? Did she have kids? Was she a career woman? Was Lancaster her real name? Francine didn't think so. Why would she be so keen to keep her features in shadow and then use her real name? That made no sense. Lancaster was an enigma, and it was probably best not to even think about her.

75

Theo Stead had just entered the surreal world of his dream when a loud bang shocked him upright. Confused and still somewhere between two states of consciousness, he listened and rubbed his eyes before flicking the switch on his bedside lamp. Another bang. It was his door. This time it was followed by several hard knocks. There was someone at the door. He checked his watch – Four-thirty. What the fuck? Who the hell would call at this time? It had to be bad news. No one would ever call at this time to tell him something good. All kinds of scenarios played in his head. Had something happened to Samantha? His twenty-year-old daughter had gone off the rails and explored all kinds of drugs. The last he had heard; she had become addicted to heroin. His ex-wife had blamed him, of course. He had never been strong. Never put Sam in her place. Never told her 'No.' Stead grabbed his dressing gown from the wardrobe handle and hurried down the stair and opened the door on the safety chain. Two men in well-worn suits stood in the amber glow from the hall light.

"Theo Stead? I'm Detective Sergeant Mark Dawkins, and this is my colleague Detective Sergeant Chris Woodward. The one called Dawkins looked like a prop forward. Shorter than Stead would have expected, but broad with no visible neck. Dawkins held out a piece of paper with an official looking crest he couldn't see clearly in the subdued light. "We have a warrant to search your flat for drugs and documentation pertaining to an ongoing fraud and conspiracy enquiry," Dawkins said.

Stead froze momentarily. He knew if he had any chance of getting away with this, he would have to keep calm. "Drugs? I have no idea what you're talking about. You're welcome to come in. There's nothing here, and as for any fraud, that's just insane. I'm an accountant."

The officers entered the flat and sat down on two softly sprung armchairs that looked like they had come from an antiques dealer.

"Before we start searching, Mr Stead, I have to do things by the book and tell you that I am arresting you on suspicion of possessing class A drugs and being involved in money laundering."

Dawkins cautioned Stead and the accountant didn't reply. He slumped in a matching settee.

"We know exactly what's been going on. We know about your involvement with Ted Howe. We've been running a surveillance for many months. We also understand that you took possession of half a kilo of drugs from Justin Fellows in The Vetch casino. So, to say you're in a bit of a pickle is an understatement."

Then Stead said something the detectives didn't expect. "Will I go to prison?"

"Are you admitting your involvement?" Woodward said.

"I can't go to prison. I wouldn't be able to stick it. I'd kill myself."

Dawkins leaned forward. "It may not come to that. If you tell us everything, you could do a deal."

"Deal? What do you mean a deal?"

"Well, we could make it all disappear. But only if you are willing to co-operate."

"You mean, inform on Ted?"

"That's the only way out for you, Theo," Woodward said.

"If I do, he'll have me killed. He's a ruthless bastard."

"You don't have to tell us about Ted. We know that. Who knows, we could even put you into a witness protection programme. How do you fancy that?"

"Fancy it? You're having a laugh, aren't you. That's the end of my life as I know it."

"These are your options," Dawkins said. "Firstly, there's prison for the possession with intent to supply, and you'd probably pull a five stretch. Secondly, do the business on Howe, and everything goes away. It's your choice. Have a little think about it while me and Chris have a little look around the flat."

After a few minutes Stead answered.

"If I do what you ask, am I going to be locked up?"

"No, Theo. You'll be interviewed at length in relation to any information you are holding on Howe. We'll want to know the ins and outs of a cat's arse, all his dodgy business deals, pay offs to corrupt officials, the whole shooting match. I'm sure that you've enough evidence to put him and his cronies away for a very long time. I'm guessing you've got false accounting information on disc or ledgers."

Stead knew the game was up. There was no point dragging it out. "It's all on discs and pen drives, going back years."

"So, by that, I take it you'll co-operate?"

"Do I have any choice?"

"None at all. We'll take you and whatever evidence you can provide back to our office where we can go through everything with our forensic accountants. It may take a day or two, as you can imagine. So, do you have any evidence either in the flat, or perhaps in a safety deposit or something like that?"

"It's all here in my safe, and on my laptop. All the genuine accounts are on the laptop, and all the false data is on disc in the safe."

"OK. We'll take possession of all that, and you've made the right decision. I guarantee that me and Chris will look after you, so don't worry about Howe. He'll get his just deserts. Now go and put a few things together in a holdall."

As Stead gathered his things, Woodward gave DCI Lancaster a ring.

"Boss, it's Chris. We've just had a good chat with Stead. He's co-operating fully. We've taken possession of his laptop and a fair quantity of discs and pen drives. We'll get him back to the office and we'll bleed him dry."

"That's a fantastic result, Chris. Once we've got it all on record, we'll do the business on Howe, and the rest of the bent brigade."

"Probably be a few days, boss."

"Not a problem. Does Stead understand the enormity of what he's going to do?"

"Yes, boss."

"OK, Chris, I'll leave you get on with it."

76

"Morning Francine, have you seen Theo? I've been ringing him all morning. All I'm getting is the answerphone," Howe said as he walked into the casino reception. "I need to speak with him. See if you can get hold of him for me."

Francine wanted to drop the news on Howe's head, but the game wasn't over yet. She couldn't wait to get away from the place. "He did mention going away for a couple of days for a bit of a break. Said he was stressed."

"Stressed? If anyone needs a break, it's me after everything that's gone on."

"Any news from you know who, Mr Howe?"

"No, nothing, Fran. Probably wants to make me sweat."

"Are you going to pay him?"

"Don't think I have any option."

"You need a bit of protection."

"I've sorted that, Fran. Don't worry about me."

Worrying about Ted Howe was the last thing that could bother Francine.

***

Howe sat on bench on the marina promenade between two blocks of apartments and in the shadow of a large sculpture he could make no sense of. The sun had broken through the morning clouds and a light breeze was puffing the remaining trails away to reveal a cobalt sky. He fished his phone from his jacket pocket just as it rang.

"Morning, Ted, I take it you know who this is?"

"Oh, I know who it is. What do you want?"

"My money, of course." The voice was full of humour. This was a game for the bastard, but Howe would get the last laugh.

"I haven't got that kind of cash at the minute."

"You'd better get it. You've got until eight this evening. I'll ring you then, so you'd better have it, or else I'll blow it all wide open."

***

Howe held the next call as a mother and her brood of noisy children ran rings around the bench. Howe was in no mood for kids and growled an expletive at the eldest.

"Mam, this arsehole just swore at me," the snotty six-year-old shouted.

"If you don't piss off and take your tribe with your I'll do more than swear."

The mother gathered her kids like a mother duck and admonished Howe before they left, mother duck leading and babies following in a line.

"Karl, it's me."

"Are you OK, Ted?"

"Aye, but that twat has just been in touch. He wants his money. I think he's lining me up for a meet. What do you think I should do?"

"Are you going to pay him?"

"Yes, just to get him off my back."

"You know what they say about blackmailers?"

"Must have missed that nugget of wisdom."

"They're never satisfied, always coming back for more."

"Well, I've got to take that chance."

"Let me know what the score is when he calls back."

"Will do."

The witching hour came, and as sure as eggs is eggs, the blackmailer called again.

"Have you got the money?"

"Yes, I've got your money. What now?"

"Same as last time. Get up to the woods and park up. Make your way to the grave you dug and wait there. I'm warning you, don't have anyone to follow you because I'll be watching you all the way. Do you understand?"

"I'm not going to any fucking woods. I'm not going through that again, no way!"

"Suit yourself, Ted. I'm going to hang up now."

"No, wait, look, I'll be there with the money. What time?"

"Nine on the dot, Ted. See you later. And remember, nobody

following."

***

"Karl, he's just rung. It's the same as last time when he kidnapped me. Penllergaer woods at nine by the grave. He'll be following me. What do you suggest?"

"He sounds like he's got it covered, Ted. I don't think you've any other option but to do as he says."

"Have you any idea who this fucker is, Karl?"

"Could be anyone; Cross, your Missus, her son, to name but a few. Not exactly bloody Mr Popular, are you?"

"Do you think he's on his own?"

"Blackmailers usually work alone. But who knows with this one. After you've made the drop, ring me."

"Will do. I'm shitting myself."

"If he wanted you dead, he'd have done you last time. You're no good to him dead, are you?"

"I suppose you're right, Karl. I'll speak to you later."

Howe didn't go home. He walked the prom several times before driving down to Caswell Bay and walking the beach. The air had turned chilly, but Howe would have been shaking even if it had been a heat wave.

Penllergaer woods was a twenty-minute drive at that time of evening.

As instructed, he arrived just before nine. Howe parked up, and trudged into the forestry, carrying a holdall of cash.

Ten minutes of walking first the footpath and then over low brush and ducking beneath reaching boughs, Howe arrived at the spot where he'd partially dug the grave. But now he could see that the grave was now at least four feet deep. This was not good. Howe started to panic; he turned and began to run, then a voice rang out, and there, standing just a couple of metres from him was the blackmailer. Dressed in a grey hoodie over a black t-shirt and black jeans, the face was covered by a mask of Boris Johnson.

"Where are you off to, Ted? Just stay there and don't move." The voice was deep but now sounded different so close. It sounded odd.

Howe could see the automatic pistol with silencer attached

pointing at his head.

"I take it that all the money is there, Ted?"

"Of course, it is." Howe said. Disappointed in himself at the sound of terror in his own voice. "Do you think I'm fucking stupid, or what?"

"Oh, I know you're not stupid, Ted. No stupid bloke could make the money you have, that's for certain. Now just toss the holdall over, I'd like to check it?"

Howe did as he was ordered. The bag fell just feet in front of the blackmailer. A quick glance inside and the blackmailer resumed the threatening stance. "Looks like it's all there, Ted. Now do yourself a favour, empty your pockets of your mobile and car keys. Then stand in the grave."

"You're not going to kill me, are you?"

"Good God, Ted, that's the furthest thing from my mind at this minute."

Howe did as he was instructed, emptied his pockets, and then stepped into the grave.

"There we are, Ted. That was easy, wasn't it?" The blackmailer grinned.

"For fuck sake, are you insane?"

"Turn around, Ted and meet your nemesis."

Howe slowly turned and faced the blackmailer as the mask was revealed.

"It's you! What the fuck is going on? I should have known?"

Before Ted Howe could say anything further, the blackmailer took aim, and fired. The bullet struck Ted right between the eyes. Howe fell backwards into the grave. He had died before he his body and passed the vertical on its final journey.

The blackmailer tucked the gun into the hoody. "That should make a few people happy, Ted."

After collecting Ted's possessions, the grave was filled using a spade hidden behind a tree, concealing Ted's body from the rest of the world.

"It'll be a long time coming before they find you, Ted, my boy, and good riddance."

After the assassination, the blackmailer headed back to the car, and made a phone call.

"It's all sorted, I've got the cash, and as they say in the movies, he's got his just deserts."

"What about the Merc?"

"I've sorted that out. It's not a problem. Just behave as normal, as if nothing has happened."

***

Karl Hatcher hadn't heard a dickie bird from Howe, and just wanted to make sure that everything had gone to plan. A quick play of the tables could also help calm his nerves. Francine stood near a Blackjack table as he entered the casino. Playing the table would probably just make things worse.

"Is Ted around?"

"No. He hasn't come in tonight. I've rung his mobile a few times, he's not picking up. It goes straight to answer phone, so I've left a message. He told me he had meetings all day. When did you speak to him last?"

"Around eight. He said he'd give me a ring back in about an hour."

"You know what he's like. He'll probably stroll in later half cut."

"Guess you're right, Fran. When he comes in, tell him to ring me. Doesn't matter how late it is."

"Will do, Karl. Are you stopping for a drink?"

"No, better not. Fran. I've got a busy day tomorrow. I'll see you around."

77

After nearly twenty-four hours of interviews, Stead had spilled every single bean, giving chapter and verse on Howe's criminal activities over many years. Together with the forensic accountant evidence, there was enough for numerous individuals, including Howe, to be arrested for conspiracy.

Lancaster had been fully briefed by Woodward and made a call. "Francine, I'm ringing you first to let you know that we've got all the evidence we need to have Howe arrested, along with all his co-conspirators. So, the quicker you disappear the better. All the search warrants have been obtained, and the properties will be raided first thing in the morning."

"That's brilliant, there's only one thing…"

"What's that?"

"There's no sign of Howe. He didn't turn up at the casino last night. I've been ringing him constantly, without reply. Do you think he's got wind of Stead and done a bunk?"

"No, no way, Francine."

"I've rung his wife; she hasn't seen him for days. Something's not right."

"Don't worry about Howe at the minute, we'll sort him out after the strike. You are my main priority now. So, get back here this afternoon for your de-brief with the team."

"Will do, boss. I'll just tie a up few loose ends. Howe's wife will be calling in later. I'll see if she's heard anything."

"OK but be careful."

"Careful is my middle name," Francine laughed.

***

Pat Howe felt calm. Calmer than she had in years. She hadn't heard from Ted, but that didn't worry her because she didn't care. If she never heard from him again it would be too soon.

Francine lugged a box once used for a toaster, now filled with personal odds and ends out through the casino door as a smiling Pat alighted from her car.

"Hi, Francine. Can I help with that?"

"No. I'm fine. Just a few personal things. I've left a message for Ted to tell him I quit."

"What? But why?"

"Got a better paying job lined up in the south of France but I have to leave today. I didn't want to hang around in case Ted kicks up a fuss."

"Oh, don't worry about that. I'll sort Ted out. I'm sorry you're leaving us though." Pat did look sorry. "And on the subject of Ted, have you seen him or heard from him?"

"I've no idea where he's got to, Pat. I've rung all over. The last person he spoke to was his mate, Karl Hatcher."

"Karl Hatcher? I've never heard of him."

"One of his business associates, I believe.

Pat shrugged. "I could write a book, believe me." Pat fished in her handbag and pulled out her purse. She peeled off several fifty-pound notes and offered them to Francine. "Go on, take them. It's just a little something to say thanks for your hard work."

"No. I can't. There's no need for that."

"If you won't take my money then come with me for something to eat. We could have a few drinks to say farewell."

Francine wanted to refuse but had second thoughts. Perhaps a few drinks with the wife of her target was a good idea. She was still technically on the job. Anything else she could dig up on Ted Howe could be useful.

"OK. Let's do that."

Pat called a local taxi and the two women headed into the city centre to a local steak restaurant. Pat's favourite.

The subdued lighting was perfect, and Francine couldn't have picked a better place to talk. A corner booth would keep their conversation private, apart from the cell phone recording Francine set up as Pat excused herself to visit the toilet.

Food and a fine bottle of wine on order, the two women talked about the casino and Pat's plans. She had everything worked out and reeled off the spiel she had rehearsed. The first bottle was drained quickly but Francine ensured Pat drank two glasses to her one. Halfway through the second bottle, Pat was beginning to slur her words.

"Yes, I've often wondered about your relationship."

"When I met Ted, we had nothing. We were happy. He saved me from a pretty shitty and grim future. Not sure I ever really loved him, but I did like him. He was funny back then," she smiled. Then he went to prison, that was hard. But I stuck by him. After he came out, he went into business, and this is the result. Perhaps I should have left him years ago, I don't know. What about you, have you got family?"

"No. No one to write home about, Pat. My parents died when I was just a kid, so I was fostered out for years."

"It must have been difficult for you, Fran?"

Francine shrugged. "I've learned to survive. Been all over the world. Got into the security business. Worked in all the big casinos. I've done alright."

"I know Ted thinks a lot of you. There are not many he trusts, but I know he trusts you."

"That's good to hear. Where do you think he is?"

"God knows."

"I hope you don't mind me asking and tell me to mind my own business if it's painful, but you said Ted saved you from a shitty future. What did you mean by that?"

Pat took a gulp of her wine and placed her glass back on the table. Both hands still cradled the stem. "It's not really something I talk about. I sometimes wish I could."

"If you're uncomfortable then don't. It's just that I won't be here tomorrow, so if you want to unload, please feel free. I'm a good listener."

Pat smiled sadly. She clearly struggling with something, and Fran could see she was thinking about her offer. Finally, she said, "I was just a kid. Fourteen. Living a pretty dreadful life, mainly on the streets. My mother was a drunk. God only knows who my dad was. We had nothing and I had to steal food for us to survive. I cooked the food and mam just drank, and drank, and drank."

"You had it worse than me."

Shaking her head, Pat took another drink and topped up her glass. Francine said nothing, allowing Pat to continue when she was ready. "Anyway, I met a man. He was about twenty years older than me. He seemed nice. Ran a dodgy betting number. Had kids as runners between pubs taking bets from punters. He caught me nicking fruit from a stall in the market. Made a fuss in front of the stall holder that he would take me to the cop shop. But when he got me outside, he gave me a fiver and let me go. To cut a long story short, I saw him every day after that. We eventually started talking and he seemed nice." Pat snorted. "One night, he saw me outside the Grand Hotel, up by the railway station. I was begging outside the entrance but doing a crap job of it. He asked me if I wanted to go to his place. Turns out he had a room just around the corner. When he got me inside..." Pat's eyes started to fill.

Francine placed her hands on to Pat's.

"He raped me," Pat said.

"Jesus! I'm sorry, Pat."

Pat nodded sadly. "He made me pregnant."

"God no! What did you do?"

"My mother didn't care. Social Services did though. I had the baby. A little girl," she added wistfully.

"What happened to her?"

"She was taken off me and ended up in care."

"What about her father?"

Now Pat looked scared. "Nothing I could do. Nothing I wanted to do. He was bad news."

"Sounds like it."

"No. I mean really bad news."

"How worse could he get?"

"Oh, a lot worse," Pat said. "He disappeared shortly after he killed a man. Stabbed him to death in an alley somewhere."

"Murder?"

"You're smarter than you look."

Francine smiled. If only Pat knew her secrets too.

***

Norma Cross checked her watch, brushed lint from her jacket sleeve and stood to attention as Detective Chief Superintendent Terry McGuire entered the office. "DCI Cross, sir."

McGuire waved his hand dismissively. "Between us, it's Terry. I don't like formalities."

Cross relaxed a little.

"I've been asked to take you on. I'll make it clear from the outset that I want the best from you. You treat my team like they are your family. Respect them and they'll respect you. Jesus! I shouldn't have to tell you this. You've made some cockups and now it's time to save your career. Are you willing to do everything I say?"

If Cross felt slighted by McGuire's bollocking, she didn't show it. "Of course, sir... er... Terry," she corrected herself.

"Prove yourself to me and who knows where you might end up. Remember, we're more than a team. We're family. Nothing comes between the family. Blood is thicker than water."

"I couldn't agree more." A week ago, no, a couple of days ago, Cross would have been angry. But now she felt good. Ted was gone and her mother was free. Time to reset.

***

Thirty miles away…

"It's all gone to plan. It worked out sweet as a nut. Looks like everyone has got what they wanted since the unfortunate demise of Ted," the older man could barely supress a smile. "I reckon as far as they're all concerned, he's chip paper and has done a bunk. Nobody gives a toss about him."

"Excellent, and are you happy with your cut?"

"Not a problem," the younger man said.

"You did a good job on Ted. The clown was getting too big for his boots, lording it over everyone. He got what he deserved."

"He was well connected. He had friends in high places."

"I know that!" was the reply with youthful impatience.

"I know them all, but there's a new kid on the block now."

"Well, you know where I am if you want any other business sorted. Just give me a bell."

"I'm grateful."

"I enjoyed watching the bastard squirm and beg."

The older man shook his head. What had he released on the world? "Jeez! looks like I've created a monster."

Printed in Great Britain
by Amazon